PANHANDLE

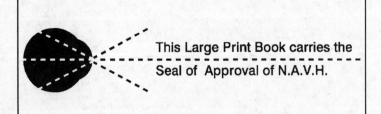

This Large Print Book carries the
Seal of Approval of N.A.V.H.

PANHANDLE

BRETT COGBURN

THORNDIKE PRESS

A part of Gale, Cengage Learning

GALE
CENGAGE Learning®

Detroit • New York • San Francisco • New Haven, Conn • Waterville, Maine • London

GALE
CENGAGE Learning·

LIBRARY OF CONGRESS CATALOGING-IN-PUBLICATION DATA

Cogburn, Brett.
    Panhandle / by Brett Cogburn. — Large Print edition.
        pages cm. — (Thorndike Press Large Print Western)
    ISBN-13: 978-1-4104-6097-4 (hardcover)
    ISBN-10: 1-4104-6097-5 (hardcover)
    1. Large type books. I. Title.
PS3603.O3255P36 2013
813'.6—dc23   2013018331

Published in 2013 by arrangement with Pinnacle, an imprint of Kensington Publishing Corp.

INTRODUCTION

The greatest thing about stories of the Old West is simply a matter of sheer space. No tale seems too tall under the scope of that big, wide-open Western sky. There is room to let your mind wander along buffalo-scarred trails, and up wild rivers that lead to the fossilized and bleached bones of a land that only once was, but forever lives on. That mythical West has a flavor like no other, with a grit and a physical feel to it as sharp as the frigid bite of a blue norther blowing down across the plains, or the scorching heat of a desert sun. It was a wild, raw land in an era where everyone seemed tougher, and there were things worth fighting for. Its stories are best told by the light of a campfire, or with a far horizon in sight. An old pioneer heart beats strongly in some of us, and we long for a place yet undiscovered.

I had the fortune for many years to make

my living from the back of a horse, in a place where cowboys still step on frisky broncs on cold mornings, and drag calves to the branding fire on the end of a rope. Growing up around ranches, livestock auctions, and backwoods hunting camps filled my head with stories. My great-grandfather on my mother's side was a former U.S. Cavalry sergeant who used to set me on his knee and tell me stories of chasing Pancho Villa in Mexico. His wife told me how she came to Indian Territory in a covered wagon prior to statehood, and how their milk cows got so sore-footed on the trail that they had to shoe them like work oxen. There were family tales of a great-great-grandfather who was a Johnny Reb turned Galvanized Yankee, sent west during the Civil War to fight the Sioux in Minnesota and the Dakotas.

While other children were dreaming of robots and caped superheroes I was fighting Indians and grizzlies with my BB gun on a frontier no one else had ever trod. I dreamed of a place and time where nervy people could throw down their old lives and strike out toward the setting sun.

Perhaps no other thing had a greater influence on my fascination with the Old West than the family stories that went with an old sepia photograph hanging on the wall of my childhood home. My great-grandfather, Franklin "Rooster" Cogburn, was an Arkansas and Indian Territory badman who had a scrap with Hanging Judge Parker's deputy marshals. He was too tough to die, and as wild as the rugged mountains that reared him.

And maybe after all those years I've absorbed a little of that Western flavor, like an old piece of barnwood soaking up rainwater. If my tales leave readers with a little taste of trail dust in their mouths, the smell of powder smoke in the air, and the feel of a prairie wind tugging at their shirts, then I'm a happy man. I'll prop my boot up on the fence and spin you another yarn.

— Brett Cogburn

PROLOGUE

Reynolds Ranch, Higgins, Texas — 1936

It's a damned shame, but the Texas I knew is just about gone. Soon, there won't be even a hint left of those days other than the prattling of old-timers with wandering minds, stooped backs, and their rheumy eyes twinkling with yesteryear. If we don't die young, maybe that's how all of us end up — nothing more than a story we keep telling ourselves, over and over.

There are folks who call me a pioneer, whatever that means. Those who say that are newspaper writers and such. Mostly, they weren't around to live the life I knew, so they naturally think the old days were something special. Maybe they were, because I miss those years more and more, hard times and all. To hear them talk, I moved out here before the buffalo, but that ain't nowhere near the truth. I was a relative latecomer to this country, but I did ride

9

into the Panhandle before barbwire, rail-roads, and farmers busted things to hell. The boys used to call me "Tennessee," and we cut a wide swath through this country once upon a time.

Nowadays, most mornings I wake up feeling older than Methuselah. I can't ride a horse anymore, but I still saddle mine up every morning and tie him to my yard fence like I've got somewhere to go. I still tug on my boots even though my achy knees creak and protest, and I'd feel naked without a good hat on my head even if I don't make it any farther than the spur-scarred rocking chair under the shade of my front porch. I'm just old whether I like it or not, but my story is that of a young man in his prime, wild and hard to handle, and yet to learn that life charges a price for every pleasure.

I still don't claim to be much wiser than I ever was, but I do know one thing for sure. Two cowboys getting hold of a racehorse is like giving matches to children. Throw a pretty woman into the mix, and somebody's bound to get burned. Looking back down the long years, that isn't exactly how it was. The horse was just an excuse for adventure, and the woman, well, she had everything to do with our trouble. But hell, I'm getting ahead of myself. . . .

CHAPTER ONE

Anyone who feels sorry for an Indian hasn't ever been shot at by one. I was a far cry from being an expert where Indians were concerned, but I guarantee you I was learning by the minute.

We ran our horses breakneck across the prairie, with those Cheyenne shooting at us every step of the way. I lay low on my horse's neck, cracking my rope on my chaps' leg, and urging the wild-eyed herd of stolen horses on before me. Some four hundred yards behind me was a whole passel of the savages, screaming like banshees and whipping their ponies furiously in an attempt to run us down. Here and there, black powder smoke blossomed, and the dull boom of a gun sounded across the prairie. They were way too far off to hit anything from the back of a running horse, but they had their mad up, and continued to bang away like it was the Fourth of July.

Occasions like that one led a man to thinking about the ramifications of his actions, and the pattern of his life. Right about then, I was thoroughly disgusted with my life in general, and was promising myself to reform from all my bad habits. It was at that moment that I swore off of horse-thieving, and any more dealings with mad, bloodthirsty Indians.

Fast wasn't fast enough to suit me so I lashed my horse across his hip with the tail of my rope to hurry him along, but he didn't have anything extra to give. He wasn't going to last much longer, and I knew I was just about two jumps ahead of becoming buzzard bait.

To the north, an immense, black wall of clouds spread across the horizon, silhouetting the buttes and canyons of the Canadian River. Lightning laced the sky with jagged brilliance. The herd of horses pounded over the rough ground, and the drum of their hoofbeats and the thunder that rumbled from the storm throbbed in my chest like maddened war drums. The dust boiled up in a thick veil, and I felt alone in the insanity of it all. I was caught between a rock and a hard place. I was running blind away from one storm and into another, and I was more alive than ever.

A bullet whistled by me, and it was entirely too close. Those heathens behind me were dead-set on collecting my hair. That was the terrible thing about Indians — they had peculiar notions about how one should go about killing one's adversaries. It just wasn't civilized at all the way they went about things. A white man would just kill you, content with the fact that you were dead, but an Indian liked to kill you slow.

They should have made doctors out of the Indians considering how they liked to remove things from the human body. They would cut off, and cut up, things that most folks just naturally take for granted. I was determined that if they were going to catch me, they were going to have to run one hell of a race, because I was fond of all my parts. I found the notion of going around missing vital components to my natural look to be highly unsettling to say the least. My scalp, my skin, and my nutsack were among the things that I'd consider especially bothersome to lose.

Where in the hell was Billy Champion?

Life has taught me that there is no such thing as easy money. I cursed myself for the stupidity of letting him talk me into such a predicament. It had sounded easy enough — just round up a few Cheyenne ponies one evening and slip them off in the night as easy as you please. Never mind the fact that those same Cheyenne might not be as high on the idea as we were. We had stirred up a hornet's nest is what we had done.

The rain started to fall in huge, scattered drops that popped on my hat brim. One of the horses before me stumbled and fell, followed by the crack of a rifle. I reined away from the crashing animal, barely missing going over the top of him. The shot had sounded pretty close and I took another look behind me.

Most of the Cheyenne had fallen back some, but one of them, better mounted, had closed to within seventy yards of me. His heels drummed madly against his horse's sides, and he was close enough that I could see the fury beneath the war paint on his face. His rifle wobbled crazily as he strained to draw a bead on me.

Another bullet thumped the ground just behind me and I drew my pistol. My horse lunged with irregular stride, rising and falling over the gullies and rolling ground. I looked down the long barrel of my Colt at the Cheyenne brave bobbing in and out of my sights, and I slowly tightened my finger on the trigger.

Before I could shoot, the Cheyenne's

horse lost its footing and cartwheeled end over end. That Cheyenne buck sailed through the air with his arms outstretched, his back arched, and his eyes as big as saucers. I swear he bounced at least three times when he finally hit the ground. He was a rolling ball of dust with an arm and a leg sticking out here and there.

Most of the starch was knocked out of him when he rolled to his feet, and he didn't look so scary anymore. His rifle was gone, his body was covered in dust, and his hair reminded me of a mad porcupine. Staggering in a circle, he tried to remember which end was up. His eyes focused drunkenly on me as I rode away. In exasperation, he sucked up a big breath, and tried vainly to blow out of the way the eagle feather that dangled limply in front of his face.

I squalled like a bobcat and raised my pistol barrel to my hat brim in a mock salute. He threw up one hand, middle finger upraised, in a universal vulgar symbol. It didn't take any Buffalo Bill to read that sign. *Now, where in the hell did a savage learn that?*

One moment I was laughing and the next I was falling. I had one instant of awful recognition as the herd vanished before me, and then my horse was sailing over the edge of a high cut-bank. My heart rose up in my throat as I prepared to meet the impact rising up to meet us. We landed in a shower of rock and sand, and when I say it jarred me to the teeth I'm not exaggerating one bit. It was at least a twelve-foot drop, but like many of those range ponies, mine was tougher than nails and he hit the ground running.

I scanned the hill above me where the plain fell off into the deep breaks of the river bottom. A big rifle boomed, and I saw the bullet strike the hill. A Cheyenne there jerked his horse up hard just as another shot stung him with dirt. The brave tucked his tail and fled back over the rise and out of sight.

Thunder clapped, and the bottom dropped out of the bucket. The rain fell in an almost impossible sheet of water. The herd turned toward the river at a wide, flat spread of sand, and I could just make out somebody riding at the lead. I ran my horse by the mouth of a small canyon where a man stood there on its lip, shooting back the way we had come. I thought it was Billy.

The horses hit the shallow crossing at a dead run. Water splashed high, and their legs churned in the deep, sandy bottom. My horse bogged up to my stirrups, but somehow he lunged free and hit the center of the river channel, where the footing was firmer. The herd was already coming out on the far bank where they turned west and raced along the river. I tried to find Billy behind me, but couldn't see anything for the storm.

It was a full hour before sunset, but it turned pitch-black in a matter of minutes. Great gusts of wind brought with them a scattering of hailstones, and I hoped I wasn't about to be sucked up by a tornado. Here and there, lightning lit up the canyon for an instant, but all I could see was rain. The little Cheyenne horse I rode was played out, and nickered pitifully for the herd, but there was no answer. I walked him blindly up and out of the canyons, hoping I was following, and not at all sure I hadn't lost the trail. Where the hell was Billy?

Like the devil, you mention his name and he pops right up. I stopped in the mouth of a gully leading up to a long rise. The dark shape of a horseman sat crossways on the trail above. It was Billy, and if I looked as bad right then as he did I was a sorry sight. He looked like a wet hen just about to run all over the place.

Many years later, I saw a book about Billy with a picture on the cover showing a masked man with a smoking pistol in one hand, and a pretty woman in the other.

17

They sure made it look wonderful. In the spring of 1881, sitting on a horse with the cold rain running down the crack of my ass, fifty stolen ponies lost in the night somewhere before me, and a pack of mad Cheyenne somewhere behind me, I pondered on those types of romantic notions. Adventure can be more fun to tell about afterward than the actual experience in the moment.

I rode up to Billy and he was smiling, if you can believe that. He was grinning like a possum, and there wasn't any pretty woman to be had, nor any gun to be found that would smoke on a night like that. I thought about shooting him.

"Reckon the rain will wipe out our tracks?" I sputtered.

Billy looked over his shoulder back down the canyon. He spit out a mouthful of the water running off the bridge of his nose, and grinned again. "I just wonder if Noah will have room on the boat for a bunch of Cheyenne nags and a couple of sinners."

"The trick will be loading those wild devils two by two when he comes paddling by."

"Won't be any job at all for good cowboys."

"You reckon Andy's still in front of them?"

"He's living it up right now if he ain't

dead. That boy doesn't seem to know that a body can break their damned fool neck running a horse in this. Coming down off the lip of that canyon back there, it was so rough I didn't know if this nag was bucking or falling with me." Billy shook his head as if he really gave a lick about personal safety.

I kicked my horse on up the caliche trail. "Let's hope he checks them this side of Kansas. That boy rides like a drunken Injun."

"Don't worry. His horse is bound to fall over dead before too long," Billy called out as he spurred his horse past me.

I had to over-and-under my horse with my rope, and punch the wore-out little devil with both spurs to keep Billy in sight. We caught up with the horses about four miles up where they were scattered out along the banks of a good-sized creek. They were a sorry sight, heads down, asses to the wind. The creek before them was rolling out of its banks. Andy wasn't to be found.

"I had hoped to bed down in Texas tonight," Billy muttered.

"That little grove of trees yonder looks accommodating enough until that creek slows down."

Billy nodded. "I guess these ponies ain't going anywhere tonight, and maybe Andy will show up."

Our saddle horses were done for, and we drifted to the herd to catch new mounts. Only a few of the horses so much as scattered before me — they were that tired after their long run. I started to attempt to pick a good one, but deemed it an impossible feat, and managed to rope the first one within my reach. It was a wonder my rain-soaked rope didn't knock that poor little fellow down, as it must have weighed twenty-five pounds.

The little horse came along easily enough, and I laughed as Billy came dragging his choice out by his saddle horn. His victim was set back on the end of the rope and shaking his head. Billy's saddle horse leaned into the pull, but stalled out after a step or two. It was just about an even match. Billy managed to face his horse up, and waited until the little paint he'd roped reared high and lunged forward to stand snorting and spraddled on quivering legs. At that, the bronc seemed to have enough and came along willingly.

"Ever notice how a horse will handle like a baby for a hundred pretty days straight, and then when it's muddy and wet, and blowing or snowing, they want to wrestle?" Billy asked. "Never try to catch your old gentle saddle horse in a muddy lot with your Sunday best on, I guarantee you."

"It's just that they ain't any happier than the rest of us with inclement weather."

"What the hell is 'inclement'? Where did you get such a god-awful word?"

"You just ain't got any education, that's the problem with you. This here" — I raised a finger to the sky — "just about fits the bill. Inclement. I'd say it is."

Billy had managed to coax the paint up beside him, and as I raised my hand, the bronc bolted and snatched to a halt at the end of the rope. Billy's horse staggered in the mud, the rope digging into Billy's thigh. For a moment I thought his saddle would roll, broadside like he was. He righted things, and managed to bring the paint back in, blowing like a buck deer and rolling his eyes.

"Serves you right for roping a pinto."

"That sore-footed nag you've got won't go five miles tomorrow. Besides, I like a horse with some flash." Billy wasn't lying. He loved nothing more than parading around on a good-looking horse.

"Well, I won't have any problem riding this one, will I? You can do all the trick riding you want, and if those reservation savages catch up to us, they might spot you first and leave me alone," I answered as smugly as a cold, saturated man who'd had no sleep in two days could.

Billy stepped down under the trees, and began unsaddling his horse. He was silent for once. I was sure I had bested him, and that was enough to make things a little bit bearable.

Billy somehow managed to saddle the paint without a wreck, and turned the other horse loose. He had the little fart tied to a tree and hobbled by the time I finished my own. If he hoped to soak some of the devil out of that paint, he was sadly mistaken.

I pitched my roll on the highest, driest spot I could find — one with only three inches of standing water — and flopped down. I could hear Billy splashing around somewhere behind me. I rolled up in my blanket, hoping to sleep, or float through the territory, one or the other.

"Riding with you is like riding with my mother. Hell!" Billy grumbled.

"Go to sleep. The rain's slacking off."

"Yeah, it's falling straight down now, and not sideways like before."

April in the Panhandle isn't exactly tropical, and that rain was cold enough to chill beer. It's amazing the conditions a man can sleep under when he's been in the saddle for two days straight. Just before I dozed off in one of the most miserable bed grounds of my life, I asked, "Reckon Andy's all right?"

"Hell if I know."

CHAPTER TWO

Andy showed up the next morning and I guess you could say he was all right. He was caked with mud from head to toe, his hat missing, gamely half carrying, half dragging his saddle along in his wake.

"I was hoping you boys had some coffee on," Andy said in his squeaky voice.

"We were just fixing to chop up the ark and burn it when you walked up." Billy was trying to wring the water from his blankets.

"Fine horse you got there." I pointed at Andy's feet.

"He quit me."

"They seem to do that to you."

"The son of a bitch stopped in his tracks and sulled up. I couldn't move him for anything. He finally fell over on his side, and I tried almost everything to get him going again." Andy flopped down on his saddle and scratched his scrawny whiskers thoughtfully.

"I like to have never dug my saddle out from under him," he added.

"He might get back up and come trailing in later," Billy said.

"No, he won't," Andy said forcefully.

"I admit you know something about wind-broke, rode-down, sulled-up horses, but you could be wrong," Billy threw back at him.

"No, I ain't."

"How's that?"

"I shot him, that's why!"

"You sure ain't a lover of animals, Andy," I said.

Andy Custer might have been sixteen, although he claimed to be older. He was just short of six feet tall, and rail thin. He was blond and fair as white linen. He wore a thin mustache and goatee that he claimed to have patterned after a picture of General Custer he saw once. He had a voice that tended to get higher and squeakier the more excited he became.

Andy fancied himself a sure-enough desperado. You didn't have to ask him, because he'd tell you without your asking that he was a bad man — hell on the men who crossed him, and worse on the women who dared to love him. He had a habit of always pulling out his pistol and playing with it when he was sitting around. Billy and I

25

wondered which he played with more, his gun or his pecker.

Andy's image of himself might have been shattered if he could have seen himself then, sitting there muddy and shivering, with his hair sticking out every which way. He idly played with the flopping sole of his right boot, and his big toe poked out of a hole in the other.

None of us had much in the way of clothes, and we were a ragged lot. Our hats were the best, our neckerchiefs were of silk, and our fancy-topped boots were too fine to walk in. But, in between, we were mostly just faded rags. My own shirt had so many holes it looked like somebody set me afire and put me out just before it all went.

Now Billy was as opposite from Andy as could be. He had a way of looking good no matter what. Even in his rain-soaked rags, he somehow stood out over us. He always seemed to find a way to spruce himself up a mite. I don't know when or where he did it, but he did. That morning he had shaped up the brim of his hat a little, and he had dug a fresh, red silk wild rag from somewhere in his bag. It beat me, but it was dry, and so was the white shirt he'd donned. He always had to have a white shirt. It may have been stained and patched, but he looked like a thousand dollars compared to Andy and I.

Some men just have a way about them. Billy Champion had that way. He did everything bigger, faster, and wilder than anyone I ever ran across. I guess that is why I followed him down from the D-Cross in the spring of '81. I've heard men say that he was a man's man, whatever that is. I know horses and women liked him to uncommon extremes, and he liked them with equal enthusiasm.

There are a lot of stories about Billy, and you can believe what you want. Billy was like that; he made people talk. Billy Champion's downfall was that there wasn't any backup in him. He was double-bred stubborn. I loved him to death, but men like him can be hard to ride with, because you will get your nerve tried from time to time.

Billy was coal-black-headed, and a little on the dark side. I always figured he had some Indian in him, but he'd have shot me had I said so. On the worst morning, I never saw him go unshaved, and that morning was no exception. Billy was always an early riser, and while I sat rubbing the sleep out of my eyes and studying Andy, Billy was already done with his morning pruning.

Striding over to me, Billy sat down on a deadfall log, pulled out his ivory-handled

Colt, and began wiping it down with a rag and a little can of oil. He always kept his shooter clean. Me, I never took much care of mine, like a lot of other boys I knew. Hell, my old Colt would have probably jumped up and ran off in shock if I ever showed it a single drop of oil.

A friend of mine, on a drive to Kansas, once stopped to shoot a cottonmouth on the banks of Red River. He found his pistol was so rusty he couldn't even cock it. It was locked plumb up. He chucked it in the water, waved good-bye to the snake, and rode off.

A lot of the boys were like that. Most of them just carried them for show, or because they thought a man was supposed to. The trouble was, when the majority of the boys on the range carried guns, and were apt to settle their differences in the most violent and informal ways, there was bound to be a number of gents who didn't carry a gun for show. Nobody ever said that Billy carried his for show.

Billy wasn't a big man. He might have been five nine, or so, and didn't weigh more than one-fifty crossing a river with his boots on. But when Billy was on the prod, or happy for that matter, he seemed as big as life. He was always smiling and flashing those pearly-white teeth. One look at him and you knew it was all fun, and damned the consequences.

Andy had pretty white teeth, except for the two front ones that were missing. He said a calf had kicked them out. I rose and started to hang my blankets to dry on the log.

"No time for that," Billy said. "That's Commission Creek, and she heads up not too far from here. We should be able to cross, as she's falling fast, and pretty narrow and shallow on up there."

"My horse might not carry this wet bedroll." Sleeping in a hurricane never made me what you could call chipper in the morning.

"That sore-footed driblet might not carry you out of camp." Billy pointed to my new horse.

"What the hell is a driblet?"

"You know, a driblet." There was the faint trace of a smirk at the corner of Billy's mouth. He was enjoying my ignorance of his newfound vocabulary.

"No, I don't know what a driblet is. I think you're making it up." I wasn't about to be buffaloed.

Billy walked a wide semicircle around my horse, making a big show of judging its quality. "Yep, that's what I thought. He fits the bill."

I waited for him to continue, and wasn't about to bite the bait he was laying out for me. Billy hacked up a little wad in his throat, and let the ball hang for a minute from his lip until it fell slowly to the ground.

"That's a driblet. It ain't quite spit, and it ain't quite drool. It's a driblet." Billy jabbed a thumb at my little horse, who stood three-legged under the cottonwoods, with his nose practically on the ground, and his bottom lip sagging. He might have weighed seven hundred pounds saddled. "That's a driblet."

Andy snorted, and whistled through the hole in his teeth. "You beat all, Billy."

"Maybe the sun will pop out later and we can stop and dry our gear." I was annoyed at Andy for no reason. But then again, I was annoyed at Andy most of the time.

"I'll go bring up the horses if I can, and catch 'Horsekiller' here a mount." I was perfectly willing to leave, so as not to give Billy the chance to gloat.

I was just about out of earshot when I heard Andy whine, "Catch me a good'un, Nate!"

Like there was a good one in the bunch. It was a pretty sorry-looking herd of horses, and only three outlaw cowboys would be stupid enough to risk life and limb stealing them. Much as those Cheyenne liked to race, you would have thought they would ride better horses. Maybe that's why they hadn't caught us, because it just wasn't worth the effort. They probably gave up chasing us as soon as they had put on a little show of trying to shoot and scream us into the Hereafter.

That might have been the case, but I wasn't taking any chances. I would keep a watch over my shoulder all the way to Kansas. When they were burning rifle friction over our heads I took them plumb serious. We were lucky to have outrun them, but Billy had figured it that way. It was early spring, the grass just starting to green up, and he claimed that if we rode horses that had wintered with a little corn, we could outrun any pursuit by Cheyenne on winter-starved ponies.

To my own way of figuring, I thought that the Cheyenne didn't have a good horse left among them, what with every cowboy wintering in the Cherokee Strip to the north driving them off, and with the soldiers around the reservation keeping the bucks from stealing any new replacements.

The horses weren't scattered too far at all, because they were mostly gutted and wore out. I roped a little bay that looked in better flesh than most of the others. Billy joined me on the paint. As he swung around to the other side of them, I laughed as the paint repeatedly boogered, jumping sideways every so often as he kept looking back at Billy on his back. That served Billy right for being foolish enough to ride him. Nobody in those days wanted to ride a paint horse.

We started the ponies up the creek. They were moving slowly without any travel to them. I left them to Billy, and led the bay to Andy. It was a five-minute ordeal saddling him, but Andy finally got a leg tied up and got it done.

"Wish I had my hat. My head don't feel right," he complained.

"I wish you had a lick of sense. Slip his foot loose and let's go."

Andy pulled loose the slipknot holding up the near hind foot and hung his rope from his saddle horn. Gathering up his reins, he carefully stepped aboard. The bay tensed and humped up like a cat with a watermelon on his back. "He don't act sociable, do he?"

The bay stood stock-still and trembling until Andy let out his version of a Comanche warwhoop and tapped both rowels into that pony's blown-up belly. Bay shot straight up and landed, all fours bunched up and too cinchy to move. Andy motivated him again, and they lit out up the creek. The bay bawled and stiff-legged all the way. Say what you wanted to about Andy, but the kid could sit a bucking horse.

The sorrel I rode had been ridden a little before, but he was a far cry from broke. His feet were too sore to give me much trouble, and I contented myself to amble along back to Billy. Andy came by me, his horse still crow-hopping a little ways and then stopping. Andy would spank him out of it, and they would go a little ways and repeat the process.

"I don't think this boy's been rode before. How am I supposed to herd horses?" Andy said as he plunged past me.

"Keep his nose pointed the way you want to go. Kick when you need to move, and pull when you want to stop," I advised.

"I hear you."

I'd never done anything but cowboy since I was big enough to count for anything. It seemed like that was a hand's job in those days. You were expected to herd wild cattle on the back of a horse just as wild. I have seen and rode some good animals, broke to death, gentle, the kind you could do something on. There were good cutting horses worth a fortune beyond me, and good roping horses that you weren't afraid to tie to and rope just about anything. Every hand had one to tell about, but most of the time it was riding some sorry bronc that would as soon stomp you as look at you.

We caught up to Billy. He put a lead on the herd, and Andy and I brought them along, pushing up on the drag until we broke them into a good long trot. We were quite the sight, all of us on green or unbroken horses. Andy's horse continued to pitch, and Billy's paint shied at everything from Billy to a clump of grass that didn't look right. Hell, I even saw it fart and spook itself. There was something about the splashy-colored devil that had outlaw written all over him. I thought Billy was making a fool of himself over that nag. A knot-headed horse has been the misery of many a man, but if I'd known half the trouble that little paint horse was going to get us into I'd have shot him on the spot.

We made our way upstream, waded across the creek, and rounded a little rock pile, a government survey marker that was the Texas line. Both Andy and Billy let out a whoop, and kicked their horses up. Andy went so far as to turn a little circle at a lope, whooping and slapping his chaps' leg in time as the bay broke into pitching again.

Crossing that little line must have meant a lot to those boys. The country in front of us looked just the same to me as what we had left behind, but then again, I wasn't from Texas. You would have thought those two were born in heaven, and had just come home after fifty years in hell.

I knew better than to say anything, or I would have to hear Billy expound upon the virtues of Texas for an hour. To my mind, that country might not even have been Texas, except by the say-so of Texans. There was nothing civilized that far north that I knew of, and damned sure no towns north of Mobeetie and east of Tascosa. But then again, those Texans would have claimed California, and part of Canada as Texas ground if the world would let them.

Maybe we all carry a touch of the old home with us, packed away in its own little cubbyhole. They say home is where the heart is, but I was a restless, traveling sort of man. Those gusting winds drifted my wandering horse back and forth across the plains of endless grass until I was an orphan by my own choosing. I'll always remember home, not as a quaint picture of the place where I was born, but as a feeling. It was a rhythm of one hoof after another cutting prairie ground.

CHAPTER THREE

Swinging west of a little stage station, our stomachs be damned, we lined out north across a rolling, short-grass country, scattered with gyp-rock canyons here and there. About noon we topped a hill and could see a long, flat descent down to a little creek cutting across our way. A small trickle of smoke drifted up from a camp below. I could make out what looked to be a cart with a couple of horses tied alongside.

Billy came loping back down the line and pulled up beside me. "What do you think?"

"My stomach thinks my throat's been cut."

Without another word, he lit out back to the front of the herd. We headed on down to the creek, the camp still some mile or so off. A hundred yards out, the horses in the camp nickered, and a few of ours answered. A sawed-off, bearded man with a Muley Sharps rifle in his hand came up to lean against the wheel of his cart.

Leaving the herd to scatter on grass, the three of us rode up and stopped about ten yards out from the fire. Billy spoke for us. "Howdy."

"Hi," the man beside the cart replied.

"We're driving north to Kansas and are all but out of grub. Was wondering if you might have a bit to spare."

"I might." The whiskered gent looked us over for a bit, and then strode to the fire. "Light and set."

All three of us ground-tied our mounts, and then stepped up to the fire, where the fellow had a pot of beans simmering. And I'll be danged if he didn't have a little batch of sourdough biscuits warming there. He dug out some plates from a kit in back of the cart, and we went at that food like a starving bitch wolf with pups. There wasn't enough silverware to go around. I came up short, but just raked mine off the plate with my knife straight into my mouth.

I slowed down long enough between bites on my second plate to study the wizened fellow across the fire from us. He sat Indian-fashion on the ground with that Sharps nestled across his thighs. He still eyed us suspiciously, or maybe there was a crafty look about him. He was extremely short, with an old, slouchy hat that hung down almost to the bridge of his nose. His gray beard draped over his potbelly. He might have been sixty, but his round little eyes were bright and sharp.

I noticed Billy was watching him just as closely as I was. I noticed too, that he was especially eyeing that Sharps Borchardt rifle on the old man's lap. It looked to be brand spanking new. Depending on who you asked, cowboys had taken to calling that model a Muley Sharps either because it kicked like a mule, or because it was a hammerless design and muley cattle were those without horns.

Now I carried only a pistol, but Billy carried a Winchester too. He was always armed like a bandit. He claimed he carried a long gun for shooting meat, and to keep some disagreements at a distance. He had a love for firearms, and that Muley Sharps had caught his eye.

"You boys taking those horses to Dodge?" Whiskers asked.

"Probably, or wherever we can find a buyer," Billy answered.

Now even at a distance a person could tell those horses for what they were. Up close, not more than four or five wore so much as a single brand. I could tell Whiskers was a trader, and he was eyeing that herd like Billy was eyeing that Sharps.

"I'm Billy Champion, this gent here to my right is Nate Reynolds, and the skinny galoot to my left is Andy."

"Andy Custer," Andy threw in. He insisted on telling everyone he was kin to the late general.

Billy gave him an impatient look and continued, "If you've got a bit to spare, we could use a little grub to get us on through. We ain't got much hard money, but maybe we could deal you out of a bit of salt and beans."

Whiskers didn't answer about the food. He looked past us out to where our horses grazed. "I heard of you. You're the man who backed John Jay down. Do you know you're on his range right now?"

Billy ignored the question just like Whiskers had done. Everyone in Southwest Kansas, the western half of the Indian Territory, and probably back down the trail south into old Texas knew about Billy's run-in with Jay.

Jay's outfit took in a big chunk of country, and was running a lot of cattle. Billy had brought a herd up from South Texas a year ago, and delivered it to Jay's headquarters in Kansas. That's how Billy and I had met;

I worked under him on that drive.

Billy and Jay disagreed on the delivery count, and things got a little heated. Like a lot of self-made men, John Jay thought a lot of himself, and he was used to running roughshod over lesser men. He cussed Billy for losing too many steers on the trail, cussed about their condition, and generally let Billy know what he thought about his poor abilities in regard to managing a trail herd. The recount on a hot day had clipped everyone's fuses pretty short. Before Jay had gotten good and wound up, Billy put his hand on his Colt and told him they could settle things between them real quick if he had the guts. Jay backed down in front of our crew, and his. He paid up according to Billy's count, and the taste of humble pie didn't set too good with either he or his hands. He ought to have counted himself lucky that Billy didn't kill him right then. In those days, nobody would have denied Jay deserved anything he got. You had best be careful how you spoke to prideful men with pistols on.

I was just damned glad it didn't end up in a killing that day. It probably would have gotten both crews into it.

"Lot of trouble, driving horses," Whiskers said.

"What trouble?" Billy answered.

"The market can be doubtful, and it can take time to find a buyer."

"That's a good set of horses, and we've got time."

"It'll be tough to sell them in their winter clothes."

"The grass is greening; they're putting on weight as we speak. They'll be fat and summer-slick in a couple of weeks."

"It's hard to see them from here."

"I don't guess I'd mind showing them to you."

Two traders had met. Whiskers went behind the cart, and untied a horse from the off-wheel. Billy rose and eased out to the paint. I mean he *eased*. The horse raised his head and snorted, and made two bounds away from Billy before he managed to con his way up to him and get a hold.

"Little wild, ain't he?" Whiskers said as he rode up.

Billy stepped aboard. "He's a little green, but he's a traveler."

He reached down to rub the horse affectionately on the neck, and that paint traveled about twenty feet sideways in one jump. Whiskers cackled like an old hen, and the two of them made off for the herd.

Never one to pass on a chance to nap,

Andy sprawled out in the grass. Me, I took the opportunity to study that peculiar little layout. The cart was not of the Mexican type, but rather a spoke-wheeled job with a single seat, and tarp on the bed. A one-eyed, brown mare stood hip-shot alongside. She was galled with harness sores, and so skinny you could almost see through her. The cart was a one-horse rig, and it was amazing to assume that she was responsible for pulling it.

The sun was busting through the clouds and hitting the ground, promising for a pretty day. Andy must have been enjoying it, because he brought out the band, snoring to a tune all his own.

I took up a piece of sourdough and wiped the last of the bean juice from my plate. I watched Billy and Whiskers in the distance. They were drifting lazily through the grazing horses, stopping to study this one and that one from time to time. I knew the haggling was getting serious when at one stop I heard, even at a distance, Whiskers go to cussing until he gagged on his tobacco.

After what must have been half an hour, I decided to leave the bean pot, and join the fun. As I rode up Billy motioned me on over to him.

"Put Driblet through his paces so this

man can see I've told him correct."

Paces? Billy sat there smugly with a twinkle in his eye, like he expected me to have something to show him. With a sigh of surrender, I rode out from the herd and put on a little demonstration of what that sorrel nag couldn't do.

I pedaled him up to a lope with a good dose of my guthooks, and with a little finesse, managed to ride him in a big circle to the left. He was so sore-footed it was a job to keep him from breaking stride, and he had a trot that would jar the front teeth out of a beaver. He wrung his tail in frustration, and jacked up his head and gaped his mouth against the bit. I pulled him down slowly to what you could call a stop, made an attempt to roll him back the other way, and loped a couple of circles to the right. I headed back to the horsetraders, not aiming directly at them, as I wasn't sure I could stop short enough to keep from crashing into their midst. I took a severe hold, and bit-bumped him into the ground.

Whiskers grunted his approval and spat tobacco juice out in a thick black arc. "Stops hard, don't he?"

I didn't want to tell him just how hard it was.

"Just like I told you, he can turn around

like a cat in a stovepipe, stop on a dime, and get back like a bad check," Billy chimed.

"Smooth, ain't he," Whiskers added.

I was beginning to get a good handle on his horse appraisal skills. "I'd say so."

"See there, and he's pretty to boot," Billy said.

The sorrel did have a flaxen mane and tail, a big blaze face, and two socks on his hind feet. Beyond that, you couldn't tell where the ugly stopped and the horse began. He was so narrow you couldn't have passed your fist between his front legs, and he had a long, thin bottle head that was disproportionately large in comparison to the rest of his body.

The horses were drifting farther down the creek looking for grass, and I left to go bring them back a little closer to camp. When I returned, Billy left Whiskers and rode up to me for a private discussion of the kind that happens when parties are horse-trading.

"You know, we might get ten to twelve dollars a head for those horses in Kansas *if* we found a buyer. And those soldiers down south may have got word we stole them, and wired the news north. It's happened before," Billy said solemnly. "If we could make a good trade here, it'd be better than going to some farmers' calaboose over a bunch of ten-dollar Cheyenne ponies."

"What's the trade?"

"Five dollars a head, and we take the cut with us, or throw them in."

"Cash money?"

"Well, that's a lot of hard money. Let's see." Billy made a show of tabulating on his fingers. "Fifty head minus one that's got a knocked-down hip, one with an eye put out, and five that a coyote wouldn't eat. Let's say ten head of cuts. That's forty head at five dollars." He fired up his finger adding machine again.

"Two hundred," I said impatiently.

"Yeah, two hundred. How's that sound?"

"Hard money?"

"Well . . ."

"How much hard money?" I could see where things were headed.

Billy tried one of his smiles to frame the wonderful price he was fixing to shoot at me. "Sixty-five cash, that Sharps gun, fifty rounds of friction for it, and a little sack of victuals."

"Who gets the gun?"

"You can have my old Winchester."

"What about Andy?" We sometimes forgot about Andy, and I felt it my job to see that he was treated in a Christian fashion.

"I've got an old converted Colt Navy in

my bedroll that he's been wanting. I'll give it to him so we all get a new shooting iron. We'll split the cash three ways."

"That old Navy ain't worth ten dollars."

"Once I tell Andy that Wild Bill Hickok favored Navy Colts he'll think he's getting a hell of a deal. He'll probably become a two-gun bad-ass himself," Billy snorted. "Besides, the boy's gotta pay something for the education we've been giving him."

"That'll work." I agreed readily, satisfied that things were divided equally enough.

"Just think, partner. We can drift down to Mobeetie and have a sure enough good time with that money." He slapped his thigh in sheer exuberance.

Billy felt it was his job to always keep my spirits up. After two years of riding with him I'd come to learn how to get at the truth of things when he told me something. When Billy was trying to convince you to go along with what he suggested, whether good news or bad, you just had to divide or multiply everything by two. Things were just generally halfway like he said they were. If he told you about a trip, and you didn't want to go, he would tell you it was only a two-day ride. It would wind up taking four. If he told about a hundred dollars to be made at something, and you went along, you might make fifty. He wasn't a liar; he just got too enthused with convincing you to go along with his plans.

"You can have my saddle horse," Billy said.

"What are you going to ride?" I was shocked by Billy's generous mood.

"I'm keeping the paint."

I threw a disgusted look at the paint, and headed out to rope Billy's horse out of the herd. I'd lost my personal saddle horse somewhere in our flight with the stolen herd, and was more than happy to take Dunny. He was as gentle and dependable as the day was long. Billy could have that flashy little pinto nag if he wanted him. He probably thought the horse matched his ivory-handled pistol.

"Who's going to help Whiskers drive that bunch?" I asked.

"That fellow looking over the creek bank pointing a shotgun at us," Billy burst out, obviously enjoying my shock and growing discomfort.

Sure enough, after he pointed out the direction I could make out somebody looking at us over a cut-bank in the creek. He had been there all along, not ninety feet from us when we were at the fire. That would have made most folks nervous.

"Old Whiskers ain't too trusting," I said.

"His name is Harvey."

"I'll call him some other things once we get out of here. I don't like anybody pointing a gun at me, especially when I don't know they're there."

We rode back to Harvey Whiskers' camp, and Billy was smiling like somebody holding a gun on him was the funniest thing in the world. I threw my saddle on Dunny, proud to have the little black dun, or what a lot of folks call a line-backed buckskin.

Harvey began pulling his saddle from the horse he was riding. "I think I might keep that sorrel for my own personal horse."

"I bet you'll love him," I replied.

I stepped up on Dunny, and Billy came up with a little canvas sack of grub that he handed up to me.

"Get up, Andy," Billy hollered.

Andy didn't stir until I walked Dunny over the top of him. He sprang from the grass in one move. "That horse could have stepped on me!"

"Mount up."

While Andy went out to get his horse, Billy handed me his Winchester, and shoved the Sharps in his own saddle boot. I took a latigo string from a bunch I carried on my back dee, and tied it to the saddle ring on the carbine. As soon as I'd hung it on my saddle horn, Harvey walked up and paid us the currency. Billy held the coins out in his palm to eye them appreciatively. Reaching down, I snatched a twenty-dollar gold piece and a few dollars more from the little pile in his hand, and pocketed them.

"Hey! We've gotta divide it evenly!" Billy cried.

"If you were an educated man you'd call that an eyeball-cut." I laughed and started to turn away.

Harvey was saddling the sorrel, and he called out across the horse's back. "I'd say that wasn't much of an accurate split."

"I'd say you'd better call in that man you got out yonder. I'm tired of my back feeling most too wide." I wasn't feeling funny anymore.

I wasn't about to try and ride out of there with Whiskers' money, only to give it back to him after I was shot in the back. Common sense and experience made me wary, and with Billy along I would have thought nothing of bearding the devil in his den.

Harvey didn't argue any and waved his man on in. A big black fellow came walking up out of the creek with a long-barreled shotgun cradled in one huge elbow. That man was a giant, and must have stood half way past six feet. One of his legs was as big around as my chest. He wore a big-brimmed, straw sombrero, a rough calico cloth shirt, and a pair of patched overalls that ended about three-quarters the way down his calves.

"You want me to hitch up the mare, Mister Harvey?" The man's voice was deep, and slow.

Andy rode up just as that fellow spoke, and I thought he'd break a spring. "Where the hell did he come from?"

"Let's go." Billy reached up and tucked some of the money into Andy's vest pocket.

Andy wasn't having any of it. His voice raised a notch higher, "Has that nigger been holding a gun on us all this time?"

I studied the black man standing there like a tree. He was as calm as can be, with that shotgun looking awfully little on his arm. A quiet man can be the one to watch in a fight, and despite his outward calm, I could tell he would scrap at the drop of a hat if Andy continued to push him.

"Let's go, Andy." I tried to relate the seriousness of the situation in my voice.

"That nigger don't scare me none," Andy sneered.

That black man's face might as well have been chiseled from stone, but I noticed his thumb ease up onto the hammer of his scattergun. I figured I'd have to shoot him, but by then it would probably be too late for Andy. That shotgun had two holes in the end of it big enough to stick your thumbs in. A double-barrel ten-gauge with full chokes at fifty feet can be a serious proposition. A man might miss, even with a shotgun, but who in their right minds would want to chance it?

Before things got too Western, Billy shoved his horse against Andy's. "Let's go."

Andy didn't want to leave without a fight, but Billy spurred into him, and Andy's horse staggered, turning away from camp in order to regain its balance. Before he could turn back, Billy cut Andy's horse across the rump with his hat. That bay horse farted, gathered itself up, and took off in a runaway with Andy hauling back on his mouth to no avail.

Billy eyed the black man for a long moment. A second seems like an awful long time in a situation like that. Billy could be a little abrupt when it came to disagreements, and I resigned myself to whatever was about to happen.

"Was there enough grub in that sack to suit you?" Harvey's voice interrupted the staring match.

Harvey must have had more sense than I had thought to change the subject. Of course, there would come a time when I would rethink a lot of the things about people I had judged in my past, some of them sooner rather than later.

"It'll do," Billy said to Harvey, but he was still looking at the black man.

Billy wasn't one to pick a fight, but I knew he wouldn't let anybody think they had run him off. We had been in the act of leaving when Harvey called up his man, but that didn't keep Billy from taking the time to roll a cigarette and study the weather for a bit. That black man hadn't said a word to us, or threatened with his gun. Still, the calm, massive presence of him challenged us, and Billy seemed to feel it most.

"I wonder if Andy has gotten his horse stopped yet?" Billy finally asked me.

He turned the paint and we took our own sweet time riding away from camp, as if there wasn't a gun at our backs. Andy was long gone, obviously unable to turn his cold-jawed pony. Once we reached the crest of a big hill we struck a lope to catch up to him, and I turned in the saddle for one more look back. Harvey had gone to saddling the sorrel we had sold him, but that black man stood in the same spot like he was rooted there. He appeared determined to watch us until we were out of sight.

About half a mile over the hill, Andy loped back to meet us. "You'd no call to do that, Billy. No nigger ever backed me down."

Andy was just about as mad at Billy as he was at that black man. However, he worshipped Billy too much to want to shoot him — or kill him anyway. While the two of them jawed back and forth, I happened to look to our east. About two miles off I could see a long plume of dust worming its way toward Harvey's camp.

"You two look yonder. I think that's those Cheyenne fogging it up our trail." I didn't wait for a response. I just stuck the spurs to Dunny and headed west.

Billy and Andy didn't take long in following suit. We ran that way for about a mile, and then hit some canyon country and slowed to a long trot. We stopped just off the edge of a big canyon, looking back the way we had come, and listening for sounds of a fight. There were no gunshots, and the wind was blowing too hard to hear anything else.

"I wonder what that nigger thinks about a bunch of mad Cheyenne?" Andy was obviously pleased.

"I hope that old man is a talker," I said.

"I hope they give him a chance to talk," Billy replied.

"He was a crafty sort, and if he does squirm his way out, those Cheyenne can read sign."

"You always look at the bright side, Nate." Billy shook his head at me.

"I'm still kicking, and I intend to be to-morrow."

I made sure to keep my eye on our back trail as we circled south. An old frontiers-man once told me that the best way to stay in some semblance of good health in Indian country was to always keep your eyes upon the skyline, and never sleep beside your fire. Maybe I was just a natural-born worrier, but I had no confidence in my luck or fate to favor me with fortune.

"I'm too busy having fun to worry." Nothing could faze Andy. "We'll have a time in Mobeetie come tomorrow, won't we, boys?"

"Hell yes, let's ride! There's whiskey, gambling, and a good-hearted whore wait-ing on me!" Billy hollered, and raced off.

Both of them were soon riding beside each other, laughing about the time they were going to have, and the trouble they might get into. Before long I was feeling it too, and my worries were slowly left behind along with what little good sense I had.

Sometimes all a man needs to forget his cares is a little recreation, and a dose of harmless misdemeanor. Yes sir, high times were coming to old Mobeetie. It was good sport, and damned the consequences when you rode with Billy Champion.

CHAPTER FOUR

There are moments when the world seems to sleep, and time passes with absolute perfection. Those times are fragile, and are to be observed in stillness.

The day after our horse trade, we camped in a draw south of the Canadian River. It was a quiet place, with a small cottonwood and hackberry grove shading a little spring that slowly seeped down to the river. We tossed our saddles on a sandy flat at the bottom, and picketed our horses close to hand. Each one of us lay down, and although it was only late afternoon, we slept like dead men until the next morning.

I awoke first, rolling out of my bed just as the sun was rising. I walked up out of the draw, and looked upon the plains falling away to the south.

In that light, at that moment, the world was a different place, and I was small upon the face of it. The shortgrass glowed golden yellow in that light. The slightest of breezes rolled the grass away from me, flowing away in rows, like ripples in the water, growing ever outward until they were out of sight. That wind swept away before me, quick and elusive, but with a sweetness that lingered.

You can't capture moments like that in memory, much less describe them with accuracy to anyone else. You only recall bits and pieces — little boxes of precious perfection that come back to you with the purest clarity, even many years later. They were things like the feel of a horse, the sound of cattle bawling out of the dust, or the smell of a certain woman floating in your head. *God, how they could linger.*

And then the moment was gone, or rather, I was gone from the moment. The world moved on and left me, and I was large upon its face again.

I walked back to camp to find Billy and Andy lying on their blankets, smoking and telling tall tales. They both looked at me curiously, for I must have seemed too quiet. My mind was bad to take hold of things, like a dog worrying a bone.

"Where ya been?" Andy asked.

"Looking."

"At what?"

"I don't know for certain."

"What?"

I watched him scratch his tangled blond mane, his brow wrinkled in irritated puzzlement. I hunkered over our little fire, my hands spread over its flame. It wasn't cold, but several days of being a little chilled had worn on me, and the fire felt good.

"I was just looking at the horizon. It's a beautiful morning." I was anxious to end the conversation.

"Nate, you beat all! I think you're a little addled."

"Let up, Andy. He's just educated, that's all. Educated folks have got a different way about them," Billy stated in a matter-of-fact way.

"Well, I went all the way to the fourth grade! Even if that was off and on a little, you could say I graduated," Andy said. "And I don't talk funny like he does, even after all my schooling."

"Nate there is a Kentucky gent. He went to fancy schools, and danced at them fancy parties. He slept in a feather bed in a big, white house, the whole bit. Didn't you, Nate?"

"It wasn't quite like that."

Billy knew a little about me, or what I'd let him know. My folks were considered big people back there. They weren't rich, just affluent in their own little world. They had a lot of land in cultivation, a big house, and some fine horses, but not enough for a second son.

My parents did see to it that I had a fair education for the time. After my stint in a little country schoolhouse, I spent two years at a college in Virginia. Returning home, I was given a small stake, my inheritance, and a merry send-off to get me started on my course in life. My oldest brother got the farm, as was his right. My sisters could marry their way to fortune, and knowing them, they would.

Me, I lit out for the West to see the sights, and I hadn't stayed in one place too long since. I made my way to Texas, and hooked up with a trail herd of horses headed to San Antonio. I went with a Blocker herd of steers north to the railroad at Wichita. From there I made my way into Nebraska following another herd, and soon drifted into Colorado, where I spent two years on a ranch there. Most of my work was taking delivery of Texas herds, and driving them one bunch at a time for sale to the miners in the mountains west of there.

I had eventually made my way back south, and wintered in the Cherokee Strip, riding the grubline from camp to camp to keep from starving. I'd met Billy there, and went with him that spring on the long drive from deep in South Texas to deliver Jay's trail herd.

Basically, I spent years in the saddle learning a trade. And in that time, I learned how those conquistadors must have felt when they came riding across that country astride those fine Barb horses, with lances in their hands, and their eyes hungry for gold. The elevated feeling of the *caballero,* the gentlemen on horseback, made even the smallest man look down on those who were lowly enough to walk on their own two legs. I was no gentleman, but I'd be damned if I'd ever do anything again that couldn't be done from the back of a horse.

I remember my grandpappy never drank but one kind of liquor. I asked him once why he didn't ever try anything else. He told me he couldn't imagine liking anything better than what he already drank, and I guess I was like that too. I had found what suited me and I couldn't imagine doing anything else.

The country was big and open to the sky, and made a man feel either awful large, or awful small, depending upon the grit in his craw. It brought out the pride in a man, blew him up, and seemed to raise to the surface the core of his character, both the good and the bad. I think it was the freedom that did that. We had endless space to ride in, game for the taking, and too little law to keep us all from going half wild. A man could be as good, or bad, as he felt big enough to be, but the country had a knack for taking a man's measure, and trying him on for size.

"My stomach's rubbing my backbone raw," Andy whined.

He reached out from his bed, and grabbed at the grub sack. I felt the same way, but didn't say so. He could do the cooking himself.

"You worried about those Cheyenne?" Billy asked.

"After a week in Mobeetie, I might not worry about them anymore," I said.

"If I didn't know you better I'd say you were scared of those reservation warriors," Andy jabbed at me.

"You've got the Injun fighter's name."

I watched him trying to find a witty reply. I cut him off before he could say a thing, and motioned toward the fire. "Why don't you go get us some chips? These damned cottonwood limbs are green and will hardly burn at all."

Grumbling something under his breath,

he dumped our groceries on the ground, and took off from camp carrying the sack. He was back before too long with an impressive pile of cowpatties.

"How far did you have to go to find a dry one?" Billy asked.

"Wind's already dried most of them out." Andy pointed to his gathering as evidence.

"Keep the fire small so it doesn't smoke too much," I said.

Studiously ignoring me, Andy fed the fire like he was stoking the boiler on a highball train. "I need a hot fire to cook on, and anyhow, Nate, I figure it is a question of bravery. Does it take a braver man to face scalping, or a slow death from starvation?"

"Hell, I'm hungry myself. I saw a chunk of side-meat in that sack," Billy said.

We were cleaning up the last of the bacon, and sipping coffee boiled in a fruit can, when Andy jumped to his feet. "Lookee there what comes!"

We all looked back down the draw, and watched that big black man come up to us. He was riding the sorrel we'd traded Harvey, and that shotgun was still in his arm.

He pulled up in front of us. "Got a bite to spare?"

Lo and behold, Billy invited him to step down. Billy and I, and that black fellow, sat

62

down around the fire, and left Andy standing there with a dumbstruck look on his face.

I figured Andy would make trouble. He wasn't necessarily a hothead, but I think he was bound to show Billy how tough he was. Despite that, he continued to stand there for a bit, looking awkward and unsure. I think he was a little awed standing up close to our visitor. Andy could climb on a man-killing horse, run breakneck over a prairie dog town, or race beside a stampede in the black of night, and never bat an eye. But I don't think he'd ever seen the likes of that black man.

"All we have left is coffee." Billy motioned to our improvised coffeepot.

"That'll do," the black man said.

He reached inside his shirt and pulled out a battered tin cup. After pouring himself a cupful, he hunkered back on his heels, apparently unaware that Andy still stood above and behind him.

"That was a good trick you boys pulled."

"We thought so." Andy's courage was returning. Even a giant didn't faze him for long.

The black man seemed not to even know Andy was there. "My name is Tom Freeman."

"What about Harvey?" I asked.

"Those Indians were on us quick. Harvey lit out for the plum thicket along the creek. Me, I rolled under the cart, and they just went on by. They'd spotted Harvey and were hot and heavy after him. While they were hooting and hollering and searching the thicket, I jumped on the sorrel and lit out before they took the time to notice there were two of us." Freeman's big hands cut the air sharply, as he described the action.

"You probably led those Injuns right to us." Andy squatted beside Billy, with his bony wrists dangling between his knees.

"I didn't owe that old crook anything, so I left him," Freeman paused and then added, "If those Indians didn't get him, the Lord will some day. You boys don't know what an old he-coon you pulled that stunt on."

"We just sold him some horses," Billy said.

"You didn't make out so bad yourself." Andy jabbed a finger at the sorrel Freeman rode up on — the sorrel with Harvey's saddle on it.

"That man owed me more than that horse yonder."

Billy removed his hat, and began to idly turn the brim in his hands. "What'd he owe you?"

"Fifteen gallons of whiskey."

"Where the hell did you get that much whiskey?" The mention of liquor seemed to embolden Andy a little more.

"I made it."

"Is that what you did where you come from?" Billy asked.

"I made the best whiskey in the Nations, and that's saying a lot."

"Reckon that's sure some recommendation in your line of work. Is that where you hale from?"

"Yeah, down in Choctaw country. Had me a good operation there. Had some land and a Choctaw woman."

"Parker's boys run you out?"

"I just got tired of their stealing. 'Confiscations,' they called it. They never arrested me, just got so they'd steal my whole batch."

"Seems like you might have made good whiskey if they thought so highly of it."

"I made some."

"What about your woman?"

"She was worse than those deputies. I might have shot me a few of those old boys, but that woman was something else. Me and her squared off one day, me with this shotgun, and her with a cast-iron skillet. It was touch and go there for a moment. I decided it was too chancy of a thing to try her, and left the country."

Billy, as usual, seemed to be enjoying the moment. I figured Tom Freeman would keep his attention for a while. Billy often claimed that entertainment was where you found it. That entertainment was generally in the form of the eccentric characters Billy seemed to draw to him.

Billy studied Freeman with obvious pleasure, like a kid with a puppy. "Now, if you had a bottle of your whiskey we could take the measure of it."

"Yeah?" Freeman seemed to be enjoying Billy just as much.

"Well, you claim to be an expert in the field of whiskey-making, and we claim to be equally skilled in whiskey-tasting." Billy motioned around the fire.

"Seems like almost everybody claims to be a sampler." Freeman's manner was as equally grave as Billy's.

Billy jabbed his thumb my way. "Yes, but most folks don't have a Tennessee boy in their midst. This long-legged jasper here is a bonified Tennessee gentleman, and he claims that there ain't any whiskey except Tennessee whiskey."

You would have thought Billy was selling a horse.

Freeman eyed me for a long moment, as

if inspecting me to see if he thought I matched my pedigree. "I've known a few of you boys in my time. Don't know nothing but coon hounds, sipping whiskey, and fighting."

He rose and headed for his horse, returning shortly with a bottle of whiskey. He pitched it to me. "Let the expert begin."

"I ain't from Tennessee, I'm from Kentucky."

Freeman didn't seem to hear me, and Billy wasn't about to let me disqualify myself. "Let's drink."

I pulled the cork on the bottle, and held it up before my eyes. The whiskey was as clear as spring water, and I gave it a shake to observe the bead. I glanced at Freeman, and he seemed pleased.

Billy noticed and said, "I imported him in just for these occasions."

Turning up the bottle, I let a slug roll down my throat. That was the smoothest whiskey I ever drank. And man, what a jolt it packed.

"That's good," I said. "Smooth as a baby's butt, and kicks like a Missouri mule."

"I'll be the judge of that." Andy's arm snaked out and grabbed the bottle from me.

Like the connoisseur he was, he turned her up like a calf sucking a bottle and didn't come up for air until he choked himself. Andy's sole measure of what constituted good whiskey was that it made him drunk enough to squall like a panther, and sick enough the next day to swear off the stuff forever.

Andy passed the bottle to Billy, and he took a pull at it. He was silent for a moment while the red flush of whiskey spread across his face. "You're an artist, Tom."

As if to reinforce his compliment, he turned the bottle straight up and took another pull. He shook off his shivers and pitched the bottle back to Freeman.

Wrapping one of his huge paws around that bottle, Freeman held it before him like a preacher holding up the Bible before his congregation. "Here's to the friendships made and lost, the women married and left, and the money won and thrown away by men drinking good corn liquor."

Two hours later, everyone had taken the full measure of Freeman corn liquor. Even Andy was warming up to the talented new-comer.

"Are you kin to General Custer, that Indian fighter?" Freeman asked.

Andy attempted to straighten himself from the drunken slump he had assumed several drinks ago. "Yep."

"He made quite a name for himself."

"I reckon he'd have whipped almost every bunch of Indians from here to Canada by now if he'd of lived." Andy's chin was bouncing off his chest as he nodded.

"Wasn't it Indians that killed him?" The irony apparently wasn't lost on Freeman.

Andy sat with a dumb look on his face. After a moment of deep thought, he announced, "I gotta piss."

This triggered an impromptu migration from the fire. Andy strolled down to the little stream that ran down the draw. "I'll flood them Cheyenne villages downstream." He started to do just that.

"Only a heathen would piss in a creek," Billy said and then joined him.

In a moment the four of us stood watching yellow streams of urine trickling off down the current.

"That's a hundred and ninety-proof Kentucky sipping whiskey." I pointed at my own stream. "It's corn-yeller, aged in my gut, and made in a clear spring."

Andy rocked back dangerously on his heels, shaking his pecker. "Take a good look, boys. I weighed thirteen pounds when I was born, until they circumcised me."

"Looks like a grub worm with the guts slung out of it," I said.

69

"Put that little old nubbin away." Freeman swung his pecker back and forth over the water, splattering piss at our feet.

"Would you look at that?" Andy pointed at Freeman's cock, which stuck out the side of the bib of his overalls. The damned thing was so long he didn't even have to bother with unbuttoning his fly. He just pulled it out the side.

"You'd better put that thing up, boy, before Andy falls in love with you," Billy said as he turned back to the fire with all of us in tow.

"I ain't your boy." Freeman stopped short of the fire and his bloodshot eyes stared at Billy belligerently. He pulled out a tattered, thin little book from his hip pocket and held it in his palm before us.

"What's that?" I asked.

"Carpetbagger gave it to me when I was a boy. It's a book about the U.S. Constitution and such." Freeman studied the book in his hand.

"Did you learn to make whiskey from that book?" Billy asked.

"We were all created equal," Freeman said. "The country fought a war over it."

Billy flopped down on his back beside the fire and propped one boot heel on the toe of the other. "Now Tom, you seem like a nice enough fellow, but some mean old Texan is going to crack your head if you ain't careful where you pitch that sassy talk."

"It's a free country," Freeman said.

"You're too damned big to argue with, short of shooting you. If you tell me you're white I'll believe you."

"I ain't ashamed of the color of my skin, and I'll be as sassy as I please." Freeman holstered that book back in his pocket like a gun.

"Tom, I'm coming to believe you've got more than a little fight in you." Billy's smile was oblivious to the building passion in Freeman's voice. "What about you, Nate? Have you got anything against this colored fellow?"

"No," I said.

"See there, Nate is a good Tennessee boy, and you've already convinced him," Billy said.

"Kentucky," I muttered under my breath.

"Humph," Freeman grunted. He turned his back on us, and went to check his horse. Somehow I got the notion he was as stubborn as Billy was.

Surprisingly enough, Andy followed Freeman, mocking a two-hand hold on a gigantic tool at his crotch. "I think I'll call you Big'un."

"I've already gotta name," Freeman said.

They argued down to the horses and back. Billy settled the matter. "Long Tom Freeman."

"Long Tom!" Andy repeated.

"Long Tom and General Custer riding to glory," I said sarcastically.

"Are you coming to Mobeetie with us, Long Tom?" Billy asked as he picked up his saddle.

"If I's smart enough to foller ya, Mistuh Billy," Freeman said.

Just that easy, Billy adopted one Tom Freeman, despite the fact that he had been ready to shoot him the day before. And then again, maybe Freeman adopted Billy. I don't know which was the case. Life has a funny way of throwing people together on a whim, and our fate often hangs in the balance.

Once we had all saddled our horses, Billy stepped aboard his and tipped the last of the whiskey down his throat. He tossed the bottle high, and Andy jerked his pistol out and let it bang. The bottle bounced off a rock and busted when it hit the ground.

"Are you ever gonna hit one?" Billy asked.

Andy jammed his shooter back in his holster while his left arm fought to hold the rein on his frightened horse.

"Get on, General Custer," Freeman

72

whooped.

"All right, Long Tom." Andy swung into his saddle without touching his stirrup. That boy should have been a circus rider. He ended up sitting backwards.

"Turn around, you drunken heathen," Billy said in disgust.

Andy studied his horse's tail for a moment, and then turned to look at its head behind him, as if he had just realized what he had done. "Well, I'll be damned. There for a moment I thought somebody had cut his head plumb off."

Billy spurred off in a shower of dust. Andy grabbed a handful of tail and belly-punched his horse with both feet. The frightened animal peeled off after Billy with Andy laughing and reeling in the saddle.

We all hit a lope for Mobeetie like some mad parade, with Billy in the lead. Freeman bounced along beside me, hugging at a canvas sack which hung from his saddle horn in order to keep it from flopping. It must have held the last of his whiskey. He grinned foolishly.

"Come on, Billy! Come on, Long Tom!" Andy had managed to right himself in the saddle.

Freeman joined in, and his deep bass voice sounded across the prairie. "Come on, Tennessee."

"I'm from Kentucky," I said, holding to a long lope behind them.

I thought they were all drunken fools. Had I not also been drunk, I would have included myself in that category. But fools or not, they were my friends, and I would follow them through hell and high water.

CHAPTER FIVE

Mobeetie didn't need us to look like the circus had come to town. It was Saturday night, and the town was burning wild. We just helped fan the flames.

We came running three-abreast down the street, popping our pistols, and carrying on like the young devils we were. We pulled up in front of the first saloon, as wild-eyed as our horses. A small crowd stood under the awning in front, shadows in the lamplight there. Andy squalled and plunged his horse into their midst, attempting to make it into the saloon. The door wasn't wide enough, and he only succeeded in scattering a few people, and knocking askew one porch post.

Despite our wild entrance, not a soul seemed to give us due attention, because we were nothing out of the ordinary. It was early spring, and apparently, the boys were gathering for one last celebration before spring works. At least thirty cowponies were tied up and down the street, standing three-legged beneath their saddles. There was a passel of soldiers, freighters, and drunks from all corners of cattle country parading the streets and bars of Mobeetie. They all had one thing in common. They came to have a good time. Mobeetie was wild in those days. She was wild and hard to curry below the knees, and we loved her that way.

As I slipped the cinch on Dunny, I noticed Long Tom hadn't dismounted. He still sat clutching his sack of whiskey. Looking at him reminded me of the old story of Jack clutching the goose that laid golden eggs while he climbed down the beanstalk. Long Tom was ragged and forlorn looking, a huge slumping figure oversized for the Texas pony he rode.

"Hide your whiskey, hitch up your britches, and come on," I said.

He eyed me for a long moment, his eyes in the lamplight showing white and large. He pondered me like an owl eyeing a field mouse below him. Slowly, he turned his horse away and headed down the muddy street. The weary step of his horse matched the slouch in Long Tom's back. It was as if both were affected by some age-old weariness, or burdened by some mysterious affliction.

"Where are you headed?" I asked.

"You've got a lot to learn, Tennessee," he called back softly over his shoulder.

"I'm from Kentucky."

"I know you." His voice was a whisper in the darkness.

Long Tom disappeared into the night. Billy and Andy had already disappeared into the saloon. I wondered where Long Tom thought he was going, but I figured he was headed for Ring Town, the joint for colored folks north of town. Maybe he knew somebody there.

I shuffled my way into the saloon, hesitating inside the doors to let my eyes adjust to the dim, smoky light. The bar was lined from one end to the other with boys in from the range. Everyone else was gathered in groups here and there, and I spied Andy talking to someone at the back. Billy was nowhere to be seen.

I made my way to the bar, sidling myself between two men like a cow shoving its way to the feed trough. I gathered up a beer, and turned my back to the bar to take in the room. The beer was lukewarm at best, but it was wet and tasted good enough to suit me.

"By damn, that's whiskey by any man's standard!" the man to my right cried.

He was a drawn-up little fellow hidden beneath the slouching brim of a large hat. He wore suspenders, and farmer boots with mule ear tugs. He looked like a freighter or such.

He turned up his glass again and finished the remains of his whiskey. When it had traveled the length of his throat and settled in his gizzard, he shivered like a wet pup.

"That's just awful enough to do the trick." He winked at me.

"Seems like a painful way to go," I said.

He eyed me craftily, making an exaggerated motion of having to look up at me.

"Beats the hell out of stringing wire."

"Wire, huh?"

"I've been stringing bobwire for Goodnight. If it's left up to him he'll fence off all hell and creation." He made a wide sweep of his arm.

"To hell with wire." I almost spat my distaste.

The T Anchor and the JA had already fenced small pastures, and I'd heard the Panhandle Stock Association was fixing to start a drift fence on the north bank of the Canadian River that would run for two hundred miles. I didn't know it then, but open range was rapidly becoming a thing of the past.

On my way to Wichita years before, a few of the older hands told about how a man could drive cattle from the Gulf Coast to Canada without hitting a fence. Now, with each passing year, the trail moved farther and farther west — first the Chisolm, and then the Western. Kansas was already full of both real and imaginary fences. In all but the western half you couldn't drive stock anywhere without some farmer getting shotgun mad because your cows walked over the single plowed furrow that served to fence in his crops. It wouldn't be long until a man on horseback would spend half his time opening gates.

"To hell with bobwire!" I said a little louder.

"Can't say as I like it, but it's a living."

"That ain't living."

There wasn't a thing he could say to that. He kept making a show of having to look up at me, and I knew what was coming, or at least where the conversation was headed. I stood six foot three in my sock feet.

I wish I could say I was handsome, but that isn't true. My nose was way too big, and my black, curly hair was a mop that de-fied taming. I was a tall, thin, big-jointed man, never seeming to find a shirt with the sleeves long enough. When I was a boy my

Mama had always told me I was all feet and hands. I might not win any beauty contests, but I'd grown into those feet and hands enough to give anybody that didn't like my looks a good licking.

"You ever get light-headed up there?" he asked.

"If I pissed on you would you believe it was raining?"

"Easy, I was just funning you. My name's Whiskey Pete."

"Nate Reynolds."

"Glad to know you. Have one on me." He offered me the bottle as a peace offering.

"No thanks, you could burn a lantern with that. Why don't you drink the good stuff?" I jabbed at the small, very small, selection of imports behind the bar.

"Not enough to it. That city stuff is sneaky. You drink it and the next morning you're all sick and pained. I'll drink honest, trader whiskey."

"Honest how?"

"It's up-front. It pains you just to drink it." He slapped the bar and brayed like a mule at his own wit. His laughter rose above the noise of the room, and his knees buckled. I dodged back as he laughed himself into a stagger.

I grabbed him by the shoulder and

80

straightened him. "Who's hiring now?"

"They're fixing to start the general roundup south of the Canadian this week. Find O.J. Wiren. He's range boss for the Lazy F. He's somewhere in town, and I heard he's needing hands."

"Thanks, I've got other places to be."

Billy was still missing, but I found Andy standing at the back door of the place. His attention was on something outside. I walked up and peered over his shoulder into the dark.

"What are you looking at?" I couldn't see a darned thing.

"It's a bear."

"You're shitting me. Let me see." I shoved him out of my way.

It was pitch black behind the saloon. All I could make out was what looked like a dog cowered up in a trash pile a few feet outside the door. "Damned dog is what it is."

No sooner than I had said it something growled and came at me out of the dark — something as big as a bear. I like to have knocked the doorframe loose getting back inside. I traveled all the way to the middle of the room before I stopped to look back. The place roared with laughter.

"Heeeeere, puppy, puppy!" Andy mocked.

"Found ol' Littlebit, did you?" someone roared.

I didn't like being attacked out of the dark, but I regained my courage at the sight of Andy standing calmly before the door.

"What the hell was that?"

"I told you it's a bear." Andy stepped aside and permitted me another view out the door.

Closing cautiously, I peered out. Sure enough there was a small black bear standing at the end of a chain. He didn't look so scary when I could see what he was.

"Doesn't that beat all?" Andy said.

"Why the hell have they got a bear tied up?"

"I guess to look at."

"Somebody ought to shoot him."

"I like looking at him. I'd like to own him."

"What would you do with a bear?"

Usually, nothing Andy said could shock me. "I'd dress him up in a suit, teach him to smoke cigars and play poker."

The boy wasn't all there.

"Where's Billy?" I asked.

"Last I saw him, he was off with One Jump Kate."

One Jump was one of Mobeetie's "ladies." Assured that I'd seen the last of Billy for a while, I left Andy staring at the bear. Walking away I heard him mumble something about riding it.

The night was cold as I stepped out of the saloon. I hunched my neck down inside the collar of my coat. Summer couldn't come too quick.

I handled the few coins in my pocket and weighed the course of the night. With Andy caught up in his bear, and Billy tending to his business, I suddenly didn't feel like cutting loose. To hell with it, I would catch a good night's sleep, and wake up without too much of a hangover. And for once, I would be able to afford breakfast after a night on the town.

Unwilling to spend what little coin I had on a bug-ridden bed that I would probably have to share with some equally buggy partner, I opted to find a place to roll out my bedroll.

I climbed back aboard Dunny and ambled up to a catch pen that served as the cheapest livery in town. It was just a big, rickety picket corral where a man could turn his horse loose. Whoever ran the pen forked out some hay twice a day and charged two bits a day for it.

I unsaddled Dunny and penned him. There was a small blacksmith shed just off from the corral with the haystack lying between the two. I carried my rig in behind the haystack and up against the shed wall. The shed served as a windbreak, and I was glad of it. Wrapped up in nothing but my old henskin, what we called a light cover made for the southern climate, and a saddle blanket wouldn't have made for a pleasant night.

More comfortable and sheltered than I'd been for a good many nights, I fell asleep listening to someone banging on a piano down the street. Whoever it was had the most unusual ear for music.

One Jump Kate got her name somewhere up in Kansas. The story was, one night, drunk as hell, some of the boys dared her to ride a certain bronc topless. The bronc was notorious for his devilment, but Kate was also equally well known for her own mischief. The boys just wanted to see her humbled as she was always bragging about her riding abilities. The topless part was just for their entertainment, and the sheer novelty of bare-breasted bronc riding.

Kate climbed aboard, and that bronc stuck his head in the ground and uncorked. Kate sailed off and landed with the grace of a sack of feed. This was much to the disgust of many of the boys, as they had hoped it would last just a bit longer and *then* they'd see her get pitched off.

But as it was, they all just hoorahed her, and somebody gave her the moniker of One Jump Kate. She took it in stride and joked that she knew several of the boys in the crowd whom the name also fit. Like the sport she was, she took their jokes about her short-lived ride. She came to accept the nickname, and like a lot of the girls, she bore it with more than a little pride.

Town was quiet early that morning, and I strolled up the street in search of Billy. Kate didn't operate out of one of the picket shacks like the crib girls, but had a room in Bill Thompson's dance hall.

Many of the cowponies stood tied where they'd been the night before, awaiting their masters' revival sometime later in the morning. I trooped into the dance hall, where several of the boys lay where they had fallen. It darned near looked like a battlefield. One of the bodies lay slumped across the table with his weapon still at hand — half full. The swamper was rolling another body off the bar top so he could clean it.

I went across the floor and into the back, where there were several rooms for the girls. "Billy?" I called quietly.

"Come on in," Billy's voice came from

behind one of the doors.

I pushed the door open. Billy was already up and about, looking like he was ready to go to church or something. Kate sat on the bed, her back propped up against the plank wall. What clothes she had on were open at the top, and one tit hung out. She made no attempt to put it back. She just smiled.

"Hello, Nate," she said mischievously.

I refused to let her get the best of me, and met her eye to eye, or something like that.

"Damned, you're a nasty slut." Billy pitched a wad of clothes her way.

She threw him a wicked, haughty look and laughed. "You keep coming around."

Kate was kind of pretty; in fact, she was real pretty compared to most of the girls we had to choose from. She was freckle-faced, and wormy, but she had blue eyes with the most mischievous twinkle to them you ever saw. And like Billy, she had a way about her. She wasn't bad, as the girls went, and we weren't hypocrite enough to think we were any better. Many were the times when she'd loaned one of the boys enough to get through the winter.

Billy and I left the dance hall and went down the street to O'Laughlin's to have a bite to eat. While we ate I suggested that when we finished we look up Wiren.

"I ran into him last night at the Lady Gay," Billy said between bites. He was obviously pleased to have beaten me to the punch.

"Did he need help?"

"There ain't any shortage of jobs for good cowboys in this country, especially with every English lord and his brother driving cattle in here."

Billy paused to wipe delicately at his mouth with his thumb. "You saw how many cattle have drifted down this way. The winter was a bad one. I saw brands on the way down here from plumb up in Colorado and Nebraska. Like I said, there ain't any shortage of work for good cowboys."

"How good are we?"

"I admit you handicap me some, but as pairs go, we're about as good as it gets," Billy raised his voice, not caring who heard him.

"This is a good country, ain't it?" I said.

"Just about perfect, I reckon."

The place was just beginning to fill up as we finished. A pistol cracked out on the street, and a few minutes later a bloodcurdling war whoop followed it. We glanced at each other for the merest instant, and headed for the door. It sure sounded like Andy.

It *was* Andy, and he was riding the bear down the middle of the street at a dead run. He was wearing some poor girl's underclothes just to make it interesting.

Andy brought the drunken dead from the night before to life. Hungover cowboys came out of the woodwork, lining the street as he tore by with that bear bawling his torment, and Andy laughing like a crazy man. Everyone cheered him on.

The ride was short. The bear turned sharply off the street, hit another gear, and dumped Andy headfirst. He made an effort to grab at the section of chain dragging behind the bear, succeeding only in getting drug for several yards.

He leapt to his feet, pulled his skirt off of his head, and yelled, "Help me, boys, I'm afoot."

It was cowboys to their horses, while others pursued the bear on foot. Andy led them on like John Brown going to war. The bear was rapidly putting country between himself and the pursuit. Several horsemen blew by Andy, and one finally slowed just enough for him to swing up behind.

Billy and I raced for the horse corral, but by the time we had saddled, the crowd was long gone. We hit the street running, hoping to catch a little more of the show.

We caught up to the crowd at the edge of town. People were running every direction, but nobody seemed to know where the bear was. Billy and I pulled up to survey around us. No sooner than we had stopped than the bear barreled around the corner of a group of houses. We'd just thought he was running before.

One of the boys pulled in behind him swinging a loop, causing the bear to swerve and run right through a little yard and tear down ten feet of cedar picket fence. Women screamed, and clutched their children. Some folks were praying for deliverance and others cursing.

Every time somebody got close that bear would swerve. No one could get a rope on him, and we all tried.

Bears must be long-winded, because it lined back out, heading north with all of us riding for the lead.

"He's headed for Ring Town," someone yelled.

Billy and I were jumbled back in the pack, fighting frantically to get to the front. Just about the time we got to the saloon a gunshot sounded, and everyone before us pulled up hard. The crowd was quieted for some reason. I followed as Billy pushed his paint through the crowd to the front.

At the edge of the crowd was Andy. He had dismounted and was standing solemnly before his bear. It was dead, and there was a man on the other side holding a pistol alongside his leg.

"That will be enough, boys," he said.

He was a tough-looking cuss with a big mustache. He eyed the crowd like a mad bull.

Andy jabbed an accusing finger at his bear lying there in the road. "Why'd you shoot my bear?"

"For the general assurance of the peace." That fellow didn't smile when he said it.

"That's Cap Arrington," someone in the crowd said.

"Get that bear out of the road. The stage is coming," Arrington ordered.

Nobody moved. Arrington pointed at Billy, singling him out of the edge of the group with a hawk's gaze.

"Do I know you?"

"Hell if I know," Billy drawled.

"That's Billy Champion," somebody behind us blurted out.

Arrington eyed Billy for a long moment. "I took you for someone else. I was obviously mistaken."

"I reckon," said Billy.

With that, Arrington stepped off, leaving

90

us to mourn over the bear, and the end of a grand chase. Andy sat down on the bear, slumped and looking dejected. I watched Arrington as he left.

Cap Arrington had made a name for himself with the Frontier Battalion of the Texas Rangers. I had heard Cap was down with a company of rangers to look into the theft of cattle, but had put it off as rumor. Rumor be damned, there he had been in the flesh. And if that wasn't enough, he had shot our bear.

"What was that all about?" I asked Billy.

Billy just shrugged his shoulders and mumbled something as he made for Andy. I don't know if anywhere else but Mobeetie — maybe Tascosa, but certainly nowhere else — could you have seen such an eccentric sight as a gangly boy wearing women's underclothes sitting on top of a dead bear in the middle of the road.

"They said you were riding that bear, General." Long Tom stepped forward from the crowd. His deep voice was filled with something akin to awe. He stood well back from Andy and the bear, obviously unsettled by what had happened, and the odd sight before him.

Andy brightened at the mention of his accomplishment. "I reckon I did."

"Why did you want to ride a bear?" Long Tom shook his head.

"To say I did it, that's why." Andy was perturbed at having to repeat what he considered an obvious conclusion.

"But why are you wearing womenfolk's clothes?"

Andy scratched his head for a moment. The question seemed to have stumped him. "I don't know, Long Tom. It must have seemed like the thing to do at the time."

Billy snorted, and then the paint snorted, not liking the proximity of any kind of bear, dead or not. Andy jumped to his feet and began dancing a little jig of some sort. Long Tom slapped his leg in time, soon joined by the crowd around us in some odd accompaniment.

Andy began to sing a little bawdy tune about riding a bear through the streets of Mobeetie, making up for a lack of voice and awful verse with sheer enthusiasm.

I looked up to see that a stagecoach was right on top of us, already pulled to a stop. I wasn't even sure how long it had been sitting there. The crowd was large, and a gully on one side of the road had blocked the stage's progress. Andy's song had just gotten to the part about the bear's butt having hair but his was bare.

I sat my horse right alongside the stage, and when I turned my head I looked right into one of its windows and found the most beautiful pair of eyes a man ever saw.

All I could see were those eyes, and a pert little face beneath one of those girly hats. I sat there like I had been struck by lightning. I gawked and I gawked some more just for good measure. Apparently she found me rude, because she turned away, making no attempt to hide her displeasure and offense at the whole situation.

I came out of my stupor and realized that I had just seen the girl of my dreams. And there I was, not only consorting with, but enjoying, the company of a boy in girly clothes, still singing and dancing his heart out atop a dead bear to the continued pleasure of a giant black man and at least thirty equally ribald fans.

Everyone else must have finally noticed her too. The crowd hushed. Even Andy and Long Tom finally ceased their merriment. She hesitated for the longest of moments, and then gave me the briefest of glances.

"Get out of the way, you hairy-legged saddle monkeys!" the stage driver shouted, and cracked his whip.

Horses and men scattered — all but our crew. The girl's look froze me again. I could feel the heat of my embarrassment rushing up my neck as the stage lurched forward. My moment was almost gone, and I could say nothing. I couldn't even swallow. And then the merest hint of a smile played at the corners of her lips.

What had I done to deserve that? It came to me in an instant. It came to me out of the corner of my eye. Billy had reined up beside me, and he was smiling and tipping his hat.

And then she was gone. The stage rolled away toward town, and Billy wasn't at all embarrassed enough not to follow. He kicked up his paint and loped right alongside. He left me sitting there too knotted up to cuss.

"Hey, Tennessee! They want to eat my bear!" Andy's high-pitched voice brought me back to earth.

"Dammit! I ain't from Tennessee!"

CHAPTER SIX

I only saw her once more that day. It was just a brief glimpse, and at a distance. She was getting back on the stage as it prepared to leave for Clarendon.

Long, Andy, and I stood in front of the Lady Gay, passing the time by watching the stage leave. Billy had disappeared, saying he had business to attend to.

While everyone else laughed and joked, I stood there with a sick feeling settling over me. I felt like I'd had my guts ripped out of me when the stage rolled off. What reason did I have to get so upset? I didn't even know her name, but I would have liked to ask. I would have given anything to have known.

Not long after the stage left, Billy sauntered up with a cocksure grin on his face. He looked like the hound that had just gotten into the smokehouse.

"What are you looking so smug about?" I asked.

"That's why you can't play poker, Nate. You just can't read faces," Billy teased.

"What do you know that's so funny?"

"I know you better get ready to ride. We've got to be on the Lazy F by day after tomorrow if we want to work."

I looked at Long a moment. "What about him?"

"They were silly enough to hire Andy, so who knows? Maybe if Long there would pass some of that liquor around they would take him on," Billy said.

"That's all right, boys. I don't . . ." Long was cut off in midsentence.

"The only reason they hired Andy was to run all the bears out of the country. He sure as hell ain't good for anything else besides killing horses," Billy said.

Andy grunted and whistled through his missing teeth. "By gosh, I'm the genuine article!"

"You couldn't find your ass with both hands," Billy said.

Before we could pester Andy any more, Long stopped us. "I've already gotten work."

There we were patting ourselves on the back for being concerned about the plight of poor Long, and he already had work.

"What're you going to do?" Andy asked.

"Freight supplies."

"For who?" Andy rattled right back.

"Myself," Long said with more than a touch of pride.

"Where's your outfit?" Andy was unconvinced.

"I've gotten me a good wagon and three yoke of oxen."

"Like hell . . ."

"Shut up, Andy." Billy's interest was obviously aroused.

"Where'd you get the team?"

"I bought it off a sick man up at the fort. I traded for part of it, and bought the rest on credit."

"Well, forgive us for being nosy, Long, but that man must have been awful sick. You don't look like any businessman I ever saw before." Billy offered his hand to Long.

Long wrapped Billy's hand in one huge paw and grinned. "He was just about to die, but it was the whiskey that sealed the deal."

Billy laughed. "You beat all, Long. Tennessee here is a good man, but he's often short of entertaining qualities."

"Don't you go to calling me that," I said.

Billy just grinned at me. Long motioned to the three of us. "You boys ought to throw in with me. I know where there's a double

97

wagon rig that could be bought right. With all the ranches starting up in this country, there is going to be a lot of business for teamsters."

"What the hell is wrong with you? We ain't freighters," Andy burst out.

"Thanks, but that goes for me too," I added.

Billy looked down at the ground and kicked at the dirt with one boot as if in deep thought. "Maybe when these two are full grown, and I can quit wet-nursing them we'll settle down to business, Long."

"What's the matter with you? We're cowboys!" Andy said.

Billy stared at the ground a moment, and then slowly raised his head until we could see the devilish smile on his face. "That'd be when I'm too old to sit a horse, and freighting won't be the business I'm talking about. It'll be whiskey making."

We told Long to look us up sometime, and saddled our horses and headed south to go to work for the Lazy F. Billy and Andy were in high spirits, but I was still thinking of that girl.

I trotted along behind as they visited between themselves. That stage turned around at Clarendon and headed back to Dodge via Mobeetie and Fort Supply. She was obviously going to Clarendon, or somewhere in the vicinity. The boys had taken to referring to Clarendon as Saint's Roost because it had been started by a bunch of Methodists and they kept it a dry town.

What was she doing there? I cursed myself for getting so wrapped up. Who was I to be thinking of a girl? I didn't have ten dollars to my name. I had my saddle and gear, the good horse that Billy gave me, and that was all. Besides, cowboys didn't get married. If you got married your cowboying was done, and I wasn't ready to give that up. Right then I wouldn't have traded my life for any man's, but I still kept wondering what her name was. She'd probably known me for what I was at first glance.

Billy broke me from my reverie when he pulled back and rode alongside of me. He always knew when something was bothering me. "What's the matter, Tennessee?"

"Why are you still calling me that? You know I ain't from Tennessee."

"I don't know. It's just got a ring to it."

"Well, Nate has always been good enough up until now," I said sourly.

"I'll call you by your given name from now on if you will quit pouting about that girl." Billy studied my face trying to read me.

99

"I don't know what you're talking about."

"To hell you don't. She didn't say a word to you, but one look and you acted like you were lightning struck."

"I was just looking."

"Uh-huh."

"Leave it be." I tried to put an end to the conversation by loping ahead.

Billy caught right up. He looked really pleased to have gotten under my skin.

"If I thought Dunny could outrun that Injun pony of yours I'd leave you behind." I tried to sound indignant.

"Well, he can't, but wait till you ride him on roundup. He's the best cutting horse in Texas." Billy wasn't one to brag, and if he said Dunny could cut a cow I believed him.

"I didn't figure to work him in my string. I was going to keep him for my high-life horse."

Back in those days, if a man had a really nice horse that he was extra proud of, he often saved him back and called him his "high-life" horse. I'd also heard them called " 'riginals," or "originals."

"Do what you please, but try him once."

Like it or not, Billy had lightened my mood, and he knew it. That's what I appreciated the most about Billy. He always had a way of picking me up when I was feeling down. I could, and had, come riding in off the range with fifteen hours in the saddle behind me, bone-tired with a gyp water bellyache, and he could still make me laugh. A cowboy's life was hard, but it was the laughing that always made it bearable.

Just when I was feeling better Billy added, "I found out her name."

"What . . . ?" I stammered.

He gave me a grin, a wicked sparkle in his eyes. And then he was off, with me in pursuit. He was going to talk, one way or the other.

Two days later, I still wasn't able to get a confession from him. I was beginning to think a village of Kiowa squaws wouldn't be able to torture it out of him. That was all I had to think about for the long ride south. I fretted and worried for over a hundred miles. We rode tantalizingly close to Clarendon, skirting it to the east in our rush to reach the Lazy F before they started roundup.

Late at night, when we finally were in camp at the Lazy F, I had all but given up. We had thrown our horses in the headquarters corral and bedded down beside a fire with the Lazy F hands.

Just as I was about to fall off to sleep, Billy whispered, "Her name's Barbara Allen. Her daddy's got a dry goods store in Clarendon."

Barbara Allen, what a sweet name to dream on. If I never saw her again I would still have that lovely name to carry around with me for a while. The trouble was, I had a strong suspicion Billy would be doing the same thing.

They woke us up just before daylight. The headquarters wasn't much of a setup. The jumbled frame and pile of lumber representing a half-completed manager's house was the only thing about the place that looked even half civilized. There were a couple of dugouts in the face of a bluff facing a flat in the bend of a clear, sandy little strip of water they called Quitaque Creek. It was a pretty name for a creek, but somebody later told me that *Quitaque* was the Comanche word for horse turds, or something like that. I don't think there ever was a white man who could interpret anything an Indian had to say.

One of the dugouts served as a bunkhouse, and the other had a pole shed built off its front with a wagon tarp stretched over the top. We lined up under the shed with the rest of the crew and had breakfast on a big piece of sheet iron propped up at one end by a stack of crates, and a nail keg at the other.

After we ate, we followed the wrangler down to a corral in a shady grove of trees alongside the creek. We studied the horses he'd penned there in the twilight. He helped us pick a string of six horses for each.

Most of the time, you were at the mercy of your own judgment when it came to picking a string. Sometimes you would just get one assigned to you, but when you were allowed to pick one you went about it with a careful eye. Many a time a crew got a kick out of someone picking a bad horse. If, on a morning where you were riding a horse for the first time, you noticed the crew gathering around in a suspicious manner, you could bet that you had your work cut out for you riding that SOB! And then again the outlaw might not do a thing when you got on him. He might have some hidden quirk that the crew knew about, and they were just chomping at the bit to see you encounter it for the first time. The horse might be scared of water, or go crazy at some certain little, seemingly harmless thing. He might be as gentle as a kid pony until you tried to rope on him.

In short, the boys on the range got a big kick out of watching someone else get in a wreck. But it was all in good fun. You didn't mind someone laughing at you who had been there themselves.

This horse wrangler was uncommonly helpful, and we warily gave him our trust, at least in part. I say we, but I only meant Billy and I. Andy, as usual, had to go his own way, and he didn't listen worth a darn. It seemed like he chose every horse in the pen that the wrangler studiously avoided pointing out.

Once we had them picked, we drove them over to a little remuda gathered out on a flat to the west of the corrals. Five of us and one cook were being sent south to work as a floating rep outfit. The winter had been terrible and the cattle had drifted farther south than usual, fleeing one norther after another. There must have been a jillion different brands mixed up along the Canadian River. And it was pretty bad to the south. The rest of the Lazy F bunch was staying behind to work the home range.

Rumor had it that Charles Goodnight and the JAs were buying out the Lazy F, and that this roundup was to be worked extra clean so that a good cattle count could be arrived at. The boys at headquarters seemed a little uptight. Usually, this time of year they were full of piss and vinegar and ready to get back to work. But I thought the pending sale must have their spirits down. When you found an outfit that you liked you hated to see it change hands. You never knew how things could change under new management.

The cook started his chuckwagon along, and we followed with the horses. A three day trip to roundup was before us. The remuda lined out and ran a while, kicking up their heels and raising hell in general. After a mile or so, we had them settled down a bit. I always liked to watch a herd of horses strung out and running in the morning. It was a pretty sight.

For two weeks we worked the country to the south, and southeast. It was fifteen hours a day in the saddle for us. Our floating outfit was bossed by a man by the name of Gruber. He was a withered-up little fellow who the boys called "Hell's Bells," or H.B. for short, because every time something didn't go good enough to suit him he would say, "Hell's bells, boys!"

He was easy enough to work with, even if he didn't know which end a cow quit first. Despite his shortcomings as a cattleman, you couldn't help but like him.

Our cook was a Mexican they called Carlito. It was a hell of a nickname, because he must have weighed about four hundred pounds. He had his work cut out for him. We were only a floating outfit representing the Lazy F and Hat brands, but when a cook was sent out on the roundup, he spent all day long feeding hungry hands no matter who they rode for. The men were sent here and there, moving various herds, and they often ate at whatever wagon they came across.

The other hand besides Billy and I was Dale Martin, a sandy-headed young man with a quick wit. He was a good hand and would put in a day's work here and there, but seemed a bit shiftless. He had a habit of disappearing from time to time, and despite his popularity among the hands I couldn't find it in me to like him. Card playing was rampant at the wagons at night, and he always claimed, after his absences, to have found a game and just stayed on to work with that crew the next day. Hell's Bells Gruber didn't seem to mind; he didn't seem to mind anything.

The rough breaks and canyons of that country had slowed the winter's drift, but we still had a lot of cattle wearing brands from far-off places. All cattle not belonging to the range that we were on were placed into the cut herd. The cut herd was driven along with us as the roundup moved, with individual owners' cattle to be relocated back to their ranches when and where it pleased them. The main herd, or herds belonging to the range we were on, was left behind when we moved to a new piece of country.

The country south of the Salt Fork and along the Pease and Tongue rivers was filling up fast. The Matadors and the Shoe-Bars held most of the range we were on, but there were several other smaller operators with crews working.

We worked our way east, and then north through the Diamond Tail range. As we left the home ranges of certain outfits, their main crews fell out to work their own country and prepare for market drives. However, many of them left a man or two to stay on and follow the general roundup and represent their brands. Our wagon became sort of a pool outfit, and camp continued to grow. We were far off from our home outfits, away from oversight, and we tended to have the rowdiest camp going. We did our work, but it was often after a long night of merrymaking.

One day, after one of the roundup bosses had "told us off," or gave us our working orders to gather a piece of country, Billy and I were working parallel to each other. It was broken country, and we had to ride closer to each other in order not to overlook any stock. We both topped out on opposite sides of a steep, narrow little canyon at the same time. Billy waved at me and continued along the far side of the canyon rim.

As I ambled along watching the canyon floor below me, I spotted a small pen of cattle in a little cedar thicket at the head of the canyon. From above I could just make them out through the trees. I looked across the canyon for Billy. He was passing right on above without seeming to notice the cattle.

Whistling to get his attention, I motioned at the cattle below us. Billy studied it a minute, and then began looking for a way down. I found a cattle trail, washed out and running to the canyon floor. I put my horse to it, and hit the bottom in a stir of dust.

I beat Billy down, and made my way up into the thicket. Sure enough, somebody had built a brush fence across the canyon, the sides and back being so sheer as to form a natural fence. There was a good trickle of water running through the pen from somewhere above.

The cattle penned were all two- and three-year-old steers. There must have been about thirty of them lying in the shade of the trees. At my approach they all rose to their feet and fled toward the head of the canyon. I recognized several of the brands, and in fact, the majority of them wore our own Lazy F or Hat brand burned into their hides.

I rode over to the improvised gate and studied the ground. It was tore up with horse and cattle tracks, all coming from down the canyon to where it emptied into a bigger one about a half a mile away.

"What have you got, Nate?"

"Somebody's penning steers, and I'd swear I recognize a couple of them from the cut herd." I pointed out a white steer with a crazy patch over one eye.

Billy studied the setup a moment. He took the time to roll himself a cigarette, and only when he had it lit did he reply. "Looks like some of the boys are making up a little herd."

He eyed me carefully, as if measuring what my response would be. There were hands who thought it no big deal if someone drove off a few head, but I wasn't one of them. I guess a lot of them felt that with so many big outfits forming up, that it didn't hurt to cause the rich a little loss. I figured stealing was stealing.

For the past year, most of the big ranchers in the Panhandle had been squawking about an increase in rustling, and they soon had old Cap Arrington poking his nose over the lip of every gully in the country looking for someone to hang. There were all kinds of stories about organized rustlers stealing cattle and driving them off to New Mexico, or Colorado. Folks loved to use the word "ring" along about then. Anything shady or illegal that was supposed to be going on, but couldn't be proved, was said to be done by some shadowy, mysterious "ring."

The newpapers could talk all they wanted about a "rustlers' ring," but from what I saw on the range, cattle theft was overblown. Granted, Billy the Kid and some of his like ran off some stock, but a lot of the rustling was done by cowboys here and there looking for a little spending money. The large losses of cattle reported were often the result of piss-poor management, or inaccurate counts to begin with.

"Help me tear down this fence." I started to do just what I said. Billy held up a hand to stop me.

"Hold on there. Let's think this out."

"There ain't anything to think out."

"You've got to live in this country. Think about that." He drew deep on his cigarette.

"You ain't in on this, are you?"

"Hell, no. I've never rustled cattle," Billy said testily.

"Well, what's holding you up? You ain't one to scare easily."

"I don't care to make this my business. You butt your nose into something like this and you won't ever ride easy without worrying about some jasper taking a potshot at you when you least expect it."

Billy made sense, but he was wrong. I couldn't figure him. He was no saint, but everything he ever did since I had known him was only in the spirit of a little devilment. He was a six-shooter man, and not a cheap thief.

"What's gotten into you?" I asked.

"I don't recall you complaining when we ran off those Cheyenne ponies."

"Stealing from Indians is different. They steal enough stock that you can't tell who their horses really belong to."

"So stealing from a savage or a thief doesn't count as stealing?"

"We're taking wages to do a job, and I've got enough pride to ride for the brand. You do too, or you used to."

Billy turned his horse away from me, twisting in the saddle to keep from looking at me. "I've had my ear to the ground, and

111

the rumor is that a bunch of foreigners are buying our outfit at book count. Further rumor has it that, as usual, the book count is a whole lot bigger than the actual range count would be."

"So while the bigwigs are getting ready to shyster some foreigners, some of the boys figure to help themselves a little?"

"Looks like it."

"And we should just mind our own business?"

"It's the best way."

I studied him a long minute, and then cussed a blue streak. It was far from the best way, but I agreed. We rode up out of the canyon together, and I felt like a cow thief.

"We're going to have to live with this."

"We've all got something to live with, Nate."

We threw our gather on a big plain that evening. I unsaddled my horse, and turned him loose to saddle another. I had first guard that evening and had to hustle to get something to eat and my bedroll laid out. There were enough hands that we didn't have to stand guard every night like you did on a drive, and Billy wasn't on duty that night. He hadn't come in yet when I sat down to eat.

No sooner than I started to wolf down my food, Andy flopped down beside me. He precariously balanced a full plate of beans on his knees. Andy had been day-herding the cuts, and I hadn't seen much of him since we had finished the last work and moved to the present location.

"That Carlito's some cook," Andy managed to blurt out between mouthfuls.

I had to admit that any man that could keep you from growing tired of eating beans seven days a week surely possessed a high level of culinary skill. There were good cow camp cooks and bad ones, but even the bad food didn't seem so bad when you had spent a day gathering cattle.

"You have a rough one?" I asked.

"Naaah. That black bucked me off again this morning, but I rode him the second time around."

"You picked him."

"He'll be all right." Despite what he said, that horse would be the same the day he died, and for that matter, so would Andy.

"A new outfit came in today, and some of them gave us relief on the day herd." He paused between mouthfuls. "We had a pretty good poker game under the wagon sheet."

"Sounds like you had it rough."

"We had it good until y'all started coming in with your gathers, and we had to quit before H.B. or one of the other big chiefs caught us."

I mumbled something in reply, and got up to take my plate to the wash barrel. Andy followed. He was still following me as I went for my bedroll. One of the other outfits in our camp had brought out a hooligan wagon to carry along our beds, or any other miscellaneous items that wouldn't fit in the chuckwagon.

The cook or his helper had unloaded our bedrolls and piled them. While Andy buzzed around me telling of his day's adventure, I searched out my roll. Andy didn't like my disinterest in his conversation, but my attention was on the two men standing down at the end of the hooligan wagon.

It was Dale Martin, and one of the Shoe-Bar hands. They were in deep conversation, at first seemingly unaware that we were there. However, I soon noticed that they kept glancing our way. They didn't say anything, but something in their manner made me uneasy. I caught them looking our way again, and I muttered some greeting. Both men nodded their heads, but didn't seem as friendly as they should have been.

"You find much down your way?" Martin

was a quirt man, and he restlessly slapped the braided leather against his leg.

It seemed like he was asking me more than how my gather had been. "We pushed a few head out of those brakes."

He passed a quick glance to the freckle-faced ShoeBar hand beside him before he spoke again. "There's some rough country north and west. It's easy to miss stock if you ain't looking careful."

I waited until he was looking me in the eye. "I rode real careful, but I'm sure I could have gathered it a little cleaner."

Martin slapped his leg again with that quirt and a little smirk was at the corner of his mouth. "A man's bound to pass by a few head no matter how hard he works, but a few head here and there ain't going to break any of these outfits."

"I don't miss much."

He shoved his Stetson back on his head with his thumb to reveal a curly little point of hair hanging down on his forehead that reminded me of a pig's tail. "No, I don't reckon you do."

Before he could slap that quirt on his leg again I stepped past him close enough that my bedroll brushed against him and forced him to step to the side. I walked away more than a little on the prod. I wasn't fool enough to think that encounter was anything more than what it was, but I considered that maybe I wasn't being fair. Finding those penned cattle had me edgy, and something about that Dale Martin just rubbed me the wrong way, cow thief or not.

"That Dale is about the best damned card player I ever saw," Andy said at my shoulder.

"I'd keep an eye on the deck."

"What's that?"

"Nothing." I tried not to trip on anything in the dark while I hunted for a spot to bed down.

Andy was still rattling on about his day as I found a likely place to roll out my soogan. We were about ten yards out from the fire, and I could see across it to the hooligan wagon. Dale and his buddy were gone.

"You seen Billy?" Andy asked.

"Not for a while."

"I thought I saw him a bit ago. He and Dale were talking," Andy added.

"Oh yeah?"

Andy had had enough of my poor company, and he headed off to find someone to jaw at. "See you later, Tennessee."

"Dammit, Andy! Are you the one who spread that around?"

He didn't answer me. He just kept walking off.

To my own annoyance, it seemed that my nickname had stuck, and I would forever be known by it. From the first day of roundup, strangers came up and called me Tennessee. My mama might as well have named me that, because most of the men on roundup knew me by no other name.

The boys could come up with some of the most original nicknames. The bad thing was, once they stuck them on you it was next to impossible to get rid of them. And often times they might be of a nature that reminds everyone of something you would rather they forgot. Just ask Dinky Dick Brown, or Smelly Smith.

I left Andy in camp, and rode out to the herd we had gathered that day. Billy met me halfway, riding from the direction of the cut herd. He seemed to be mulling something over in his mind, and I was willing to sit silent myself. I was bad to let things stick in my craw.

"You don't think I had anything to do with those penned steers, do you?" Billy was dead sincere, and doubt crept into his voice.

"I believe you."

"You're still pissed though, ain't you?"

"I'll get over it, I guess," I measured my words. "It just ain't sitting with me too good right now."

"That's just Little Carl's beans working on you."

"Maybe so." Carlito cooked the hottest beans I ever ate, and my belly was already feeling the effects. "I bet I fart like a Missouri mule tonight."

"Just don't stampede the herd."

I laughed. "I'll try not to."

"I need some of those beans myself." Billy started to head for camp.

"Billy?" I stopped him a few yards off. "That's the last time I'll turn a blind eye to rustling."

"I hear ya, and I'll stand by ya." He rode off in the dark.

I headed for the edge of the herd, my mind on Billy and rustled cows. I didn't think for a minute that Billy was in on hiding those steers, but he damned sure knew who was. Anywhere there were herds of cattle there was bound to be rustling, and it looked like the steal was on in the Panhandle.

CHAPTER SEVEN

We'd been out about a month, when Hell's Bells Gruber asked if one of us would like to make a quick trip back to headquarters. Our portion of the cuts had grown into a large number. He wanted a crew to come down and help drive them home. We were slowly getting far enough away from our range that the number of our brands was thinning out considerably. Also, there were a good number of cows and calves in the herd. A mixed herd was harder to drive, and the dust, heat, and handling were hard on the young calves.

I quickly volunteered for the ride. I was saddling my horse before daylight the next morning, when Billy joined me. Somehow he'd managed to talk Gruber into letting him go. I wondered what he was up to while we made the sixty-mile trip in one day's ride, arriving at headquarters late in the evening. Our little Texas horses were tough.

The next morning we saddled fresh horses, and found Wiren in camp with one of his wagon bosses about ten miles out. They had a herd gathered out on the plain, and were branding calves. The dust rolled up thick from beneath the hooves of the herd, and the air was filled with the sound of bawling cattle. Three crews were working on the ground with a couple of mounted men roping and dragging calves to each crew.

Wiren was working with one of the ground crews, and we rode up to him while he jumped on the next calf drug to him by its heels. Once the calf was branded, ear-notched, and castrated, he got up from the animal and wiped the sweat from his forehead with the back of one shirtsleeve.

"You boys decided to quit eating up ranch supplies and playing cards while the rest of us work for a living?"

We tried to hide our discomfort over his obvious knowledge of our rep outfit's recent behavior so far from home.

"H.B. said to tell you we need a few hands to help drive a herd back here," Billy said.

"Did he give you a tally of the herd you've rounded up?"

Wiren was a big man, with a grumpy way about him, but despite his jab about what had been going on out on the general roundup, he seemed pleased at the news we delivered. I handed him a tally written on a scrap of paper. He mumbled to himself over it for a few minutes.

"It'll be a couple of days before we finish up branding. You fellows pitch in here, and I'll send you back with a couple of hands once we're through."

"My stomach has been bothering me something fierce, and I wondered if I might get the time off to ride over to Clarendon and see if I can't get some Fletcher's Castoria." I kept a straight face while he glared at me like I was about to be fired.

"Never set much store by patent medicines," he growled, "You know there's no liquor in the Roost, don't you?"

"They tell me it's dry as a bone."

"Is the pain in your gut bad?"

"Terrible." I rubbed my belly and grimaced.

"Well, go on then. I wouldn't want anybody saying I ignored a dying man's wishes." He dismissed me with a wave of his hand as he turned back to his work.

Afraid he would change his mind, I whirled my horse around and took off for Clarendon without so much as a good-bye to Billy. The thought of being able to look up that girl from the stagecoach, with no competition from him, lifted my spirits. He could work his butt off branding calves while I did a little romancing.

My elation was short lived. I hadn't gone a mile before Billy caught up to me. I knew he was coming along by the grin on his face. I just couldn't figure out how he'd managed it.

"I told Wiren you were so sick that I was worried about you making it to Clarendon."

"He fell for that?"

"No. He's just a good boss, and I offered to mail some letters for him."

"You're quite the charmer, aren't you?"

Billy shook his vest pocket, and it jingled. "I got us a ten-dollar-apiece advance on our wages to cover the cost of your snake oil."

"Why does all this surprise me?"

We loped north through the breaks of that country. I was tickled to death that Wiren let us go, but there was one nagging thought that put a little bit of a damper on my general good mood. I felt guilty, but, for once, I was wishing Billy wasn't along. I didn't intend on sharing that girl's attention when I found her.

We camped that night in Palo Duro Canyon, where the endless prairie falls abruptly over immense cliffs down into that giant gash that divides the plains. The canyon was miles wide and shallow where we camped, but deepened and narrowed farther west, until the world above might not have even existed at all. We made a fire beneath the chalk-marked red rock bluffs of the north rim, and sat watching the sun melt into the high caprock miles to the west. The red stone of the canyon walls combined into a single orange glow, and then turned to shadows.

Once, those timeworn bluffs, at the jagged head of the canyon, had sheltered and hidden the Comanches in winter. That was years before we arrived, but the appearance of a band of Indians dragging their travois from the dark wouldn't have surprised me. In fact, it would have seemed right. The Comanches and the buffalo were gone, but the Palo Duro was still there — a forever place where you didn't have to close your eyes to envision the wild scope of a land that once was.

I wanted to get an early start the next day, so as to make Clarendon by morning. I attempted to go to sleep, but Billy wouldn't have any of it.

"I never knew you to take sick." Billy poked the fire with a piece of shinnery oak.

"You come with me out of a concern for

my health?"

"I guess I came along hoping to get a dose of the medicine you're looking for."

"I don't know what you're talking about." It didn't take much acting for me to play dumb.

"Damn, can't you just admit that you've been thinking about that girl for a month?"

"And I suppose you can?"

He didn't hesitate for a second. "Hell yes! This is just about a perfect country, except it's a long way between water and women."

"We don't even know that we can find her," I said lamely.

"Speak for yourself." Billy didn't lack in confidence. And he had reason where women were concerned. I'd never seen him around decent women, but the girls along the row were crazy about him.

I went to bed grumpy and jealous over a woman I'd never met. I didn't have a claim on that girl, but it was like he was busting in on my own private little dream. I went to sleep with Billy still sitting by the fire.

Morning came and we left camp for the short ride to Clarendon. Billy seemed to have slicked up a bit, and I grumbled to myself. I felt I probably looked like I ought to be thrown out with the wash. I don't know how he did it.

Clarendon wasn't much to look at early on. You could pass through it at a run and never wind your horse. It showed signs of building, but was still pretty hardscrabble looking. The buildings were a mix of different types, lumber being in short supply out on the treeless plains.

We stopped in the middle of the main street. Both of us were silent, thinking the same thing. Two could be a crowd sometimes.

Billy beat me to the punch. "I need a new shirt. Think you could handle the mail?"

An angry protest started to form on my lips, but I had second thoughts. Looking at Billy made me wish I was cleaned up a bit. I decided to find a place to knock the dust off and curry and brush up a little.

I took the mail from Billy and we parted ways. Before I went looking for that girl, I intended to find a barber and a bath. I was going to outshine Billy this time, come hell or high water.

I had to settle for a haircut given by the blacksmith's wife, as Clarendon hadn't as yet acquired a barber. The same woman mended and laundered my best white shirt for a half dollar. I washed up the best I could in a tub out back of their shop. When I headed down the street to the post office I was feeling quite dapper in my damp, semi-white shirt, and half-dollar haircut.

By the time I had finished my preening and mailed Wiren's letters, it was early afternoon. I hadn't as yet struck any sign of Barbara Allen, or Billy either for that matter. Careful questioning of a citizen got me directions to Allen's store.

I found the store, and as I'd suspected, I found Billy also. I saw him through the window. He was at the back of the room appearing to study a new hat. Barbara Allen was helping him, and he was making her smile.

She laughed just as I stepped into the room. It sounded rich and husky, tinkling across the store and filling my head. I fought the burn of jealousy.

My courage threatened to fail me, and I hesitated in the doorway. There I was, the same man who climbed on bad broncs, swam swollen rivers, roped outlaw cattle, and generally dealt with some danger to my general health on a daily basis, and yet I was scared as hell. I was scared of a little red-headed girl who had stopped her conversation with Billy to study me.

Like I said, she was red-headed. Auburn was what most folks would call it. Her hair was dark except when some light hit it, and then it shone with a red hue. She was tall, and slim. There was something about her carriage that bespoke pride. Or maybe that was the way she held her chin up just a touch. It wasn't in a snooty manner, just like she knew something you didn't. There was that same bright gleam to those green eyes that I had thought on for more than a month. I could have loved her for just her eyes.

I never had words enough to tell anybody else the proper way I felt about anything important. Looking back on that moment, a lot of things come to mind. However, I can think of no words to do justice to the way she looked, or what she stirred in me. She was simply the most beautiful thing I've ever seen.

A male voice cleared his throat and startled me out of my trance. That girl was looking at me like I was daft, and I was feeling hot around the gills about then. A snooty-looking gent wearing glasses stood behind a small counter. He cleared his throat again, and I stepped into the room.

"Can we help you, sir?" His sounded like a Yankee, and said "sir" like that may have been a questionable subject where I was concerned.

Lifting one foot at a time, I made my way

into the room. I was suddenly conscious of my spurs rattling. Awkward didn't begin to describe the way I felt right then.

"I said, can we help you?" The man raised his voice a little like he thought I might be hard of hearing.

"I just came to look," I muttered.

He tipped his chin down and looked over his glasses at me. He waved his arm at the stacks of goods in shelves behind him, and scattered about the small room. "Feel free to survey our stock, and tell us if we can help you find something in particular."

"I'm just looking," I repeated.

"Seems to be the trend of the day." The storekeeper cast a glance at Billy, who continued to make the girl giggle. Those giggles sped my heartbeat and cast small frown lines on the storekeeper's face. I wondered if he was her father.

"Hello, Nate." Billy was smiling like I was the funniest thing he'd ever seen.

My throat felt like I had swallowed a chunk of rock, and I strained to force myself, through sheer willpower, to speak.

"Have you met Miss Allen yet?" Billy waved his outstretched hand to gesture to her like he was the Prince of Persia or something. He was quite the gent, our Billy.

Triumphantly, I managed to mutter something totally incomprehensible under my breath.

Billy stepped forward and put a hand on my shoulder. "This is my friend, Nate Reynolds. He's a real talker when you get him going, and when he decides to speak something other than Comanche."

I wondered if the store could sell me a place to crawl into and hide, or if there was an undertaker to give Billy a proper burial when I cut his bloody guts out. I managed to smile appreciatively at the obvious concern of my dear friend.

"What brings you to our fair city, Mr. Reynolds?" Barbara Allen asked.

Like with Billy, I had the sneaking feeling that I was the source of the greatest amusement for her. Her eyes held the same mischievous glint.

I didn't give myself time to register what she said. I was too caught up in the sound of her to listen. My tongue took off before I was ready, and I blurted out, "I came a horseback."

Billy staggered off to compose himself, but he didn't laugh, I'll give him that. I don't guess he felt it was a laughing matter to watch a man shoot himself in the foot. Hell, I had shot my leg off at the knee.

Barbara Allen held her composure as still

as a corpse. I watched the strain in her face, and the tight-lipped straightening of her mouth. Once she had gathered a slow, deep breath, and let it out in a little shudder, she pointed a finger out the store's front window.

"Is your horse out front?" she asked dramatically, and I thought her acting technique decidedly unskillful and over-played. "I so love horses, especially these wooly little Western ponies." She started for the door.

What did she mean "wooly little ponies"? I might refer to our horses as ponies, but that was just a habit. I didn't mean cart ponies, or something. And Dunny sure wasn't wooly. His coat was summer slick and shiny as moleskin. I followed her, and I was thinking of plenty to say.

Out the door she went, and Billy and I like to have torn the doorjamb off going out it at the same time. We stopped at the edge of the street, and both of us took our most nonchalant and favorite stances. Dunny stood tied at a rickety hitching rail before us. I don't know where Billy's paint was.

Barbara Allen stepped lightly to Dunny's head, and he eased against his tie, eyeing her carefully.

"You gotta move softly around these

Western horses, Miss Allen," Billy advised.

"Oh, fiddlesticks! He's as gentle as a baby." And to prove it, she wrapped her arms around Dunny's head, and pressed her face against his jaw.

Now Dunny was generally a quiet, gentle horse who never got in a storm over anything, but he was always a touch skittish about someone handling his head. I'll be danged if he didn't just put his head in her chest like a lap dog. He stood there three-legged with his eyes half-closed, and ate up every bit of the petting she gave him.

"He's a sweetheart." Her voice had a strange tilt to it that I couldn't place.

"Billy claims he's the best cutting horse in the country."

"Is that so?" She seemed mightily impressed.

"He's all right," Billy mumbled weakly.

"Come on, Billy, tell her about him. I ain't going to brag on my own horse."

Billy looked like he had bitten into something sour. "You wouldn't want Dunny to seem immodest, would you?"

"You and those big words, Billy. You're sure a talker when you get going."

"Piss on you," Billy hissed under his breath.

"Sore loser," I said quickly.

"What was that?" Barbara Allen asked.

Billy returned my slap on the back and answered, "Why I was just telling Nate what a fine day it was to be out on the town with a good friend with such a wonderful horse."

She eyed the both of us for a moment. "He is wonderful, isn't he?"

"You could ride him if you want," I said bravely.

She cast a glance down at her dress and then back at me. "I don't think I am attired for it. And besides, we don't properly know each other."

The red rose in my face and my ears burned like fire. "Perhaps when you get to know Dunny *properly* you might ride him."

Our eyes met across the space between us, and for a minute I thought she was going to let me have it, but it never came. And then she did the damnedest thing, and winked at me. It was just one little quick flick of her eye, and the slightest hint of a smile. For a second I wasn't sure if I had seen what I saw, and then I was glad Billy hadn't seen what I saw.

Her hands continued to stroke Dunny's forehead. "Perhaps, Mr. Reynolds."

In the matter of seconds I was made mute again. A moment ago I had been riding high and tight, and now I had blown a stirrup and was one jump away from landing on the seat of my britches. And she knew it.

The door behind us swung open, and the storekeeper stuck his head out. "It's the heat of the day, daughter."

She stepped away from Dunny's head, and paused at the doorway. "Are you gentlemen's names written in the Lamb's Book of Life?"

Now neither one of us knew a thing about sheep, and nobody was apt to be writing our names down in any kind of books, much less one about the lambs. That didn't stop us though. It didn't even cause us to hesitate.

"Why no, Miss Allen, but I have always felt a strong interest in that subject," Billy said gravely.

"It is a shame that our work finds us rarely in the vicinity of church houses," I added.

Both the girl and the man eyed us carefully. "Call me Barby. That's what everyone calls me." She looked to the storekeeper as if to confirm her statement. "Isn't that right, Father?"

He looked as if he had just as soon we didn't call at all.

Billy stepped forward and offered him his hand. "We haven't met yet."

"Yes, we didn't," her father said a bit

smugly, or maybe it was just that funny wang to his speech that made it seem that way. He was a stiff sort, and very proper.

"Father, this is Mr. Champion and Mr. Reynolds." She pointed us out. "And this is my father, George Allen."

We shook hands all around, and he looked like he was ready for us to vamoose. The talk had come to an abrupt end, and both of us had just about enough of the uncomfortable silence. We were trying to find a way to leave when we didn't want to do any such thing.

"You should come to the church picnic with us this afternoon," Barby said. A look passed between her and her father that I couldn't interpret, but could have guessed at. "Wouldn't that be nice, Father?"

Even put on the spot like he was, I was surprised that he quietly, if not fervently, agreed. When she giggled and hugged him for it, I didn't feel like the only sap on the street right then. If she had been my daughter I wouldn't have let the likes of us within ten miles of her.

"I always enjoy a bit of picnicking. Don't you, Nate?" Billy's voice was stuffy and imitating Mr. Allen's accent.

"But of course."

CHAPTER EIGHT

Whenever I think about picnics, or Sunday camp dinners I shall always remember my way back to that little cottonwood stand on the banks of a small creek at the edge of Clarendon. All picnics should be held there with the sunlight scattering down through the tree limbs, and a little breeze coming cool through the shade now and again, rustling the cottonwood leaves above.

There was a long plank table heaped with the potluck offerings of the women of the community, and they fussed over it like hens in the barnyard while their children ran wild beneath, around, and through them. The men gathered in casual clusters to visit with their fellow men, while remaining within easy striking distance of the food. There was a slight hint of pride in their bearings, as if some ancient office had been placed upon them, and their roles and positions were necessary and invaluable to the whole process of the dinner.

Clarendon wasn't called Saint's Roost for nothing, and a long, tall galoot in a black wool suit was asked to say grace over the food. He was sure fervent, and I figured that was the reason they had chosen him for the job. He missed his calling and should have been a lawyer, because after what seemed like five minutes of praying even I was looking around me expecting to see the Lord himself waiting to eat. The violent noise of growling stomachs must have reminded that sky pilot of Daniel in the lions' den, and rather than face such rampant and terrible hunger he called it quits. Everyone put a little extra wallop into their amens.

The line shuffled along single-file through the dust like cattle will travel. If I had listened close I am sure I could have detected a few hungry, pitiful bawls, as we all came to the feed trough.

I stood there quiet and slightly out of place, a part of things, but slightly removed as all strangers are. Barby was helping in the buffet line, and Billy, God help his little politician's heart, was far back in the line jabbering about farming with a few of the locals — like he knew the first damn thing about farming.

My celluloid collar — Billy's idea of dressing up for such a formal occasion — was scratching my neck and coming near to choking me. A man can't relax yoked up like that. I was glad that I wasn't fool enough to sweat it out in a wool suit coat like several of those around me. Any more sweat and wool, and the place would have smelled like a sheep pen. It was bad enough to have to button a collar on to my shirt, but then again, I never was one to suffer for the sake of style.

Billy, on the other hand, would have worn a cow chip on his head if he thought it would look good. I glanced at him while I made such an observation about his character, and the devil grinned back at me like he was fixing to be elected for something. It made me feel good to take some starch out of him if only by imagining him with a turd on his head.

I came near to starving to death before I made my way up to the food, but it was worth the wait once those ladies started helping me mound up my plate. I had been on beef and beans, and the sight of those makings like to have coliced me.

I got to stand in front of Barby Allen for about two seconds while she helped me top off the precarious monument of food I was building on my plate. The threat of being trampled from behind was so great that I had to move on from her company.

An older woman at the end of the line asked me something, and I didn't understand a word of what she said. I don't know where she was from, but I am certain she came from somewhere other than Texas, because nobody but a foreigner could talk that funny. Come to think of it, there were a lot of accents around me. Most of them were Midwestern Yankee, but there were a few accents that I couldn't place.

That foreign woman jabbered something at me again that sounded like German, and I went to looking for a translator. Finally, she motioned at the coffeepots on the table before her, and to a gathering of glasses with some strange, pulpy concoction in them. I was impressed enough with the sight of so much glassware in one place, but after she had repeated herself for the third time I figured out that she was asking me if I wanted coffee, water, or lemonade.

I hadn't ever drank any lemonade, but I would be damned if I would pass up such an opportunity. It was real, live lemonade in the middle of nowhere — somebody was showing out. I took myself a glass and found a likely spot to eat. I sat down cross-legged,

Indian style, and contemplated that lemon-ade.

I wasn't sure just how to drink it, and wondered if I should hold up my pinky or something when I turned up the glass. I looked around to see if anyone else might notice me drinking such a kids' drink, but nobody seemed to pay me any mind. In fact, I saw a few other grown men holding glasses themselves. I am not ashamed to admit that the same fellow who often bragged that he never drank water, only whiskey and good beer, enjoyed every last drop of that sweet nectar.

I drank my lemonade, slicked off my plate in record time, and kicked back to ruminate. To pass the time, I studied the line of people still gathering their food. Mainly, I studied Barby Allen, or to be correct, I studied Billy while he held up the line talking to her. She was smiling again, and my collar started to make me itch even worse.

It was just like Billy to be holding up the line. Didn't he know that we were guests, and those hardworking people deserved their food the same as us? It was plainly a blatant case of rudeness and a sheer lack of good manners. And what was she smiling about?

I couldn't help but wonder what he kept

saying that was so all-fired interesting. She just kept smiling, and even laughed once while he kept right on talking, smiling, and holding up the line like no one cared. *Little Prince of Persia.*

I imagine somebody got tired of waiting and said something to him, because he finally quit the table and made his way over to sit down with me. He grinned at me like I hadn't noticed his behavior in the chuck line.

"Glad you finally took that turd off your head," I mumbled.

"What's that?" He looked perplexed, but I knew that it was just his way of acting innocent.

"Ah, nothing." I made a show of being a whole lot more interested in studying the tree limbs above me than I was in hearing him.

Billy eyed me carefully and then turned up his lemonade. He took a swallow, and then smacked his lips a time or two, as smug as a cat licking his whiskers.

"I reckon you like that kid stuff," I scorned him, all the while keeping my glass hid at my side.

"What's gotten your dander up?" A little irritation crept into his voice.

We studied each other a minute, and then

140

Billy looked back over his shoulder to where Barby stood at the tables. "I reckon more friends have fallen out over whiskey, cards, or women than just about anything."

I managed a weak smile. "But not us, huh?"

"Not by a long shot." Then he added, "I'd guess we can both handle a little friendly competition."

"Why have you got to horn in?"

"I can't see that she's wearing anybody's brand, although I haven't got a chance to check her over close enough." The devil was dancing in his eyes.

"Damn, Billy! That's a lady you're talking about," I said, a little too loudly, and several heads turned our way.

Billy kicked his legs out in front of him and leaned back on his elbows. "Are you saying a lady ain't got any parts of interest?"

"You had better quit that talk. You ought to know better." I managed to keep my voice down that time, but the red was creeping up my neck.

"Are you saying a lady doesn't have parts?"

He just couldn't take a hint. I decided that as a last-ditch effort I could end his low talk

141

by offering some answer. "No, I ain't saying that."

"Well, what are you saying?" He was as quick as a rattlesnake.

"I'm just saying that you shouldn't talk about them."

Billy craned his neck around to look at Barby Allen again. "I've already talked about them, and I've thought about them enough to wear them out. I can't tell from the look of her to have done any damage at all."

I was up on my feet as quick as a cat. Billy didn't move from the ground, but he was wary. As mad as I was I recognized that. With a slow motion of his palm down he motioned me back to the ground.

"All right, Nate. You've converted me. I'll not speak slanderously of yonder maiden anymore. I'll keep all mention of her body to myself from now on." He used his most consoling tone.

The pressure in my ears abated a little, and I started to slowly unwind. Then I reconsidered what he had said. I didn't know what kind of bargain we had just struck, and sure didn't know if I was going to like it.

While I stood there halfway between sitting and standing, froze like a kid caught with his hand in the cookie jar, Billy jabbed a finger at my lemonade glass.

"Good stuff, ain't it?"

"Ain't it." I plopped down in resignation. I just couldn't help but like him, even when I was about ready to kill him.

No sooner than I had sat back down than Billy jumped to his feet. "Come on. They're pitching horseshoes over there. Let's go show them a thing or two."

Billy headed off, not waiting for an answer. I looked longingly back to where Barby Allen had been, but she was gone. I would rather Billy go pitch horseshoes by himself, or piss in the creek for that matter, if it would keep him occupied long enough for me to have one more little visit with her. I made a quick scout of the crowd under the trees, but still couldn't spot her. Disgusted, I took my plate to the washtub and followed after Billy. Horseshoes could only give a man so much enjoyment.

We didn't teach those milk cow dudes a thing about horseshoes; we just barely could make enough of a showing to keep from embarrassing ourselves. They knew how to pitch them, and our experience with horseshoes was limited to nailing them on, or wearing them out from between our horses' hooves and the ground.

I kept my eyes peeled back the way we had come. After about three games with the locals I spied Barby Allen playing with a small group of kids. Billy was tied up in an argument over scoring. It was obvious to me that our opponents had gotten the points they needed to finish us off, so I made my escape.

I wound my way through the scattered groups of people, impatiently returning pleasantries. Barby was gone again and I couldn't find her, but I wasn't about to give up. I could track a wild cow across a rock pile and I ought to have been up to the task of finding one freckle-nosed snip of a girl. I wasn't, not quickly anyway.

My search led me to meet darned near every inhabitant of Clarendon, or maybe half the population of the Panhandle, or so it seemed. Every time I ran across somebody I had to talk about the weather with them, and give a short autobiographical account of my young life. I usually enjoy friendly country folks, but right then I was a man on a mission.

When I had about given up hope my perseverance paid off — sort of. I found Barby Allen, and I found out that Billy had found her too. They were walking alongside the creek, and I was left out in the cold, or rather the hot sun. I scampered my way back to the shade to lick my wounds.

Barby failed to appear after an hour's wait, and I was ready to admit defeat, at least for the day. As I was leaving I ran across Mr. Allen down where the horses were picketed. There is more than one way to skin a cat, and maybe it wouldn't be a bad thing at all for Daddy Allen to get to know me. I was getting as devious as Billy.

"It's a fine day for a picnic, Mr. Allen."

He was a plump little man with a balding head, and wire-rim glasses perched on his nose. I couldn't tell whether he was uppity, or just looking down his nose at me in an attempt to focus his lenses.

"Mr. Reynolds, is it?"

"Yeah, but you can call me Nate."

"Well, it is a fine day, *Mr. Reynolds.*" My smooth talk had yet to take effect on him.

I couldn't help but notice again the strong Yankee twang to both his and Barby's speech. "You don't sound like you're from around here."

He seemed to be weighing whether that was an accusation, or a question. When he finally answered, it was with more than a little pride. "My daughter and I came from Ohio."

Yankee or not, I didn't hold it against

them. As pretty as Barby Allen was, it stood to reason that there must be some good people from Ohio. It wouldn't do to be discriminating against emigrants.

"I hale from Kentucky."

He didn't seem impressed. In fact, he began untying his horse from the picket line. Their buggy was close by, and I followed beside him while he led the animal over to harness it.

"Do you need some help?"

He stopped in his tracks and turned to me once more. "Is this about my daughter?"

I tried not to squirm under his gaze, and found it a highly unsettling question to be put before me without warning. "Well, I would like to call upon her at some later date."

"I don't even know you, except for the fact that you come from Tennessee."

"Kentucky."

"Just the same, that's little to go on in my book. I haven't been in this country much more than a month, and already I've got cowboys loitering around my store every day and mooning over my daughter."

The realization that Billy and I weren't the only ones to have discovered Barby was worrisome. "I understand your concerns."

"Have you a career, or an occupation?"

"I'm riding for the Lazy F."

"I am serious."

"So am I."

I could tell he was a little frustrated with me. "That's no career. Are you a man of property?"

He apparently didn't know a damned thing about cowboys. I held down the urge to tell him a thing or two about my line of work. "I've never had any trouble finding work."

"What is the condition of your soul?" He gave me that beady-eyed preacher look that made me feel like he could see right through me.

I was at a loss for words, and he was firing off questions like a rifle volley. "Are you right with Jesus?"

"That's something he'd have to tell you."

"A heathen, and a smart aleck too!" A great sigh escaped his chest, and he began hitching the horse to the buggy.

"I meant no disrespect," I said honestly.

He turned back to me, and he spoke as if to a child. "Listen, we are a Christian family. When Barbara's mother was lying on her death bed, God rest her soul, I promised her I would raise our daughter right, and see to it that she married well. When, and if, my daughter finds a husband he will be a

147

man of substance, in good standing with the community, and the church. He will not be some drunken, half-wild cowboy."

"Have you got something against cowboys?"

"I am sure that you have some admirable qualities, but forgive me if I don't see you as an acceptable suitor."

He couldn't see anything through those glasses he kept shoving back up his nose while he lectured me. *Blind fool.*

"I think you're mistaken."

"Big hats, forty-dollar pistols, and rackety spurs aren't the measure of a man where I come from." He finished with a huff, and a straightening of his coat front.

Nothing was going as planned. Instead of welcoming me to pursue Barby's affections, the pompous windbag was belittling and lecturing me. He seemed bothered by the fact, that at my age, I wasn't governor or something. He could go on about a man's success and achievements all he wanted. If he was so all-fired rich and prosperous, why did he leave Ohio to come to Clarendon and sell dry goods? From the sound of him, God probably sent him there with a title and a salary.

What the hell was success anyway? Colonel Goodnight once told me that being a big man in the country meant owing the bank more than anyone else around you. I'll be damned if I've ever heard a better explanation.

I kept my thoughts to myself. Maybe he would reconsider our conversation, extol my virtues to his daughter, and invite me over for supper one night. Granted, I wasn't ever going to like the SOB, but it wouldn't do for me to get too crossways with Barby's father.

"I'd best be going. I have a long ride ahead of me." I started for my horse.

I hadn't gone two steps when Mr. Allen, formerly of the greater civilization of Ohio, recently come to Clarendon to sow the seeds of righteousness in the wilderness while making his fortune in dry goods, confident in the wisdom of his years, and generally too all-fired full of himself, asked, "Young man, have you thought about where you're going in life?"

Talking to him was like talking to a fence post. I swung aboard Dunny, pulled my hat down tight, and gave him just about as good an answer as he was liable to get before I spurred Dunny off.

"I am going east until I decide to stop, or turn around, or my horse quits me one."

I left him in my dust, without a look back

at him. *Old Fart!*

I was ten miles east before Billy joined me. I could tell by his sweaty horse that he had traveled fast to catch up. Neither one of us said anything for a long while. In stark contrast to my foul mood, he was all grins. I expected the overly happy little fart to start whistling a merry tune at any moment.

You will notice that I often refer to Billy as little. In fact, he wasn't that short, even though I was exceptionally tall. It was just my way of taking him down a notch in my mind when I was riled at him. A lot of the things I did seem childish, but women have that effect on a lot of men. And besides, Billy had plenty of room to come down a little. I guessed he was gloating over beating me to Barby.

He chattered away at me for a few miles, but I ignored him. I didn't especially want to talk to him right then, but not knowing what had gone on between him and Barby was driving me crazy. I could keep my jealous silence no longer.

"I saw you walking with Barby." It sounded like the accusation it was.

"We took a little walk, and talked a bit."

"What'd you talk about?"

"Aw, just stuff. We didn't get to talk long. Her daddy hunted her down and shooed her off."

"That's too bad." Maybe Mr. Allen did have a few good points.

"We'd just walked a little ways down the creek, but he set in to fussing at Barby about what he called 'scandalous behavior.' "

"What scandalous behavior?" Damn Billy. He was already getting scandalous with Barby before I could.

"Nothing. We just were talking and wandered out of sight of everyone. You'd have thought he caught us skinny-dipping or something. I was sure I was going to have to whip the old devil, but Barby lit into him first. They had quite a set-to."

"They fought?"

Billy let out a slow, quiet whistle and shook his head. "There were some harsh words said. I get the notion that they've been butting heads ever since her mother died a couple of years back. Seems like he is pretty strict on her, and she ain't too happy with some of his nonsense. She called him an 'overbearing, old-fashioned tyrant,' and that was one of the nicer things I recall."

"I can see where a person might butt heads with her daddy."

Billy looked a question at me. I went ahead and told him about my encounter with the "old fart," as we called him from that time on.

When I told Billy about the man's views on occupations and cowboying, he stopped his horse and looked me dead square in the eye. "He doesn't know anything, does he?"

"Nope."

"That shirt-folding, button salesman ought to be glad we get down off our horses long enough to talk to the likes of him." He paused for an impressive string of profanity. "I'm certain of something, Nate."

"What's that?"

"He doesn't know one damned thing about cowboys."

"Not one thing."

"We've got good horses to ride, plenty of open country, and we go where we please. That means a whole lot more than money."

"He doesn't know anything at all." My blood was getting up all over again.

"Now you're talking, Nate. If we want to sweet talk his daughter, we'll do it, and if he doesn't like it he can kiss our callused asses!"

Damned if Billy wasn't right. We had it all, and thought it would last forever.

CHAPTER NINE

The summer rolled on, and neither Billy nor I laid eyes on Barby Allen for a long time. The roundup south of the Canadian worked east to about sixty miles west of Henrietta, and then north up into the Territory. We worked both the Comanche and the southern edge of the Cheyenne Reservation, where various brands were operating under leases. We logged what must have been ten thousand miles on horseback.

I thought about Barby Allen constantly, and Billy did too. I know, because he told me. Both of us were set on being the object of Barby's affection, and jealous of the other's intentions. For a good bit after our Clarendon picnic there was a touch of the uncomfortable for each of us in one another's company.

It was just a subtle contention between us, nagging and chewing at us, until we talked less, and the old banter between us was all but gone for a time. It was like wearing a pair of baggy, sweaty britches to work. After a while a man gets pretty chafed and blistered, and soon he's sore as hell and walking funny around his best friend.

We recognized the change that had taken place between us, but I figure we were both too proud and stubborn to do anything about it. Barby Allen was just too damned good-looking for either one of us to let go of, even if it wasn't the actual woman that we both claimed to possess, but rather the notion of her.

She was something glorious to carry around inside of us and think upon. Those storybook writers will tell you that we all spent all our nights in camp singing to a bunch of cows, or yodeling and plunking on guitars around the campfire. But many a man passed the quiet hours lying alone in his bedroll, awake and staring at the dark sky overhead — lost in his own thoughts. You might work up a picture in your mind of the old home you'd left long ago, or maybe dream on what you'd like to do or see. Barby was our little dream, and night after night, Billy and I lay down to sleep, each begrudging the other a hard-on.

Given a little time, we seemed to have made our peace over that girl. Maybe we both realized how foolish it was to fight over a girl neither of us had a claim on. That doesn't mean we forgot about her, not by a long shot. We talked about her frequently. It might sound silly, us acting that way over her, but there were few women in the country, and none at all like her. I guess we were about as female starved and girl-crazy as men can get. If Billy told about her just right I would get a picture of her so stuck in my head that it would be an hour after I lay down before I could go to sleep.

And I know it was the same for Billy, because sometimes, when I had lain there unable to sleep, his voice would come quietly out of the night, whispering like some blind oracle.

"She's sure something, ain't she, pard?"

And he was right.

There was another thing that helped smooth things over between us, and that was a change in our fortunes. I mean to say, that we suddenly had more jingle in our pockets.

Nobody ever got rich cowboying, and by the same turn, nobody ever took up the trade who had such lofty financial aspirations — all those types became bankers, lawyers, railroad men, or pimps. A little extra money to spend on liquor, gambling, or trinkets was always a soothing thing.

Our path to riches came to us in the form of one certain paint Indian pony in Billy's possession. That crazy little pinto was faster than greased lightning. And once we determined that Little Paint, as we had taken to calling him, could run, there wasn't anything short of an act of God that was going to keep the money out of our pockets. None of my crew held anything against a little easy money as long as it came by honest means — like gambling.

We ran Little Paint a few times against some of the Lazy F horses that were known to be quicker than usual and none of them could even give him a race. Word soon spread among the outfits on roundup that our camp had a fast horse, and it didn't take long for someone to propose the first race for stakes. Little Paint put the dust in their faces, and we put their money in our pockets. All the riches in the world looked like gravy to us. One after another, week to week, cowboys brought their fastest stock to match against Little Paint. He outran them all like they were standing still.

If someone should ever build a museum in honor of all the good Texas cowboys who ever lived, I would think it fitting for them to paper the walls with playing cards, and plow up a nice sandy lane leading up to it suitable for a horse race. For if there's one thing most cowboys had in common it was the love of gambling.

A lot of us loved a good game of poker, but horse racing was the best of all. In an age where everyone rode a horse there was bound to be a large percentage of people who felt they were experts regarding all things equestrian. Given the frontier's propensity to gamble, there were also a lot of folks willing to wager that they knew more about a horse than the next fellow did.

Horse racing was especially rampant in Texas. There were about as many little brush tracks as there were outhouses in certain parts of the state. There was tale after tale of entire towns losing their fortune backing a local favorite in a match race. And a horse race didn't require any official, organized track to take place. A race might spring up anywhere two riders met.

Most of the races were sprint races, matching good quarter horses over short distances. They were usually under a quarter of a mile, but one might see any kind of a race imaginable here and there. The Indians loved to run longer races where their mustang ponies' endurance played to their favor. A bunch of the high-rollers down in

South and East Texas had even been importing good thoroughbreds.

I don't guess it's any wonder that men who spent most of their living hours in a saddle should love horse racing so much. It's safe to say that I don't know if I ever felt more alive than when I was standing at the finish line and cheering on the fast horse that I had bet on at the time. And like every other damn fool for a horse and a dollar, my favorite races were when I won.

After a few weeks of racing Little Paint around the roundup camps, our outfit took on a new air. It's a wonder every one of us didn't lose our jobs, but even Hell's Bells hauled himself right into the mix. He was as proud as any of us that our outfit had the fastest horse on the roundup. Being a bit older than the rest of us, H.B., without nomination, took on the role of manager and trainer. Every night he came into camp and informed us of potential matches, giving us his opinion of different horses and their merits, and the prospect of getting a race up.

Carlito, the cook, took on the role of groom, and against all cow camp etiquette he started keeping Little Paint tied to the chuckwagon. He managed to scare up a bit of grain to feed the horse, and he rubbed the little devil until his coat was shiny and slick. You never would have known he was the same long-haired, knotty little pony we stole off the reservation.

Andy became our official jockey on account of his slight stature. We all strutted around some, but he outdid us all. After every race he insisted on recounting the affair in a play-by-play fashion, highlighting the brilliant strategy he had deployed, and the subtle jockey techniques he had made use of to bring about victory. We were all so happy counting our winnings, both past and future, that none of us pointed out the fact that Little Paint was so damned fast that a monkey could have rode him to a win.

The biggest part of the general roundups in the Panhandle was over by the Fourth of July and we were finishing up our last work just east of Mobeetie four days before the holiday. We had worked a big circle between the Washita and the Salt Fork of the Red and had a herd gathered to work about two miles south of the Sweetwater. I was castrating a calf when High Card Henson rode up to the fire I was helping work. I rose to meet him, wiping the bloody blade of my pocketknife on the bottom of my chaps' leg. Two strangers were with him, but stopped off at a distance and waited.

Now old High Card weighed about a hundred pounds, stood about six foot six, and the only thing longer jointed than him was the handlebar mustache he kept tugging down below his jaw while he pulled up his horse and hooked a leg over his saddle horn. He was a professional gambler, and if you doubted the fact all you had to do to was ask him. I even heard that for a while he introduced himself with business cards he had printed in Austin that presented him as such. The thing about High Card was that he spent more time following cow tracks than he did sitting over a card game. Any time you asked him why he wasn't gambling it was because he had had to go to work to replenish his stake. It took High Card about two hours to lose any kind of stake, and at thirty-or-forty-a-month cowboy wages, it took him a hell of a lot longer to rake another one up.

If I was to have summed him up I guess I would call him a determined sort of a fellow. And then again, he wasn't all that much different from a lot of gamblers I knew. Even poor gamblers know that there are very few regular winners and a sight more losers that just show up with their donations. The trick is that almost every gambler identifies himself as a winner, suffering from an eternal case of chronic optimism whereby the rest of the world is just a bunch of suckers.

"Are you winning so much you've taken to traveling with bodyguards?" I pointed to his fellow travelers sitting off behind him.

High Card's face brightened and he seemed pleased that I could expect so much of him. "Naw, that ain't it at all. Those are some of my professional associates."

"That a fact?"

"We've a camp back up the Sweetwater a little bit — tents set up with tables and such. There's liquor, women, cards, roosterfighting, and well . . . just about everything a man who's been out working all summer could desire."

"Are you making the rounds advertising?"

"Yes and no."

"Speak your piece. I've got a man fixing to need a hot iron." I gestured back at the bawling calf being drug by its hind legs in a trail of dust toward us.

He twisted in the saddle and glanced back at his friends, followed by a studious observance of the sky. Finally, as if slipping something of the utmost unimportance and trivial nature into the conversation, he slyly said, "We heard you boys have a racehorse in camp."

"We might," I replied with equal uncon-
cern and nonchalance.

He continued to make a show of gauging
the sun. "That's a coincidence, because
there are a couple of gentlemen in our camp
that are sure getting frustrated."

"If it was winter, and it's that Mobeetie
crowd you're running with, I'd say the
watered-down whiskey froze again and
busted the barrels."

He didn't like my measure of his newfound friends, but he was quick to cover it
up. He yawned and stretched and adjusted
his tempo before he answered. "They hauled
a couple of good horses all the way up from
San Antonio a month ago, and ain't been
able to find a single bit of competition for
their animals."

"Is that so?"

"That's a fact. It seems they're beginning
to doubt the quality of horseflesh in these
parts."

"Maybe they ain't been looking in the
right places."

"Maybe."

"Maybe they're long on talk and short on
funds."

High Card shook his head solemnly. "No,
sir. Those boys got money by the sackfuls,
and are game and ready to risk a little of it

162

should a worthy challenge for their horses come along."

"You're meaning they would like a little match race with our horse?"

He appeared to be in serious contemplation. He winced as he said, "Well now, I don't doubt you boys have got a horse you *think* is fast, but how's your financial situation?"

"Have you gone to banking too?"

"No, it's just that those racehorse men up on the Sweetwater are getting pretty bored with the action around these parts and are willing to entertain a little betting on a much smaller scale than they're used to."

"Why don't your high-rolling racehorse men come down here themselves if they want to dicker up a match?"

"You saying y'all might be interested?"

"We might." I paused before adding, "Of course we realize that it would be professional horsemen and imported stock that we would be dealing with, and would expect certain considerations."

High Card nodded his head in satisfaction. "They've invited y'all up to our camp to palaver with them tonight."

"Where do we find you?"

"Just ride west until you hit the Sweetwater and turn up it until you see our fires."

"I reckon we can find you if we're interested."

The men behind me had already worked two calves shorthanded, and I turned as if to go back to work. For kicks, I stopped and motioned for High Card to get down. "You might as well lend a hand to keep in practice."

He made a show of brushing the dust off the cheap suit coat he was wearing, and then pulled a pocket watch from his vest and studied it as if his schedule required him to be off to better and more important places. "I believe I'll pass. I've had enough of the dust pneumonia and the gyp water squirts."

"The work here is honest," I said.

He turned away and, as he was riding off, he called back to me, "A man should work in the vocation of his calling."

I watched him for a minute before turning back to my calling. What I mean is that there were three fellows behind me calling me all sorts of foul names for standing around while they worked.

Andy watched me from his perch atop the neck of the calf just drug to him. He wiped the back of his sleeve across his dusty face, leaving a ragged, muddy streak. "What are you looking so happy about?"

I grabbed up a hind leg and flopped myself down to take a hold on the calf. The calf bucked against the hot iron laid on him while I grinned at Andy and held on. "You smell that?"

"The shit, or the burning hair?" He wrinkled his nose as the branding smoke rolled across his face.

"No."

"What the hell are you talking about? Has the heat gone to your head?" He got up from the calf and kicked at it as it rose and trotted off bawling for its mother.

"Can't you smell it?" I asked again.

"What?" he almost yelled back at me.

"Money. Lots of money."

"Where?"

I jerked my thumb back over my shoulder toward High Card's bunch loping off on the horizon. "It looks like we found ourselves a horse race."

Andy leapt into the air and clicked both spurs together before he hit the ground. He did a little Indian shuffle in a tight circle, and without hesitating he bailed on the next calf drug to us while I slipped the rope off of its heels. We grinned at each other like we had both just escaped the loony bin.

"I want to know one thing." He sounded very serious, and I patiently waited while he

paused for dramatic emphasis.
"Where did you find those suckers?"

CHAPTER TEN

Billy took the news just like I'd walked up to him and handed him a draft on the entire funds of the Denver Mint. All of our camp was excited by the prospects of a horse race for bigger stakes. None of us seemed to have the sense to be concerned about our challengers. That Mobeetie crowd was a bunch of holdout men and shysters that made their living skinning the likes of us. Dealing with those boys could be like sticking your hand in a sack of shook-up rattlesnakes.

Billy had the final say in any proposed race, as it was his racehorse, and he asked me to go with him to visit the Mobeetie gamblers' camp. Andy wanted to come along, but we knew he'd get drunk and wouldn't make it back to work the next day, or maybe for even longer. H.B. seconded our opinion, and ordered Andy to stay in camp.

We headed for our horses and H.B. like to

have trampled down the back of our britches' legs following us. It seemed like he was set on going with us. Besides being our boss, he was a stubborn old fart, and it was usually wasted time trying to change his mind once he'd made it up. Billy had to try anyway.

"Won't you miss your beauty rest, H.B.?"

H.B. snorted, "Why hell's bells, you boys need a grown-up along for wise council and a mature outlook."

Showing some good sense, Billy gave up the argument and climbed aboard his horse. He and H.B. took off in a lope, with me following along behind. The old man's horse was a cold-backed SOB that had to be ridden a bit before he could be trusted, and he tried to pitch. Old H.B. Gruber just jammed his pipe in his teeth and cracked him across the butt with the tail end of his reins. He had him lined out in a few stiff little hops, and was soon tearing along with his long beard whipping down either side of his face. He looked like some mad general charging off across the battlefield.

The ride to the Sweetwater was only a two-mile jaunt, and we had the fresh rode off our horses by the time we hit its banks. We turned up the creek and followed it for a few miles until we saw big fires lighting some trees ahead.

They had picket lines strung up between the trees and we slipped our cinches and tied up there. Somebody helloed us and we made our way over to the fires. There were two or three tents, and a couple of tarp lean-tos set up with a few long tables laid out between them and the fire.

The crowd wasn't the sort you would see in Sunday school. There must have been twenty or thirty men gathered around the fires, a couple of what passed for women, and five or six mean-looking dogs tied to the trees. I don't know who looked mangier and meaner, the dogs or the people.

As we walked up to the largest fire a big, burly, greasy buffalo-hunter type shoved a bottle at us. Billy eyed the amber contents swirling around in the bottle, and the filthy hand that offered it. It would have taken a box full of forty-five shells to knock the lice off that fellow.

Billy wasn't about to drink after the likes of him, but before he could offend him H.B. took the bottle and turned it up. He snorted and wheezed and smacked his lips and brayed like a jackass before handing the bottle back.

"You other fellows ain't drinking?" One of the whores, who was sitting on the lap of a man in a bowler hat, snickered. You could have planted a crop of potatoes on her, and braided the hair under her arms to drag a wagon with.

Before any of us could answer a deep voice interrupted. "I believe they are here on other matters."

We all turned to place the voice. Back at the edge of the firelight a man sat propped on the tailgate of a wagon. One elbow rested on a crate containing a fighting rooster, and the other arm was hooked by a thumb in one armhole of his vest. The firelight shone on the gold of his watch chain and the elk tooth hanging there.

And when he spoke again his voice was silky smooth and decidedly Deep South. "I think these are our racehorse men."

"We've got one," Billy answered.

"Good. It so happens that I do too — several of them in fact."

Quick as a whistle he barked out something in Spanish, and before long a little Mexican boy came leading a horse into the firelight. The crowd made room and the horse stepped nervously up to us, turning on its forequarters and bobbing its head against the lead. The boy held him there for a moment and then paraded him back and forth in front of us a few times before standing him again.

The gelding was huge, and he obviously was a thoroughbred. The long, flat muscles ran smooth and sleek over his large frame. He must have stood sixteen hands and was as long as a freight train. He was fine-boned for his size and his hocks and cannons were high, flowing down into pasterns that were long and springy. His long ears twitched alternately above his slender head, and his big, soft eyes were dark pools. Reflected tendrils of intertwining flame and shadow floated upon their depths.

"Hell of a horse, but he ain't a sprinter," Gruber whispered beside me.

At some unseen gesture or signal the boy led the horse away. He soon returned leading another animal. The same scene played itself out, but with an altogether different horse.

The second horse was a chestnut filly with a flaxen mane and tail. They had rubbed her until she shone in the firelight like fire itself. Her pale mane and tail almost sparkled. She stood just short of fifteen hands, and where the thoroughbred spoke of distance and fast endurance, she bulged with muscle. Her chest tied down low into her forearm, running down into good short cannons, and sturdy flat bone. She was short coupled and her long underline flowed up into where hip, stifle, and hock articulated the power of her hindquarters.

We watched with more than a little envy as she pranced with quick, dainty steps about the fire. Everything about her spoke of a sprinter's quick power. She was quite the lady.

"You've got some awful good-looking horses there," Billy said to the man on the wagon as the filly was led away.

"And runners too," the owner quickly replied.

"Who might you be?"

The man quickly stood to his feet and approached Billy, offering his hand. He was tall and he towered over Billy.

"Colonel Andrews, at your service." They shook hands, and I could tell by the length of time they held the shake, and the look on Billy's face, that the colonel was putting the clamp on the smaller man.

"If we stand here any longer we're going to have to dance," Billy said flatly.

The colonel gave Billy a long look as he let go of his hand. The little Mexican boy came back up dragging some chairs. We were all soon flopped down in them while the colonel returned to the courtly position of his elevated perch atop the tailgate.

"I haven't seen your horse, but I have heard that he is a runner," the colonel said.

"You might have heard that." Billy spat in the fire.

"Would you be interested in a little match race?"

"Depends on what you've got in mind."

Colonel Andrews seemed to consider things for a moment before he spoke again. "I'll race you for five hundred dollars, and let our associates take up what betting they will between themselves."

Billy rocked his chair back on its hind legs and began to build a smoke. Only after he had the cigarette lit and going did he reply.

"That gelding looks to be quick, and you can't hide his breeding." Billy paused to draw on the weed and then continued. "I'd have to have some odds."

The colonel chuckled softly. "No odds."

"Even money?"

"Even money and you race the filly."

"You don't think we're good enough to run against that Bluegrass Special?"

"No, as a matter of fact I think you know he isn't a sprint horse. I went to New York and purchased him. I shipped him by boat to Galveston and then trailed him overland to here. I did all this at quite some expense and trouble."

"And after all that money and trouble you won't run him?" H.B. threw in.

"Yes, I'll run him. I've run him at Houston, San Antonio, and I plan to run him at Denver," the colonel said flatly.

"Why not here?" Billy asked before H.B. could butt in again.

"If you wish to race him at eight and a half furlongs or more, I would seriously consider it."

"What the hell is a furlong?" H.B. squawked.

"It's an eighth of a mile," I told him.

H.B. did some tabulating on his finger digits and blew a quick gust of air out his cheeks when he came to a conclusion. "Why, that's over a mile."

"Exactly," the colonel said.

Billy had remained quiet during the exchange. He waited for a long count of three before he set the front of his chair back down on the ground and flicked his cigarette butt into the fire. "A quarter mile against the mare?"

"Even money?" The colonel was quick.

"You give me two to one."

"On what grounds, may I ask?"

"Why, you probably imported her here from China in a balloon or something."

"I can't hide her quality, and wouldn't at-

174

tempt to, Mister . . . ?"

"Champion."

The colonel faintly smirked and continued, "Mr. Champion, I am not going to attempt to doctor up some horse to look slow when it isn't, or trick you into believing I don't have an honest-to-goodness racehorse when I do. On the contrary, that filly is out of the Denton Mare."

We didn't know whether to take him serious or not. The Denton Mare was the outlaw Sam Bass's good horse. Legend had it that it was she who led him to gambling, and thence to shadier things like robbing trains and such. She was supposed to be one of the swiftest horses ever to hit Texas sod.

The last anyone had heard of her Bass had taken her to San Antonio. Then he lit out up north to go rob the U.P., and she disappeared to certain history. Some said he sold her in San Antonio, and others claimed he took her north and she died of colic in Deadwood. Sam wasn't around anymore to tell the straight of it, because the Rangers shot him to death at Round Rock in the Summer of '78.

"Wasn't the Denton Mare by Steeldust?" I asked.

"Steeldust died along about the end of

the war. The Denton Mare wasn't old enough to have been out of him," H.B. corrected me.

Steeldust was the horse that broke half of Collin County Texas in '52 by outrunning the good horse Monmouth, or at least the half that bet against him. That race happened before I was even born, and folks were still talking about it. Most conversations about Texas running horses started and ended with Steeldust and his progeny — those big-jawed, heavy muscled sprinters that gave the word "bulldog" to the early quarter horses.

The colonel swirled a glass of clear liquid around in a jar before his face, and then took a pull. He waited until his whiskey hit bottom before he answered. "No, she was in fact sired by Cold Deck, who was a son of Steeldust."

"They say he was a hell of a horse," I said.

"I would venture to say that he was the best sprinter of our time."

"They always claimed that nothing ever outran him." I'd heard about that horse all my life.

"They say that about all of them." Billy didn't appear overly impressed.

"It is his propensity to pass on that speed to his offspring which interests me," said the colonel.

"Who's your filly's sire?" Billy asked.

"She is by Old Billy, who was a son of Shiloh. Old Billy's dam was a daughter of Steeldust called Ram Cat."

"Two times back to Steeldust," I whispered.

"Her second dam was a daughter of Printer that raced with some success."

H.B. whistled through his teeth and slapped his leg. "With blood like that she ought to eat her feed off of a silver platter."

"I went to some trouble to find that filly and buy her."

"What's her race record?" Billy asked.

"I always let the handicappers do their own work."

"That matters a lot."

"My filly is open to world, given terms of the race can be agreed upon. If I suspected you lacked a competitive animal I would have showed you some of my other horses."

"You've got more?" H.B. exclaimed, and he was looking around in the trees incredulously as if he expected them to come charging out and trample us.

The colonel tamped the ash off the end of a cigar and smiled as he spoke. "I have others with me, but not so fast as Baby."

I thought that a fitting name. "Is that what

you call her?"

"Yes."

Nobody spoke for a while, and I could almost hear the wheels turning in our heads. That Colonel Andrews thought he had himself a horse and made no bones about it. And it could have been that our little Cheyenne pony was stepping out in some pretty fancy company. But, damned, that paint could run.

"Two to one on four hundred dollars and we run at a quarter of a mile," Billy offered.

The colonel thought he knew his business and was quick to counter offer. "Five to three on your horse, and we run at three hundred fifty yards."

"What's five to three figure out at, Tennessee?"

"We put up four hundred and he puts up roughly six-sixty." I glared at him for calling me that, but he was too caught up to notice.

"Call it six-fifty." The colonel's white teeth shone in an oily smile, and he looked like the devil himself by the firelight.

Billy was counting money in his head. "Call it five hundred your end, and we run at four hundred yards."

"Six hundred my end and we run at three-seventy-five, catch weights, 'ask and answer' start."

"Who steps off the distance and picks the course?"

"You and I will step off the distance in a matter equally agreeable to each of us, and the course will be laid out here along the creek to both of our satisfaction."

Billy rose to his feet, and we followed suit. The colonel once more stood and offered his hand to Billy.

"When?" Billy asked.

"Day after tomorrow at noon."

Billy nodded his head.

The colonel lifted an exaggerated eyebrow. "We have a deal?"

Billy took his hand and shook. The colonel seemed pleased, and turned to his bottle on the tailgate.

"Shall we have a drink to seal our agreement?"

"You already shook on it," H.B. said.

"Ah yes, but a drink is a much more enjoyable format. Don't you agree?"

That Mexican boy was there lickety-split with some cups, and once he had poured us all a round, the colonel lifted his glass high in a toast. "Here's to honorable men and fast horses."

Just like honorable men, we all showed our agreement by tossing them down our funnels. That liquor was smooth, but it

179

burned like fire once it got where it was going. Looking at that slick dude again through teary eyes I was sure we had just taken a drink with old Lucifer himself, and made a pact with him to boot.

H.B. must have been worried that we hadn't gone far enough to consummate the deal, because he held out his cup for more. The boy poured him another, and he hardly had time to pull the bottle back before H.B. was holding out another empty glass.

"That's damned good whiskey."

The colonel nodded in agreement. "I bought that off a man I met down the trail."

"Well, they sure know how to make it where he comes from." H.B. downed the third one.

Three glassfuls were enough, and Billy finally shepherded him off. We waved goodbye to our hosts. There was some grumbling and attempts by their crowd to get us to stay and let loose of a little of our money, but we wisely let on that it was a long ride back to camp.

H.B. was already feeling his liquor, and I had to pull him out of the clutches of some old snaggle-toothed, swaybacked hag that was hanging on him. It was all I could do to keep him from squealing and rearing up on her right then. For an old codger — he must have been at least fifty — he sure was a randy demon when he got to drinking.

We tightened our cinches and mounted up. Billy turned his horse to face us. We parked nose to nose to talk.

"How do you think we made out?" he asked.

"The distance is too short. That mare looks like she could jerk a stump out of the ground," H.B. slurred.

"I agree she looks like she ought to have early speed, but we got some odds." Leave it to Billy to paint a pretty picture.

"All in all, I'd say you done well," I threw in.

"That fellow back there doesn't race for a hobby," said H.B.

"Do you believe that filly is really out of the Denton Mare?" I asked.

"No. He's full of shit." Billy was adamant.

"Might be true, you never can tell." H.B. was getting so drunk, he was merely a singsong in the background.

"I know one thing. That filly of his may not be out of the Denton Mare, but I bet that we're going to find out if Little Paint can run." Billy only reiterated what we all knew. We were worried and excited at the same time.

We let it go at that, and for sheer orneriness Billy took off at a lope. H.B.'s horse was too coldbacked to be jumped right up to a lope like that after a long rest, and he set in to bucking again. H.B. was too tipsy to have thought to shorten his hold on the horse, and the bronc-riding exhibition was on right there.

It was pitch black and all I could make out was a vague shadow twisting before me. I could hear that horse bawling and thumping the earth with all fours. Soon I heard a different thump, a string of cussing, and the sound of a horse running off.

"I'll go get his horse," Billy called out of the night.

I eased up to where I thought H.B. had gone down. He was moaning something awful, and I thought I could make out the shadow of a man down on all fours. He sounded like he was dying. He sounded worse than that — like he was dying slow and terrible.

I dug around in my vest pocket until I found my matches, and struck a couple of them to see by. Sure enough, H.B. was down on the ground. He had gotten up on hands and knees and was still moaning. There was a string of slobber hanging out of his mouth danged near to the ground, and he was covered in grass and dirt. He set in to cursing and wheezing, and I was worried that he was hurt bad.

"Are you all right?"

"Hell, yes, I'm all right," he growled.

"Well, why are you bawling so? What's the matter?"

He cussed a bit more before answering me. "What's the matter with me? Hell's bells! Can't you see I've lost my damned pipe?"

CHAPTER ELEVEN

Early in the morning on the Fourth we hitched up the wagon and headed out to meet our destiny and write our names in the immortal granite of racing history. Little Paint traveled jauntily behind the wagon, and we could hear money jingling every time his feet hit the ground.

There were at least ten of us traveling together, and about three times that many were still back on the roundup grounds awaiting the opportunity to come and see the show. A rotation had been worked out whereby all of the hands could get a little time in Mobeetie for the holiday. Those left on guard with the herd would be relieved by others who had already spent their allotted time enjoying the sights. The only problem was that, no matter what, somebody was going to have to miss the race, and nobody wanted to. They say a good cowboy never left the herd, but I had a feeling that there were going to be some cattle in a certain neighborhood left unattended for at least the duration of an afternoon.

A hundred yards from the gamblers' camp we were hailed by a chorus of drunken yells and pistol shots. From the looks of things their camp had quadrupled in size. Half of Mobeetie and Ft. Elliott must have turned out to see the show, and we could see more folks coming down the river from the northwest.

As we neared the camp we passed a wagonload of Bill Thompson's dance hall girls trying to string up a tarp between two trees. A few of the boys naturally stopped to help, but the rest of us rode on.

Not all of the people were Mobeetie's night crowd. A couple of Army officers and their wives were spreading blankets on the ground and breaking out a basket of goodies in preparation for a picnic. Down around the gamblers' tents a pack of wild kids ran screaming and laughing in and out of the melee'.

Colonel Andrews's Mexican boy met us and guided us under the trees to where they'd roped off a little area for us. H.B. tied Little Paint up, using the rope strung around the trees as a picket line. About twenty yards separated us from the colonel's big tent, and we could see his racing string tied side by side in the shade, eating from the feedbags tied to their heads.

The little Mexican untied the Baby filly and led her over to a helper to hold. He wove his way through the crowd of men gathered 'round her and dug out a brush and a rag from a large wooden tack box. He returned and began to work over the horse's coat. The filly seemed to take notice of our horses and raised her head and nickered long and loud. Little Paint twisted and faunched around on his lead and answered her as if it was a challenge.

Folks were naturally curious to see what kind of horse we had brought. They all stopped to gather in small groups to visit. Little Paint was still a touch on the wild side, and he spooked back on the end of his lead rope several times as the crowd pressed close. Billy had Carlito take a position alongside the horse to act as a guard. He was there to ward off the kids who threatened to run under Little Paint's belly, the women who would offer him sweets, and those who just naturally wanted to touch what they had come to see.

I wondered if we shouldn't have kept the horse back away from the crowd, and kept him as quiet and stress free as possible. Billy had considered that earlier, but decided that this might give the animal time to acclimate to things before the race. Besides that, we doubted if we could avoid a crowd around our camp anyway.

Billy soon strode off to find Colonel Andrews and lay out the race course. Andy and most of our crowd had followed H.B. over to look at Baby, and Carlito assured me he had things under control. Our Mexican cook was about half bandit, and he patted the pistol and knife at his belt. I figured Little Paint was safe enough.

It was still a good three hours before the race was to be run, and with time to kill I wandered my way along through the crowd to see who I could see.

Just past the colonel's tent somebody had set up a refreshment stand. A wagon tarp was laid over a rope between two trees, and staked at the ground on either side, forming a tent. A large wagon was parked at the back opening, thus blocking admittance from that side, and the front opening was blocked by a plank laid over a couple of wooden kegs. This makeshift bar lay just far enough back into the tarp roof to allow customers at the bar a narrow strip of shade.

I made my way up to the bar, and it was already doing enough business at that time of the morning that I had to wait for a gap at the plank to appear. Two men and a woman were tending drinks, and they had to hoof it to keep up with the orders. It seemed like there were a lot of gentlemen set on getting the morning off to a good start.

I tossed down a half-dollar whiskey, and then bought a beer, which cost me another fifteen cents. I took my beer and continued to walk down through the camp. Just past the tent bar they had a long mess table set up, and every chair was full. Behind the table they had a barbecue pit and the smell of smoky beef filled the air. I wondered whose beef it was, but it was like an old Texas cowman once told me. The best eating beef always belonged to someone else.

Nursing the lukewarm beer I ambled my way along, greeting many I didn't know, and stopping from time to time to visit with some old acquaintance. I looked back over my shoulder and observed two young boys following in my wake. I stopped and they stopped. They stared at me intently, as if expecting something of me.

"What do you two want?"

The boldest of the lot said, "Your bottle. That barman is giving a penny for every bottle we find for him."

I stared them down a bit, and one of the boys lowered his head and went to digging at the ground with one bare foot. The bottle was just about empty, and rapidly losing what little cool and refreshing qualities it once had. I turned it up and drained the last of it, and then tossed the bottle over the top of the boys' heads and out into the grass.

They whirled in an instant and dashed for the bottle. I was reminded of stepping out of the door of a house with a plate load of table scraps for the hounds. Both of the boys spied the bottle at the same time, and those two kids went after it root-hog-or-die. They rolled around in the grass, and a punch or two was thrown before the bigger of the boys jumped to his feet and took off in a run with the bottle waving proudly in his grasp. The smaller boy raced at his heels, matching every turn as the other sought to dodge and evade him. They zig-zagged away like a pair of mad hornets.

"Boys will be boys," a deep voice sounded behind me.

I turned around, and who should I see but Long Tom standing there with a smile on his face. He was looking a lot more prosperous than the last time I saw him. A new felt hat, not even yet broken in, sat atop his head. He wore a white shirt tucked into duck pants held up by suspenders, and a pair of tall topped boots with long, flapping mule ear tugs.

"Looks like times are changing," I said, and offered my hand.

"Slowly, slowly."

"How's the freighting business?"

"Better than I'd hoped."

We took us a walk to catch each other up on what had been happening during the past summer. It seemed like Long had latched on to a good deal. He was then running not one wagon, but three. He had his original wagon and three yoke of oxen, and had purchased another large wagon about the same. He had also acquired a smaller wagon with four big mules to pull it. The ox rigs could handle about four thousand pounds of freight apiece, and the mule rig between two and three thousand.

"Sounds like you have been doing real good and real quick."

"There's a lot of business, and the money's good, but not that good. I've been busy, and a banker up at Caldwell offered to loan me some money to, what he called, 'expand my operations.' " Long hooked his thumbs in his suspenders and rocked back on his heels as he was speaking.

"You're going to get rich if you ain't careful."

Long smiled even bigger and took me by the shoulder to tell me about his business as we walked along. "My freighting business ain't all that I've been expanding."

There was a cousin of his back in the Chickasaw Nation who, it seems, was equally talented where the making of whiskey was concerned. Long was hauling some government supplies periodically down to Ft. Reno, and as of late he'd been going on down into the Chickasaw Nation to load out corn. The hiding of a few boxes of whiskey in a load of ear corn was a simple matter.

There were a lot of Indians who dearly loved to get hold of a little of Satan's Tonic, and a growing number of cowboys filling the Cherokee Strip and other parts of the Territory who approached the stuff with equal enthusiasm. It seemed that Long had the business acumen, the good sense, and the moral depravity to take advantage of such a ready and lucrative market.

He was picking up most of his freight out of Kansas and covering a big swath of country. His deliveries covered several of the various forts and Indian agencies in the Territory, and many ranches in the Texas

Panhandle. The trade in whiskey was strictly prohibited in the Indian Territory, but that made for a good market. There is nothing like a little illegality to create demand.

As I later learned from Long, there were a few rules to operate by when you were peddling whiskey. The first one was to be on the lookout for John Law. The government was hell bent and set on keeping liquor away from the Indians, and probably just as set on collecting taxes on liquor made and sold to its citizens. A man had to keep on the lookout for tribal Light Horse, Federal Deputy Marshals, and even the U.S. Army at times. The only thing that stopped a man from peddling a little whiskey in the Indian Territory was the law, and there were too few of its representatives working a whole lot of country.

Second, a man always collected his money before the goods were handed over, and you never gave more than a sip for a sample, or you would soon have more friends than you had liquor.

Third, and last, you never stayed around too long after selling Indians a bunch of whiskey. Given their warlike nature, and the fact that, to white men, they were considerably unpredictable at best, they were liable to get drunk enough to scalp you and take the rest of your makings.

Some might think that it was prejudicial to suppose that liquor had any worse of an effect on the Indians as a whole than it did on white folks, but it was the truth. I've heard people talk about how we whipped the Indians by killing their buffalo, and the Army burning out their winter camps. To my way of thinking, formed by a life lived in that time and country, we whipped them because we brought three things that the Indians were lacking — smallpox, lawyers, and whiskey.

We continued our rounds while Long questioned me thoroughly about Billy, Andy, and myself. I filled him in as best I could, and he was especially curious when I got to the part about our racehorse.

"Are you boys the ones that are going to run against Colonel Andrews's horse?"

And when I nodded in affirmation he asked, "That little old pinto of Billy's is your racehorse?"

I again confirmed, and he shook his head and whistled in disbelief. "Is he fast, sure enough?"

"You ain't the only one that's come into good fortune."

"Y'all had better watch your money. Do you know this Colonel Andrews?"

"We've met him."

"But you don't *know* him."

"We ain't foolish enough to believe he ain't a professional if that's what you're asking."

"He's sure enough a professional. You had better be careful not to bet all you've got with that man and expect to win."

"How is it that you know him?"

"I met him coming up the trail a week ago and sold him some whiskey."

"And you know all about him now?" Long was trying to rain on our parade, and it was making me a little testy.

"No. I was just starting my story and you interrupted."

"Go ahead then."

"I'd already heard about the colonel a long time back. It seems like your bunch is the only ones that don't know about him." Long flopped down in the grass and picked a stem to play around with in his mouth while he talked. I could tell I was in for a story and sat down with him.

To hear Long tell it, Colonel Andrews was darned near famous for his sporting ways from the Gulf to Denver. He traveled the roads and trails of the West dragging a team of racehorses, fighting roosters, a few pit dogs, and even a foot racer from time to time. He was a high-stakes man and there wasn't anything he wouldn't bet on, and even less that he hadn't won money on.

"All I'm going to say is you boys had better be careful with your money," Long cautioned.

"You don't seem to have a very high opinion of our good senses, or our judgment, where horses and character are concerned, do you?"

"I've had more practice than you. White folks like him have been skinning me since I was knee high to a mule. When you're black you learn that white people don't make any attempt to cover up the fact that their only aim is to get something out of you, and no more. It's just natural that over the years I've come to know their look."

Long paused to adjust his grass stem and then continued, "He's one of those Southern boys who don't know nothing about nothing except for riding horses, playing cards, beating niggers, and sipping fancy liquor. He'd shoot you over nothing, while he read his paper and talked about the price of cotton, and he wouldn't miss. He was raised in white diapers, and his mama told him he was the best thing since grits. He came naturally to assume he was better than most folks, and he's on the look-out to take advantage of that. All the while he is smiling at you, he is figuring on just how smart you are and how much he could take you for."

"You seem to know a lot about your fellow man," I said sarcastically.

"I ought to. One of those just like him was my daddy."

Long looked at me close and hard for a long minute. I met him eye to eye and waited until he smiled.

"Well, at least half of you is all right," I said.

"Which half?"

"The half that can make good whiskey."

Long jumped abruptly to his feet and motioned me up. He wanted to see Billy and Andy and take a look at our racehorse. I led the way toward our wagon.

Somebody rode by at a run screaming like the world was on fire. "Indians! Indians are coming!"

The crowd stampeded over me and like to have trampled me to death. In three shakes of a hound's tail everyone was gathered up tight around the tent saloon like freighters circling their wagons and throwing their oxen to the inside.

There were enough gun barrels sticking out of the crowd to have fought Gettysburg all over again. Some officer had formed up the black soldiers into a firing line with their Springfield rifles loaded and ready. Long and I rounded up a little girl we found crying and alone. We brought her along until we had joined the group, and set her down with her daddy. In the rush to protect the saloon I guess she had been forgotten.

All eyes were looking to the east, and sure enough a long line of Cheyennes was pouring over the top of a rise toward our camp. I guarantee you it was some sight to see. They were dragging their tepees and travois behind their ponies, and every one of them was decked out in their best outfits. Strung beads and feathers blew in the wind and the sunshine made the white buckskin a few of them wore all the brighter.

There must have been a hundred of them, squaws, children, warriors, and all. Their camp moved to some age-old migratory rhythm set to the time of their ponies' shuffling hooves and the creak of travois poles. The people laughed and the camp dogs yapped and ran in and out of their midst. The braves, half-naked and armed to the teeth, rode at the perimeter of the tribe for security. A good-sized herd of grass-slick horses was driven alongside the line of their march by a gang of rowdy boys.

And wouldn't you know it. Old Chief Blue Knife was riding at the head of the procession. He sat straight on the back of his horse, a long, wickedly sharp lance in his right hand, and a brace of pistols in his beaded belt. It wasn't feathers blowing around him, but instead it was several human scalps tied to the bridle reins of his horse.

When he neared, his face was a mask of stoicism, and his eyes were like to chunks of coal. If I was right, our location on the creek was south of the Cheyenne Reservation, but they might not draw the same boundaries. Nobody knew if Blue Knife came to burn us out or shake our hands. In his younger day he was known to be a temperamental sort just as apt to befriend you as he was to cut your heart out and feed it to his dogs.

I couldn't help feeling that he looked to be on the prod, and I was remembering a few things I would have liked to have forgotten just then. I swear I could feel every individual hair on my head tingling as I remembered three damned fools who had stolen some Cheyenne horses the spring before, and most of them belonging to a certain chief named Blue Knife.

Just when you think things can't get any worse is just when they are bound to. Long poked me in the ribs to get my attention. "There's one more thing I forgot to tell you. You remember old Harvey? He was the man you traded those Cheyenne horses to."

"Yeah."

"He and the colonel are brothers."

I thought that it was a small, small world indeed when in the course of one day a man ran into so many folks apt to kill him.

"I saw him this morning," Long added.

"Who?"

"Harvey."

"He's here?" I couldn't help but look around.

"He is, and he was looking for Billy and some other boys with a paint racehorse. Seems he had a near miss with some Cheyenne who caught him with stolen horses."

I am not the nervous type, and have at times taken great pride in my feats of daring. However, right about then I must admit to being a bit overwhelmed, and more than a little disturbed by the fact that I was either about to be shot by a disgruntled horse trader and his gambler brother, or scalped by a tribe of Red Indians.

Chapter Twelve

The Cheyenne uprising was put down before it even began. Chief Blue Knife stopped his bunch about forty yards out from us. He sat his horse patiently, and didn't have long to wait. Cap Arrington stepped from the crowd and walked out to talk to him, or shoot him with his long-barreled forty-five should it become necessary. It seems that the good people of the newly formed Wheeler County had elected the Ranger as their first sheriff. I guessed that dealing single-handedly with a hundred blood-thirsty savages must have fallen within his official duties.

The captain jawed a while with the old chief and then came back and had a conference with the military officers. When that was over he marched right back out to Blue Knife and they talked some more. I couldn't make out what they were saying, but it must have been agreeable to Cap because he didn't shoot anybody.

Blue Knife turned his pony around and rode back to powwow with some of his warriors. After a meeting of the aboriginal minds, the whole band of Indians started off again, angling for a point farther upstream. I was thinking that perhaps Cap Arrington's wicked mustache and long-barreled Colt pistol weren't enough to turn the Cheyenne back to their reservation, and he had to settle for detouring them around us as a matter of saving face.

Everyone continued to watch the Cheyenne almost hypnotically while they paraded by. A murmur went up from our crowd when the Indians stopped and started pitching camp on the north bank of the Sweetwater about a hundred and fifty yards upstream from the race grounds. Our group began to get a little loud and anxious, while the Army troops mingled around informing everyone that the Indians were here to take part in the festivities, and had promised not to steal any white women or scalp anybody out of hand.

That quieted the cool and calm types, but there was quite a little uproar from the scared-shitless-of-Indians faction within our midst. Cap Arrington waded among those still gathered, and informed them that our camp sat astraddle of the boundary between Greer County and the Cheyenne Reservation. Not only were we trespassing, but we were introducing whiskey and gambling on to Indian lands. After he had listed the hundred and one laws we were breaking, he then subtly suggested that we all just try to get along with our new friends.

A lot of folks formerly prejudiced to Indians were converted on the spot. Having to choose between playing well with others and leaving the party before things got started, most everyone became instant Indian lovers, humanitarian philanthropists, and activists for the red man's cause.

Like most of the Plains tribes, the Cheyenne loved gambling, especially horse racing, and they had their share of those who lusted for the bottle just like we did. Before long, Indians were mixing in and out of the camp, and everyone settled back down to the fun at hand. There is nothing like the commonality of shared depravity to break the ice between cultures. So much of the Indian Wars could have been avoided if somebody had recognized the social benefits and soothing nature of a little drunkenness and the casting of lots.

The Cheyenne had brought along a few swift horses themselves, and before long the number of scheduled horse races grew. At about eleven o'clock Cap Arrington climbed on top of a wagon and shouted to gain everyone's attention. He announced that there were to be two races before ours, and several afterwards. The first race was to be a mile long with five entries. The second race was to be a match race between one of the colonel's horses and a runner that some men from Weatherford had trailed up.

Long and I made our way back to the chuckwagon and found Billy and the rest of our gang already preparing for the race. Long and Billy had a quick, friendly hello, and Andy like to have shaken Long's hand plumb off at the shoulder.

"How are you, General?" Long asked.

"About to be rich and famous."

We all laughed at Andy's immodesty, but secretly we were all riding a wave of optimism and high spirits. Billy had put up two hundred of his bet with the colonel, and the rest of us chipped in to make the other half. Most of our crowd had already made their own personal bets, and from the talk I heard, many of them had bet everything they had on Little Paint. The gamblers, once they had most of the money in the camp on the line, were offering to allow bets of just about any personal property, providing an appraisal of its value could be agreed upon.

H.B. warned us right then and there not to bet our saddles, but I could tell by the squeamish look on several of the boys' faces that they had done just that. If you had asked what time it was you would have been out of luck, because there wasn't a pocket watch left among them. They were all piled on a table in front of Colonel Andrews's tent along with a miscellaneous pile of firearms, jewelry, and other assorted valuables. A man stood guard over the table with a double-barreled shotgun cradled in his arms. Two more artillery-toting tough sorts stood guard at the door to the colonel's tent, where all cash bets made with the coalition of Mobeetie gamblers were being held.

The rumor was flying around that there was ten thousand cash in the tent. That sounded pretty steep, but I guarantee you a pile was bet that day, and not just with the Mobeetie bookies. Many citizens made their own bets with each other, and nobody knew just how deep the Cheyenne were bailing in.

There wasn't much time for socializing, because Billy and Andy were furiously working on a saddle they had acquired. The colonel had a special, lightweight racing saddle; since we lacked one ourselves, Billy had purchased an old cavalry McClellan to avoid the weight disadvantage one of our heavy stock saddles would have caused.

I managed to gather Billy off to the side, and hurriedly informed him about Harvey and the colonel. He didn't seem to give that much thought. I could tell by the look on his face that he had already decided that Harvey and the colonel could go jump in the creek. I realized it was useless to ask him what he thought about racing Blue Knife's paint right in front of him, because he apparently had decided that right then he had more important things to worry about than who was likely to kill us.

Then again, Billy wasn't given to worry anyway. Tough men like Billy and Cap Arrington probably went to bed with clearer minds than most. It stands to reason that they figured they could get up in the morning after a good night's rest and just shoot anyone who might make trouble.

Somebody was calling for the first race to start. We left Andy and Carlito to take care of our horse and made our way down to the start line. Stakes with red painted tops had been driven into the ground to mark the race course. They ran in a line dead away from the creek across the flat for a long,

long ways, turned in a big loop, and arced their way back to finish where they had begun.

There were three Cheyenne horses entered and their jockeys rode up to the scratch mark bareback and half-naked. Their horses were painted up with all kinds of circus marks, their tails tied up, and bells and feathers braided into their manes.

Bill Thompson had a black horse entered and he joined the Cheyenne buffalo runners at the line. He snorted and bowed his neck at the wildly decked-out Cheyenne horses, and his rider fought to keep him from turning tail and running off with him.

The crowd parted to admit the last entry. It was one of the colonel's horses that we hadn't seen before, and he stuck out like a sore thumb. He was another thoroughbred for sure, although he wasn't the looker that the big gelding we had seen a few nights before had been. The colonel's Mexican boy was riding a funny little saddle set way forward on the horse's withers.

The horse was trimmed in a loud coordination of matching colors, from the saddle blanket to the jockey's silk shirt and cap. The boy wore a pair of goggles and carried a long, stiff quirt. The horse's head was covered in what appeared to be a modification of a set of workhorse blinders.

Cap Arrington was to start the race, and he stood atop a wagon at the start/finish line. He stood grim faced with his pistol pointing at the sky like he was threatening God Almighty himself. The horses jostled around as the jockeys tried to get positioned at the mark. It was Arrington's duty to fire the shot to start the race only when all horses were fairly and properly at the scratch line in the dirt.

The strategy and complications of getting five fractious horses all standing reasonably well at the line simultaneously seemed to go on forever, and then Cap's forty-five cracked and they were off and racing in a cloud of dust.

The crowd roared and the Cheyenne jockeys whooped like they were on the warpath and whipped their mounts with long, limber quirts. The horses were bunched for a while, but soon lined out head to tail in a tight line, with one of the Cheyenne horses leading. The colonel's thoroughbred was last, but his rider looked to be holding him in check.

They raced away into the distance, and then were rounding the far turn. The same Cheyenne horse held the lead, but the colonel's horse had moved to second by the time they came out of the turn and started the long straight stretch back to the finish line.

Three hundred yards away and it was a two-horse race. The Cheyenne horse and the thoroughbred ran neck to neck, and so close you couldn't have walked between them. They were two hundred yards out when the brave leaned out and cracked the Mexican boy with his quirt. The Mexican returned the favor with his stiff bat, and even from that distance you could see the dust fly off of the Cheyenne's chest.

When they came across the line it was the colonel's horse a winner by two lengths, and the Cheyenne with the big red welt across his chest a faltering second. The people at the finish line cheered wildly, and their raucous noise was matched by the agony coming from the Cheyenne gathered on the other side of the track. I watched as one of the squaws fell to her knees wailing, and then jerked out a knife and hacked off one of her braids.

The jockeys had gotten their horses pulled up and were coming back to the line. The Mexican boy made his way toward their camp, and he was followed by the Cheyenne who had come in second. I was returning to our campsite, and so got to see the Cheyenne dismount in front of where the colonel stood at his tent. Solemnly, the brave handed the reins of his lathered horse to the colonel and walked away. The colonel looked over his prize with several of his friends while the dejected Cheyenne trudged back to his people.

You can't keep a good man down, and seeing Little Paint being shined up and readied for his race drove all doubts from my mind. When I walked up, Andy was putting on a new, bright red shirt with a large C embroidered on the back of it in white. Kate and a couple of the other girls, wanting to be part of the action, and just through friendship and good nature, had made the shirt for the occasion. They stood around waiting for him to model their handiwork.

Andy tucked the shirt into his checkered pants, and strutted around for all to see. He turned red as his shirt when one of the girls pinched his ass and kissed him on the cheek.

The girls hadn't forgotten Little Paint either, they had braided up his mane with red ribbons. Together, Andy and that horse were going to look as gaudy as those Cheyenne buffalo runners. Although, I was just as proud as Andy was, and from Billy's smile I could tell that he was too.

The second race was starting, but we were

too busy running into each other while we frantically went about searching for something to do to get ready to race. The only calm one in the bunch was Billy. He was wearing a new white shirt, and a green neckerchief with white polka dots. He leaned against a tree with the sole of one boot propped back against the trunk and calmly smoked a cigarette down to the butt in ten seconds. The way he was puffing on that thing made him look like a locomotive with the coal bin heaped full and the throttle laid wide open.

Being of a cautious nature, and overly wise for my age, I hadn't bet a single dime on the race other than the twenty dollars required for my part of the two hundred Billy hadn't had to bet. I had only parted with that money out of loyalty to a friend short of funds, rather than giving in to the gambling urge like the rest of those boys. Most grown men realize that money earned is easily lost and hard to come by. A bird in hand is worth two in the bush, and so on. Realizing that I had very little time before our race was to start, I ran like the fool I was to the gamblers' tent. I had forty-two dollars in my pocket, and I bet every red cent of it. I even threw my pocket watch and pistol in for another twenty-five at even odds.

As I was walking back to our wagon I heard Arrington's pistol pop again, and I knew the second race had started. On my way back I met two young Cheyenne girls walking toward me. They were both pretty, and I couldn't help but smile at them and tip my hat. Both of them ducked their heads shyly as we passed. There was a Cheyenne Dog Soldier following them, and the look he gave me was a heap full of bad medicine. He hurried the girls away from my vicinity, while keeping an eye on me over his shoulder. The Cheyenne were awfully protective of their women.

Not that I was anything to worry about. Barby Allen was the girl for me, and I wondered what she was doing for the holiday.

A representative from the colonel's camp came over and asked if all was ready with us. We agreed that it was, and he went back to where he came from. Billy untied Little Paint and led him out into the open. Andy started to mount, but H.B. stopped him.

"Get those spurs off, they're too heavy."

Andy quickly shed them and started once again to mount, but he stopped himself. He dug into his pockets and pulled out a handful of small change, and his pocket knife. Then he pulled off his belt and took his tobacco makings out of his shirt pocket.

"Here, Tennessee, hold these for me. I need to lighten up."

I took his belongings while he swung a leg over Little Paint. We watched while he walked the horse out into a big circle and brought him back again. Little Paint seemed to be feeling good and traveling fine. Andy continued to walk him around while we waited.

Soon the people down at the start line parted and made a long alley of bodies opening up to the race course. That was our signal and we started in their direction. Several of the cowboys off roundup walked with us, and we were followed by Kate and a group of the "girls." Before we had gone very far one of our crowd started playing "Dixie" on a harmonica. Billy loved that Rebel stuff, and even I felt as proud as if we were marching in a parade and going off to war.

As we passed the colonel's tent, the Mexican jockey came out on Baby and pulled in alongside of Andy and Little Paint. If something had happened and the race had never been run that day, it still would have been something to see those two horses together in one place. Baby looked like a queen with her neck arched proudly against the bit, her little nostrils flaring in her muzzle, and her feet moving over the ground like snowflakes in the summer.

Little Paint may have not been as professionally outfitted in race colors and shiny tack, but he knew he was "the man" on that afternoon. He wasn't as pretty as Baby, but he was ready and rearing to go, and the closer he got to the crowd the more his spring wound up, until he was going sideways. The sheer vitality of him leapt out at you. Anyone looking at him knew that he was a runner, and was ready to race.

As we walked I kept my eye on the people lining either side of our path. When we came to the track I saw the colonel waiting, and Harvey stood at his side. He didn't say a thing as we walked past, but I noticed Billy kept his hand near his pistol until we had reached the far side of the finish line.

The course Billy and the colonel had agreed on was three hundred and seventy-five yards of the first straightaway that the earlier races had been run upon. They had taken a team of horses and a homemade drag, made out of a large iron cauldron turned upside down, and knocked the top off the grass for the length of the three-hundred-and-seventy-five-yard race. Everyone had chipped in and walked over the track, removing the larger rocks, grass clumps, and clods. Two poles had been cut and placed in the ground on either side of the track at the far end. The horses were to start there and race back to the line the other horses had been starting from.

The crowd grew strangely quiet when the two horses paraded down the track, especially considering the level of excitement and the amount of whiskey consumed by many. Maybe everyone knew they were about to see something special, or maybe they were just catching their breaths for a bit.

They had moved Cap Arrington's wagon down to the far end, but he stepped out into the middle of the track and called for everyone's attention. All talking ceased while he spoke.

"Ladies and gentlemen you are about to witness a match race at three hundred and seventy-five yards between Colonel Andrews's Baby and Billy Champion's War Bonnet," Cap announced.

I turned to Billy in confusion. "What the hell?"

Billy looked equally as confused. The jockeys walked the two horses around Cap as he spoke, and as Andy came by we tried to motion him over to see if he knew what was going on. He grinned sheepishly. "They asked me earlier what we called our horse, and I couldn't help it. War Bonnet sounded better."

We didn't have time to argue; what was done was done. Besides, if we murdered him we would be short a jockey. So that's how the famous race between Baby and War Bonnet came about. When folks talk about that race years later, and they mention War Bonnet, they have the imagination of an ignoramus kid to thank for it. But I have to admit, it did sound better.

Cap Arrington continued, "I will judge a fair start, and sound the gun when both parties answer at the mark. Scratches and false starts will be called back, and we will restart. Please keep back from the course and give them room at the finish line."

He started to make his way up the track, and then stopped and turned back to face the crowd. "I'll personally shoot anyone who gets in their way."

Being the old Ranger he was, everyone believed him.

Our bunch stood on the far side of the finish line opposite of the colonel and his gang. While two boys stretched a long length of ribbon across the finish line the colonel raised a glass he held up to us in salute. Billy returned the gesture with a tip of his hat.

We all waited expectantly as the two horses lined up. Both horses were a little high and were hard to get ready at the mark in coordination with the other horse. Finally, Andy and the Mexican started both horses side by side at the walk and approached the scratch line at the same time. It worked, and they only paused a split second before Cap fired off his pistol and they were running.

That race was one of the most glorious things I have ever seen, and a sprint race doesn't last but a few seconds. Both horses shot out of the hole and ran nose to nose, necks outstretched, bellies down, and tails a flying. The crowd was so loud in my ears that I hardly realized I was yelling myself.

They came to the finish line and for a minute I thought we were beat. Baby looked to have a nose on us, but in the last instant, thirty yards out, Little Paint, or War Bonnet if you will, seemed to drop even lower and gather more speed. When they came across the line it was War Bonnet by a nose.

We all ran onto the track jumping around like schoolchildren. And I'll be damned if I didn't hug H.B. and pat him on the back like I loved him. After a moment we realized that the race hadn't been called yet, and all of our attention turned to the two Army officers appointed to judge the finish.

Both of them stood conferring in the center of the finish line. They didn't keep us waiting, because they announced War Bonnet the winner by a nose. If we cheered wildly the first time, it was nothing compared to what we did then. Andy came back with our horse and bailed off right into our midst while Carlito took the bridle.

We were all dancing around and acting silly when H.B. quieted us. In the middle of the throng of people who had rushed on to the track he faced us all.

"Boys, we're loaded," he said with tears in his eyes and a quivering lip.

We all shouted in agreement and started to celebrate again. He waved his arms frantically for us to quiet. "Boys, you don't understand. I said we're loaded. I took the money Wiren gave me to make payroll for the summer, and I bet her all."

Billy shouted to the sky and grabbed up old Hell's Bells and lifted him plumb off the ground. We all beat on his back until he lost his pipe and his hat. Andy grabbed him by the ears and planted a big kiss on his grimy forehead. H.B. took a wild swing at Andy, but the kid was too fast and ran away.

Some of us were already heading out to collect on bets, and I was left standing alone for a moment in the middle of the track. A big Cheyenne came walking right up to me and it was Blue Knife. I danged near went for my gun, but I had bet it on the race. Before I could fight or flee he was upon me.

"That is a fast horse." His face was unreadable, his coal-chunk eyes burning into the back of my skull.

I didn't know what to say. I just stood there like I was shot.

"You picked a strong Cheyenne pony. Won me lots of money."

His face cracked into a big smile and he turned and walked away. I never said a thing, I just watched him leave with my mouth hanging open. It took me a moment to even untrack one step.

I had taken about two of those shaky steps when Andy came running toward me. I thought I heard him, but it took a second time for me to register what he was yelling.

"Dutch Henry and his boys have robbed the stakeholders and got off with all our money!"

CHAPTER THIRTEEN

Ours was a rags-to-riches story, and in the manner of the turbulent fortunes of the high-stakes gambling world, we didn't have long to enjoy our fortune before we were back in rags. We never even got one sniff of our winnings before some damned highwaymen held up the guards and took off with our stakes.

A holiday in cow country can be quite a fracas, but nothing could compare to the pandemonium that set in following the announcement that Dutch Henry's gang had taken off with most of the loot in camp. I guess a lot of the camp held a vested interest in the stakes. You would have thought that everyone was a winner, because all of them at the same time stormed the tent where the stakes had been held. What must have been fifty or sixty booted men tried to enter that tent at the same time. Despite the numerous assurances that not a red cent was left, everyone had to see for themselves.

Once the robbery was confirmed some-body gathered up the guards, shook them a time or two to get the straight of things, and in the matter of moments almost every man in camp was mounted and ready to ride. Most of us were impatient to go, and a little hard to rein in, but Cap Arrington took a stand before us.

"I'll shoot the son of a bitch who messes up the sign left by these bandits." The old Ranger was tugging on his mustache with one hand, and the other rested on the butt of his holstered pistol.

We gathered in a rough semicircle before him to listen.

"They're just getting farther away while we sit around here and jaw," somebody in the crowd all but shouted.

Cap's beady-eyed gaze raked the group to discover who had spoken up. "I've already put scouts on the trail."

Billy was sitting his horse beside me. "This is about the sorriest-looking posse I've ever seen."

Looking around me, I had to agree with him. A lot of the cowboys, and more than a few others, had bet their saddles and pistols on the race. It seemed that Dutch's boys had taken all the shooters with the rest of the loot. To top things off, they ran a rope through the swells of every saddle held in the stakes, and drug the whole pile of hulls across the prairie while they fled. As a result half the boys in the posse were bareback and unarmed.

"Those Cheyenne don't look anywhere near as ridiculous riding bareback." I pointed to the wild group of braves that was then racing up to go on the warpath with us.

Billy looked over at one of the fellows beside us who was sitting bareback on an exceptionally thin horse. The man was squirming around uncomfortably and had one hand between his crotch and the high, thin blade of his horse's withers.

"That's because folks that ride bareback all the time just naturally know not to pick a raw-backed horse," Billy said.

"Our bandits are definitely a bold, sassy bunch to have pulled this off," I said.

"From what I've heard about Dutch Henry, he's got balls as big as church bells."

Without evidence it seems that Dutch Henry was nominated for the theft as the only outlaw in that neck of the woods with enough stature to have pulled it off. He was a salty German who had scouted in the Indian Wars. He had some grudge against the military at Ft. Elliot, and a strong dislike for Indians. Naturally, he and his gang had been waging a horse thieving war against the U.S. Army and the surrounding tribes for many years. He claimed to leave white civilians alone, but a long list of thievery and murder was attached to his name.

"That damned Dutchman is going to be a handful if we corner him," an old-timer beside us said.

Cap must have heard him. "Dutch Henry's retired. We're just going after some outlaws of the average sort."

The whole posse grumbled a little under their breaths. It seemed that most of our group preferred the thought of being robbed by such a notorious character as Dutch Henry, instead of any old run-of-the-mill bandits.

"Cap's right. I know for a fact that the Law caught Old Dutch and hauled him to Dodge City." H.B. spit for emphasis any time he thought he had said something important.

I studied the tobacco juice staining his whiskers. "Is he in prison?"

"No, Dutch is wily enough to know you won't get far in the outlaw business without the best lawyers money can buy."

"If he ain't in prison, where's he at?"

"He moved on to other parts. This damned country is getting too civilized for an outlaw to operate with the proper aplomb and bold manner which he was accustomed to."

Somebody listening behind me scoffed at H.B.'s tale. "Bat Masterson shot Dutch dead at Trinidad, Colorado in '78. My uncle saw it happen."

H.B. cast a frown back over his shoulder at the man who'd contested his story, but seemed content to let it rest. I listened to men behind me continuing the discussion for a bit.

I leaned over and spoke quietly for only H.B. to hear. "I was up in that country in '78, and I didn't hear anything about a shootout between those two."

H.B. grunted and growled around the pipe clenched in his teeth. "Famous folks all have more than one version of their life story."

"You men pay heed to me and we'll catch these robbers," Cap said loudly.

The mass of mad men was about to grow mutinous if held back any longer, and Cap had to take an occasional step back to keep their nervous horses from trampling him. I guess he saw the blood in our eyes, because he cut short his instructions on the professional manner of catching bandits.

"Just remember, don't go shooting these bandits if you can help it. Let the Law deal with them." Cap hurried for his horse.

"That just means he doesn't want us killing them before he can hang them," Billy said.

Cap stuck a foot in the stirrup and loped off toward the Sweetwater with all of us at his heels and threatening to run him down. Being in the lead must have been important to him, because he sure had to get his horse up to speed to stay ahead. We were an impatient bunch used to dealing with our own troubles after our own fashion, and we didn't need anybody on a white horse on yonder hill to wave us on with the brim of his hat and a few fighting words.

We followed a line of torn-up ground where the outlaws had drug the saddles. Here and there was a chunk or a piece of some poor fellow's kak, and you could hear the groans of misery go through our posse like a dose of salts.

A couple of the Cheyenne scouts were waiting for us on the bank of the Sweetwater about four miles down the creek. They had found where the outlaws had crossed and, figuring a bunch of dumb white men couldn't track an elephant through a snow bank, a few of them were waiting to guide us.

One of the Cheyenne told us that the outlaws had dumped our saddles in the creek. Just like that, several of our own jumped down and hit the water. It was swimming depth out in the middle, and they looked like a bunch of ducks bobbing up and down. Before long, one of them came up to the surface and shouted that he had a hold of the rope that the saddles were strung together with.

Soon, more of them were in the water and had taken hold of the rope. After several minutes of choking and straining they managed to work their way closer to wading water. Somebody rode out and took the end of the rope, dallied it to his saddle horn, and spurred up the bank. Something broke loose, and as a result, only about half of the saddles ended up on dry land. The rest of them were left to posterity in the bottom of the creek, despite the repeated attempts of some of the boys to salvage them.

There was a mad scramble as those who had ridden bareback sought their saddles from the muddy pile of offerings. You can understand that not all of them came out of that scrap with a saddle, and even the ones who did weren't necessarily carrying the saddle they had lost. If you couldn't find your own saddle, you might get lucky and commandeer one belonging to somebody who wasn't present. For years afterward men were still swapping saddles trying to find their own.

We loped off that day from the Sweetwater leaving several of our men behind to continue their futile river salvage operation. A few of the men who had firearms but no saddles lent out their weapons to those who were blessed with a saddle. If our numbers were somewhat lessened when we left the Sweetwater, we were at least better armed.

I couldn't blame most of the bareback brigade for staying behind, and I myself would have had to have lost a kid sister or something to go along without my tack. You can't begin to imagine the indignant nature of riding along bareback with a group of properly equipped men.

Our posse was somewhat better equipped when we left, but there remained several men riding bareback, and you could easily spot the men lacking firearms by the shameful looks on their faces. You would have thought they had been forced to troop across the country naked or something. Then again, when you're used to having a pistol on your hip to flop around and fondle as a sure sign of a swinging dick, removal of said item is bound to cause discomfort.

Right then I thought that it was safe to say that those bandits had made a grave mistake due to a miscalculation of human nature. The stealing of a citizen's money is bound to cause a certain amount of desire to chastise and punish the guilty party, but the bandits had acted in such a way as to cause a degree of bloodthirsty need for revenge never seen in simple matters of financial loss. To force a man to pursue his losses in a fashion where he feels naked and missing his parts before his clothed and properly equipped comrades is a sure way to get hanged.

The trail led straight west, mile after mile, hour after hour, and every time our horses' hooves hit the ground somebody was either propping themselves up off a galded crotch, or reaching for the comfort of a pistol that wasn't there anymore. And with each and every step of the way, they got madder, and the thoughts of many in our posse dwelled on the torturous manner with which they would deal with the bandits once they captured them. It was more than justice that we demanded; it was revenge. Yeah, it was going to be a short trial, a quick verdict, and those money-stealing, ass-torturing, emasculating sons of bitches were going to hang — if we could catch them.

The afternoon of the second day, the trail split between the headwaters of McClellan Creek and the Mulberry. The Cheyenne scouts determined that there were five men in the outlaw gang. Three of the men had headed northwest toward the Canadian, while the other two had turned off to the southwest. A quick powwow was held and it seemed that Arrington had received the Army's assurance that they would proceed at haste westward up the Canadian looking to cut the sign of the outlaw gang. Riders had also been sent to Tascosa to notify authorities in that locality of the possibility of our bandits passing through in the near future. It appeared that the three outlaws who had turned north were riding into our support, while the two who had ridden away from the Canadian had the greatest chance for escape.

Arrington quickly divided our posse. One group, led by Colonel Andrews, was to pursue the three outlaws headed for the Canadian as closely as possible, and strengthen their numbers by rendezvous with the soldiers if feasible. The Cheyenne went with the colonel, as they claimed the country to the southwest had always been bad medicine for them, fit for nothing but Comanches and Mexicans.

Meanwhile, Cap would lead the other party in pursuit of the two outlaws who had headed southwest. All of our Lazy F crowd, including myself, went with Cap at his request, because of our supposed knowledge of the country where we were headed. For my own part I didn't know squat about that country except for the fact that most of the water out there was bad when you could find any. Billy informed me that there was plenty of water all the way to New Mexico if you knew where to look, but even he made no claims about taste.

Cap Arrington was reputed to be of the old frontier mold, but despite his survey of the country beyond the headwaters of the Red and his much publicized discovery of the Lost Lakes, he had come near freezing and starving to death himself and a whole company of Rangers the winter before on the Yellow Houses. Even though many of the men had worked some of that country, and were at least familiar with parts of it, H.B. just had to volunteer. He assured us that, should we need his services as a scout, he had once carried the mail and two gallons of whiskey from Mobeetie to Roswell.

No matter the quality and quantity of the whiskey, he was sure he had a good feel for the country.

It seemed that our knowledge of the terrain and its finicky waterings would counterbalance the cunningness of the outlaws and lead us to their inevitable capture. However, I was beginning to get the feeling that we were going to eat a whole lot more dust before that happened.

We lost the trail several miles down the Mulberry, but continued on, looking to pick it back up. Our way led us down the creek to where the JA boys were building a set of pens on the flats there. A crew was digging postholes, and a wide, stocky man with a set of white whiskers put down his crowbar and walked out to meet us. Even after Cap informed him of our mission to apprehend the outlaws the man continued to eye us with more than a little disdain. Either he seemed to doubt our ability to capture bandits, or he suspected our party of being equally guilty of similar crimes worthy of legal sentence. He would do nothing for several minutes other than cuss and spit.

Upon hearing Cap out with only a few interruptions of profanity, he tugged at his whiskers some and called one of his hands over. Upon questioning, the hand told us that two horsemen had come by the camp that morning and stopped to eat. They had tried to trade horses, but the JA hands had suspected what they were and sent them on their way astride the horses they came in on.

"Which way were they headed?" Cap asked the JA man.

"Where in the hell do you think?" the whiskered man interrupted before the other could answer.

Cap looked perturbed and was pulling irritably on his killer mustache, but he kept his voice calm. "Colonel, when I catch them I might ask them where they were headed."

Texas seemed to have a colonel or a captain behind every bush, and I began to feel a little left out. I began considering a title for myself. This was my first acquaintance with Colonel Charles Goodnight, and despite the fact that I was never to know him well, I got the impression that he was a man who felt great impatience with the portion of the world outside his operation. I was more than a little surprised that he would curse so much and seem to have so little respect for a Ranger of such reputation as our staunch captain, and sheriff of Wheeler County no less — a man of two titles.

"They sure as hell didn't go up my canyon, so they'll have to ride up the Tule. At the head of the Tule the old Comanchero trail forks three ways. They could go west to Las Escarbadas, northwest to the head of the Trujillo and Puerto de las Rivajenos, or southwest across Double Mountain Fork and to the Yellow Houses. You should split your men and send one bunch up the Palo Duro and across to the Trujillo. The other bunch can ride like hell to Las Escarbadas. You ought to be able to head them off or catch up to them." Colonel Goodnight eyed the cap rock to the west like he could see them traveling right then.

"What if they go south?" Cap asked.

"Well then, you can chase them some more, but it's been my experience that most bandits are headed for Fort Sumner or Las Vegas, and your average bandit is just smart enough to know that he needs to go west and not south to get to either one." Goodnight sounded like he was lecturing a ten-year-old.

"I came through that country and didn't go just like you tell it," Cap said.

"Yeah, and you like to have killed yourself too. Not many men have any sense of direction or the skill necessary to navigate such a country beyond the bounds of its known trails, and I doubt your bandits are any exception."

I could tell Cap started to relate the bandits' actions concerning the taking of our saddles and firearms as evidence of their unusual abilities, but he thought better of it considering the nature of who he was conversing with. Instead, he tipped his hat and started to turn his horse around.

"We bid you good day, Colonel, and leave you to the romantic undertaking of building an empire."

Goodnight squinted in the sun and gave him a look that would sour corn on the stalk. He hollered back over his shoulder at one of his men. "Farrington, saddle up and go with these horse racers and catch their bandits for them."

"To hell with you, Colonel. I am perfectly capable of catching my own bandits," Cap snapped back at him.

"Well, go on then. You're impeding my progress in this construction." Goodnight waved us off and took his digging bar back up.

On his way back to the posthole he had so recently left, he spit and cussed everything in general, from the weather, cattle prices, lawyers, and bankers to bandits, and the incompetent vigilantes who chased them.

As we rode off I heard him telling a couple of his men to head up the Palo Duro and over to the head of the Truijillo to look out for the bandits that we were bound to miss.

I rode off thinking that he must have thought a lot of the two men he was sending, or else he didn't think much of us. For some reason, I decided I liked the cantankerous devil, but Billy rode by me cussing Goodnight under his breath. I think Billy just didn't like too much authority in any one location, namely in his location.

We crossed the Tule at Mackenzie Crossing and made our way up the canyon for several miles. Not long after sunset we began passing the scattered, bleached bones of what must have been hundreds and hundreds of horses. The varmints and such had scattered them over a broad swathe of the canyon floor, but in the mouth of a side canyon the bones were still piled thick.

I was soon informed that the remains were Mackenzie's Bone Pile. It seems that about seven years before, Colonel Ranald S. Mackenzie had come through there in possession of about a thousand Indian ponies captured when he surprised the Comanches in Palo Duro Canyon. Fearing the warriors would follow and retake the horses, he ordered his men to shoot the lot of them.

The light in the canyon was dimming fast and the bleached bones almost glowed with a light of their own. You wouldn't think a grown man would be scared of a few horse bones, but I admit that the hair on the back of my neck stood up a little as we passed the eerie graveyard. Some of the others must have felt the same thing, because they were unusually quiet until we left it all behind.

About an hour after dark we stopped to rest and water the horses at a spring Cap knew. Somebody started to make a fire, but Cap like to have had a fit. He claimed that the outlaws could be camped nearby, and no man in his outfit was going to risk ruining the expedition on account of wanting to boil a little coffee. Those old Rangers were of a determined sort, so no one argued much. We settled for what little cold rations we had along, and a sip of brackish water.

When every man had lain down in his blankets to catch a little shut-eye, I could just make out Arrington squatting on his heels in the moonlight and looking to the west. I don't know if he was looking for campfires in the dark, expected the bandits to charge down upon us, or was just planning out his brilliant campaign against outlawry. It must take that kind of thinking to get a title in front of your name.

I didn't ponder on the subject for long. I'd only slept about three hours in the last two days, and I was dead set and determined to do a little catching up. It wasn't that I was any less fervent to catch the bandits. I just always believed in leaving the worrying to the higher-ups, because position has responsibilities and worries all its own. Let all the leader types stay up all night fretting and planning. Come morning, I was going to boil myself a pot of coffee — all the captains, colonels, and horseshooters in Texas be damned.

CHAPTER FOURTEEN

The bandits fled up the Tule and then west to Las Escarbadas just like Goodnight predicted. For years I had heard about Las Escarbadas, or "The Scrapings," but there wasn't much to them except for the water seeping into several pits dug in a desolate draw. The West was full of romantic-sounding place names that made you want to get up and travel. When you got where you were going you usually found that the only thing significant about the location was its ability to keep you from dying of thirst, or that the finding of it let you know that you weren't entirely lost.

While our thirsty horses sucked up their fill, we argued over the freshness of the bandits' tracks. Most agreed, from the amount of water yet to seep back in one of the pits, that the outlaws were only an hour ahead of us at the most. As you could see farther than that ahead of you at times in that country, Cap told us to be ready for a horse race at any moment. Billy, riding his famous War Bonnet, and several other men with good horses pushed to the front of our posse, ready to run down the outlaws when we spotted them.

We never came into sight of them that day, but at daybreak the next morning we spotted smoke coming up out of a wide shallow draw to the north. We were a good four miles off when we spotted the smoke, but we smelled the sheep at about the same time. The bandits' tracks led straight toward the smoke. It seemed that even a sheepherder's camp in the middle of nowhere was prone to visitors.

When we had neared to within a quarter of a mile, Cap had us dismount and walk. Just back from the lip of the draw a couple of the men took the horses' reins while the rest of us began bellying up to the point where the ground fell away so as to avoid skylining ourselves. Sure enough we could hear sheep bleating, and the ground over which we crawled was ate off short and covered with their droppings.

Just about when we were beginning to have enough of sneaking up on sheepherders, a shot was fired and then two more. Thinking our bandits had seen us, and that we were under fire, Cap rose to his feet and waved us forward with the barrel of his gun.

Instead of a bold cavalry charge, we huffed and puffed our way the last few yards up the rise, and skidded to a halt. Below us about four hundred yards away was a wagon and a camp surrounded by sheep. The outlaws' two hipshot, worn-out horses stood teetering off to one side, and what looked like one dead man lay by the campfire still in his blankets. An outlaw with a pistol in his hand stood over the dead man, while a pack of sheep dogs barked furiously at him. Someone who we presumed was the other bandit came out of the wagon cursing and shot one of the dogs.

Some of our boys were a little edgy and took the shot as a sign to open up on their own account. Despite the fact that less than half of us had rifles, we all began to bang away. At that range with pistols a man stood little chance of hitting anything, but we did manage in our first volley to kill another dog, and terribly distress a herd of about two thousand sheep.

The outlaws were obviously professionals, as they didn't waste time returning fire with their short guns, but instead raced for the sheepherders' team of wagon horses staked nearby. Some of our crowd managed to speed them along some by hitting close enough to them to dust them a little.

Amidst the gunfire, Cap was calling our horses forward. The handlers were having a hard time leading them because of all the ruckus. Cap was soon hollering for us to cease firing, and after the boys had shot their guns empty once again, he finally convinced them to mount up and take the fight to the bandits.

All but Billy started for their horses, and he remained kneeling on the ground with his Sharps to his shoulder. By the time I hit the saddle both of the bandits were racing bareback out of the camp on fresh horses. They were slowed considerably when they entered the herd of sheep.

Billy continued to hold his aim while we came thundering up behind him. Cap was yelling something about the distance being too great for accurate marksmanship just about the time Billy touched off his cannon. That Sharps rifle roared and coughed smoke and one of the outlaws and his horse went down in the middle of the sheep.

Strange little war cries went up from our bunch as we charged down the slope toward the camp. I managed to be near the lead, but I held my fire. I'd lost my pistol after betting it on the race, but I still had Billy's old Winchester. My fellow compatriots were less inclined to save cartridges, and continued to shoot from the backs of their horses. I wondered if I wasn't in more danger from behind than in front of me.

The surviving sheep dogs had decided to hold the herd against the prevailing tide of anarchy. They raced furiously around the bleating, milling animals, and the bandit still on horseback had hell getting through the woolies. The other bandit and his downed horse were lost in the stir of wool and dust.

Just as we raced past the camp and veered around the edge of the herd in pursuit of the mounted outlaw, I caught a glimpse of a man standing beside a dead horse in the middle of the sheep. I pulled up my horse and somehow managed to get down off him with my Winchester still in my hand. A bullet cut the air near me, and I struggled to steady my aim while at the same time holding on to one rein of a maddened horse that threatened to drag me off.

Visibility was poor due to the dust, and the bandit in the herd was no longer in sight by the time I could still my horse long enough to shoot. Something knocked my leg from under me, and I knew he was still there. I hit the dirt with my whole foot and

241

lower left leg throbbing like it had been hit with a sledgehammer.

I flopped myself around in the dust and fought to aim my rifle from a prone position. I was too close to the sheep, and down low like I was I couldn't make anything out. Despite the fact that I had no clear target, I rose to my knees and fired two rounds somewhere close to where I thought I had last seen my adversary.

While I held my fire and cursed my throbbing foot, several of the posse rode back and dismounted around me. Gunfire was thick there for a bit as they poured it to the bandit in the herd. I don't know if they could see any better than me or were just shooting to be shooting. The sheep continued their racket even after the gunfire finally quieted down. I took the time to examine my wound, and to determine how much of my leg had to be amputated.

There wasn't any blood, but the band of my left spur had a shiny dent in it, and the heel of that boot was gone. I was considerably relieved, because the heel off a fancy Ft. Worth boot is a small price to pay to save a limb. I would have danced a little celebration right then, but the fact that there was still a bandit in our midst distracted me from the elation of keeping one of my legs.

Andy came tearing up to me astride a lathered horse. "Are you hit, Tennessee?"

"I'm all right, but you had better get down from that horse."

Realizing that he was the tallest target in the neighborhood right then, Andy scrambled down out of the saddle and took a post beside me.

"Don't worry, I won't let them take us," he said dramatically.

The only gun he had been able to acquire was a one-shot derringer about the size of your palm, and he was squinting out of one eye and aiming it toward the herd when he spoke. His peashooter popped even before I could point out the ridiculous nature of his weapon and pose.

"You couldn't hit that herd of sheep from here with that thing."

"Can too. I've already hit one." As proof he pointed out one of the animals on the edge of the herd that was humped up with blood slowly staining the wool of its side.

"Yeah, well, you weren't trying to hit the sheep, were you?"

"They already got the other bandit." He evaded my question.

"Who did?"

"He and the captain shot at each other on the run until they were both empty, and then Dale Martin ran him down and roped him."

"Is he still alive?"

"They drug a little hide off of him bringing him back."

Our brief conversation ended when the other bandit called out from the herd, "I'm shot to pieces. If you boys will quit shooting I'll come out."

"Come ahead," Cap's voice called back at him.

He managed to limp out of the sheep in pretty good fashion for a man shot to pieces. He had thrown down his gun and our men had tied him up with a catch rope in no time. Cap appeared on horseback with Dale Martin, and they were leading the other bandit at the end of a rope behind them. The two criminals were reunited, and we all made our way back to the campsite.

I was one of the last to arrive on account that Andy had to go catch my horse for me. When we got to camp we found that every single man in our crowd had stopped to gather around the campfire in silence. They were as quiet as a church mouse when I rode up. Billy was standing next to the captain at the center of the circle the men had formed, and I looked at him as I shoved my way beside him.

"What the hell is the matter?" I asked.

He never even answered me; he just pointed a finger at where everybody was staring. I looked down in that direction and I saw the murdered sheepherder's body beside the fire. The blankets were disarrayed and did little to cover the condition of the corpse. A dark, ugly bullet hole between the victim's shoulder blades was still oozing a thick rope of blood, but the gore wasn't what had us all speechless.

"Well, I'll be damned" was all that I could manage to say.

There wasn't just one body in the blankets but two, and they were naked as the day they were born. It wasn't their nakedness that had everyone silent, but their positions in relation to each other.

"Those two must have been really close friends," somebody finally managed to say.

"You don't reckon they were shot and just landed that way do you?" another asked.

The bottom body was face down with the other laid atop it in similar fashion. It didn't take me long at all to have seen more than enough, and I walked away with several of my friends in a similar state of mind.

"You don't reckon they're still attached do you?" Andy asked as I left.

The prisoners were seated on the wagon

tongue with a guard watching over them. The interrogation was a little slow coming as most of us were still wearing confused looks on our faces, and our attention was half diverted. Cap came forward and stopped before the two prisoners. Neither one of them would look him in the eye.

I didn't recognize either one of them, but I hadn't been in the country long. It seemed that most of our crowd knew one of them. He was a clean-cut young man dressed like a cowboy. He was fair-haired and couldn't have been much out of his teens.

The other man was a grimy sort like you could see in the last remaining dregs of the buffalo hunters hanging around Mobeetie or Fort Griffin. You couldn't tell where the dirt on his face ended and his whiskers began. He was the one Billy had shot down in the sheep herd, and the same lowdown devil who had knocked the heel off my boot. Despite his claim to have been shot to pieces, his only wound was a bullet hole in the leg. Granted, that Sharps took out a pretty good-sized chunk where it exited, and his britches' leg was heavy with blood.

"Where's the money at?" Cap asked.

The catch ropes had been removed, and their hands had been tied behind their backs with pigging strings. The older man reared his head back to swing a long, greasy lock of his hair back from his face. He met Cap's gaze, but not boldly.

"What we've got left of it's in our saddlebags."

Somebody had already caught up the bandits' original horses, and the saddlebags on each were soon removed and brought before Cap. He continued to eye the prisoners while a couple of the boys dug around in the saddlebags. A rough count was made of the contents, and only about three hundred dollars was found, there being only two small bags of coin and one bundle of paperbacks.

"I told you we only had our cut of it," the older bandit repeated.

"I'm figuring that what you stole split five ways comes up to a hell of a lot more than what you've got here," Cap said coolly.

"We were robbed," the bandit said.

An angry murmur went up amongst us, and we began to crowd in a little. The bandit glanced around frantically, his eyes wide.

"I'm telling the truth. I swear it."

"I'll bet they figured we were close and buried it somewhere along the way," someone said. It has always been common knowledge that bandits and pirates would rather bury good money than spend it.

"He's telling the truth," the younger bandit almost whispered without raising his head. He had a strong accent, maybe English.

"Who robbed you?" Cap asked.

"We got robbed on our cut." The older again spoke.

"You split the loot on McClellan Creek?"

"Yeah, and that damned . . ."

The younger bandit raised his head and quickly cut him off. "You keep quiet, Lem. Do you hear me?"

"You'd better talk, Hughes. You're in a pinch here," Cap said quietly.

"To hell with you. I'll kill him if he can't keep his mouth shut."

"You aren't going to kill anybody, because we're going to hang you."

"I'm not scared of dying."

"That's good, son."

The older man was getting pretty shook up by all the talk of dying and he looked around the crowd. "Don't any of you boys have a smoke, do you?"

"Who'd you split the money with, Lem?" Cap asked.

"Give me a smoke and I'll talk. Maybe you'll catch him and hang him later." Lem ignored the wicked look his partner passed him.

After a lit cigarette had been pushed into his whiskers, he took a few drags to calm himself. "It was Harvey Andrews. His brother put us on to the job, and Harvey led it."

Billy and I met each other's eyes across the group, and Billy blurted out, "Do you mean Colonel Andrews was in on the take?"

"Hell yes, we were to split the loot in Las Vegas, and Harvey would take his brother's share to him later. We got worried about who was behind us and stopped to split our shares on the McClellan."

"You loose-mouthed bastard, if I had a gun I'd kill you," the kid swore.

"Cake, you've spent too much time reading those 'penny dreadfuls.' There's no such thing as honor among thieves," someone behind me said.

Later, I learned that the kid's name was Cake Hughes. He was the son of some English dude with a handful of titles who had sent him out west to learn the cattle trade. Cake had earned his name when several of the men he was working with had discovered that he was hiding something from them that he had received in his Christmas mail. Not long after, he was caught out behind a shed eating a fruitcake out of a box his mother had sent him.

It seems that Cake Hughes had been working around our neck of the woods for about two years, and in all that time, the only thing anybody remembered about him was that he spent a lot of his spare time reading about outlaws, and the rest of it practicing with his pistol. From what I heard, his daddy must have given him quite a stipend, because he used up about a hundred dollars' worth of ammunition shooting into a dirt bank out back of his line cabin his first winter in the Panhandle.

Lem kept a cautious eye on the kid, but continued, "Before I could count my share, Harvey, Mexican Joe, and Handles McElroy threw down on us and told us to get packing in another direction."

"I thought the Comanches killed Handles years ago on the Pecos," Cap said.

"No, but he does have less hair than he did back then."

"They scalped him?"

"Yeah, and cut off his ears too." Lem paused to take another drag of tobacco before he continued. "He's been meaner than a shedding rattler ever since."

"He was mean enough before," Cap remarked. "Who's Mexican Joe?"

"Just another Mexican outlaw as far as I know. I guess that country is so full of thieves that they have to come north to find work."

While Lem puffed on his cigarette, Cap pulled out a little tally book and the stub of a pencil. He wrote the names of the alleged gang inside. Either his memory must have been poor, or he was planning on writing a book in his retirement years. Once that was done, he turned his attention to the kid.

"Cake, what have you got to say about that deal over yonder?" He jerked his thumb back over his shoulder in the direction of the dead men.

"They were queers," the kid sneered.

"That don't explain why you had to sneak up on them and shoot them."

The kid laughed and looked around him. "They were too busy rutting to have to be snuck up on."

"Did *you* do the killing, or the both of you?"

"Him?" The kid gave Lem a disgusted look. "He was too worried about being followed."

"And all you could think about was killing. Is that right?"

"Hell, they were just sheepherders, and queer ones at that."

"Get up." Cap looked mad enough to go bear hunting with a switch.

Some of Cake's bravado left him, and he failed to meet Cap's hard gaze. Cap was silent for a moment, and that seemed to make the kid all the more uneasy. I think he was beginning to realize the serious situation he was in.

"What are you aiming to do?" he asked.

"You're going to dig a hole, boy. You're going to dig it deep and proper so we can bury those men. I aim to work some of that meanness out of you."

While the young bandit stuttered around trying to come up with something bold to say, somebody went and found a shovel in the wagon. Another man untied his wrists and stuck the tool in his hands.

"What about Lem?" the kid asked.

"He's going to help," Cap said.

"But I didn't shoot nobody," Lem protested ever so softly.

"No, but I guess you were a well-wisher to it."

Lem was untied, and both of them were marched over to a spot of ground near the bodies. Somebody had finally had the decency to throw another blanket over Cake's victims. Cap took the heel of his boot and began to mark out the dimensions of a grave. Once he was finished, he gestured for the prisoners to get to work. There was only one shovel, but a large tin can was rounded up and given to the pair for another digging instrument.

Lem must have known that the captain was the kind of man you didn't dicker with, or else he understood what was to come. Anything that prolonged his eventual demise was good enough for him. He got down on the ground, bad leg and all, and went to scraping with the can.

"I want it dug deep," Cap ordered.

"It will take me all day to dig two graves in this ground. It's hard enough to wear out a dozen shovels," the kid complained.

Cap studied the bodies for a moment before answering. "I guess one grave, extra big, will work. I don't think they would mind."

CHAPTER FIFTEEN

Most bandits are by nature and inclination just too lazy or too smart to work, at least on a full-time basis. After all, who coined the term "easy money"? In spite of their shortcomings, those two managed to dig a grave about five feet deep. They took turns at the shovel, while the odd man scraped away with the rim of the can. They squashed the rim to a point to facilitate digging. It was slow going, but they managed. I can close my eyes and still picture those two bandits slaving away to earn a hanging.

The kid tried to sull up and quit the digging a few times, but we convinced him he had to keep it up. We passed half the day listening to the scrape of metal on the hard ground and swatting flies. Late in the afternoon, Lem threw his can up out of the hole and rested his hands on his hips. The sweat was rolling down him, and dripping off the ends of his beard.

"Well, boys, she's finished. I reckon I've just about dug myself to Hell."

He came up out of the grave almost reluctantly, and the kid crawled out with a lot less piss and vinegar than he started with. He asked for a sip of water, and when he was handed a canteen I noticed his hands were shaking a little bit.

We just folded the bodies of the sheep-herders up in the blanket they lay on, and set them down in the grave. Cap asked if anyone would like to say a few words over the deceased before we pitched the dirt in on them. Nobody said anything at first, but H.B. finally stepped forward. He said he knew the men, but not well. We all put our hats in our hands despite the sun, and stared down into the hole.

H.B. cleared his throat. "Their names were Berry and McGurty, and they weren't always sheepherders. When I knew of them they were freighting in whiskey south of Doan's Crossing, and trading a little with the Indians north of the river. I sure don't know what caused them to lose all their morals since then. Lord, I don't know much else to say, but please have mercy on these Sodomites, because I don't think they were always such."

When he was quiet for too long, we all

thought he was finished and started to filter off.

"And Lord —" H.B.'s voice stopped us, and he continued high and clear. "Let this be a lesson to the boys here to avoid herding sheep, because once a man starts living like that it's just a long slide to the bottom."

A few of the men said amens, and then our prisoners began shoveling again. I stepped off with Billy to have a smoke and to chew the fat awhile. He seemed quiet and thoughtful, and I had to do most of the talking at first. He spent his time trying to call one of the sheep dogs away from the herd while I jabbered.

I made some brilliant observation about stock dogs while I watched him try to bait the animal with a chunk of meat. The dog came close a few times to sniff around a bit, but he eventually slinked back to the sheep. Billy watched him go and turned to me.

"That's a loyal animal there."

I agreed and started in again about dogs, but Billy interrupted. "Say what you want about sheep men, but they've sure got some fine dogs."

"Seems like that ain't all to be said about them."

His mind didn't seem to be too much on dogs, despite the talk. "You once told me you spent time in church. Do you reckon God hates their kind?"

"No, I don't think he hates them. He wouldn't like their ways, but then again a lot of us are paddling that canoe."

Billy didn't answer, and I could tell he was turning it around in his mind some.

"My mother always told me that God loves us all, and that we're all sinners," I added.

Billy looked me in the eye. "You think they could go to Heaven?"

"I don't know just how much God would hold their being queer against them," I answered weakly.

Billy threw me a disgusted look. "No, that ain't what I'm talking about at all. Do you think God would let a sheepherder in heaven?"

He gave me that mischievous grin of his, and I admit to being thrown off a little. I thought I was following him for a moment, then I thought I wasn't, and then I thought I was again. Billy had a way of getting you to tell him how you felt about something, without telling you anything.

About that time Andy walked up. I could see Billy measuring him for what was about to come out of the boy's mouth.

"I grew up with an old boy like that back

home." Andy mistook our looks of dread for interest and kept talking. "We always figured he was a little off — you know he talked kind of sissy like, and didn't like the way us boys played sometimes. Turns out later that he ran off with some drummer, and his daddy caught them down the road apiece in a hotel. He shot them both, and rode home and had breakfast like nothing had happened. His wife asked him what went on and he told her straight out. He said he loved his son too much to see him carrying on that way."

"Damn, that's rough," Billy remarked.

"His daddy wasn't like that, or none of his kin. His daddy sired eight kids, and his grandpa about that many."

"What makes a fellow that way?" someone wanted to know. It seemed like most of the boys had gathered around to hear Andy's tale.

"His mamma said the drummer took advantage of his youth, but we all knew he was a little bit girly. Other than that he was all right. Hell, we used to shoot bean-flips and throw pocketknives, and go skinny-dipping down behind the schoolhouse just to make the girls giggle and run home."

"You swam naked with him?" Billy was quick to pounce, and as merciless as a cat.

"There were several of us boys swim-ming," Andy attempted to defend himself.

"There was a whole bunch of you?" Billy returned.

Andy started to stutter, and Billy kept right after him. "Did you feel him looking at you?"

"He acted all right."

Our crowd was enjoying the entertain-ment and Billy made a big show of shaking his head solemnly as if hearing sad news. "I don't know, Andy. You might ought to be careful."

"Why is that?"

"Oh, it's nothing at all. It's just that something like that could rub off on you."

Andy glared around at the group. "Noth-ing got rubbed off on me!"

"I believe you, partner. I was just worried that your friend might have thought you liked swimming with him."

Everyone, including Billy, made a show of walking off while stealing doubtful glances back Andy's way. Andy was ready to pull his gun, and probably would have if he could have remembered which pocket he had put it in. Billy came back to him and offered his hand before we ended up dig-ging another grave.

"No hard feelings, huh? I was just joshing you."

"There wasn't anything the matter with it. We were just kids swimming. None of our daddies had to shoot us in a hotel." Andy was about mad enough for his lip to quiver, but Billy seemed to be calming him. "That ain't something to joke about, Billy."

After rolling him a smoke, and continuing his line of soft talk, Billy soon had Andy calmed somewhat. The two of them started back over to where I and a few others waited.

It didn't take Lem and Cake near as long to fill in the grave as it did for them to dig it. Cap ordered everyone to break camp while they finished up. We drew straws for who had to drive that stinking sheep wagon. Luckily, I drew a long one, and only had to help hitch the team. Billy had shot the wheeler so we had to hitch Cake's horse alongside the remaining animal.

When we had loaded the wagon we asked about the sheep. Cap said we were going into Ft. Sumner to leave the wagon and belongings, and to hell with the sheep. Somebody else could ride along and round them up later. It was a good thing Cap knew cowboys, because not one of us was going to herd sheep.

When everything was ready, Cap rode over to where the prisoners were sitting atop the new mound of fresh earth. They both looked up from spelling themselves when Cap pitched his rope down on the ground before them. Cake jumped to his feet looking wild.

"My father wouldn't hear of this!"

Cap stared down at him like he was an ant. "You're a long way from home, son, and he probably won't hear of it at all."

Dale Martin stepped quickly to pick up the rope, and both Lem and the kid jumped back a little. Martin looked to Cap, and the Ranger just kept staring at Cake.

Like a rabbit flushed from his hole, the kid couldn't take it any longer and he blurted out, "You can't hang me here!"

"No, son. We're going to ride west until we find a suitable tree, *and then* we're going to hang you." He left it at that and turned his horse away.

"Get them both up on that horse," he said to Martin.

Lem climbed up on their remaining horse, and it must have belonged to Cake, the tallest of the pair, because the stirrups hung far below the older man's feet. He acted so weak he barely made the saddle. Maybe the blood loss and the hard work had gotten to him, or he just worried about where we were taking him. The kid climbed up behind him, and Martin led off their bridleless horse at the end of a rope. The animal was just about used up, and plodded along with its nose a foot above the ground. The dust rolled up slowly beneath its feet at a gravedigger's pace.

Lem was hatless, and he had torn a rag out of his shirt to wrap around his wounded leg. He placed both hands to either side of his saddle horn, and rested them there on the swell. The kid clutched uncomfortably at his partner's waist. Both of them stared ahead into an indifferent horizon.

There was something sad and desolate and timeless about the way the pair looked, like two refugees fleeing the plague of a distant land. Nobody ever painted that picture on the front of any books — the way men look when they are at the end of their rope and all hope is lost.

I came across a dirt farmer one time sitting in the door of his claim shack watching the dust roll across the withered remains of his last attempt at a crop. His wife rocked a crying baby, and hummed a soft, senseless tune. And yet the tune was familiar. Both man and woman had that look.

I have seen that look on the faces of folks

burying a child that they shouldn't have outlived. It's the look of the flooded-out, burned-down, misbegotten, left-behind widows and orphans of a world that has grown too old to notice our passing. It's the feeling that all you have to do is sit still long enough and wind will grind you up as fine as the dust and carry you long past caring.

As we were leaving I noticed Billy still hadn't mounted. Nobody had been able to coax the dogs into coming along, or catch them and put them in the wagon either. The sheep had quieted and only one of the dogs remained at his loyal post with the herd. I looked around and spotted the other dog lying on the new grave with his head rested on his paws.

Billy was trying to call him over, but the animal only stared up at him from under his brows. I heard Billy cuss as he mounted his horse. I pulled up and waited for him to come alongside. He was pretty subtle, but I saw the chunk of salt meat he dropped to the ground on his off side.

We rode out of the draw and past the herd of sheep. The other dog was still with them, but they had begun to scatter and go to grazing. Their midst was dotted with the dead scattered around the floor of the draw. High overhead I could see the buzzards already circling.

"Hell of a day for sheep and dogs," Billy said, and I couldn't have agreed more.

We found a grove of big cottonwoods along a dry branch less than a half a day's ride east of Ft. Sumner. We didn't even unhitch the team, or loosen our cinches. Without a word from Cap, Martin led the prisoners into the trees. Cap asked for another horse, but nobody wanted to volunteer their mount. I guess none of us liked the thought of a man being hanged from the back of our horse. Cap didn't volunteer his either, but remained on its back while we all stood around on foot. I guess it wouldn't have looked right for him to preside over an execution from the ground.

H.B., being of mature years and possibly more used to such occasions, brought his horse forward by the bridle. He looked up at the kid. "Swap horses, Cake."

Cake got down, but he refused to mount. "You ain't hanging me. Give me a gun and I'll fight the lot of you."

I was beginning to think he had a little sand, but then he started crying. "My father is rich. You just let me go and he'll make it right."

The kid's knees buckled, and H.B. had to

264

catch him and hold him up for a moment. H.B. didn't seem to know what to do.

Finally, Cap rode forward. "Get on that horse."

I guess when the kid met Cap's hard gaze he knew it was over, and he just died right then and there. He climbed right up on the horse and only sniffled a little while his hands were tied behind his back.

Two catch ropes were thrown over two big limbs on the same side of the tree. The prisoners were led under them, and their horses stood nose to tail facing opposite each other. We gathered around while Cap and several of the boys placed the loops over the bandits' necks. I don't know how they managed it. I could have shot the thieves in pursuit, or in a fight, but for some reason hanging them was different. It was justified, but easier said than done.

I stood holding one bridle and Billy the other. Cap stepped back and looked up to the kid. "Have you got anything to say?"

We all thought the kid would break down again, but instead, he spoke in a tight, controlled voice. "Don't tell my father what happened to me. Bury my belongings here with me and let him think what he will. What he can imagine is bound to be better than the truth."

Cap waited him out and then turned to the other man. "What about you?"

Lem looked each and every one of us in the eye like a preacher in the pulpit looking back at his congregation. "I've shot buffalo when there were so many you couldn't see where they began or ended. I've found water where there wasn't any, and the worst of it was plenty good. I remember when it was nigh a week's travel to the settlements, and the Indians were thick as flies and bound to take your hair. I came to this country in '67 and saw her while she was still fairly new. I remember when the sight of any kind of white woman was rare, and not even that could keep a man from going back out in this forsaken country."

We were all listening, and we heard him too.

"I never thought it would come to this," Cake said to no one in particular.

Lem leaned out to spit, careful not to lose his balance on his horse. "I've killed, and robbed, and whored, and cheated my whole life. I reckon hanging is an even swap for just getting to live as long as I have."

"Are you through?" Cap asked after waiting for a polite bit.

"Hell yes, I'm through."

I saw one little tear trickle from the corner

of Lem's eye, but he kept his chin up and stared straight ahead. He was a grubby thief that we all knew was just as likely to lay out to rob and murder you as he was to smile at you, but he was the real deal. Say what you want, but being bad doesn't make you a coward.

Cap stepped back and motioned Billy and I away. We both eased off, lest the horses try to follow. I was scared to death the horse I held wouldn't stand still.

"Sudden" is the only word that I can use to describe the way it happened. No sooner than I had cleared out of the way than Cap cracked one horse on the hip with his hat and then doubled back across himself and hit the other. And just like that, two men were kicking in the air. God help me, but I don't think a man can talk about justice unless he has seen a man hanged.

We all saw it through to the vicious end, but that didn't make it any better. What little personal effects the deceased had had were placed into a hole quickly scooped out at the bottom of the hanging tree and covered up. Quick wasn't quick enough, and we all headed for our horses at the first chance. Cap held off a bit before leaving, and continued staring at the hanged men.

"You want to keep that picture in your

head so that it will never be an easy thing," he said as he walked by me to his horse.

"It's a hell of a thing, Cap." I meant every word of it.

We rode out of there at a walk, and not a single man looked back. Billy and I rode alongside Cap.

The Ranger turned to Billy. "That was quite a shot you made yesterday."

"Even a blind hog will find an acorn now and again," Billy said.

"What part of the country did you say you hailed from?"

"I didn't."

"I sure think I ought to know you." Cap had nothing else to say, and he looked straight ahead of him all the way to Ft. Sumner.

Goodnight's two hands met us on the edge of Ft. Sumner. They were riding east and stopped to palaver some. They claimed to have missed our bandits, but we told them not to worry. They asked why, and Cap told them there were a couple of saddles hanging on cottonwood limbs and two good catch ropes a half a day's ride to the east. That was enough said.

As far as I know, way out east of Ft. Sumner in a rare cottonwood wash, lie the bones of two outlaws. They might even still be hanging there, but I don't know. We rode away from that place, and I haven't ever been back.

CHAPTER SIXTEEN

We had only recovered a little of our fortunes and were anxious to head east and find out the whereabouts of the other posse. Despite our hurry, we took the time to ride into Ft. Sumner for resupply, and so Cap could leave word of the abandoned sheep at Pete Maxwell's trading post. The old fort was in fact a fort no longer, the military having left and sold everything years before. Maxwell's enterprise now occupied the former post. It was a low-slung affair of several adobe buildings forming a rough plaza of sorts, surrounded by the settlement that had grown around it over the years.

Cap went to Maxwell's big house down by the river to palaver while the rest of us stood around under the shaded veranda of the old barracks and smacked our lips over a jug of tequila. None of us were especially fond of the sticky concoction, but it was the cheapest thing available.

I looked to Billy reclining on a stack of salvaged lumber beneath the roof beside me, and then to the horde of tough-looking characters standing around and eyeing us with no love at all. Our posse had been under constant observation since we arrived. A mixed congregation of both Mexican and Anglo men with weapons bristling about their persons kept the vigil

"Those old boys wear too many guns to hold honest jobs." Billy nodded his head toward the nearest group of suspicious locals loitering across the plaza from us.

"I'd bet you the government's advertising for most of them."

"I believe you're right. Posses do seem to make them nervous." Billy flipped a cigarette butt out into the sunlight in the direction of our watchers. They didn't even blink.

I watched the scattering of Mexicans working for Maxwell going about their business timidly, making sure not to hang around too long, or to look anybody in the eye. They obviously saw trouble in the making and wanted no part of it.

"There's bound to be some good folks around here, but they seem overrun by the sort that'll steal your horse just to welcome you to the Pecos Country," I said.

"Not just your horse. This bunch would

peel you right down to your skin."

"Billy the Kid's liable to be wandering around here. I hear he's extra mean."

"I reckon we'd know him if we saw him. From all the talk about him I'd guess he's bound to be exceptional."

"Well, I just hope old Cap can resist the temptation to hang New Mexico's bandits."

"We've already got other irons in the fire."

H.B. sat down beside us with a sigh. "Billy's right, I've had the drizzling shits for a hundred miles, and I've about scratched out what little hair I've got left." He dabbed at the sweat on his balding forehead with a handkerchief while he fanned himself with his hat. "Let me tell you, you ain't ever been truly worried unless your head's broken out in itchy bumps."

Our lust for revenge was slowly being dampened by other concerns. Most of our posse consisted of men who should have still been with the roundup. Every one of us was probably returning east to be fired for leaving the herd, because none of us were on the payroll for racing horses and chasing outlaws. And H.B. had the loss of Wiren's payroll to think about.

In the course of one week we had managed to engage in licentious drinking and gambling on company time, embezzle company funds, and introduce vice and wanton behavior on to Indian lands. In our defense, the punitive expedition to New Mexico did result in the failure to save two innocent citizens, the hanging of two criminals without recourse to the courts, and the murder of fifty sheep and a dog. One could prejudicially argue that the murdered citizens weren't all that "innocent," and I doubted that anyone would question the hanging of a couple of murderers when there was such a thick supply to choose from. However, our assertion that the deceased sheep and the dog were somehow accessories to the crime was sure to be considered as of a dubious nature. The worst alkali water in West Texas couldn't have given us as bad a case of the shits as the worries we had right then.

Cap soon returned and we made ready for the long ride back to Mobeetie. We left the wagon and team with Maxwell and rode out with a puny sack of victuals to feed us, and a bait of corn for the horses. Our entire posse was thus equipped to travel over a hundred miles.

"Here's a little something to fortify the inner man." Billy held a fresh bottle of cactus juice aloft for all of us to see.

H.B. stopped his horse at the edge of the

273

settlement and eyed the bottle doubtfully. "You just got one?"

"I'd have gotten more, but Cap's a stickler for discipline."

"Well, I've been worse supplied. All a man needs to travel in wild country is a few cartridges to shoot some game, a little salt to cook your meat, and some whiskey to shorten the miles."

"What about a good sense of direction? They say Goodnight can find water out here when nobody else can, and he's never been lost," I said.

"Water, you say? I never touch the stuff." He shivered and stuck out his tongue and made an awful face. "You and Goodnight can have your sense of direction, and I'll take the whiskey. I remember when that know-it-all old windbag was wandering his ass all around this country Rangering after Comanches, and didn't have a clue where he was most of the time. Just because he's finally learned this country doesn't mean he's a homing pigeon or something. In my opinion, knowing where you're at all the time is just damned unrealistic."

We traveled up the Pecos a bit and then cut northeast, arriving at Las Escarbadas by a slightly more northern route. From there, we angled to the north headed for Tascosa.

The game was scarce and we went hungry for the most part. The liquor ran out as quickly as our food, and sober, we still managed to overshoot our route by twenty miles. We found the GMS headquarters on Tierra Blanca Creek and were provided there with some beef, but no whiskey. One of the hands informed us that the Army was camped at Sanborn Springs, and we continued north.

The Army was gone when we got there, but the half of our posse we'd left at Mc-Clellan Creek was still in camp. They were glad to hear of our success in catching our bandits, but not near so happy to find out that we had recovered so little money. Colonel Andrews was nowhere to be seen, and we immediately asked his whereabouts. It turns out that they'd had just as an eventful, even if less successful, journey as we did.

After our parting at McClellan Creek, they followed the outlaws' trail up to and westward along the Canadian River. Before they had gone too many miles they were greeted by a fusillade of gunfire. One of the Cheyenne scouts was wounded scouting a crossing of the Canadian. The posse took shelter on the river bank in a rare stand of timber and looked to return fire on the bandits they were sure had doubled back to ambush them.

They soon recognized that the fire was too heavy to come from just three men. It turned out that the bandits had passed through the country telling all they met that the Cheyenne had left the reservation and were on the warpath, scalping every person they came across. A contingent of the Tascosa crowd, several riders from the LXs, Bar Cs, and the Quarter Circle Ts joined them to ride down and battle the native horde.

The attackers held a position on the north side of the river in the gyp rock bluffs opposite the timber. Long-range shots were exchanged for about an hour, and then the U.S. Cavalry arrived to help our posse. At that point the war really broke out.

The soldiers had been to the south, and upon hearing the gunfire they came up to join the fight. The commanding officer set up his men in a skirmish line behind the cover of the timber, and brought the two cannons he had with him forward. I guess the soldiers had arrived unseen by the party north of the river, because the first two rounds out of those field pieces surprised them greatly.

The two rounds whistled across the river

and struck smoke from the bluffs. Firing on that side ceased and men started running everywhere. Two more cannon rounds landed over there, and a good volley of concentrated rifle fire before those on the south realized that something was wrong. Those on the north had also come to a quick conclusion that it wasn't Indians they were fighting.

All firing ceased, and a few of those men on the north bank peeked their heads out of the gullies and rocks they were hiding behind to ask for a parley. The commanding officer and a small detail rode out and met them on the south bank. Soon, all parties involved joined the discussion whereby matters were attempted to be smoothed over.

The Army and our posse were sorely vexed at having been fired upon in the course of their duties, while the attacking party of cowboys and Tascosa toughs were still a little put off by having artillery shells dropped on them. To complicate matters, the Cheyenne thought it had been a heap good fight, and were hard to get under control, much less convince that the fight was over. After much heated discussion, the attackers agreed to disband and ride back to whence they came, and the Army decided to escort the Cheyenne back to the reservation, lest similar misunderstandings happen again.

All in all, the Battle of the Canadian counted none killed, two wounded, and several disgruntled men. The attackers left as they'd promised, no worse for their wear other than a bad case of shell shock and a scrape here and there. The Army started off down the river with the pack of happy Cheyenne who were ready to go home and recount the battle to their people. Our friends in the other half of our posse were left alone to chase the three bandits, who were probably long, long gone by then. Due to the excitement of the fight it was way up in the evening before anyone realized that Colonel Andrews was missing.

Thinking their leader might have fallen in combat, a search of the battleground was quickly made. The colonel hadn't left with the Army so he must have crossed the river and headed north or west. Some thought he must have gone to scout ahead for sign of the bandits, but things were so trampled on the north side of the river that no hint of him was found.

The excitement of the fight was soon replaced by the depression of having such bad fortune befall their pursuit of the bandits. They had killed half a day of valuable time, and now their esteemed leader, a man of many admirable leadership qualities, none of which anyone could quite put a finger on, had disappeared. That gray melancholy that can come upon us without warning struck the party, and they sat in camp and brooded for two days until our arrival.

When we informed them of the colonel's participation in the robbery, the color came back to their faces, and they were ready to fight again. Our only chance lay in going to Tascosa in search of the colonel. Our sister posse, eager to make up for the failure of not having hanged anyone yet, led the charge across the Canadian. None of the horses were up to a long run, and we had to settle for a slow walk to Tascosa.

The colonel, it seems, had avoided the settlement, possibly having gone west along the Ft. Smith road. Cap had thought it unwise to split the party again, considering the events thus far, and we took up residence in one of the saloons to work things out. Cap volunteered to go to Denver via Las Vegas, New Mexico, and keep a lookout for Andrews and his gang. He advised the rest of us to return to our work. He would contact us should he need our help.

Our horses were played out, and we were without funds except for the little money we had recovered. Decisions would have to be made before further pursuit of outlaws could be funded. A long meeting was held right then and there to settle the matter of finances.

There were bound to be far more claimants to the money than there was money to go around. Many people who had suffered monetary losses on the Sweetwater were not even present to petition our meeting. Several arguments were presented over the course of a couple of hours. Determined to come to a just and amicable decision, we stuck to it, only adjourning the meeting a few times to allot funds for refreshments.

Finally, we decided that there wasn't much to go around, and anyone who had lost their money should have had enough gumption to go after it. All parties not present were thus barred from financial settlement. There were twenty-five men present, not counting Cap Arrington, who had no financial interest in the outcome, having been smart enough not to gamble. According to the claims of those present, three hundred dollars, minus the purchase of some drinks, didn't begin to pay back losses. There was no way of knowing who had bet what, and each man had to be taken at his word. It seems, however, that every man present was a high-roller, and had bet the ranch on the outcome of the race.

H.B. was known to have one of the largest losses, and Billy was recognized with him by his portion of the race stakes, which was a larger bet than anyone else claimed. Most of us somewhat agreed that the two of them should split the money, but they refused. We five Lazy F hands offered to eat our wages for two months to let H.B. make up for the loss of the payroll Wiren had given him.

It was further agreed that Billy would take only fifty dollars for his losses, being deserving of a large share due to his ownership of the winning animal in the race, but not wanting to hog all the money. Another fifty dollars was to go to Cap to fund his trip to Denver. This act was looked upon as having some small value as an investment should he capture the bandits and get the rest of our money back. The remaining hundred or so dollars was divided equally among twenty-four men. I remember getting about four dollars for my part.

Cap wasted no time in procuring a fresh horse and riding for Las Vegas. We were left to our own accord, none the richer, but a little wiser. It was nightfall before we managed to round everyone up to start back to Mobeetie. Then it was decided that it would be better to lie over for the night in town and get an early start in the morning. We did stay the night in Tascosa, but we failed to get an early start. I don't guess we had gotten any wiser.

Fortune had put a little jingling money back in our pockets, but the dives of Tascosa managed to get most of that before the night was through. I had to loan Andy a dollar to have his horse shod the next morning, and I borrowed that from Billy, who had to dig to come up with the amount. It seems that our financial lot in life was always to follow a predetermined course of misfortune and bankruptcy.

It takes no short amount of time to ready and outfit such a large group. We had managed to put our purses together and come up with the price of a few bottles of whiskey sold to us at a volume discount by one of the earlier rising saloonkeepers in town. He must have been determined to see us leave broke to have given us such a bargain. After I had tasted the whiskey I decided that we had overpaid.

It was a prompt and punctual noon when we left Tascosa. I remember the approximate time because the sun was making my head hurt.

Andy rode up alongside me, and he didn't look like he was feeling as dapper as he tried to let on. He was sweating pure rotgut, and his eyes were bloodshot and sagging. He offered me a drink from one of the bottles. "This'll chase the wolf out of your head."

"No thanks, I believe I've had enough." I was too sick to consider curing a hangover by getting drunk all over again.

"You've gotta be tougher than that. Hang'n rattle, cowboy." He offered me the bottle again.

"You can go to Hell. I ain't got the stomach for it."

I heard somebody retching, and looked down the trail behind me. Two of our party were off their horses and emptying their guts in the grass. Andy's face turned a shade paler and he fought down a gag as he quickly rode ahead. Even Billy looked like something the cat drug in, and didn't have a word to say except to grumble something incoherent every now and then. It seemed I wasn't the only one without the stomach for it that morning.

Only H.B. seemed no worse for the wear. He rode up beside me with a grin on his face, and looking fresh as a daisy, if slightly drunk. "You youngsters are sure soft. Maybe we'd best stop and eat a bite. I've been thinking about food all morning. What I'd really like to have is some fresh, raw buffalo liver to sink my teeth into."

I tried not to listen.

"Indians taught me that. There's nothing better than biting into a big raw liver with a little gall juice poured over it, unless it's a good batch of boiled cabbage, or maybe some of that German kraut. All I've got to do is think about it and I can get a whiff of that strong smell of cabbage cooking."

I bailed off my horse at the side of the trail and let him go ahead. I never did like liver or cabbage.

"The coyotes are going to be trailing us before long." H.B. laughed to himself as he rode off.

If you ran with cowboys in those days, you drank. And if you think we drank too much, you're right. It was whiskey that led us to most of our troubles, but if it hadn't been for the whiskey there wouldn't have been near as many fascinating stories to tell. Whiskey, or cards, or a combination of both led to more killings and general felonious behavior than anything else. I'm ashamed of the fondness I have had for both.

The ranchers of the Panhandle weren't

teetotalers themselves, but most of them realized the problems that go along with drinking and gambling. As a result, both were banned from most of the ranches in that country. Any man caught doing either on the ranch was fired on the spot, and many of the big ranchers had agreed not to hire anyone who had been fired elsewhere for such violations.

Clarendon's citizens had signed agreements prohibiting liquor, and a bunch of Quakers down south of them practiced the same. For miles everything south of the Canadian River was dry. The whole country would have been sober if it weren't for Mobeetie, Tascosa, and the itinerant whiskey peddlers selling from the back of their wagons.

That year Goodnight funded a school in Clarendon, and at least five white women were living outside of Mobeetie or Tascosa. You knew things were starting to get civilized when women arrived. Along with them came churches, schools, courts, and outhouses. The list of unacceptable offenses would grow to such a state that your average man couldn't have any fun.

The Panhandle Stock Association was determined to rid the country of rustlers, and to put a judge and jury just around every bend. I didn't hold with rustling, but with the Comanche gone, it was one of the few things holding up progress. Before long nothing of any consequence was going to happen in that country if they didn't slow down with the civilizing.

No liquor, no cursing, no spitting in public was about the sum of things to come. We might as well have all sold our saddles and joined the ladies' bridge club. I don't know why they wanted to tamper with a perfectly good layout, but I guess progress has its costs.

CHAPTER SEVENTEEN

We were fired before we even got back; we just didn't know it yet. We met Wiren and some hands driving the Lazy F herd, the one we were supposed to be with, long before we reached the Sweetwater. There was nothing to be said in our defense. If we had been in his boots we would have done the same.

Wiren was mad, and he ranted and raved a little. Even a fellow in the wrong can only listen to so much. We all got a little on the prod, but nobody's mother was brought into question, or honor severely impugned. To a man, we prided ourselves on our independence and willingness to get stubborn at the drop of a hat. We figured we could ride off from that outfit just as easy as we rode in there. H.B., Andy, Dale Martin, and I jumped down and jerked our saddles off the company horses we were riding while Billy and a couple of the hands rode over and roped Dunny and our other personal mounts out of the remuda they were driving.

Wiren was a pretty good sort, and we were just in the wrong. Before we could ride off he asked us if we were broke, and then gave us seventy dollars to tide us over on the way. He told us not to take the firing too hard, because the JA was buying the Lazy F, and Goodnight's tolerance for fun and leisure was far less than his own.

The following spring, Goodnight and Wiren had a pretty big fuss over the counting of the Lazy F cattle. I don't care what Charlie Goodnight had to say about him, Wiren will always be all right with me. He understood that a man has to be let loose every now and again. If it hadn't have been for us cowboys, every head of cattle in the state would have drifted off to Mexico and those big shots would have starved out for want of foolish labor.

It wasn't winter, but it was still a tough time of the year to land a job. The roundups had all moved far to the north and the outfits around had settled down to the work around their home ranges until time to ship cattle in the fall. However, we had some hope due to the number of new outfits moving into the country.

Billy wanted to try his hand at running War Bonnet a few more times. My financial situation made me less bold than he. We both hated to part, but we separated at Mobeetie, and he and Andy headed south to try their luck on the horse tracks at San Antonio.

Dale Martin shocked us all and took a job teaching school in Clarendon. Goodnight had offered him the job, and that shocked us even more, because the rumor was that Martin was suspected by the stock association of rustling — a lot of rustling. He was a smart devil though, but I still didn't like him.

I was left with H.B. and he wanted to ride down to Clarendon to talk to a man he knew about jobs for us. I didn't put up much of an argument, and I didn't tell Billy where we were going before he left. It seemed like my competition for a certain girl was thinning out for a while.

I convinced H.B. to take a little swing to the northeast to the Cheyenne Reservation. I wanted to talk with Blue Knife some. A little yellow Cheyenne horse had caught my eye during the race day, and I knew just the girl that needed it. I explained my reasons and he agreed to the detour with only a little grumbling. It tells you the situation I was in to want to visit with a savage who I still wasn't convinced didn't want to gut me. Love will do that to a man.

Blue Knife's band was camped on a creek off the Canadian many miles above where we had left them. When we had neared to within about a mile and a half from camp we came across a squaw. She was wailing and cutting herself with a knife. After cutting herself she would rub sand in the wounds and wail some more. At times her cries sounded like a song.

We rode over close thinking she needed help, but she didn't even recognize our presence. I thought she might have been crazy and in need of our help. Before we could come too close two Cheyenne warriors rode up and motioned us off. We tried to sign with them some about the woman, but they just shook their heads and motioned us away. When we didn't scat along quick enough they both rode up and took our horses by the bridles. I put my hand to the butt of my pistol, but H.B. motioned to me to sit tight.

"They don't mean us any harm, but you can get us killed just the same."

H.B. kept talking to them about Blue Knife. I didn't think they understood a word he said, but at least they led us off from the squaw in the direction of the camp. In sight of the tepees we came across another squaw doing the same crazy things. If anything, she was going at it even worse. She had hacked off her hair, and she was bloody from the neck down.

Several more bucks rode up and surrounded us, most of them placing themselves between us and the squaw. We repeated that we were looking for Blue Knife. One of the men nodded his head and motioned toward the camp. I rode along looking back over my shoulder at the last squaw we had passed.

There were at least thirty lodges in the camp and at least twice that many dogs. Our escorts dismounted and motioned us to do the same. We hobbled our horses, loosened cinches, and slipped our bridles off right there. Our original two escorts led us to the far side of the encampment, where Blue Knife sat under a brush arbor out in front of what must have been his lodge. He was watching a passel of his women cutting up beef. Blowflies were everywhere and the carcass stank to the high heavens.

"I believe they let that one age too long," I said to H.B.

"It was probably dead when they found it.

They've been about to starve for a long time."

"If this camp is all that's left of them I'd say they've been more than 'about to starve,' " I observed.

"There are several camps of the Southern Cheyenne scattered about under different chiefs, and there ain't any of them any better off. The government is supposed to feed them beef and educate them," H.B. scoffed. "I don't know which part of the system ain't working."

One of the braves left us to wait while he went over to Blue Knife and talked a while. Blue Knife rose to his feet and greeted us in surprisingly good English.

"Come and sit down, white men." He waved expansively toward his buffalo robe under the arbor.

He seated himself only after we had taken a spot. I waited for H.B. to start the conversation, but he just looked at me with a blank face. I sat facing Blue Knife across the space of the robe, and I was a little skittish. Looking into those dark eyes set deep into the leathery folds of his face made me damned glad I'd never run into his like out on the plains in the old days.

"I don't have any whiskey," Blue Knife stated. No white man can look at an Indian's face and tell what he is thinking. I thought he was begging for liquor.

"We don't have any either."

Blue Knife stared at me and I stared back.

"Good," he finally said. "Whiskey is bad for all Cheyenne. I like whiskey, but it makes me do bad things. It makes me want to kill cowboys."

I started to say I was glad that we hadn't any whiskey. Instead, I motioned off along the creek where I could see some horses grazing. "I've come to trade horses with the great chief Blue Knife."

The only reference I had for dealing with Indians came from having read *Last of the Mohicans* as a child. I didn't know just how well Blue Knife spoke English, and I felt a little self-conscious making trade talk. I decided to try and talk to him just like I would anybody else.

Before I could practice this radical theory of communication Blue Knife asked, "Did you see any rain to the west? We need rain."

I shook my head in the negative, and once more tried to breech the subject of horses. "I saw one of your squaws riding a good yellow horse the day of the races."

Blue Knife nodded his head some, but he didn't mention the horse. He studied the clouds to the northwest and scratched at a sand flea gnawing his belly. I was rapidly learning that Indians, like Mexicans, have a whole different sense of time. Trading with them was a test of patience and nonchalant discourse.

Despite all accounts of such meetings between white men and Indians, Blue Knife didn't offer to pass the peace pipe around with us. Instead, he pulled out a cigar and promptly bit the suck end off of it. He produced a box of matches and lit the stogie. He cupped the flame of the match in his hand and leaned over close to me. Tobacco is a religion in itself among the Indians, and I started rolling a cigarette when he produced the cigar, lest I break some unspoken rule of etiquette. His black eyes seemed to twinkle a little bit as he lit my cigarette.

"You have come before to trade for Cheyenne horses?" He remained close to me, leaning far forward at the waist.

I scrambled to think of an answer, but he was too close to allow me proper thinking room. His eyes were as unblinking as a snake's.

"I came, but did not get to visit. It made me sad to have ridden so far and not have gotten to meet with your people." I didn't stutter a lick.

Ever so slowly he leaned back against a willow backrest, eyeing me all the while. A slow, slight hint of a smile moved at the corners of his mouth, and the folds at the corners of his eyes wrinkled a bit. "I too am sorry that we did not meet the last time you came looking for horses."

H.B. wasn't privy to the necessary information, but he still caught wind of something that wasn't just right. He stared a question at me, and he was starting to look a little white around the gills like his pipe tobacco wasn't setting well with him or something.

I refused to ask about the horse again as I was determined and willing to wait for the chief to mention it in his own good time. We passed a good while just smoking and watching the squaws cut up the rancid beef. They were cutting the meat into about three-inch strips and hanging them over poles rigged up horizontal to the ground. They were handy with a knife, and some of the pieces were cut so thin you could see daylight through them. I'd always heard that it was the squaws you wanted to avoid if you were a captive.

Watching the squaws made me think about the two we had passed coming there, and I broached the subject to Blue Knife.

"What's the matter with your women that we passed on the trail here? Are they crazy?"

Blue Knife thought on the subject for a while before answering. "They are sad."

"I've seen a lot of sad people, but never any that cut themselves up. Can't you stop them?"

"Don't you know anything, Tennessee? They're in mourning and you'd best go easy," H.B. warned.

"Is that how you are called? Tennessee?"

I started to give Blue Knife my Christian name, but it hadn't taken hold anywhere else, so I just nodded my head.

"I know Smokes the Man," Blue Knife gestured to H.B. "I nearly had his scalp when I was a young man."

An exchange of glances between H.B. and me was enough to let me know that I wasn't the only one holding out information.

"Blue Knife, you have a long memory," H.B. said.

"Your friend likes horses too. He and the Dutch Man used to visit us from time to time," Blue Knife said.

"Dutch Henry?" I couldn't hide my shock in spite of having known that H.B. had a shifty side.

The old chief merely nodded his head in agreement. "They were in the big fight we had with Custer."

"Damn, H.B.! Why'd you offer to come along?"

H.B. shrugged his shoulders and sucked hard on his pipe, while Blue Knife continued. "Some say Smokes the Man has a bad heart, but he and the Dutch Man always took more horses from the soldiers than they did from us. Anyway, that was a long time ago."

"That's what I think. Let bygones be bygones," H.B. muttered.

It seemed that I had brought two horse thieves into the Cheyenne camp. I was getting edgy and felt the need to keep the conversation going. "What are those squaws we passed out yonder mourning about?"

"Cowboys poisoned a dead cow with strychnine, and their children ate the meat and died."

I didn't know what to say, but like a fool I kept talking. "What cowboys?"

He didn't answer except to point to the north. The Strip was filled with Texas herds grazing on a lease with the Cherokees. The Apple outfit was grazing cattle on a lease in the Cheyenne and Arapahoe reservation. As far as I had heard there had been no trouble between the Apple hands and the Cheyenne.

The boys along the Cimarron River adjoining the northern boundary of the reservation were a whole other story. I'm sure they weren't all bad, but there had been a lot of shots swapped around the river. The cowboys claimed the Cheyenne stole and begged around their camps, and the Cheyenne claimed that a lot of their ponies ended up in Kansas. The law didn't bother too often about stolen Cheyenne horses. The feeling about Indians in that country at the time was pretty hard.

"How come they cut themselves up that way? Why don't you stop them?" I asked.

"They are mourning. That way their children know they will miss them, and the world can hear that their hearts are very sad."

"White men don't carry on so."

"It's our way."

"How long will they go on?"

"Until they are through. There is no set time." Blue Knife looked at me like I was a little on the slow side.

Nobody in the village seemed to notice the noise, but we could plainly hear the wailing squaws from where we sat, despite the distance. "It sometimes sounds like they're singing."

"They are." Blue Knife paused to adjust his cigar stub in the corner of his mouth before he added, "Sometimes they sing, sometimes they cry, sometimes both."

We listened to them for a while. They sang and cried and their voices drug out long and sad like the bawl of a good hound. I didn't know what they were saying when they said anything at all, but their sorrow was alive in the air. Two braves had sat down at the foot of a lodge at the edge of the camp and set in to beating small skin drums. They sang something themselves in quiet voices that continually rose and fell in pitch and volume. The drums beat and those poor, wretched women wailed.

"What do they sing about?"

"Sadness."

I had a heap more questions, but I figured I'd already been rude enough and decided to let it go. I sat quiet and listened to the drums and screaming women until I was sad myself.

"Once they are through mourning most of the sad will be gone. It will not eat them inside. It is a good way. We cry and sing to show how sad we are. Sometimes we just sing when we are happy. Mostly now we sing when we are sad."

He put the short butt of his cigar out against the dirt, and then ground the remaining tobacco between his fingers. The grindings were placed into a small pouch at his side. I held forward my tobacco sack, and he took it. He eyed my shirt pocket and I pitched him my papers. With deft, quick fingers he rolled himself a cigarette as neat as any saddle monkey in Texas.

Bull Durham has eased a lot of negotiations in its time, and the chief smoked three more cigarettes while he talked.

"I have had five sons and they are all dead. They have gotten sick and died, they have been shot by soldiers and died, and they have been scalped by the Comanche and the Kiowa and died. They are all dead, but I am alive. I too have fought, and been sick. Why am I still alive? The buffalo are gone and the white man says to eat the wohaw. He gives us money to graze his cows; they eat the grass all around us, but we go hungry."

"You should tell the government about your problems."

He ignored my remark like I had suggested he go to the moon to take a nap. "I sometimes think I should paint my face and go fight the Pawnee. The Pawnee don't fight good, but I am too old to fight. Now I just sit and watch the women and children."

There was a gaudily decorated stick propped up atop his plunder at the front of his tepee. A whole string of scalps hung along its length, and I gestured to them.

"Are those Pawnee scalps there?"

A sly look came across his face. "I am too old to remember."

Two boys came running by and the chief said something to them in Cheyenne. They took off like a shot and the old man continued. "Nobody would care if I fought the Pawnee. Nobody likes them. They fight for the soldiers, but the soldiers don't like them either. Now they have moved them close to us. It is close enough even for an old man to ride."

You could tell that he was reminiscing about the good old days. He had sort of a savage, dreamy look about him as he thought about raiding and pillaging. From what I'd been able to see, about all Indian men did was hunt and fight. The government wouldn't let them fight anymore, and had killed off their main source of meat. There wasn't much to do except reminisce.

One of the boys the chief had spoken to returned astride the yellow horse I wanted. I hadn't even mentioned the particular animal I sought, but the chief knew. He worked on finishing off my makings while I got up and looked the animal over.

The palomino horse was as cute as a button. He had a long white mane and tail, and his coat would have been dark gold except for the bleaching of the sun. All four legs were covered by white stockings, and a broad blaze reached from eye to eye and all the way down to his nose. The boy rode him around some while I watched. The little gelding seemed gentle and willing.

"Do you like the horse?" Blue Knife asked.

"He's close to what I'm looking for." I sat back down on the buffalo robe and pretended to lose a little interest.

"What have you to trade, Tennessee?"

I had come prepared, and I motioned for him to wait while I went to my horse. I led Dunny back to the brush arbor and pulled two pouches of Bull Durham tobacco from my saddlebags, a pound sack of Arbuckle coffee, and a brand-new pocket knife. I placed them on the robe before the chief. He put the tobacco in his lap along with the coffee, and then opened and closed the knife a few times before laying it back down.

"What else have you brought?"

"That looks like a fair trade to me."

Blue Knife appeared to consider my offer while shaking his head somberly. "One of my women rides that horse. She likes him very much."

"I'll just bet she does."

"She will get very mad if I trade him to you. She has a bad temper, that woman." For a warrior that had sent more than a few fellows to the happy hunting grounds, he made a passable attempt at looking scared.

"Have we got a trade?" I asked.

"No trade. What else have you got?"

I knew I should sit down and wait him out, but I was an impatient sort, and was anxious to take that palomino to Clarendon. I went to my saddle and brought back the Winchester Billy had traded me. The chief was now paying a lot of attention; in fact, he rose to his feet and met me halfway. I handed him the rifle and he worked the lever a few times and examined the ejected cartridges. He shouldered the rifle and sighted down it before setting himself back down with the barrel across his thighs.

"Good trade." He motioned me to take the horse.

"No trade. What else have you got?"

The way he looked at me for a minute I was glad he didn't have any whiskey.

"The rifle was given to me by a friend and he will get mad if I trade it to you. He has a bad temper," I said.

Surprisingly, the old savage laughed loudly and motioned me to sit back down with him. I ended up trading the rifle and the other plunder for the horse, a good Gallatin saddle with a fancy braided Mexican bridle, and wool blanket thrown in to boot. God only knows where the saddle came from. I put it on the palomino and led him to my horse. We mounted up and made ready to leave.

Blue Knife walked out to our horses and placed his hand on Dunny's neck. "I think your heart is good, Tennessee. Come back and smoke with me sometime."

I nodded and turned my horse away. As I was riding off I heard him say, "Cry when you are sad, or you will let it live in your heart and it will eat you. Come here when you need to, and we will show you how to mourn."

As we were riding off H.B. said, "You paid too much for that horse. Now if old Dutch was still operating we could show you how to come by a horse the proper way."

We passed the mourning squaws on our way back. The sight of the wretched women made me turn to H.B. "Those Indians were bloody fighters, and they were constantly trying to wipe one another out until we come along and whipped them all. They don't know any other way than war, and somebody always has to lose."

H.B. just nodded his head. "I reckon

that's right."

I pulled up my horse and looked back at the village with its mutilated women, rotten meat, and skinny, potbellied kids. "I'd be damned if I was them if I wouldn't take up my gun and try and kill every white son of a bitch in the country — man, woman, and child. I wouldn't live like that."

Charlie Russell, back before he quit cowboying and got famous painting pictures, said that the Indians had lived in paradise until we came and ruined it. He said that a cowboy was about the closest thing to an Indian, and I guess he wasn't too far off the mark. We lived about like them, and there would come a time when civilization would be trying to shut us up somewhere. They'd run us down and starve us out, and in the end they would parade the last of us up and down the street to lament our passing while they fired a cannon shot for Old Glory. In the end, it was just a simple matter of geography. We needed a lot of room, and the country was just growing too small for cowboys and Indians.

Chapter Eighteen

The smile of a truly happy woman is a thing to behold. When I rode into Clarendon and showed Barby Allen what I'd brought her she squealed like a little girl, and wrapped her arms around that palomino horse like he was her long lost baby. If I was to live ten thousand years, the sound of her laughter would ring just as clear in my mind as it did that day.

When I looked at her there was no understanding of her, any intuition, or supposition of what was in her soul. The smallest things she did held me spellbound, and yet she shed no light on the mystery that she was to me. I simply beheld her and knew that I wanted her. The wanting of her was almost more than a man could bear; there was nothing I wouldn't have done to possess her.

"Is he gentle?" Her hand took up the bridle reins.

"Oh yes."

She took a quick look back over her shoulder into the store, and I couldn't make out her father anywhere in the windows. "I couldn't take such a gift. It wouldn't be proper."

"I wouldn't be proper, or your daddy wouldn't approve?"

Her spine stiffened, and she met my challenge eye to eye. The stubborn look on her face changed in an instant to a mischievous one. She made a study up and down the empty street on which we stood, and for some reason I was already beginning to feel part of some secret that I was not yet privy to. I took up Dunny's bridle and followed her as she led the yellow horse around the corner into a narrow alley beside the store.

"Tighten the cinch for me." Before I could even reach the horse she had disappeared into the store's side door.

I hadn't even finished tightening the cinch when she reappeared. She was carrying a metal washtub, and with little aplomb she plopped it down beside her horse, who was no less startled than I. I was getting a little red around the gills at the thought of her riding astride, but I have to admit that I had enough foresight to have shortened the stirrups for her before I'd even made it to town.

"Get up on your horse and close your eyes."

Who was I to argue? I stepped right up on my horse and sat there with my eyes squinched shut. I felt silly and excited at the same time. I heard that tub thump, and the stamp of her horse's hooves as he shifted under her weight.

"All right."

I opened my eyes and she was sitting her horse before me. She had managed to arrange her skirt around the saddle as good as could be expected. I didn't know where to look or not to look. Before I even had time to make up my mind she took off down the alley at a lope, and I had to hustle to follow her.

I had seen skirted women ride astride before, but it's a whole hell of lot different when it's some old granny or little girl riding to the neighbor's house. At first I was feeling kind of bashful, but I ended up feeling pleasantly wicked. I was determined to match her nonchalant daring, and I quickly gained a position beside her and stared straight ahead while we made our escape from the peering eyes of town. I didn't want her to think I hadn't seen a woman's calves before, even if never so lovely a pair.

We loped over the plain in silence for miles with the hot wind to our faces, and the sun behind us. When our horses had worked up a light sweat we settled to a walk, and still we said nothing to each other. We wandered aimlessly the dips and folds of the land with both of us caught up in the silence of our own pleasures.

When we had ridden down the sun, and the shadows started to crawl across the land we stopped atop a rise and sat our horses where we could watch the lights of town glowing on the horizon. I wanted to say something, but nothing seemed to fit, and everything I thought of seemed like only small talk. I took in her shadowed profile there beside me, and I drank it in like I was dying of thirst.

She turned her head to me, and her face was all but hidden in darkness. "Do you think me too bold to go riding off with you like this?"

"I don't know what to think of you." I meant every word.

"And how should I take that?" Her voice was filled with mock indignation.

"Take it the best way."

She seemed to think on that for a moment. I rested my forearms on my saddle horn and waited. My mind raced with the idea that there was something I should do or say before the moment was lost. The fortunes of a man in love and war are made at such moments when courage cannot fail.

"I've never seen anything as pretty as you." I fully expected her to flee for the safety of town, but she held her ground.

"Are you making love to me, Tennessee?" And again there was that playful hint to her voice.

"I'm doing a poor job if you have to ask."

She was silent, and I knew that I was right. I made up my mind then that I'd already waded in up to my neck, and I might as well go ahead to swimming.

"I've thought about you a lot since the first time I saw you on that stage." I sounded like I was taking an oath instead of confessing.

"It must be hard to pay attention to your work with all that on your mind," she said.

"I'm serious."

"Maybe you are a little too serious at times."

I guided Dunny over alongside her horse until my leg was right up against hers, and our faces were close in the dark. She didn't pull away, and I looked at her for a long count of three while I built up my courage.

"I haven't begun to get serious, yet." I leaned out toward her, ready to steal a kiss.

I admit to having thought about kissing her on more than one occasion, and I guess you could say that I was determined. When our faces were only inches apart she laughed and rode away. I was left behind with a goofy shape on my lips, and a humming down in my drawers. It didn't take me long to set in after her. She was hard to catch, but like I said, I was determined.

I caught her on the outskirts of town, or rather she pulled up and let me catch her. The chase had my blood up and I turned my horse crossways before her like some bandit blocking the road.

"I'm dead set on kissing you."

She must have taken me seriously, because the play was gone from her voice when she spoke. "All right, you can kiss me."

Well, there it was, and I began to falter. She sat her horse calmly, staring at me, and acting like she was waiting on the coffee to boil. I managed to position myself back alongside her, but I was taken aback. I leaned close to her again, but she made no effort to ease my discomfort. She kept her face to me, but she made no move to meet me halfway. I hung up there almost to her lips with that goofy-lipped feeling coming over me again.

I cussed, and then cussed again for cussing in front of her. I drew back, not sure at all what to do, and feeling defeated. The tide of the battle seemed to have turned against me, and I was at a loss what to do about it. She kept looking at me, and that was making it worse. What the hell did she expect?

"Well?" she questioned.

"Well what?" I snapped.

I made to turn away, but the old devil started coming up in me. I leaned out quickly and kissed her. It was no more than a peck, and I barely felt her lips. I reared back just as quickly as I had closed in on her, and I wasn't at all satisfied with my actions. Before I could make up my mind to have another go at it, she reached out and grabbed me. She pulled me slowly to her, and I guarantee you I could feel her lips that time.

When she pulled back I was too busy readying myself for another go at it to talk. Her hand on my chest held me off, and I halted my assault. I could feel her hand slightly quivering against me, and the warmth of her was still on my mouth. I pushed lightly against her, but she stepped her horse away until there was space between us again.

"I'd better get home."

That couldn't have been any farther from my thoughts. "Ride with me some more."

"Don't follow me home. I'm probably in enough trouble already."

"Ride with me." I pointed my horse away from town, and beckoned her with my hand.

"I think there is more trouble in what you ask." She stepped her horse near again, and her hand once more touched my chest, if only briefly.

She started off toward home, and I made as if to follow her. She turned in the saddle and held up a hand for me to stop. I sat and watched her ride away into the darkness, and long after she was out of sight I listened for the sound of her horse. When I could no longer hear her I turned and rode east with my heart outsized in my chest, and a smile on my face. I began to whistle a silly little tune to the jig of Dunny's feet on the trail. I was still whistling it the next morning when the sun climbed up out of the ground to the east, and I was forty miles long gone from her.

H.B. and I went to riding for the Horseshoe outfit south of the Canadian. We spent the latter part of the summer over in the Cherokee Strip receiving and working trail cattle on the T5, another ranch owned by the same syndicate. The cattle were all from down below the tick line, and the managers planned on wintering them in the Strip and then moving them to the Horshoe the following spring. Folks will tell you that we didn't know what caused Texas fever back then, but just about every good cowman had the right idea by that time.

The South Texas cattle had built up immunity to the fever, but stock they mingled with farther north invariably got sick and died. It was the ticks those southern cattle were carrying that spread the disease. Nobody had the whole thing figured out, but most had learned that once the southern cattle were wintered in our country they no longer spread the disease.

The Panhandle Stock Association was barring passage to all herds from that "way down" part of Texas. Trail herds coming north had to pass to the east of the Association members' land holdings by going up the Western Trail, which was the original trail to Dodge City. Once a trail herd made it north of the Cherokee Strip, the going got tougher. The settlers were growing thicker every year. It wouldn't be long until a man couldn't drive a herd through western

Kansas without stomping on somebody's crops. It had already proven true with the trails farther east.

The Texas Land and Cattle Company, the "Syndicate" as we called them, was a Scotch outfit, and they were big operators. However, the T5 wasn't much to brag about. The cattlemen occupied the Strip on a lease basis, and not much was put into improvements in those camps. Their hands were a rough, outlaw bunch, better at stealing horses and robbing travelers than they were at handling cows. They had some fellow's skull with a bullet hole in it hanging on a peg in the bunkhouse, and liked to hint around about the killing. Later on, it was a couple of T5 hands who helped Marshal Henry Brown and his deputy rob the bank at Medicine Lodge, Kansas. They killed the president and a teller, but were soon caught and hanged.

I won't say every man on the T5 was of that sort, but I figured that those who weren't outlaws were at the least well-wishers to that sort of thing. I hadn't any use for the outfit, and was glad when we were released to go back to the Horseshoe. H.B. and I took our time riding back, because we wanted to see some new country. We rode from camp to camp all the way across the Cimarron and the North Canadian.

H.B. noticed me scratching at the back of my neck. "You eat up with them too?"

"I feel like I've got mattress critters crawling all over me."

"Let's stop and turn our clothes wrong side out." H.B. got down off his horse and proceeded to undress.

"That ain't going to get rid of them."

H.B. stomped his spindly, fish-belly-white legs out of his long handles, and stood there studying the ample curve of his belly. He scratched around and came up with a big gray louse and cracked it between his fingers.

"It won't get rid of them, but it'll get us some relief for a while."

I jumped down and started peeling off my clothes. The insides of my shirt were crawling with lice and various other parasites. I went over myself thoroughly, and hunted down as many of the little varmints as I could.

"I ain't ever been eat up like this," I said.

"I waited out a blizzard in the Winter of '76 in a dugout on the Concho with a bunch of buffalo hunters. I got me the worst case of seam squirrels I've ever had in my life. That spring I found me a camp of

316

Mexican sheepherders, and bought a set of clothes off of them. I burned everything I'd been wearing, and paid one of those peons to peel off all my hair with a set of sheep sheers."

"I'm gonna burn mine when we get somewhere to replace them." I gave all my clothes a good shaking and then started putting them back on wrong side out.

"Somebody's coming." H.B. stood in all his radiant splendor and scratched at his balls while he studied the wagon coming down the trail about a quarter of a mile off.

"Shit!" I fumbled hurriedly at my clothes.

H.B. didn't seem bothered or hurried. By the time we were dressed and up on our horses I saw that a man and his wife were sitting on the seat of the little covered wagon. I was wishing H.B. would veer off the trail and go around, but he rode right up to them.

"Howdy," H.B. tipped his hat to the young couple.

The husband's only reply was a scowl, and the pretty little thing at his side stared at him with big eyes for a split second before she gasped and ducked her head against her man's shoulder.

I was feeling pretty peaked, and thinking we might get shot. I gave a little tip of my hat, and tried to stare straight on ahead as we passed along the wagon. Two little kids, a boy and a girl, were riding on the tailgate with their feet dangling. The boy had a long stem of Indian grass in his hand and was picking at the milk cow tied to the corner of the wagon with it.

The boy looked up at H.B. with big eyes. "Gosh Mister, how come you were standing in the road naked?"

The little girl giggled. "Daddy's mad."

"You kids are going to get a whuppin' if you make that cow set back on her rope." H.B. gave them a big wink.

"Damned, ain't you even the least bit embarrassed?" I said when we got out of earshot of those folks.

"I bet their mama liked it." H.B. puffed out his chest, curled up his tightened arms, and tried to suck in the gut that shaded his saddle horn. "I bet it ain't every day that she gets to see a fine figure of a man like me naked."

"You sure ain't a gentleman."

"A gentleman ain't got a chance with any woman I ever met."

The timbered bottoms along the Cimarron were loaded with game. I saw more deer and turkey along that river than I had ever seen in one place in my life. A man with a good rifle and a steady aim never need go hungry in that neck of the woods.

We came across one big camp, and then another. The last one had a well-beaten wagon trail leading to it and looked to have seen at least a couple of years' use. There were two big wagons parked under a shade tree, but nobody was around. I counted twenty-three deer hanging from cross poles tied up high between trees.

"Kansas market hunters. They come down every fall and spring to haul wild meat out by the wagon loads," H.B. said.

We continued up the river for a few miles, and came upon a set of fresh wagon tracks cutting a beeline for Kansas. We turned and followed them, and soon started finding dead turkeys littering the trail. It looked like somebody was just tossing them out of the wagon as they traveled along. I counted forty-three turkeys in the course of four or five miles.

I was so mad I couldn't see straight, but I was also wondering why anyone was shooting turkeys just to throw them out to waste. I looked to H.B. to see if he knew the why of it.

"It's still too hot this early in the fall. They spoiled in camp before they could get to town to sell them," he said

"The damned farmers and settlers are eating off this country as clean as a plague of locusts."

"Yep." H.B. didn't like the matter any more than I did.

The market hunters and the game they sold were probably about all that was keeping most of those dirt herders from starving. Most of them didn't seem to have the sense or the means to grow anything, and the only thing admirable about the whole bunch of grangers was their sheer, stubborn audacity, and a willingness to starve. I didn't think it took any genius to recognize that this was cattle country. A lot of us at the time thought that Western Kansas would never grow anything for a farmer but blisters on his hands. Damn, were we wrong.

"All the buffalo are about shot, there's too many cattle grazing this country slick, and now the farmers are going to plow up everything into dust." H.B. waved his pipe in a wide sweep around us. "Soak it in. At least it was a damn fine country while it lasted."

We swung west until we hit the Ft. Elliott Trail at Buzzard's Roost on Little Wolf Creek. I liked the country where the Little Wolf dumped into its namesake, Wolf Creek. Just northwest of the junction of the two was a high white caprock overlooking a wide expanse of prairie that stretched to the northeast as far as the banks of the North Canadian. The grass was good there and there was no better water in that country.

I don't know why I was looking so close at that country, and thinking how I'd like to find a place like that for myself. It seemed lately that my mind was given to wandering into some strange corners. What the hell would I do with such a place? My home was the wagon that called me to chuck.

The fact of it was that I'd started saving my money, and some scary thoughts were beginning to take hold in my head. The scariest notion of them all was the thought of giving up my trade. In my day there wasn't any such thing as a married cowboy. Owners and managers might get married, but if you were going to be a big outfit hand you had to be single. Nobody provided houses for married men, and it wouldn't have mattered if they did. A cowboy spent seven or eight months out of the year in the saddle, twelve if he landed a winter job riding line.

I'd known a few hands who had married and managed to cowboy a little. They started up little rawhide outfits in some small nook amidst the country of the big operators. They ran a few cows, not enough to live on, much less prosper with, and supplemented their income with whatever work they could find. To my way of thinking, a man might as well hang up his spurs for good when that happened. He wasn't doing anything but dragging out his misery. If it came to that you might as well just buy yourself a milk cow and put in a garden.

Freedom is just a word to those who have never felt free. When I woke up in the morning I knew that I was beholding to no man. I owned nothing, owed nothing, and fear of traveling never got in the way of my pride. The world had no effect on the way I thought, because nothing can be dictated to a man that won't take it, except death itself.

I was considering trading it all for a woman who I wasn't sure would have me, and who I had only seen three times. She would probably laugh at the fool I was should she know how I was carrying on. For all I knew I could have just been suffering from a case of inflamed glands or something. It was no surprise that in a land of few women that a man was bound to get a little silly at the sight of one. I told myself to just forget her, but the thing was I couldn't — not until the end of all things when the sand scoured my bones, and the wind rattled the gravel in my empty skull.

CHAPTER NINETEEN

We hadn't been back on the Horseshoe
range a day when we heard that Billy had
returned to his old stomping grounds.
Somebody had seen him in Mobeetie, and
they said he was cutting quite a swath down
there. We heard that he and Andy had
showed up leading a whole string of good
horses, and sporting a roll of cash big
enough to choke a mule. We figured the racing in San Antonio must have been really
good.

The second week of November we were
on the north bank of the Washita sorting
out three- and four-year-old steers to make
up a market herd to drive to Dodge City. I
was adjusting the neckerchief on my face in
the downwind side of the cut herd when I
saw Billy and Andy come riding up. Sure
enough, they were leading a string of horses,
and every one of them looked to be the kind
you would like to own.

Andy waved to me from afar, and went on to the river to take care of the horses while Billy came on our way. The first thing I noticed was that Billy did indeed look to have prospered. He was still dressed like a hand, but his outfit was brand new right down to the saddle he rode. There was a new light gray beaver atop his head that looked to never have seen any weather, and a diamond watch fob dangled from his vest pocket. He was smoking a cigar when he offered me his paw. We shook hands and grinned at each other like two wiggly hound pups.

"Where are you two pilgrims headed?" I asked.

"We're going to winter in Dodge. I hear there's some racing up there."

"You already cleaned out those suckers in San Antonio?"

Billy pitched me a cigar before answering. "Those boys down there know a trick or two, but there ain't any substitute for a horse that can *really* run."

"Have you still got that paint nag?"

"Now you ought not to speak of War Bonnet that way. They'll be writing songs about him before long."

"I take it he measured up to the competition."

"It was robbery the way we took their money. That Cheyenne pony outran everything they had. I'd still be down there, but we ran out of anyone willing to race him that I had enough money to wager with."

"Looks like you've added a few more to your string that might run a little." I pointed to where Andy was leading them.

Billy studied them a might before he answered. "There's a few there that show promise. A man has got to offer more than one flavor if he is to succeed running match races."

It looked like Billy had learned more than a few tricks on his outing down south. I looked forward to hearing about the time they had in that old town. "Why don't you make camp with us tonight? All that high-rolling ain't made you allergic to beans, has it?"

"I ain't changed any. I've just got a little more to jingle in my pockets, that's all."

Several of the hands working the herd waved welcome to Billy, and he obviously enjoyed the attention. He waved back and passed a little banter with some of them. I pushed a new steer into the cut herd, and then rode back beside Billy.

"Why don't you come to Dodge with us?" he asked.

I gave it some serious thought, but decided against it. "No thanks, Billy. I ain't got the constitution to handle the ups and downs of the gambling life. It looks like they'll keep me on for the winter, and I'm going to play the pat hand."

I could tell my refusal bothered Billy, though he didn't let on like it did. "That's all right. I'm thinking of leaving my horses with a man in Dodge come spring. I'll be back to work the roundup come hell or high water. We'll show these jaspers who the top hands are, won't we?"

I grinned in agreement while I made to push a steer back that threatened to run off from the herd. Billy dove right in and helped me turn him back.

"You don't mind if an old hand hangs around awhile, and shows you how it's done?"

I didn't mind at all.

Billy helped us hold the cut herd while a part of our crew cut out what didn't shape up in the other herd. Those cattle that didn't fit the requirement for the fall shipment were driven out of the herd and over to the cut herd. Only a few of the hands entered the main herd at one time. It was somewhat of an honor on most ranges to be chosen to cut cattle. If you were sent into the herd, that meant the bosses judged you to be a top hand, smart enough and skilled enough to work the herd quietly and with as little fuss as possible. Another prerequisite was the possession of a good cutting horse in your string.

Many a hand bragged about his roping horse, or a horse that could go all day without falter, but the most prized horses of the range were the cutting horses. Trail men valued a good night horse, but the cutting horses were kings.

Each ranch or outfit had one that they bragged about, and every cowboy had an opinion as to the greatest cutting horse he had ever seen. It was not unusual to see men with a lifetime spent on the back of a cow-pony, and witnesses to a million cuts, stop and intently watch a good horse and rider work. When we gathered around the campfire at night, it wasn't just bad men and whores we talked about. We had all heard the names of good cutting horses that we had never seen from way down in Mexico to up yonder in old Calgary.

As for those without a good cutting horse in their string, or not known for their skill, they held herd. I patted Dunny's neck and wished we were riding into the herd to cut something out. There I was on what Billy claimed was the best cutting horse in Texas, and that meant the world, and I was holding the cut herd.

I am not ashamed to admit that I watched enviously as Hoos Hopkins, the foreman's brother, eased into the main herd on the back of a little brown horse we called Booger. Through the dust I could make him out, easing a small bunch of cattle to the outer edge of the herd. Hoos and Booger had their eyes on the steer they wished to cut, and the other cattle in front of them were allowed to slowly slip by them and back to the herd.

At the right moment, he guided Booger up into the steer to block his way and stop him from returning to the herd with his pals. That was when the dance began. The steer's instincts were to return to the herd, and he would try anything to get there. Booger's job was to prevent that from happening, and to drive him away to the other herd.

Booger was good enough that the rider had to guide him little once Booger knew which steer was selected. With his ears pinned flat against his neck, and his neck stretched out like a snake, Booger went to work. The steer ran right and left trying to get by the horse and rider, but Booger would head him off every time. He ran until he headed the steer, stopped hard, and rolled back into a turn to match each change of direction the steer made. The steer faced up to the horse and darted in quick spurts, right and left, back and forth, trying to get by this nemesis that blocked his way.

With his butt to the herd behind him, Booger locked down on his hindquarters, and his front end rocked from side to side mirroring the steer's movement, each time just far enough ahead to pin the steer in place. Old Hoos sat high and tight, his legs and hips in rhythm with the wild movement of his horse. It was a beautiful, dusty animal ballet.

Finally, the steer threw up his tail and angled away from Booger, giving up the fight, but attempting to gain distance and circle the herd. Booger drove out at him, still counteracting the steer's moves, but at each turn driving him farther away from the herd he had left.

When they neared the cut herd Billy and I rode in behind the steer and finished driving him on to where he belonged. We pulled up and bragged on Booger a little, and Bee Hopkins, the foreman, heard us.

"Why I saw Old Possum once drive a

jackrabbit from the herd with his bridle off. They won a bet on that, a thousand dollars," he said.

If I had a nickel every time some cowboy told me he had seen a cutting horse so good that he could cut a jackrabbit I would be a rich man. It was just like the fact that every cowboy in Texas had drank out of a muddy hoof print at one time or another. If you didn't believe them, all you had to do was ask. Actually, you didn't have to ask, they were prone to volunteering the information without provocation.

I had no response for Bee. For one, because there was no response, and secondly because despite the fact that the boss was easy to get along with, I didn't think it was too smart to go arguing with the man who had offered me a winter job.

"He ain't near as good as Dunny," Billy said.

"You sound pretty sure of that." Bee didn't seem to mind arguing.

Billy eyed Hopkins for a moment like a he was eyeing a wasp nest, and thinking about bumping it just to see what havoc he could cause. "This ain't any place for a fine horse and a top hand."

Before I could inform him that was just where we were, Bee was telling me to go

331

make some cuts. "Have at it, and let's see this horse."

Billy motioned me to the herd with a grand gesture, sweeping his arm in a wide arc while slightly bowing at the waist. "They just don't know who they've got working for them."

There was about a thousand head left, and two other riders were cutting out cattle. A man entering the herd had to know a steer old enough and big enough to ship from one too young, small, or lacking in the requirements given by the bosses. All these cuts had to go to the cut herd. Billy had stuck his neck out for me by risking his own reputation to vouch for Dunny and me.

Once I had Dunny deep into the herd I had no doubts about him. He walked on cat feet among the cattle, alert but soft and waiting. His ears worked nervously back and forth, and his head worked ever so slightly from side to side. He was waiting for me to move him toward an individual animal long enough for him to know what I had selected.

Guessing about the kind of horse I rode, I deliberately worked my way toward a high-tailed yearling crashing crazily away from me through the herd. There were still twenty head between him and us when I became aware that Dunny already knew what I was after. He, like I, looked over the animals in front of us, his attention solely on the wild-eyed red roan steer at the edge of the herd. We worked the bunch to the edge of the herd hardly without even stirring up the dust.

The steer was so wild that when the bunch hadn't gone thirty feet out from the herd he tried to double back and forced my hand. Before I could spur Dunny toward the steer he was already leaping forward, ears pinned flat. Dunny was locked on to him, and in two strides he had a neck past him. The yearling tried to stop and suck back to the right. Dunny's butt dropped out from under me in a ground-rending stop, his hocks almost parallel to the ground. Like a spring he seemed to coil back on himself, launch his head and neck back the other way, and uncoil in one smooth explosion of muscle. The rest of him flowed out of the ground in succession, like water turning a bend.

Where Booger had been graceful, Dunny was brutally powerful. Instead of holding a line and not attempting to drive the cow away until it turned tail, Dunny worked forward at the cow a little bit each time before a stop and turn. After each stop Dunny changed direction in an explosion of dust; his mane and the heavy tails of my split reins flew out flat beside me when he turned.

In a matter of seconds Dunny had the yearling confined to a ten-foot run, and at each turn he drove the yearling farther away. The yearling faced us and threatened to charge right by us. Dunny crouched to meet him, his nose outstretched and inches from the ground. The standoff seemed to last forever. I could feel Dunny's muscles quiver with anticipation. He buckled at the knees slightly, getting ever lower into the ground.

The yearling started right and Dunny jumped out and headed him, the two of them almost colliding. The yearling whirled away, beaten and ready to head for the high country. Dunny came out of his tracks like a sprinter, racing after the yearling and driving him to the cut herd while biting at his rump. He got close enough to bite a clump of hair from the steer's tailhead, and I thought he was half alligator. I raised my rein hand for the first time, taking a light hold on the bit to back him off a little.

Dunny immediately slowed, and I felt him slowly relaxing beneath me. He knew his job was all but done. A rider circled behind us, and took the steer on into the cut herd while I pulled Dunny up and patted his neck. I've seen a lot of great cutting horses, but I never got to see the greatest one of them all, because — damn me for a braggart — I was always riding him, and his name was Dunny.

Billy let out a long, low whistle as I rode near, and I grinned like a schoolboy, as proud of Dunny as I would have been of my own flesh and blood. Both the Hopkinses loped up to me. They were all smiling.

The boss pointed at my horse. "What will you take for that horse?"

"He can't be bought."

"I've got a thousand that says he can."

Billy chimed in before I could answer. "A man could start a little outfit of his own with that money."

"That's just enough money to start a little rawhide nester outfit and starve out the first winter." I didn't consider the offer for one second. Call me a sucker for a good horse if you want to.

"And I'll stake you to twenty-five yearling steers," Bee challenged.

"Think about it, Nate. He's your horse," Billy said quietly.

I've never been accused of being a good talker, but that was one time when I said just what I wanted to say. It didn't take me long to do it either.

"This horse ain't for sale."

I don't know why my color was up, but Bee didn't take it personal. He knew cowboys, and you didn't have to explain much to him. He just shook his head and grinned. I stared back at him, and he motioned to the herd.

"Are you going to cut anything else?"

"You bet." I had to fight the urge to lope into the herd like a greenhorn.

That night Billy and I laid in our bedrolls talking a bit before going to sleep. "How come you gave Dunny to me?"

"He's a great horse, but the fun in great horses for me is finding them or making them."

"You reckon the good ones are made, or born that way?"

"I guess it's a little of both."

"You can have him back if you want him."

"No."

"But . . ."

"I gave him to you, and after today I don't regret it at all."

I was quiet for a minute.

"Billy?"

"Let's go to sleep. We're starting to sound like some of those old saddle partners who have been together too long."

"You're right."

"I know it. Go to sleep."

"Go to hell."

"Piss on you."

I felt better now that we had things squared away and Billy was back for a while. All was right in the world. We slept in the middle of a country where a man could ride forever, and where good horses and good friends were the only riches worth having.

CHAPTER TWENTY

About four weeks before Christmas, we left with a trail herd headed for Dodge. I guess the higher-ups thought Hell's Bells was management material, because they put him in charge of the crew. Ours would be the last Horseshoe herd up the trail that fall, and as many of the boys weren't certain of their prospects for a winter job, we traveled at a leisurely pace, even for a trail herd. We weren't in any hurry to join the ranks of the unemployed. Besides, a slow traveling herd always brings more money at delivery.

The fifth day we were trailing in to Mammoth Creek, ready to make camp for the evening, when we saw two riders coming down from the north. I was sitting my horse wide of the point and talking to H.B. while the herd spread out to water. I was still passing the small talk when I noticed he wasn't hearing anything I said. His attention was on the two riders who were still a good mile away.

"They look like Rangers." He packed his pipe, all the while never taking his eyes off the oncoming riders.

"I don't know how you could tell at that distance."

"I can tell. I could spot one of those badge-packers at twice that far."

I was studying them hard wondering what there was about the two riders that was any different. It was true they were coming fast, but many a man left Kansas that way. To my mind they could have just as well been bank robbers, or firemen headed to a fire for that matter.

My attention wavered back to H.B., and I found him dismounted. He was checking his cinches and still eyeing our soon-to-be visitors. By the time I began to smell something funny about the deal he was back on his horse and turning south.

"Yep, those are Rangers. I'll catch up to you later," he said over his shoulder as he ran away.

"Where are you going?" I yelled at him. I can still remember his fading cry as he raced out of earshot.

"To hell if I don't change my ways."

And yes, it was two Rangers who came

roaring up on lathered horses. They were awful curious as to who had fled in their wake, but we all played dumb. Their horses were too tuckered out for pursuit, and they didn't press us too much on the matter. They knew as well as we did that it was somebody who wasn't taking any chances on who they might be looking for. For that matter, I don't know who they were looking for. Back in those days there were a lot of men who got the urge to be a long way off when the Law showed up, and you never knew who was on the scout.

Old H.B. said he'd see us later, but that has been thirty years ago, and I still haven't come across him or his like. I sometimes wonder where he got off to, but hell, he's probably still running yet.

What can I tell you to make you understand the life we led, or the hardships we faced? How can I describe the cut of a norther blowing down across the prairie with the sharp edge of a knife? When I say that we were caught in no-man's-land in an early blizzard, will anyone living know the feeling of such a quickening cold threatening to rupture the very marrow of your bones, and nothing to battle it but cheap coats, and bitter constitutions?

One minute the weather is fine, but you

are eyeing the horizon to the north and the slate-gray sky spreading above your head. Any man reared on the plains knows that first harsh burst of cold wind cutting his face for what it could be, and then you can't see a foot in front of your face, because the snow is blowing so hard. You stay on guard not because you are getting anything done, but because that's what a good hand is supposed to do.

I know what it feels like not to know where camp lies, or where you are for that matter. I know what it feels like to be so totally blind and alone in the storm and full of a fear as cold as the norther itself. My fingers have been long past the hurting kind of cold, and when my teeth stopped chattering there was only a numbness of body that must be closely akin to death itself.

Nine men tried to stay with the herd as it walked blindly southward with the wind. We somehow managed to make our minds fight the cold and find the good sense to stumble to a cow chip fire that was impossible to find — a fire that went out no sooner than the last man had found its feeble glow. We hunkered miserably wrapped in our blankets, and each of us was alone in his suffering and the knowledge of his own impending death.

Eight hours later, the storm ended as quickly as it had begun, disappearing into the nowhere from whence it came. We were all alive and kicking, and we should have said grace, or sang a hymn of thankfulness and glory to be alive. Instead, we staggered out across the prairie in search of our horses that we had turned loose to fend for themselves as best they could. We found seven good mounts froze to death — those last ridden with the energy necessary to keep warm sweated out of them, and the milk blue glaze of their dead eyes the only remnant of the horrible cold that had taken them.

That morning I saw brave men shaken, and I do not know if they grieved for a favorite horse, or from the shock of dead men finding out they were still alive. They were hard men, but that was often the way of it. Each man carries most of himself to himself alone, and some so much so that they could never know themselves after the fashion that we seek to know our friends.

We gathered our herd back and rode on a short mount of horses all the way to Dodge. We gathered in the bars and dancehalls and laughed at fate and blizzards. We talked of men and horses and wars long gone, and sought to convince the world that we were invincible. Our brush with mortality along the trail slowly turned to a good story, and like all misery, eventually became an adventure purely by the recounting of it.

That was Christmas Day 1881, and I had turned twenty-five two days before. The bright lights of Dodge called to a cowboy like a siren's song, but I had no ear for her then. All I could think about was a certain girl down south.

We had permission to spend a few days in Dodge after handing over our herd, but I wasn't having any of that. The morning after Christmas I saddled Dunny and hit a lope down the trail for Clarendon. I was bound and determined to ask that girl to marry me.

So I rode south with my heart swollen in my chest. I was worried and happy all at the same time. There was a cheap new suit on my person, a ten-dollar gold wedding ring in my saddlebags, and there wasn't a clue in my head as to whether or not she would have me. To this day I don't know why I put the suit on in Dodge instead of keeping it wrapped up until I reached Clarendon. I rode fifty miles that first day, and at the end of it I couldn't put my finger on one concrete thought I'd had all day. I've seen hounds take off running game and be gone for days — immune to anything of the outside world except the bawl of their own voices and the thought of the chase. I guess you could say I was sure enough in a mess.

By day I rode as a man possessed, and only long after nightfall did I lay down beside my fire with Dunny's picket rope beneath me and the stars shining overhead. Each night I stared into the fire and my thoughts whirled around in my head like fireflies.

Alone in my blankets I wondered how there could be so many stars, and what it was that made coyotes howl. I thought about how my cowboying might be over with, and wondered what Billy would say to that.

It became a ritual for me to lay out all my money on the ground before me each night before I fell asleep. I would sit there and count it as if it might have grown since I last beheld it. Like all poor folks, I could wish all I might, but counting doesn't stretch a dollar any more than a camel can pass through the eye of a needle. Should Barby Allen marry me, we could start a life with thirty dollars, and two player piano tokens courtesy of the Long Branch Saloon. What a hell of a way to start marital bliss.

I was coming down the Tuttle Trail, just

west of Zulu Stockade, when I saw a bull wagon coming up from the south. I could tell who was whacking those oxen when I was still a half of a mile off. There wasn't anyone else in the country as humongous as Long was. He was packing a ten-foot whip in his right hand that cracked like a pistol shot, and stomping size-fifteen footprints beside a three-yoke team.

When I neared to within two hundred yards of him I thought he was cussing, but I soon found out he was laughing and talking to somebody. That somebody was perched atop the lead wagon, and it was a she. She was the prettiest little Indian gal you ever saw, and she was all dolled up in fine buckskin and beads. When I rode up she ducked her chin down shyly, and I couldn't see anything but the top of her head and two little moccasins poking out from under her skirt.

"Hello, Tennessee," Long bellowed like the old bull of the woods.

"What kind of load are you hauling, Long? She doesn't look big enough to need freighted."

Long puffed out his massive chest like a gobbler gone full strut, and placed his mighty hands on his hips. I could tell he had a happy inside him every bit as big as he was.

"I'm a married man now."

"I thought you were through with Indian women."

"I am just through with Choctaw women. Those civilized Indians expect too much of a man."

"Cheyenne, ain't she?"

"Yeah, and she's a princess."

"I can see that for myself."

"No, she's really a princess — the daughter of a chief," Long said.

"What chief?"

"She's old Blue Knife's girl."

Well, it was a small world after all. It seemed like I wasn't the only one who had been trading on the reservation.

"How did you get him to let you take off with her?"

"I asked him."

"You just *asked* him? That's all?"

"Well, it seems he's a little partial to my product."

"I know you make good whiskey, Long, but you mean to tell me that he let you marry his daughter because he likes it so much? Those Cheyenne are more partial to their women than that."

"She liked me." Long was beginning to

346

sound a little defensive.

"And that's all?"

"Well, I did a little trading too."

"A little?"

"It seems like Blue Knife had recently acquired himself a Winchester, and needed some cartridges. I gave him two hundred rounds of .44 shells, a good horse, a box of cigars, and two bottles of my finest for a wedding gift."

"You mean to tell me that you are arming the hostiles? What kind of man trades firearms to Indians?"

Long ignored me, and I was wondering if he already knew where Blue Knife had gotten the rifle. While I was thinking of something else smart to say, Long walked over to his new bride and motioned her down. She hopped down beside him and followed him over to where I sat on my horse. I tipped my hat to her, and she blushed before looking back at the ground.

"What's her name?"

"Fawn."

"Does she speak English?"

Long lifted his hat and scratched his head some before he said, "Not much. I've had a hell of a time trying to talk to her since we left her pa's lodge."

She was beginning to get over her shy-

347

ness, and she looked at me with a frank curiosity. I must admit that I was pretty impressed with Long right then.

"I guess this makes you a chief or something, Long."

"I just want to be the chief of my own house. That Choctaw woman wouldn't let me be chief of anything."

"Are you going to marry her proper?"

"Her pa married us before we left, and I'm taking her with me to Dodge to get a preacher's say-so."

"I wish I had the time to go along with you."

"I'd be proud for you to stand up with me."

"I'm on my way somewhere important, so I'll have to miss the wedding."

"That's a shame, because you're sure dressed up for it." He eyed me up and down carefully.

I decided not to be outdone where women were concerned. "I'm going to try and fetch a wife myself."

"Are you going after that Clarendon woman?"

Long always seemed to know more than you would expect. He was like a buzzard when it came to the comings and goings in that country. It must have been the miles he traveled and the folks he ran across. But then again, in a country sparse of people, folks just naturally had a lot to tell when they finally ran across somebody who would listen.

"I'm going to marry her if she'll have me." I was pretty proud of myself right then for the way I confessed my innermost plans to the world.

Long had a troubled look on his face when he spoke. "Billy done took her off and froze her to death."

"What do you mean?"

"He stole her off from her pa to take her to a Christmas dance and they got caught in a blizzard."

There was a lot I wanted to say, and there was a lot I wanted to ask right then, but nothing would come out of my mouth at that moment. I felt like I'd had all my wind knocked out, and the world was falling fast out from under me.

I mumbled my good-byes, and left Long and his bride standing in my dust. If I had ridden fast and hard before, then I must have looked like I had hellhounds on my trail the way I left out of there. That damned Billy had killed my wife.

CHAPTER TWENTY-ONE

It was New Year's Eve when I found Barby Allen laid up at Ft. Elliott with the post surgeon to tend her while she was on the mend. I felt like somebody had reached in and tore the heart out of me when I first laid eyes on her swaddled in fever blankets up to her chin. A weak, faint smile lit her face, and for once where she was concerned, I knew just what to do. I took a chair at her bedside, and proceeded in earnest to tell her how I felt about her. I told her about the hopes I had for the two of us, and the kind of man and husband I'd try to be for her. I swore by my soul and damnation that I'd never fail her, and that I loved her so much I was of a mind to kill my own best friend for putting her in such a shape.

"Put your little hand in mine, Barby, and say you'll marry me."

All eternity's prospects seemed to hang in the balance for me, as suspended as the empty hand that I held out to her. That hand seemed to weigh twenty pounds as I waited and hoped for her to bring her own hand out from under her covers and to place it in mine. Barby's eyes turned down, and I heard the quaver of her chest as she sucked in a quick breath.

"Give me your hand, Barby," I asked again, more softly than before — so softly in fact that my voice was lost to my own ears. It was as if I was afraid that even so subtle a thing as my own breath could blow away that fragile moment and tip me over the void above which I felt suspended.

"I'm going to have a baby," she whispered, and her eyes never rose.

The knife fate had driven toward my heart never struck home. I have a lot to be ashamed of in my life, but that moment wasn't one of them. My hand steadied, and my heart grew strong. I knew that I wasn't worth one little drop of sweat on her upper lip even if you had chopped both the legs off of her right then, and damned her soul to perdition for the taint of her very name.

"Look me in the eye, and take my hand."

Her eyes slowly rose to search my face for I don't know just what. After a long moment she timidly removed her hand from under her blankets and reached out to me.

Big tears slid down her cheeks and she stopped her hand just short of mine.

The little hand she held up was missing the last two fingers — frozen to the quick in that terrible storm, and cut off by the surgeon. It was as if she purposely held it for my examination, as if to say, "This is what I am."

I grabbed that beautiful, pitiful little hand and hung on for dear life. I kissed the bandaged stumps of those fingers of the past. "You're still beautiful."

"You're a blind fool for wanting a crippled woman already carrying a bastard child two months grown," she sobbed. "You don't want a loose woman."

I stopped such talk with my finger across her lips. Half of a day went by while I pulled her to me and fervently plead my love, coaxing and comforting like some maddened priest from the mountains, come down to whisper prayers in the ears of all the wretched and abused.

"Will you marry me?"

"I love you, but I don't deserve you."

"I had hoped you wouldn't figure out what a sorry catch I am until after I had a ring on your finger."

She laughed for the first time, and smiled a little like her old self. I propped open the door to our room, and sat beside her on the edge of the bed where I could hold her. The two of us sat long into the night watching a full moon glowing so big it seemed just outside the door. The cast-iron stove in the corner ticked away the hours while I fell more in love with her than ever.

Long into the evening she finally looked up to me and whispered, "I'll be a good wife, I promise."

I was sitting in a rocking chair watching her sleep when the surgeon walked in at daylight. After one of those doctor lectures about how much she needed her rest I decided to go see if I could find Billy and settle whatever needed settling between us. I shoved my hat on my head and headed out the door with bad things on my mind. "Remember your promise." Barby's voice caught me at the door.

Right off the bat I was learning that women often couldn't be made to wake up when you wanted them to, and never seemed to sleep when you needed them to. I turned in the doorway to look at her, for I thought it could be the last time.

I had ridden to Mobeetie half ready to kill my best friend if Long's story proved true. Somewhere in the night, after hearing Barby's story, I had promised to forgive Billy, partly because she gave me no other options. If she and I were to have a life, then I had to act as if she and Billy had never met. I had to act as if my best friend had never lain with the woman I loved, and then dragged her into a blizzard to freeze her and the unborn child near death.

I nodded to let her know that I would keep my word, and walked out the door. The peaceful look on her face was no match for the hell in my heart. I had agreed to act like I forgave and forgot, but there was no forgiveness or memory loss in me right then. I would try my best, but Billy and I were going to come to an agreement about certain things, one way or another.

I made a long walk down the length of Mobeetie looking for Billy. Barby had told me the truth about her and Billy in the blizzard, and I could find no fault that belonged to him, except, perhaps for bad judgment in his choice of timing and weather. Still, a man set to steal my woman away and carry her across the plains horseback should keep his eyes on the skyline.

I guess what I aimed to settle with Billy was the fact that Barby belonged to me from then on. I was going to marry her, and be a father to the child he sired but would never know as his own. I didn't have a lick of give in me when it came to that. I knew how I felt about Barby, and thus assumed that Billy could feel the same way. Given that assumption, maintaining possession might end up a matter of the last man standing.

When I asked around for Billy I got a funny feeling and curious looks from people, even if they hadn't seen him. It seemed that folks were already forming their own opinions about Billy's escapade with a certain young lady of good standing currently healing up at the Post. Given that almost everybody knew that Billy and I were friends, nobody would tell me what rumors were going around.

I passed Barby's father storming up the street. He was making his way from the stage stop, and the driver was yelling after him about what to do with his luggage. Mr. Allen didn't stop, or even turn back to answer the driver. He was so wrought up with going to see his daughter for the first time that he didn't even acknowledge the friendly nod I passed his way; he just kept marching to the hospital. I decided I could deal with him later, and kept on my course.

When I stepped into the Lady Gay I immediately noticed one thing, and failed to notice another. The thing I noticed was Billy standing by himself at the far end of the bar. The thing I didn't notice was that everyone in the place was giving him so much room to himself that they had crowded back against the walls.

Billy looked at me over his drink, and a face that was momentarily hard started to soften, but didn't quite make it there. I still didn't have a clue just what I was going to say when I asked for a drink beside him. The bartender was taking his sweet time, and that left me standing at a loss.

"We've got some things to settle, Billy."

He acted like he knew what was coming, and it bothered me some how he was standing with his right hip well clear of the bar and his right thumb hooked in his gun belt. But the look on his face wasn't threatening; in fact, I could see the emotion welling up in him.

"I'm sorry, Nate. I'm sorry for it all." He said it like he really meant it.

"You like to have gotten her killed."

I watched as he quietly soaked in what I'd said, and he never dropped his gaze from mine. He looked tired all over, and his eyes were bloodshot and haggard. It dawned on me that the five-day stubble of whiskers on his face was the first time I'd ever seen him unshaven.

"Some people are saying I got scared and

left her out in the cold to save my own hide," he said quietly.

"I know that ain't true."

"You've been to see her?"

"I sat with her most of yesterday."

"She told you all about it?"

I merely nodded my head at his question. She had indeed told me all about it. She had told me how she'd saddled the palomino before supper time, and then sneaked out to meet Billy outside of town that night. She told me how they laughed and talked on their way across the plains on the way to the dance, unaware of the cold marching rapidly down upon them. I held her while she relived the fear and the cold when they suffered their way blindly into the face of the norther, only to finally seek shelter in the lee side of a cutbank, where Billy failed to start a fire from the leftovers of an old wagon bed. And I had almost cried with the wishing I had been the one there to hold her close while they shivered and hurt as the storm tore over them.

"She told me she begged you to leave her and save yourself, and she told me you wouldn't go."

"I didn't leave her until daylight when the blizzard was over. I didn't have a single match left, and we'd lost both our horses that night. I went to find them or somebody, because I knew I had to get her out of there. She didn't have anything left in her to get up and go with me."

Even though I had heard it all from Barby, I could tell Billy had to tell me himself. I nursed the drink I really didn't want, and listened.

"I headed south and walked ten miles looking for those drifted horses. Every mile I was looking back over my shoulder, knowing I was getting farther from her and that the day was ticking by.

"The odds were long against it, but I found our horses still alive about late morning, but I couldn't catch mine. I took hers and struck out for where I'd left her, but he didn't have any speed left to give. It was just about noon when I rode up to where she should have been, only she wasn't. A bunch of the boys from down south were headed to Mobeetie late, and stumbled across her."

As he told it, I remembered how she said she had crawled to the top of a rise and waved at them, and cried out for help with her voice so weak she was sure it wouldn't carry all the way to the passing men. She had been sure they would ride on to leave her to her fate, and that same fate she had already decided the departed Billy must have shared.

"I followed them up to town, but they were a half day ahead of me," he added.

"I know, Billy, you don't have to tell me more."

"Just want you to know I'm sorry, because I know how much you think of her."

"Then why were you taking her to a dance?"

"Because I think just as much of her." His tone left no doubt that he meant what he said.

There it was, out between us. The problem was that only one of us was to have her.

"We're getting married as soon as she's well," I said without a clue as to how he would take it.

I believed him when he said he cared for her, and I understood the knife I'd slipped in his gut right then. His face turned harder, and I looked at a man close to the raw edge of something.

"I suppose you took the opportunity to talk me down a little, and talk yourself up pretty high at the same time."

"You know me better than that. I asked her, and she said yes. That's all there was to it."

Billy didn't like it any more than I would

have, but he offered his hand. I was as false right then as Judas, because I took that hand. I shook his hand like all was settled when it wasn't, at least not on my part. I took his hand, because there was growing in me a terrible, weakening fear of his finding out about the child if I let on like he had more to answer for than just a blizzard and a dance.

"She couldn't have done better." We both knew he said that only because that's what a friend and a good loser is supposed to do.

Deep down I knew how far I would have gone had things went differently. I was willing to lose my friend for Barby, but the same didn't seem to hold true for Billy. Right then, some of the anger in me toward him started to slowly seep out, if even by the stain of my own guilt.

"Nate, you'd better go along." Billy's voice was as hard as nails.

I thought maybe he'd put up a front as long as he could where Barby was concerned, until I noticed he wasn't looking at me at all. Instead, he was looking over my shoulder toward the far end of the bar. I turned and saw Rory Donnovan was standing there facing us with a sneer on his drunken face.

"That man's been spreading it around

that I ran out on her and left her to freeze to death," Billy said.

I'd like to tell you that I tried to talk Billy out of what I could see was going to happen, but I didn't. I knew Billy too good to waste my time, and had I been in his shoes I wouldn't have taken it either. I'd never liked Rory Donnovan anyway. He was a loud-talking, greasy runt that cowboyed some, but spent most of his time out of work and hanging around with the Mobeetie crowd. Rumor had it that he had killed a man or two, but folks said that about everybody who acted tough those days. All I ever knew he'd done was beat a whore half to death in Caldwell, Kansas.

There were about ten men scooted back against the wall on the far side of the room, and I joined them. The bartender had disappeared, and I realized then that this trouble had been brewing long before I'd arrived. I'd failed to notice why Billy had one end of the room to himself. I was as dumb as the rest of the bystanders who didn't haul themselves out the door and out of danger, but like them, I was determined to see the thing.

Who knows what led Rory to that moment? He spent all his time hunting trouble, and that morning he found some. Rory had a mouth on him, and once Billy got wind of what he was saying there was no stopping what was to come with both of them in town, short of Rory crawling into a hole somewhere. Rory was as proud as he was mean, and he wasn't going to crawl anywhere.

I had never known Billy to kill a man, but somehow I knew he could handle Rory Donnovan. Up until that time, nobody had seen any of Billy's graveyards, yet most recognized him as a man to avoid trouble with. There was just something about him in that regard.

Billy stood with his thumb still hooked in his belt, and his left forearm resting on the bar. He looked calm if not peaceful, while Rory just looked disagreeable and nasty like he always did. He drank the last of a beer and slammed the empty bottle down on the bar top, then wiped the wet from his lips with the back of his hand. He studied Billy with obvious contempt, and let out a loud grunt of disdain.

"I'll say what I please about you," he said.

Billy said nothing, and that seemed to embolden Rory all the more.

"You're a damned coward to run off and leave a woman in a snowstorm." He put a hand on his pistol butt.

"And you're a lying little son of a bitch." Billy's voice never changed or rose in volume when he said it.

And that's all there was to it, no long speeches men are supposed to make before they die, or any band to play melancholy music and beat slow drums. There were just two men mad enough to kill, and willing to do so.

Rory's gun was out quick, and his first shot went into the wall behind Billy. Billy seemed too slow, but he took that little bit of time to do it right. Even at that short of a distance Billy leveled his pistol at arm's length and shot Rory through the guts. Rory was falling when he let off his second shot into the floor at Billy's feet. He fell to a sitting position on the floor with his shoulder and head against the bottom of the bar. He was cussing Billy and struggling for another shot. He didn't get a third, because Billy put one through his skull just above the left eye.

We all watched Rory die out with his brains splattered on the bar, and his life-blood leaking out on the floor. He looked like a twisted, grotesque ragdoll pitched down there at the foot of the bar with Billy standing over him with a Colt's revolver leveled in his hand. It takes a man time to absorb such as that and we all stood there bound by some unknown law that kept us like silent and immobile Romans, until Billy either moved, or spoke.

He turned slowly to eye every man in the room except me, and every one knew that all they had to do was ask for it. Apparently nobody there had any issues with Billy, or was willing to take them that far. The old saying that you could have heard a pin drop was never more apt than right then. Billy was still holding his Colt when he walked out the door.

I was the first to move as I followed Billy outside, taking care not to step in the blood-spot as I passed Rory's body. I was just in time to see Andy ride up with a spare saddled horse and a pistol in his hand.

"I guess you got the bastard," Andy said.

"Yeah, I got him." Billy got on his horse.

Andy grinned at me. "I'm glad you were there to help in case anybody decided to gang up on Billy. A man can count on his real friends when he's in a bind."

Before I could answer, Billy cut his horse between us, looking up and down the street before he looked at me. "I'm going some-where else while this cools off. Anybody sticks their nose outside that door with the wrong intentions, you kick them in the shins."

With that, he and Andy rode off at a trot down the middle of town, with the gawkers already rushing to the scene giving them wide berth. I had to admit that even Andy looked the part of a bold, bad man come to the aid of his leader. The two rode leisurely away while Mobeetie's finest showed up to purvey the gore.

So that's how it was there early in '82, fresh off a blizzard and a killing. I got married to the woman I loved and Billy rode off with a reputation grown even larger by the killing of Rory Donnovan. What a way to ring in the New Year.

CHAPTER TWENTY-TWO

I don't think Barby laid eyes on another woman for the first three months we were married. I went into the freighting business with Long as soon as I built us a half soddy, half dugout for a home, and turned out a small herd of cattle on the range. I was so caught up in trying to get ahead in life that I didn't think about a pregnant woman left alone in the middle of nowhere being bothered by it all. Maybe I was just dumb enough to think that the garden and three chickens I left her with were enough to keep her company, or that it was all right as long as I made sure to worry about her while I was gone.

Imagine a woman bellied down with a child five months' grown working herself silly carrying water, weeding gardens, and chasing centipedes and pack rats out of the house almost every night. She would tell me all about it when I was home, not complaining, but as if the sharing of her thoughts lifted the worry from her shoulders, at least for a time. The work didn't bother her as much as the being alone. She loved the chickens and her horse, but they were lacking where conversation was concerned.

The night sounds like to have driven her crazy at first, but she learned to love the coyotes' howls, and to interpret the stirring of the horses in the corral for what it was. Thunder, lightning, and the wind rattling the plank door on its hinges still made her heart flutter at times, but after a few months she could lie down oblivious to most of the sounds of the night. Most of all, she hoped to hear the sound of my freight wagon rolling up the hill to home.

Despite her many adjustments to fit in with her new and extravagant surroundings she never learned to more than tolerate the seemingly continuous onslaught of prairie wind. Its constant tug and pull irritated her tired body, and every day was a war whereby she fought to remove the dust driven into every crack and crevice of her home, clothes, and person. At times she felt as if a broom, a bucket of water, and a stubborn will were not enough to combat the dust and wind. She loved the day or two after a rain when the ground was too wet for the wind to pick it up and throw it at her. It was a sandy country, and a little bit of mud was a welcome change.

All the while she could feel her baby growing inside her, and she listened while I told her what I hoped and dreamed for us. She must have believed me when I laid out the ranch we would own someday, and just like me, maybe she could picture the beautiful home I would build her with white rail fences and fruit trees edging the road to the house. Maybe, like me, she could see it all as clearly as if tomorrow were today. All she had to do was to hold out and persevere. It was a bold hope, but dreamers often make the best pioneers.

Barby's forced exile from humanity came to an abrupt end exactly three months from the day we were married. I had been out on the trail for over two weeks on my second freighting trip when Long and I decided to stop by my home for a few days on our way back down to Colorado City to pick up freight. What I found at home was a woman who had had enough of the kind of living she was getting from me.

The proverbial straw that broke the camel's back came in the form of a yearling steer that decided to use the corner of the soddy as a scratching post one morning just at daylight. Being a frightened, but brave woman, Barby steadied her nerves and let fly through the wall with the new Winchester I left her. After two good shots into the direction of the scary noise, the threatened invasion of her home was at an end. It took her a while to get her courage up to look outside, but she eventually came out to find the intruder dead from her rifle.

I can attest to the thorough nature of her home defense, as Long and I drove up that very morning to find a crying, crazy woman sitting in the doorway, and one of my steers dead at the corner of the house. Both bullets had hit him broadside, and he had died in his tracks. Early on I had some doubts as to her mental stability, but never questioned her marksmanship.

One might assume at the time that an up-and-coming cattleman like me ate a lot of beef, but that would be incorrect. The small herd we had was for multiplying or selling, and not eating. My rapid plans to achieve riches in agriculture could not be slowed by the needs of our palates. However, I did not stop on this occasion to consider the loss of future income and prosperity, due to the fact that I had a wife threatening to go home to her daddy. That was the same daddy who had warned her staunchly not to marry a man with so little promise as I showed. My entire attention was on said threat, and absorbing the list of complaints thrown at me by my aggrieved spouse.

"Nathan Reynolds, I love you to death, but I'm not spending another night here alone!" Her green eyes were glistening, and her little fists were clenched at her sides.

"I've gotta work, Honey." I had found that women liked sweet little pet names, and I was hoping to smooth things over.

"Don't you patronize me!"

I wasn't sure what "patronize" meant, but I promised myself not to do it again. "I'll try not to stay gone so long at a time."

"You'll try?" Her voice raised three octaves, and I was glad her rifle wasn't handy.

Bless Long's heart, he tried to help. "Mrs. Reynolds, he's just working hard to build a home, and he's new to this marriage stuff. You've gotta be a little patient with him."

Barby chased Long backward with a stiffened finger wagging under his nose. "Don't you go to taking up for him, Long. There's more to a home than just a roof. I've had it up to here with this pioneer stuff." She chopped the air above her head with a wicked slice of her hand.

Long and I were pretty tough, but she

soon had both of us treed up on our wagon seats. She huffed and puffed back and forth in front of us for a while until she wore out and started crying again. I watched helplessly as she trudged to the house.

There is nothing like an emergency to spur a good man to action. I quickly tallied up the things that bothered her — dust, chiggers, wind, noises, loneliness, vagrant cattle, etc.

"What's gotten into that woman?" I asked Long, truly at a loss as to what I should do.

"You're leaving her alone too much." Long eyed the house cautiously as if unsure it was safe to get down from the wagon.

"What about Fawn? You're gone just as much as I am."

"She's got her family on the reservation to keep her company when she doesn't go with me."

"I'd take Barby with me from time to time, but she's too far pregnant to be taking a beating on a wagon seat."

"That makes it even worse. She's pregnant and alone."

"I can't help it. I promised her I'd quit freighting as soon as we can get this ranch paying." That was going to be a long time, considering our small herd.

"I don't reckon she married you for your

money."

"If I hang around here we're soon going to be wearing nothing but buckskins, and I don't think she wants to live like a squaw." The same notion hit both of us as soon as I said it.

"We could bring Fawn to live here." Long was already smiling.

"That just might smooth things over at that."

A little feminine companionship was just what Barby needed. Both of us patted ourselves on the back for such a clever and wise solution. Neither one of us claimed to be experts where women were concerned, especially unpredictable and volatile pregnant women, but our plan seemed solid nonetheless. I could hardly wait to break the news to Barby.

"You're going to do what?" was all she could scream once I made her aware of the plan.

She threatened me with far worse things than going home to her father, bodily harm among them. I was shocked that the promise of the company of a strange woman of foreign affiliation, and who spoke not one bit of the English language, should come as small comfort to her. After I was able to endure what seemed like an overly drawn-out session of wailing, biting, and gouging, she allowed me to give her a good hug. She was at least closer to her usual self once I had the steer removed and butchered that evening.

I was determined to leave with Long that night in order to fetch his wife to Barby's side as quickly as possible. Yet, once again, I showed my ignorance of the opposite sex, and Barby *convinced* me that leaving her alone one more night was out of the question. I was quick to agree that her idea was much better than mine, and waited until morning to fetch Fawn.

We returned home two days later with Fawn and her household in tow. That household consisted of a bundle of what appeared to be various animal hides and by-products, a tepee, and three or four Cheyenne camp dogs. Barby was not so unladylike as to appear other than pleased at her female guest's arrival, but I noticed her eyeing the dogs with a little displeasure. They were an ugly, mangy set of mongrels that were too wild to catch most of the time, but always under your feet and growling if you stepped on them. I started to offer Barby comfort by telling her of the value of Cheyenne dogs if we should suffer an unusually hard winter, but thought better of it when I considered her recent state of humor.

A meeting of the minds was held and a site beside the house was chosen to place the tepee. I chewed on Long a little when he lounged about instead of helping his wife erect the lodge, but soon discovered that she was even bossier than my own wife. Fawn scolded me and set me off knowing that she didn't want or need my help. I joined Long in relaxed repose in the shade of a wagon, where we smoked away half a sack of tobacco watching the proceedings.

I was astonished by the fact that Fawn seemed happy enough for Barby to help her, and without one word between them they went about getting Fawn's house in order. Long told me that Fawn considered it woman's work, and a man's job was to hunt enough to keep the family in meat. Given the time and inclination, a man could make love or war at his warrior leisure. Long was obviously proud that idle time found between such demanding duties could be spent making sure that he got plenty of rest to fortify him in his exhaustion. I admit to being shamefully envious. It's not racism that makes me certain that Barby had not one drop of Indian blood anywhere in her pedigree

Surprising as it may seem, pairing Barby

and Fawn together worked out fine. By the time of my next return home from freighting, the two of them were getting along like sisters or something. They communicated in a mix of English, Cheyenne, and women's intuition. I hadn't been around them five minutes when I began to feel left out of the loop. Both of them would laugh, or exchange funny looks at times when I couldn't even tell anything had happened.

Apparently, the two women had had no problem communicating from the get-go, or they couldn't have come up with the list of homemaking demands they soon presented Long and I with. It seemed they needed more flour, more chickens, a shotgun for Barby to shoot quail with, two glass windows for the soddy, and a shed built for their horses. A milk cow and a butter churn would be nice when we had the money for it. You can't believe how shocking the accumulation of a household is to a man who has lived out of his saddle and bedroll for many years.

Barby brought an iron bed frame and feather mattress to our home as part of her dowry, and Fawn insisted that she too have one. She was a proud Cheyenne, but had to admit that the whites were on to something in that department. Not only did she want the bed, but showed Long where she had laid out a spot for a house on the side of the hill beside our home. I wondered if Long was regretting bringing his wife under the influence of a white woman.

Being men, Long and I sought to deny these extravagant wants on the basis of budgetary concerns, but of course the girls won out in the end. Soon my soddy had two glass windows, and Fawn and Barby were serving up buttered bread and fried quail. It didn't seem so out of place in our little cultural menagerie, but the specter of a feather bed in a tepee might seem a novelty to some.

Apparently it was novelty enough to have half the cowboys north of the Canadian coming by to look at it.

I was just about home one day when I met two cowboys coming down the trail from my house. They were both even younger than I, and looked a little sheepish. One of them was carrying a little cloth bundle.

"Your wife is about the best cook I ever saw." He held up the package as if it was evidence.

I watched his Adam's apple bob up and down nervously. I scowled a little, maybe on purpose and maybe because I couldn't help myself. I had my suspicions as to what had brought them to my humble abode. Two pretty women sounded like more of a draw to tourists than buttered bread, especially where cowboys were concerned.

"Is that so?"

"We just stopped by to meet you folks and maybe see if what we'd been hearing about that big fancy bed in a tepee was true. That missus of yours is real nice. She and that Fawn loaded us down with food."

"We hope you don't mind. We were real respectful," the other of the two added.

You're damn right I minded.

"Yeah, she's quite a gal, but she can be a little nervous. She gets scared so far from town, and from time to time she's had to shoot at sounds before she sees what she's shooting at."

"Oh?" they said in unison.

"Yeah, she shot and liked to have killed a fellow who knocked at the door a while back. Me and Fawn's husband like to have never smoothed that over."

"Is that fellow she shot all right?" That Adam's apple was wiggling around like a turkey waddle.

"Sure, he just took a little lead. He said there weren't any hard feelings, even though it takes a while to heal up from two .44 holes."

I could tell they were mulling around in their heads whether to believe me or not. "You boys come around sometime and we'll visit again. Just be careful she sees you plain, or that you find me first."

Neither one of them said anything, and I was glad to see I'd given them something to think about. I waved good-bye and drove down to the soddy. Long was gone, but Fawn and Barby already had supper waiting for me. I studied the two women while they scurried around setting the table. They seemed in an especially good mood.

"Would you say grace?" Barby asked me.

I folded my hands but didn't say the blessing just then. "I met a couple of fellows leaving here."

"Yes?" Barby was giving me a funny look.

"They didn't pester you, did they? They looked ornery."

She looked to Fawn and then back to me with the hint of a smile playing at the corners of her mouth. "No, they were real polite, and seemed like nice young men."

I felt like I was the butt of some inside joke, like when you've got a piece of food on your face without knowing it, or a booger on your nose. I tried to read Fawn, but she lowered her head and tinkered with her plate.

"Are you going to say the blessing?" Barby asked again.

I bowed my head and tried to get my mind on a prayer. "There aren't any more of those cowboys coming around, are there? If word gets out that you'll feed them they'll eat us out of house and home."

Barby leaned back in her chair and a broad smile spread across her face. "Why, I think you're a little jealous."

Fawn was smiling too, but looked back down when I caught her at it. I never could guess what an Indian was thinking, much less a woman.

"I am not."

"You are too." Barby giggled mischievously, and then reached out and laid her hand on mine.

"How many cowboys are pestering you?"

"Well, it seems there are a lot of ranches around here."

"How many?"

"I don't know. Different ones show up from time to time, but they've all been nice. Why, one of them even split some cook wood for Fawn the other day."

"I know cowboys, and they ain't coming around just to split firewood."

"They're harmless. Word has just somehow gotten around about the bed in the

379

tepee. Folks are just naturally curious to see it, and then we gave away a little buttered bread and plum jam." She was still smiling, but I could tell she was losing patience with me. "Those boys don't get any good food, not woman's cooking."

"I'm just saying, you're going to have every cowboy within fifty miles of here coming around and mooning over you two."

Barby looked at Fawn and then put both of her hands on her hips. "This has gone about far enough, Nathan Reynolds." When she called me by my full name I knew I was in trouble. "It was funny at first, but you're taking this a little too far. I'm beginning to think you don't trust me."

Fawn gave an angry grunt as if to reaffirm what Barby said. She spouted out something in Cheyenne at me.

"I can't understand a word you're saying."

"Big dummy." She rose and folded her arms across the front of her buckskin dress. She gave one angry stomp of a little moccasined foot and stormed out the door.

"Now you've gone and hurt Fawn's feelings." Barby clucked her tongue in disapproval.

"I didn't say anything to her. Hell, she can't even speak our language." I couldn't help but feel the two of them were ganging up on me.

"Don't curse at the table. She speaks more English than you know."

"She only speaks it when she wants to."

"You've got a thing or two to learn about love and trust." Barby followed Fawn out the door.

I hurried after her, but she avoided my attempts to hug her, and ducked back inside. I heard the latch fall into place to lock the door right after she slammed it against my nose. I sat down against the outer wall and bided my time. Surely she would get over her mad before too long.

It was near midnight when she finally came out and woke me. Two of Fawn's dogs were piled up against me. They smelled, well, like dogs, and I smelled just like them after lying with them for hours. I started to pet one of them, but it growled at me and both of them walked off with their hackles standing up over their shoulders. Those damned dogs were as hard to figure as the women who gave them scraps all the time and kept them hanging around my door.

"You can come in the house if you'll promise to quit being so jealous," Barby said.

"I was just worried about you, that's all."

She gave me a wry look and blocked the

doorway. "Promise?"

I had a kink in my back and a chill from the night air. "I promise."

She hugged my neck and kissed me. "Now come to bed and we'll forget about it."

I never meant to make her mad, but I was sure I knew cowboys better than she did. I had no desire to sleep outside with the dogs, and decided I could wait to confer with Long about the whole matter when he got back. Surely two of us could put the sum of our ignorance of women together and come up with a plan to keep away all the tepee seekers and bread addicts.

As it turned out, there was no keeping them away without getting myself in trouble with my wife for rude behavior. But I did grow a little more at ease with the whole situation. The cowboys were a bit sheepish the first time they showed up when Long and I were home. We tolerated them long enough to learn it was clear that most of them were just looking for the opportunity to eat and talk to a woman. They went out of their way to be courteous, and most of them were too bashful to make much of a nuisance of themselves.

There were certain fringe benefits that came along with our wives' popularity. Several times various cowboys brought large lots of flour, or other staples in exchange for the treats they ate up. They thought it a more than fair trade to exchange a fifty-pound sack of company flour for the little bit they ate when they happened by. Our home larder became bountiful.

Another side effect of their worship and devotion to our queens of prairie biscuits and feminine conversation was the increase in my cattle herd. Not only did those cowboys help keep an eye out for our cattle to ensure their welfare on the range, but they did such a fine job that a few of our cows had twins. I had originally bought only two hundred cows and a small bunch of yearling steers. By those cowboys branding every supposed maverick with our brand, those cows had a tremendous calf crop. It was not so much to cause our outfit undue suspicion, but enough to greatly affect my books in the coming years.

I am ashamed that I made such a feeble effort to stop what they were doing. I justified it at the time by telling myself that many of the big operators started by branding everything they could put a loop on, but that doesn't make it any better. In short, my initial steps toward becoming a cattle baron were due in large part to a bunch of good-hearted cowboys with twisted notions of what was fair. They were lonely for the sight of a good woman, and hungry for the dietary change she offered.

Long adjusted to the cowboys' visits easier and quicker than I did. He was soon suggesting we should be glad they popped in now and again to look in on the safety of our wives while we were gone. I acted as if I was in agreement and finally at ease with the whole situation. However, I couldn't help the pang of jealousy when I saw any man around my Barby.

I was wickedly pleased to come home one day to find Long's father-in-law camped out on an extended visit. He and his harem of womenfolk, Fawn's mother included, had pitched a lodge on the creek below the house. Fawn had erected her father a brush arbor in the yard, and that was where the old savage was sitting when I rode up.

I hugged my wife, admired a papoose she and the womenfolk were fawning over, and took a seat with Blue Knife. While I looked him over, I was thinking what a scare he might put in some of those boys showing up all the time. The more I thought about it, the more it seemed a good idea to get him to move in his whole clan. Perhaps he could recommend a few warriors that liked to chase and scalp nosy cowboys.

"How are you, Blue Knife?"

"I'm good, Tennessee." He patted his belly with a gesture at the empty plate beside him.

On second thought, should one of those cowboys come upon a bunch of Cheyenne surrounding my house it might lead to the whole country believing that the Indians were off the reservation and on the warpath. It wouldn't do to have half the country riding to the aid of my household. Since the Cheyenne scare in '78, people were still a little jumpy.

"You've got a good woman, Tennessee."

I hadn't had time to measure just how well Barby was taking the presence of her latest company, especially the fearsome Blue Knife. I watched the women while I talked with him. Apparently Fawn was now speaking enough English for her to translate to her family for Barby.

"I'm proud of her." I regretted immediately that I sounded like I was talking of my horse or something.

"She didn't run the first time she saw me." His black eyes twinkled with devilment as he spoke.

"Maybe you didn't yell and shoot as much as usual," I shot back at him good-naturedly.

"Smoke with me, Tennessee."

That meant that I was supposed to pull

out my tobacco, and I gladly did so. No doubt, he had a sack of his own, but I gave the devil his due. Besides, I was coming to like him.

We sat silent for a while, enjoying our cigarettes and watching our women play with the papoose. I felt unusually content right then. My cattle were fattening on good grass, I had a home and a soon-to-be baby, and no cowboys were going to run off with my woman. I felt like taking a peaceful afternoon nap with a clear conscience and an easy mind.

"I saw your old friend this morning." Blue Knife interrupted my daydreams.

"Long?" I hadn't seen him in two weeks.

"Billy," he said, like he'd known him for a long time.

It was no wonder Blue Knife and Long got along so well. You couldn't guess what either one knew, or didn't know.

"I saw him down by the creek this morning. We smoked and talked some," he added.

"How was he?"

"He was good. I guess he came to see you, but you were gone."

I hadn't seen him since he shot Rory Donnovan the day before my wedding. I'd heard he was in Dodge, but hadn't run into him on any of my trips there. I still thought of him as my best friend, but there was Barby between us. I didn't know how to solve that. I figured things have a way of working out if given a chance, and in the meantime I wished I had been home when he called.

"I wish I'd been here. There's no telling when I'll see him again."

"He will come again soon." Blue Knife sounded confident in his assertion.

"What makes you think so?"

Blue Knife's black eyes twinkled again, and seemed to look right down to the inside of me. I had a sick feeling I already knew the gist of what was to come.

"I saw his tracks down by the creek and up the hill. He's been here many times."

"Is that so?" I knew damned well that it could be.

I'd almost paid off my debt to Long for the money he'd loaned me to buy my freight outfit with, and that Caldwell banker's payment on the cattle loan wasn't due until the fall. I figured I was due at least a little time at home with my wife. Maybe I'd been gone way too much the last few months.

CHAPTER TWENTY-THREE

Billy never showed up to visit again that spring, and I heard he was down south picking up a trail herd. I stayed around the house for most of the month of May, loving my wife, and trying to make her home a little better. I built us a horse shed, and helped her transplant some flowers from the creek where she found them to the little window boxes I made for her. I enjoyed going to sleep every night with my hand on her baby belly, and the sweet smell of her in my nose as I lay my face against her neck.

My stay at home lasted through the roundup of my home range during the first week of June. That done, I knew that the lard can we kept our savings in was nearing empty, and I had to get back to freighting. I drug my feet at leaving, but Barby knew the situation just as well as I did. She regretfully sent me on my way.

I met Long in Dodge, and we picked up a

load of military freight we had on subcontract for delivery at Ft. Elliott. It was while at the fort that I heard Billy was just south of the Salt Fork with his herd of cattle and headed north for delivery somewhere in Colorado. I also heard that the Panhandle Stock Association had formed up an army to see that he turned east or west of their ranges. The Association had a quarantine on all cattle coming in from the south, because of the Texas fever scare. They sent thirty-five tough cowboys to make sure that he went around. That's a lot of men to suggest to a trail boss that he follow a certain route, but they knew Billy like I did. He might not be of a mind to go around anything.

Mobeetie was buzzing with guesswork as to what would happen when the Association tried to detour Billy from his chosen trail. There was no state law backing the quarantine. The only authority it had was the Association's guns, and that was what had folks excited.

The Association members were steadily fencing off large holdings of private and state leased grassland, and it wasn't going to be long until the little man wasn't going to have a place to graze his herds for free. The big ranchers complained that they invested lots of man power to operate the roundup on open range, paying a disproportional and unfair amount to tend small operators' cattle in the process. They also said that without legally claimed grazing territory and fenced holdings, the cheap old longhorn cattle that many of the little men or old-time cowmen owned would crossbreed with the fancy European Hereford and Roan Durham cattle that they paid high dollar for to improve their herds. Also, open range would let us poor folks enjoy the benefits of their high-dollar bulls servicing our cows without having to pay for them. In short, rawhiders like myself who couldn't afford to operate on a big scale were seen to be freeloading off their attempts to be cattle barons.

I had to admit that the beef industry was changing, and that the time was probably coming when a man had to run better cattle and fewer of them. That meant fencing off land to protect your breeding program. Land was expensive when you had to buy it, and a man with limited space needed to run meatier cattle like the Herefords and Shorthorns that would bring a premium at market. Nobody wanted to eat tough longhorn meat unless they had to. The farmers were bound to come once the railroad came through the Panhandle, and they'd suck up the available government land. Maybe Colonel Goodnight was right to preach that the future of the country was livestock farming, or a blend of cattle and crops. I wasn't ready to trade my rope for a plow, but what he said made some sense. Of course he and the English dude who was his investor could afford enough ground to still cowboy and not have to farm.

The town was heavy on the side of the "free-grass" faction, as it was labeled by some. Despite the Association's claims to equal representation for both large and small stockowners, many folks refused to believe that it was anything but a way to keep a few power-hungry men in control of the country. Our ranks were reinforced by a few stubborn ranchers and fence haters with large outfits who didn't see eye to eye with the Association. Open range was a time-honored tradition in Texas, and a lot of us wanted it to stay that way.

I myself wasn't too blind to see some of the good the Association was doing, but I was too late and too poor to have any say in things. So, in the American tradition of self servitude and unmitigated revolutionary spirit, I was ready to fight them tooth and nail. Leave it to Billy to pick the fight.

I hired a man to drive my wagon until I returned, and saddled Dunny for war. Within five minutes of hearing the news I was ready to ride to the aid of my friend, but I wasn't quick enough to get out of town before Long cornered me.

"Are you coming?" I asked impatiently.

"Too many outlaws and whiskey peddlers already give you free-grassers a bad look, without adding a proud black man to the mix." Long's tone left no doubt as to the fact that he intended to ignore the situation and keep right on about his business.

"That's Billy I'm going to help." I thought that was good reason enough.

"Billy's likeable enough at times, but he doesn't feed me."

"What if it was me down there?"

"It ain't."

"It could be."

"You've got a family to take care of, and a business to tend to. You can't hire some drunk out of a saloon to entrust your livelihood to while you go off looking for fights that you own no part of." Long's calm tone fell far short of soothing me.

"I help my friends when they're in trouble."

"Do you think Billy and I are friends?"

"You sure ain't acting like it."

"Being friendly and being friends are two entirely different things. I might have broken bread with him, but that doesn't make me his good friend."

"At least you've made it plain."

Long shook his head slowly in frustration while he continued, "When I was a boy white folks used to put me up on a keg and get me to dance. I never once mistook all their clapping and backslapping praise for any more than what it was."

"Billy didn't put that chip on your shoulder," I said, only half-hearing him.

"No, he ain't put me to picking cotton, but when he laughs and slaps me on the back I might as well be up on that keg again. I'm just a funny nigger with a big dick doing tricks," Long said quietly, but I could see the color of passion rising in his face.

"I don't know anything about all of that."

Long probably could tell that everything he was trying to say was just bouncing off my hard head. He was silent for a long moment, looking like he was trying to figure out what one says in an insane asylum to calm the patients down. I was getting madder by the minute at him; the more he talked, the madder it made me.

"You run with an outlaw, and you'll end up like one." He pointed a finger at me for emphasis.

"He's in the right, and don't point your damned finger at me."

"Listen" — Long held up his hands to me in appeasement — "you do what you're going to do, but remember this. There are two kinds of outlaws. There are those that are outlaws because they're too mean, too greedy, or just too evil, if you will, to abide by most any kind of law. The other kind of outlaw is of another sort."

"What's the other sort?"

"The other sort just doesn't give a damn about consequences."

"I suppose you think Billy's that kind?"

"And he won't live long because of it." Long paused to spit in the dirt for emphasis. "The world won't tolerate him."

Talking to Long was like talking to a fence post, and I had no more time or patience for it. I promised to catch up with him as soon as I could, and asked him to tell Barby where I'd gone if he saw her first. However, before I could show my heels to that town, One Jump Kate came running up and latched on to my arm. Great big tear tracks streaked her makeup, and the little wampus cat looked like she was more mad upset than sad upset.

"They've arrested Billy for cattle rustling,

and they're bringing him here for trial," she blurted out.

The Association kept Billy's herd from crossing their holdings, but they didn't give him a chance to decide whether or not to push through the wall of Winchesters they had waiting for him on the far side of the river. Instead, they snuck up on his camp in the dark of the night, and caught him in his bedroll. He woke to a bunch of rifle barrels staring him in the eye, and found out that he was under arrest. I heard that Billy told them all to go to hell and he counted out loud the number of rifles pointing at him.

Back in the days when cattle were cheaper than cheap in Texas, and as many wore brands as did not, a lot of cowmen thought nothing of killing cattle that didn't belong to them on the range. You damned sure didn't do it under the owner's nose, but nobody would label you a cow thief for doing it unless you didn't own stock yourself. What kept the practice going was everybody's suspicion that it was impossible to stop, and the unwillingness of most to make an issue of it.

Our faith in the common man's good sense told us that most folks weren't going to kill a beef that they paid for or worked to gather and deliver when they could shoot one belonging to somebody else. Nobody liked supplying free beef to their fellow man, but a lot of folks figured to make sure they ate as much of others' beef as they were bound to lose in kind. It sounds an awful lot like stealing, but at least if everybody did it, then maybe the scales would balance out in the end. The custom persisted in a backdoor way until the likes of the Association decided to make an issue of it, and they had the man power and money to do it.

The word had been out for a good while in the Panhandle, but due to adherence to his training, or because he thought he could get away with it, Billy had his boys kill a range steer and butcher it just as they were about to camp one night. The Association got wind of it and found a means to dodge a showdown with Billy's herd, as well as show the country they intended to enforce all of their laws.

They arrested Billy as the boss who ordered the steer to be slaughtered, and they arrested Andy because in the heat of the arrest he got mad enough to tell them he shot the steer. Two criminals were apparently enough to serve their wants, because the rest of the crew were left with the herd under the watch of the Association cowboys.

The upshot was that Billy and Andy were taken to Mobeetie to face charges, and stand trial like common rustlers.

I waited with the rest of Mobeetie for the arrival of Billy and his captors. A large group of us greeted them when they rode into town and gave the Association posse a fair share of catcalls and insults. There like to have been a shooting, but nothing was thrown around but hot tempers.

The prisoners were turned over to Cap Arrington to jail, and charges were filed with the district attorney. There was some talk of storming the jail that first evening and busting Billy and Andy out, but before the crowd could get drunk enough, Cap came walking down the street with a twelve-gauge coach gun across his elbow. He never said anything to the crowd; in fact he acted like we weren't even there. He went inside the new courthouse, which contained the jail, and came out with a chair. He took himself a seat beside the front door and proceeded to clean his shotgun. From time to time, he quit swabbing the bores of that gun, and gave us a friendly smile.

A lot of the crowd decided it would be best to take their complaints back to the saloons and leave Arrington to his gun cleaning. If that lawman had a problem with our stand against injustice he knew damned well where to find us.

The Association gang that had arrested Billy stayed in town for a show of force, but they kept to their own. The sporting crowd at Mobeetie was dead set against the law-and-order business that the Association was pushing on all fronts. That's not to say, by any means, that everyone in town was against the Association. There were a lot of good people who liked many of the things it was doing. I myself counted some of its members as friends, despite my feelings about open range.

Things had calmed enough for the law to let me visit Billy by the next morning. After they checked me for hidden weapons, I was led down the narrow hallway fronting the cells and allowed to take a chair in front of the one containing Billy and Andy. A deputy manned another chair at the far end of the hall. He was leaned back against the bars of the last cell, reading a newspaper and trying to appear as if he wasn't listening.

One night of hard time in the calaboose didn't seem to bother Andy, and he was grinning when he reached through the bars to shake my hand.

"Don't make any suspicious moves." Andy nodded his head toward the guard. "They know there ain't any jail that can hold me."

"You're a certified desperado now," I kidded him.

Billy didn't look as tickled with his surroundings as Andy did. He gave me a quick handshake, and began to pace the floor of the cell. I had the impression he had been pacing before I arrived, and maybe the entire night before. In fact, Billy looked more than half pissed-off about the whole situation.

"Where's the cake?" Billy asked me, disappointment in his voice.

"What cake?"

"The one with the hacksaw and a forty-five in it."

I was glad to see he still had a little of his sense of humor about him. He brought his pacing to an abrupt end, and dragged his cot over to the front of the cell for a seat. He leaned back in the corner of the bars and rolled himself a cigarette while we talked.

"They act like they aim to see this through," I said to the both of them.

"There's still some that won't stand for this," Billy said.

"Have you got a lawyer yet?"

Billy was licking his new cigarette closed, and could only nod, but Andy was quick to blurt out, "We've got Temple Houston on his way here."

I made no attempt to hide the fact that I was greatly impressed. Temple Houston was one of the best known lawyers in the western half of Texas. Besides being the son of the late hero of the Republic, Sam Houston, he was a real fire-eater with enough flamboyance to keep him in the newspapers, and he was quickly rising among the state political ranks. He packed a pistol that he was more than willing to use, and it was he who killed Al Jennings's brother in a saloon gunfight over to Woodward, Oklahoma in later years. Little Al was never more than a wannabe outlaw and train robber, and I reckon his brothers weren't much shakes either. But it's safe to say Temple Houston had a little bark on him. Besides shooting straight, he could get every man in a courtroom standing up and cheering him on when he was laying his defense talk on thick. Maybe it was just lawyer parlor tricks, but many of the common folk thought he was one of their own.

"How'd you get him to come?"

Billy eyed me with a crafty grin. "All the cattlemen in this country don't belong to the Association. There are a lot of the old-timers who don't like bloated old highbinders like Goodnight and his rich cronies telling them how the cow should eat its corn."

"I figured Houston would side with the power. I heard he wanted to run for the Senate or something." I vaguely knew what I was speaking of.

"Nope. The talk is that the Association cut him out of things when they were setting up the law here, and he's dead set on fighting them on the State Land Lease Act they're pushing for," Billy said.

"We'll keep open range if Houston has his way," Andy said like he'd read it in the Bible or something.

"It's bullshit, but at least it looks like you're going to get a fair trial. Maybe Houston can make them eat crow."

Billy jumped up out off his cot like he was ready to fight. "Hell, I killed a crippled Spur steer for some beef, and they arrested me for it. I've got a trail herd going nowhere that I spent every dollar I had to buy. It's costing me about fifteen dollars a day for the crew, and I've got a delivery date in Colorado that's getting too close for comfort." Billy paused long enough to kick his cot over before he continued. "A man can't drive a herd of longhorns where he needs, because a bunch of bigwigs who got here first are claiming twice the country they own."

Billy started in again before I could answer. His unlit cigarette punched through the air like an orchestra conductor's wand. "You can believe their spiel about law and order and honest dealing, but you remember that they're paying bonus salaries to every county official and the district court. They claim it's to help keep talented, honest men in jobs that the government pays too little for, but that's a load of sheep crap. They want to make sure that no honest-to-goodness Texas cowman and his raggedy-ass old longhorns set foot on the state land they're fencing. That's what they're doing."

"I'm with you, but when you pick a fight, you sure don't look for a little guy."

"Open range was good enough for most of those shysters when they were small operators, but now that they're rich they want to change the rules," Andy threw in.

"Some folks say the railroad is going to bring in farmers by the boxcar load, and that they'll latch on to all the state land the Association ranchers are trying to hold," I thought aloud.

"That'd be about right. Between the railroad, farmers, and the dumb-ass Association there won't be anywhere left to run a cow. If they had any sense they'd buy us all some dynamite to blow up the railroad and stop it from leaving Wichita Falls." Billy cussed and kicked his cot over.

"The country is going to hell in a hand-bag," Andy moaned. "We ought to cut down every damned strand of bobwire we run across."

"I'll tell you one thing, Tennessee, if they don't let me out of this jail in time to get my herd to the delivery grounds by my contract's date, they can't even imagine the trouble I'm going to cause them." There was a chill in Billy's voice.

Before I could say anything else, Cap Ar-rington stepped into the hallway. "If you're going to stay any longer I'll have to get you a cell."

It seemed visiting hours were over, and I rose to go. I stood up between Cap and Billy, and the two were staring at each other. Cap glanced down at the overturned cot, and the bedding strewn about the cell floor. One hand played at a corner of his mustache while he looked at Andy and then Billy again.

"Are you boys taking it hard?"

Billy smiled an easy smile, turned his cot right side up, and pitched the bedding on it. He propped one foot on the cot's edge and struck a match on a cell bar. Once his cigarette was lit he shook out the match and pitched it against the far wall of the hallway, where it lay smoking on the floor. To all appearances Billy looked like he might have just finished reading to a Sunday school class.

"I was sleeping like a baby until that cot threw me off."

Cap's face didn't so much as twitch. An old tom turkey like him knew not to gobble over just anything. He stepped aside to let me by to the hallway door, and when I was just about gone I heard Billy call to me down the hallway.

"How are Barby and the kid doing?"

Arrington was right behind me blocking my view into the cells, so I couldn't see Billy's face after he said it.

CHAPTER TWENTY-FOUR

The trial that brought so many to Mobeetie was never to be. The Association dropped the charges within five days of Billy's arrest, and the opposing sides had massed their forces for nothing. They didn't stand a chance in convicting Billy, but I expect they knew that from the start. They held him long enough that he had to send orders to his herd to make the dry swing to the west of the settled country, lest he go broke, and his arrest served notice to the country that bucking the Association wasn't worth the hassle.

I heard a lot of people made themselves scarce when Billy was let out of jail, and I reckon it was like accidentally catching your neighbor's dog in your steel trap. Catching him isn't all that difficult, but letting him go is a whole other story. Billy didn't appreciate having his toes pinched any more than the dog would.

The law may have turned Billy and Andy loose on the public, but they made sure to shadow their every move while in town. Arrington, his deputies, the city marshal, and two Texas Rangers made sure that Billy didn't go to the outhouse without friendly escort. Billy and Andy paraded their entourage around town for most of a day, poking a little fun at all the attention they were getting and giving everybody time to notice the high number of absentee citizens.

As for me, I returned to freighting, and I hustled through the summer work, trying to make every cent I could. I'd promised Barby I'd come in for the last month of her pregnancy, so I had to make hay while the sun shined. I learned every trail from Dodge to Colorado City, and from Wichita Falls to Tascosa. By the time the summer ended I was becoming a regular muleskinner.

Despite my good intentions to be with Barby in the weeks just before our child was to be born, I cut my scheduling just a little too fine and arrived home a week later than we'd planned. I knew I'd catch hell from her, but at least I'd made it before the baby was born.

Nobody was out and about except for Fawn's dogs when I drove into the yard. They all sat facing the doorway of the soddy with their ears perked forward, whimpering and whining and wagging tails in some strange excitement. I hollered to let Barby know I was home, but received no answer. I was making my way to the door, half angry at the poor reception I was receiving after having been gone so long, when I heard a strange cry, and one of those stew-meat curs let out a long, mournful howl that would have put an old lobo wolf to shame.

There was a stirring within the house, and Fawn appeared in the doorway brandishing a broom in her hands. The dogs scattered instantly in all directions while the broom swished around them. Fawn looked up from her attack and instantly cut loose on me in a long breath of angry Cheyenne. At that time, I still couldn't understand half of what she said, but I knew enough to know that she was a little put out with yours truly. I thought about following the dogs' example and getting out of her reach, for I am sure a tomahawk wouldn't have looked any more dangerous in her hands than that broom did.

As it was, I headed for the door in a display of sheer bluff. That little savage gave me a vicious poke in the gut with the business end of the broom, and another spout of Cheyenne let me know in a hurry that I wasn't going any farther. Once she was sure she had me stopped, Fawn started back inside, but threw a suspicious look back over her shoulder to make sure I was going to mind.

I waited impatiently for what must have been a quarter of an hour after she shut the door and disappeared. I could hear all kinds of muffled noises from inside, and I was relieved to think that I heard Barby whispering more than once. The mules needed unhitched and put away, but I was beginning to surmise that my sweet wife had something special planned for me since I was home for a while. The thought put a happy inside me, and I decided the chores could wait a bit longer.

The sun was setting, and the lights were showing through the windows when Fawn finally cracked the door open and stepped aside for me to enter. I ducked into the low doorway and the first thing I saw when I straightened up was Barby lying on her bed with our newborn bundled in her arms. She had the baby wrapped in a frilly little blanket, and I couldn't see so much as its nose poking out.

"Are you going to just stand there, or come over here and look at your son?" Barby teased, but I could detect a little note of tension in her voice.

I took a seat on the bed beside her and placed my arm around her shoulders. She leaned against me and brushed the blanket back from around our son's face. The little face looking back at me held me spellbound and all I could do was stare.

Out of the corner of my eye I noticed Barby watching me intently, and I knew she wasn't sure what my reaction would be. When we had first married I'd worried some about how much the baby would look like Billy. Afraid that I wouldn't give the child a fair shake, I had reminded myself for months that the child was mine, no matter who had sired it. I was ready to be a family man, but the baby had only been an idea to me when in the womb, intangible and unknown. As I sat with him before me, I was like a kid under the Christmas tree with something totally surprising and wonderful just unwrapped.

For the time being, the flood of emotion I felt left me content to simply look at the child, but Barby placed him in my lap even though I was timid about holding him. I'd never held a baby before, and whether or not it was from the fear that I could not handle seven pounds of baby without dropping it, I was afraid I'd do something wrong.

To my surprise, the little tyke didn't seem to mind me holding him at all, and I swore he seemed to like it.

"His name will be Owen Daniel, if that's all right with you," Barby said softly.

"Howdy, Owen." I touched his hand, and I'll be danged if he didn't grab a hold of my finger.

Barby and I sat for a long while laughing and talking. She clung to my arm and pointed out everything from the baby's feet to the strength of his tiny hands. She told me she'd made the little quilt herself, and Fawn showed me a little papoose sack she'd made from soft doeskin and lined with rabbit fur. There was a wooden frame for it that Long had whittled out and put together in his spare time. I couldn't imagine Barby packing Owen around on her back like a squaw, but she informed me it would be handy to have around the place while she worked.

Next, the two women showed me the contents of a great pile of gifts mounded by the front door. It seemed that over the last week every cowboy in the country had stopped by and left something or another. There were little silver bells, baby shoes, rattles, and wooden toys. I couldn't for the life of me figure out where they had found them, or imagine grown men walking up to the counter and requesting such items. Looking at my baby, I thought I understood; it's all right to be silly where babies are concerned.

Fawn retired to her tepee, and left us alone. I could have stayed up half the night talking to my wife, but I could tell she was awful tired. Fawn had told me of her long labor, and advised that I let her get some sleep. Barby didn't argue with the suggestion, and reached out to take Owen from me.

"It wouldn't hurt if he stayed up with his daddy a little longer, would it?" I asked sheepishly.

"Nathan" — she was the only one except my own Mama who ever called me that — "he's been asleep for an hour."

"It won't be any trouble for me to hold him a bit longer."

Once she was asleep I took him outside into the night where the stars shown down as far as the eye could see, and the nighthawks dipped and dove in the light of the moon. I walked and told him of the things I'd do for him, and told him of the country where he now lived. I informed him of the good mother he had, and thanked the Almighty that I was lucky enough to have them both.

Barby had gone into labor in the middle of the previous night and she'd been at it throughout the day with no doctor within a hundred miles, and nobody but Fawn to help her. The hardware company thermometer I'd tacked to the wall beside the door read a hundred and two degrees in the shade of the eave that day. The West had a reputation for tough men, but somebody ought to give credit to the women brave enough and tough enough to survive in the early days on the frontier. The women of Troy who cut their hair for bowstrings didn't have a thing on the pioneer women of the West.

The night air was growing cooler, and I took my boy back into the house. I laid him down against his mother, and she opened her eyes for a second and smiled faintly at me as she clutched Owen to her chest. Once I had the mules put away I returned to the house to slip into the bed beside Barby with Owen snuggled between us. I threw my arm across them both and lay awake long into the night, staring into the dark of the room and wondering how I wound up at such a point in life.

Just before I fell asleep I heard that dog again. Somewhere out in the night he howled long and deep, sad and happy at the same time, and my heart went out to that mutt so alive as to find reason to sing in the dark.

That winter was one of the happiest times of my life, and even the cold couldn't dampen my spirits. My wife was happy, the baby was healthy, and the weather wasn't too terrible. Every morning I rose early, and after my chores I'd walk down the path to where Long was building his house. We'd have us some coffee and talk about the day's carpentry plans and other such things until the women had breakfast ready. Then we'd troop back down to my soddy, where we all gathered at the breakfast table.

When the weather wasn't bad, I helped Long with his house some, and kept an eye on my cattle. Other than chopping a little ice, and keeping my mules close to home, I didn't work too hard. Long freighted little that winter, spending most of his time building his house. He mostly used oxen to freight, and they didn't work as well as mules in the wintertime with the grass not growing. You could operate a mule team giving them some feed, and it wouldn't get into your profit too much. I thought I had enough jingle in my pockets to get us through to spring, and I was having too much fun to work, so my mules stayed turned out for most of the winter with only a little corn to keep them closer to home.

By the time spring finally rolled around, Long had a nice three-room frame house built, and the novelty of Fawn's featherbed in a tepee disappeared forever. Being wiser than most, Long and I kept the tepee up in case after a domestic dispute our wives accidentally locked the doors for a night.

My season of leisure left me cash broke, and I was anxious to remedy that. My team was paid for, my cattle had wintered well, and I planned on making some real money for once in my life. I'd promised Barby that this would be my last summer away from her so the pressure was on me to make the next several months extra profitable. So one fine morning in April, I kissed my wife and child good-bye and left home once again to seek our fortune.

Poor folks know in their hearts that no matter how good life is going, things are just bound to get worse. My team was a little on the thin side after the winter, and my first load was too heavy for them even if they'd been in good shape. My trip from Dodge was a slow, difficult journey to say the least. Before I reached Tascosa I busted a wagon axel, had a mule go lame, and I was coming down with some sort of sickness.

By the time I returned to Dodge to pick up another load I was more than sick — I was just about dead. Somebody had the sense to pull me from my wagon seat, and I spent a week in bed with pneumonia. I don't remember much about that week, but the doctor said it was touch and go with me for a while, and he'd just about given up on my living.

Even after I was up and going again I was still so weak I couldn't stand without my heart racing, and threatening to cough up a bloody lung. I was in no shape for much of anything, but Barby would be worried, and I needed to get back to work. I paid off the doctor, and went to get my outfit. It was easy enough to find, and the crooked livery man presented me with a board bill that was unreasonable to say the least, especially to a man in my condition.

After beating him about the head and shoulders with a singletree for a minute or two I had him just about ready to adjust his bill when the Law showed up. They returned the favor by buffaloing me over my head with a pistol barrel and throwing me in jail. My fever came back and I ended up on my deathbed again at the doctor's place with a concussion added to my list of ailments.

Another week passed, and when I was ready to leave again, the Law took me before a judge who promptly extracted a hefty fine from me, and my livery charges, plus damages. The law in Dodge must have placed a pretty high value on the headache I gave that liveryman, because they just about took all the money I had. I had about two dollars left in my pocket, and couldn't help but wonder how many more times they would let me hit him for that price.

I figured it was time to cut my losses, so I took a load of freight bound for Mobeetie and left good old Dodge City. If anybody was watching they sure didn't see me wave good-bye. I drove out of there hunched over on my wagon seat with the fever shivers racking me under my blanket wrapped carcass, and my hat sitting crooked on a head too knotted up to fit inside it.

The upshot of the matter was that I had been gone over a month from home, made one freight haul, and had lost fifty dollars on the trip. Not only was I broke, but I was in debt a hundred dollars to the company of Wright and Rath for a replacement mule they fronted me. My body couldn't seem to shake loose from the sickness, and the promise of me making much money that summer looked pretty dim right then.

By the time I'd detoured down Wolf Creek to stop by my home I was more than ready to see Barby, and allow her to baby me around a few days. The thought of a little of her pampering and a willing ear to hear my troubles lifted my spirits considerably, despite the dark funk I was in. I was anxious for my home place to come into view, and maybe Barby would come to meet me down the road like she sometimes did.

Nobody came to meet me even after I had driven all the way up to the yard in front of the house. Both of Long's ox rigs were gone, and there was a strange horse tied to the corral fence. I set the brake on my wagon, and climbed down from my seat when a movement in the distance caught my eye. It was Fawn standing on her porch, and I waved at her. She went inside her house without waving back.

I was studying the tied horse as I made my way to my door. I didn't recognize the brand it wore or the rig on its back, but assumed it was probably another cowboy who had come by to pester Barby. The door was open, and as I reached it I heard the sound of a man's voice and Barby's giggle. The combination of the two began to build a pressure in my head and chest.

CHAPTER TWENTY-FIVE

"Hello, Tennessee," Billy said merrily as I stepped inside, and then he tried to correct himself, "uh, I mean Nate."

He was sitting at my table and holding Owen on his knee. My eyes darted to Barby where she stood across the room at the stove. Her eyes were a little big, and one hand nervously smoothed at her dress front. I brought my attention just as quickly back to Billy. Owen stared at me, and then turned away and let out a playful squeal as he ducked his head into Billy's chest.

I was a man right then who felt he was at the end of his rope, with nothing left to lose or win, because I knew what was coming before Barby said a word.

Misery has a way of building upon itself by reminding you of every other single thing that is wrong and equally miserable in your life. Seconds seemed like hours while I stood in my own house where I should be king, and my mind compiled the list of sins laid at the feet of my wife and best friend. I knew in my faltering heart that what I imagined would hurt no more than the truth I was determined to hear.

"Nathan . . ." Barby stopped short of whatever she was going to say, and started across the room to me.

She was wearing a new dress that I'd never seen, and that I hadn't bought for her. I stopped her at arm's length and held her before me, running my eyes over the dress, and recognizing for the first time that she was wearing a fancy silver hair pin I'd never seen either.

"Billy bought it for me as a wedding present." Her voice told me she knew how I was going to take it before I even opened my mouth.

Maybe I was too sick, but nothing I told myself seemed to quell the anger rising in me. When I looked at Billy smiling at me with Owen in his lap all I could think was that he'd come back to get what was his in the first place. The more I looked at him the more I knew that he already had figured out that Owen was his, and that Owen knew it too.

I started to speak, but a fit of coughing buckled my knees and I had to grab for the edge of the table to steady myself. Barby threw her arms around me, and steadied me in her embrace. The table slid away under my weight and Owen started to cry.

"How long have you been here, Billy?" The phlegm from my throat choked my words.

"Not long." He stood where he had risen to dodge the flying table with my son clutched in one arm. It was obvious to me that the bewilderment in his voice was no more than an act.

"You're sick," Barby cried out like she gave a damn.

Weakly, I shoved out of her grasp and reached for Owen, but my legs banged against a chair in my way and knocked it against the wall. Billy held Owen out to me with a look on his face like I had gone stark raving mad. He never knew how right he was.

I pulled Owen to me and stepped back to place both Barby and Billy under my glare of judgment and condemnation. Barby was crying, and that started Owen crying again, which set the dogs outside to barking at the door. She reached for him with her face twisted with hurt, all but begging me to let her lay hands on her husband and child. For a moment I wanted more than anything to let her touch me again, but the hurt I felt was tearing me apart.

"How many times has he been here?" It was plain that it was a question I'd already formed an answer to.

The color drained from Barby's face, and I saw a little of the life slowly go out of her right there like blood seeping into the sand. I hurt so bad that I needed to hurt her, and I hurt more seeing that I had done it. My head swam with a weakness that was more than the pneumonia, and I whirled at the sound of Billy moving beside me. My hand clawed clumsily for the butt of my pistol, but could not seem to find it with a proper hold. Billy stepped by me and out the door.

I was left standing with my pistol shaking in my hand and only Barby before me. She slumped into a chair and buried her face in her hands. I didn't know what to say, and felt sure that it was Barby who had some talking to do. I waited to hear what lies she would tell, and if she could look me in the eye and say them.

She looked up at me with her tear-flooded eyes begging me to let her have Owen, and held out her arms pitifully for that much mercy. I couldn't resist the need I felt in her, and I handed him over. She pulled his face to hers and kissed his forehead, and rocked back and forth with him pressed into the fold of her. Those wet, green siren eyes of hers looked at me again and I saw anger instead of shame.

"He's been here pulling bogged cattle for you for two days, you jealous, ignorant man," Barby sobbed.

It took a moment for her words to soak into the middle of the storm I'd worked up in my heart. The cheap suspicions I felt had taken a hold of me, and wouldn't easily let go. I strained to interpret the look on her face for what truths it might contain.

"If you trusted me so little, then why'd you marry me?" Her voice gained strength, and cut at me with a razor edge.

I reached out for her, but she ducked her head down away from my gaze, and balled up protectively over our son. I was left a man standing in the middle of nothing, with nowhere, or no one to reach out for. Just as quickly as I had been ready to accuse, I found myself feeling the fool. Maybe I needed her so much that I would grasp on to any hope she threw my way, but I believed her — I wanted to believe her. I stumbled to the door and stopped there braced against the jamb, frantically searching the yard for the sight of Billy.

He was mounting his horse and I holstered my pistol and ran to stop him. I headed him off and he turned the horse so fast he almost ran me down. I grabbed at his bridle, and Billy looked like he would put the spurs to his horse if I didn't let go. The horse slung his head, lifting me off the ground and swinging me wildly about at the end of my arm. It was only a death grip, willed by the realization that I had to make peace with Billy if I were to find forgiveness with Barby, which allowed me to hold on.

"Wait, Billy."

I could see no disgust in the way Billy looked down at me. Instead, I saw only disappointment on the face of my friend who I believed might be no friend at all.

"Maybe I'm a jealous fool." I was torn by the feeling that I might be apologizing for nothing, and thus, even more the fool.

"You're wrong, Nate."

I sought to catch my breath as much as I sought what I should say. Neither wish would come to me, but I had to keep talking or Billy would leave and Barby might go right after him. I hated myself for the weakness and indecision I felt right then. Easy answers eluded me and I could not decipher truth from lie, or love from loss.

"She said you've been saving my cattle."

Billy didn't answer immediately, and I

knew if I was as innocent as he let on to be, I would ride right out of there and leave me sitting in the dust. I also knew that nothing would be the same after this, because a mended fence isn't the same as the fence you started with. I was sure of that because I knew that I could not forget, or entirely forgive, if I had been in their shoes.

"Heel flies," Billy said.

"What?" Mention of flies had no place in the turmoil of my mind right then.

"Heel flies are bad this year, and your cows are getting bogged in the creek trying to get away from them."

"I'm sorry," I croaked, and no two words ever came harder for me.

It came over me then that Billy was telling the truth, and that time would prove it so. I'd come home and accused the woman I loved of adultery with my friend who was instead working to save the small herd of cattle that I had worked so hard to put together, and could not replace.

"The dress and comb were just presents for the wife of a friend." Billy didn't mean to, but he cut me a little deeper.

"I just took it different."

"I'm just as happy for her as I am you, that you two married and have got a kid." Billy paused to let that soak in before he added, "Remember, she was my friend before you were married."

I remembered, and that was the thing I couldn't let go of, no matter how hard I tried.

"You shouldn't buy another man's wife a dress."

Billy nodded. "I can understand that. It was just a dress, and I didn't mean anything by it."

"Get down and stay. You are welcome here anytime," I said.

We looked at each other, and both of us knew the lie in what I said. Good intentions would have to serve in place of truth where our friendship was concerned. I had won Barby, but it was me who felt the lesser man.

"I'll go find something to do while you patch it up with her," Billy said.

"You understand, don't you?" I wasn't sure myself just what I was asking.

"I reckon I do." He stepped from his horse and slapped me on the back just like nothing had ever happened.

"I'll totter around the corral a little, and you go talk with your wife."

I knew I had it to do, but that didn't stop me from being scared to death. The awful thing about apologizing to a loved one is that by the time you are ready to say you are sorry, you realize just how wrong you were. The walk up to the house was a long one.

Barby was waiting for me, and I guessed she had been watching out the window. I had hoped she would say something first and maybe that would lead me to that perfect thing to say that would make everything alright between us. She said nothing, but at least seemed willing to hear me out.

"I'm sorry." I have never said anything that I meant so earnestly, and yet sounded so weak to my ears. "I love you and Owen more than anything," I added.

What I said had no miraculous effect on the hurt I saw in her, nor did she offer me the comfort of appearing soothed by my words.

"He doesn't know about Owen," she finally said.

Intuitively, she knew what I feared, and put it before me. My knees weakened and the room swam around me, and Barby became a vision that I could not keep in focus no matter how hard I tried. I could feel the sweat popping out on my forehead, but I was determined to stand until I was sure she still loved me. Still, I welcomed the pain of the floor rushing up to slam into me, and Barby was there holding on to me and crying again.

"Do you love me?" was the last thing I remember saying.

"Yes," she whispered in my ear.

I wanted to hold her, but I couldn't find the strength to lift my arms. I wanted to make her understand that I'd never meant to hurt her so, but not a word came out. I feared to let her out of my sight, but my eyes succumbed to the weariness that weighed me down and the pressure that had threatened to burst me open floated away.

"Don't ever hurt me like that again," Barby whispered.

I would have promised her had I heard. I would have lied, stolen, or murdered if she had asked me to. The devil be damned if good intentions led to sweet lies and heartache ahead.

CHAPTER TWENTY-SIX

In a matter of days Barby had me nursed back to health, or at least had me feeling good enough to want to be out and about. I think it was as much the company of her and Owen as it was the home remedies she applied, or the bed rest she enforced. My chest felt normal again, and I was simply a weaker version of my usual healthy self.

Billy was staying in the tepee and riding my cattle every day. He was pulling not only bogged cattle that belonged to me, but nearly every brand in the surrounding country. The heel flies were bad, bad that year, and the cattle would head into the creek to dodge their bites. There were other cowboys from the country around working just as hard, but that didn't make the work any easier. Billy would pull one or two out and drive them off from the creek just to return only to often find that more cows bogged while he was gone. It was nasty, hard work, and he'd injured his horse's back pulling them out by his saddle horn. Once I was home, he took a pair of harnessed mules along to drag the bogs out with.

I rode out with him one morning against his insistence that I was still too weak. We only found one lone steer that day stuck up to his belly, and I operated the mules while Billy dug him out a little and put a rope around his middle. He rigged another rope inside the loop where we could pull the noose open and back through the honda after we got him out. Without that second rope we'd have to throw the steer to get the rope off. Sometimes we had to anyway, but it often worked, and a rope around the middle beat breaking the steer's neck pulling on his horns.

The mules sucked the steer up out of the mud, and Billy came sloshing out right behind him. The slip rope worked and the steer trotted off shaking the mud from his back, seemingly no worse for the wear. On the other hand, Billy was covered from head to toe in mud, and looked about give out.

I suggested we stop and eat the lunch Barby had sent with me, and Billy readily agreed to a break. We found a high rock ledge atop a little butte, and laid our vittles out where we could watch the country below us while we ate. After I finished eating, I lay back on the rock, and pushed my hat down over my face to shade my eyes. I must have dozed off for a while, because the next time I looked Billy had moved to the edge of the drop-off, and was sitting with his feet dangling out over space, and his eyes upon the horizon.

"This is one hell of a good country," Billy said to himself, as much as he did to me.

"That it is," I said as I swung my legs off the ledge and took a seat beside him.

"Maybe we should have let the Indians keep it," Billy muttered.

Being a tried and true Texan, Billy was no lover of Indians, so his words surprised me a little. "Hard to run cattle with Comanches on the loose."

"That's a fact, but we ain't going to last here near as long as the Comanche did." Billy dropped a rock and watched it fall and bounce down to the bottom of the hill.

"This is cattle country, and there will always be cowboys here," I said.

Billy shook his head and pointed to the east and then to the west. "Do you know what's out there?"

I waited for him to tell me.

"Look just as far as your eye can see," Billy instructed me, but all I saw was prairie grass rolling in the wind and miles of sky.

"The railroad is just out off the edge of where the world drops off. It's getting closer everyday, and every mile of track they lay shrinks this country down a little more. Soon it won't be such a big piece of country at all," Billy said. I noticed for the first time the sadness in his voice, and the melancholy mood about him.

"That railroad will be the ruin of it all, I guarantee you. The farmers will come in here by the droves hungry for land, and ignorant enough to think they belong here. It'll be the farmers and the railroad that end open range, and not the damned Association."

"A lot of them say that's why they are organizing, so that they can hold on to a big chunk of this before the railroad brings the farmers," I said, just to play the devil's advocate.

"Damn it all!"

"Times are changing. I guess that's the way of things." I was thoroughly convinced of the sad truth of what I said.

"And that's the shame of it," Billy said with a long sigh. "I liked it just the way it was."

"You're still driving herds north."

Billy nodded agreement, but didn't seem

comforted at all by the thought. He stared off at the skyline, and I could tell that in his mind's eye he was following the North Star along trails once passed, and driving herds with friends long since gone to market.

"I went all the way to Fremont's Orchard with that herd." Billy reached a hand to point north to a far place only the map of our minds could see in the distance. "And the Association, and the lawyers, couldn't stop me."

"I wish I'd been with you." I knew that kind of life wasn't to be for me anymore, but I meant what I said just the same.

"I'm going to tell you something that I've never told anybody," he said.

Billy wasn't given to speaking of himself, but something moved him that afternoon — something so powerful that he opened forth the flood gates of his memory and I listened while he talked the sun down from the sky. He told me of his family, and of his life before I'd met him, when Texas had been a damned hard place to live. I listened to every word he said, and I've never heard its like again.

"You came to this country later Nate, but my daddy brought my older brother and me out of Mississippi when I was four. My name was Cavenaugh back then. Daddy had one good horse and a rifle, and he scouted the trail while my brother drove the oxen and I rode the lead steer all the way to the country southeast of Henrietta. He built us a dog-trot house, and we set in to farming crops, and running a few cattle and hogs in the Cross Timbers. My brother was just in his teens when the war broke out, and Daddy told him to stay and watch over me while he went off to fight. We never saw him again, but we heard he was killed at the Battle of Pea Ridge up in Arkansas.

"The Comanche had always been bad in that part of the country, but with most of the men of fighting age gone they got worse. My brother and I slept out in the timber away from the house when the moon was full and the Comanche were raiding. He wanted to join one of the companies of Rangers, but he had me to take care of.

"When I was ten we put in a watermelon patch and made a fine crop. We hitched up our wagon and set out to take a load up to town to see if we could sell them. We had been out of just about everything for a year, and hadn't any hard money to buy what we couldn't make. A bunch of Comanches came upon us on the prairie, and it was a good mile to the nearest timbered bottom.

"My brother had an old rimfire Henry

rifle that Daddy had left with us and he leveled it on the bunch, but was afraid to shoot unless they were close, since we had only one full magazine of ammunition to our names. They scared off for a while, and stayed back out of easy rifle range whooping at us and scaring us silly. We tried to drive on with our oxen, but they raced in and stuck them full of arrows.

"We decided to make for the shelter of the timber, and started in that direction with my brother walking backwards with his rifle leveled the whole way. The Comanches set in on us about two hundred yards from the timber, and both of us were hit with arrows more than once. My brother picked his shots carefully, and every time he squeezed the trigger one of those braves took some lead. He may have been short of full grown, but that long Henry rifle in his hands kept the Comanches from overwhelming us. He was about the bravest man I ever knew, even if he was still a big kid himself."

Billy stopped, and I heard him take a deep breath, and steel himself for the rest of what was to come.

"We made the timber with both of us carrying arrows in our bodies and took shelter behind the first tree we came to. My brother was hard hit and dying, but he laid his rifle up across a limb and dared them to keep coming. They rode off out of shooting range and had them a powwow about how to get hold of us without my brother putting a bullet in their briskets.

"While they were talking my brother died and left me alone just before nightfall. There wasn't a shell left in the Henry, but I kept pointing it at the Comanches as they rode back and forth in the dusk, and they finally gave it up and rode off. I think if they had known it was just me left they would have killed me. I watched our wagon burn in the night, and took off walking for Henrietta, thirty-five miles away.

"Folks at the settlement pulled the arrows out of me and doctored me up some so I could lead them back to the body of my brother. They buried him, but there wasn't much more they could do to help me. A good family took me in as an orphan, and I went with them when they moved back to Fannin County that year. A lot of folks were going back east a bit to get away from the Comanches until the men came home from the War. Within a year there wasn't one family left in that whole settlement."

Billy stopped his story and seemed to study on whether he should go on. You can't speak of the hard things in life without reliving them just a little bit, and maybe more than a little bit. However, Billy seemed bound to finish what he started, and he continued his tale.

"By the time the War ended those people who were looking after me decided to move to Arkansas, and I didn't go with them. A man named Bob Lee came home from the War, and he kind of took me under his wing and his family gave me work. I thought he was just about the finest man I ever saw, and although I was only twelve, I took to wearing a pistol in a sash around my waist and a feather in my hat just like him.

"That part of Texas had too many Unionists before the War, and Reconstruction was damned bad there. The carpetbaggers, Union Leaguers, and homegrown ne'er-do-wells seeking favor with the government thought Bob's family had a little money they could steal, arrested him on trumped charges to blackmail him, and hounded him in about every way they could. Everybody who claimed to be a Unionist with a grudge against the Lees had free rein to do as they pleased. Davis's State Police and Union troops had control of the country, and no ex-Confederate officer like Bob had a leg to stand on with the government.

"Bob and his family were proud, and they took on all comers. They didn't ask for quarter, nor gave any either. Bob hunted his enemies and shot them down where he found them, and he didn't hide the fact. The night riding got so bad in that country that we never stayed home for the Union men to find us, we just slept out in the woods, and folks brought us supplies at arranged places. Many of those foolish enough to sleep at home were called out in the night and shot down on their porches, or hanged. Just being seen talking friendly to Bob and his family was enough to get you killed.

"To be arrested by the state police or the soldiers meant you'd never make it to jail, because they would shoot you down or hang you by the roadside for the womenfolk to see. Bob said I wasn't old enough to fight, but I held the horses on many a night while he and his friends tried to even the score a little.

"The odds were too long against him, and they shot Bob down from ambush while he rode down the trail from home in '69. A lot of his kind stayed a while to fight, but his good name had kept us in favor with much of the public while he was alive. After he was gone it was only a short time before every last man that had fought on Lee's side was either killed or left the country.

"I was known to be a Lee man, but I hadn't killed anybody, and was too young for them to come after me if I stayed out of their sight. There wasn't anything left for me in that country, but Bob had been awful good to me. I reckoned to settle a few of his accounts before I headed for other parts.

"The Comanches had showed me how to use the full moon, and on one such night I made the rounds and paid call to the house of a family that had given Bob hell. I called two men out and shot them down in their yards with my Navy Colt, and I got another down the road apiece, going to his well for water that morning. The law came after me hot and heavy, but by the time they knew what I'd done, I'd thrown away my desperado sash and plumed hat, and was halfway to South Texas on the back of a horse too fast to catch.

"I changed my name, and hired out with a trail herd being put up for a drive to Abilene. I took the name of Billy Champion, because I was young enough to like the sound of it, and the state had put my name on the wanted list. The state police were looking for a boy that didn't exist anymore, and I never looked back, not once. I just kept following trail herds and wearing out horses until I was sure the Law had forgotten about me, and I was another person entirely."

I waited for Billy to continue, but he was silent in the growing dark.

We often assume to know our friends best simply by the fact that they are our friends, and accordingly their souls must be most apparent to our detection. I learned that day how little I knew of my friend. Perhaps you never really know anybody any more than a face, a voice, and a loose sum of jumbled assumptions.

I could tell Billy had lost whatever urge had moved him to talk, but I was too full of questions to leave it alone.

"The Law ain't still wanting you after all this time, are they?"

"I saw my given name a couple of years ago in one of those criminal books the Rangers carry."

"East Texas might as well be in another state. That's been long enough ago that everybody, including the Law, probably forgot about you."

Billy turned to me, and from his voice I knew he was giving me that faint, tolerant smile of the kind normal folks often grant the imbecile.

"Like I said, you're still new to Texas.

We're taught here from birth never to forget a wrong until we get the chance to make things right. The Rangers won't forget a crime, they just ain't found me yet."

We were five miles from home and it was getting time we headed back, but I couldn't bring myself to move if Billy had more to say without me pumping him. He didn't, and after several minutes he rose to his feet to walk to the horses. I followed him and we rode all the way home in silence, and turned the mules and horses loose in the corral.

I started with Billy to the house for supper, but he stopped at the edge of the lamplight spilling weakly out of the windows on the yard. He stood there and stared up at the full moon glowing bright in the sky above.

"I don't know why I told you all that," he said.

I had no answer for him, because I didn't know why he had told me either, except maybe we were still good friends despite loving the same woman.

CHAPTER TWENTY-SEVEN

Times were changing indeed, and I couldn't seem to keep up with the pace. It seemed like no matter how hard I tried, I couldn't get ahead for going backwards. My teamster business was just enough to keep my family fed, and it was going to be a long time before I had enough cattle, if ever, to make my living with them. The interest rates that Caldwell banker was charging me threatened to put me under even before I got started as a cattleman.

I was too long getting over the pneumonia, and missed a lot of business that summer. I had a bank loan to pay off that fall, and didn't have one red cent set aside for it with only two months until it was due. Worry was riding me with the devil's spurs, and if I could have donated the time I spent worrying about money to more constructive thoughts, I could have solved half the world's problems in a matter of days.

To top things off, Barby told me she was pregnant again, and that I could expect another child in late winter.

That was just another big log thrown on the fire burning under me, and I cast my fortunes back on the prairie with my mules before the banker started sending folks by to see if I was going to work. As usual I cast one last glance back at my home before I drove out of view, and wondered if I'd ever make it look like I'd promised Barby it would. Maybe I had some long lost uncle who had died and left me a fortune that I didn't even know about yet. Or maybe it was just going to be one long, hard pull to get where I wanted to go.

Long and I were making a trip together down to the Tule Ranch when we heard a pack of dogs coming our way just north of the Washita. We stopped our wagons and studied the prairie for signs of the bawling animals, or for whatever they were chasing. Before long, six long-legged, grizzled mutts of a kind I'd never seen before came racing out of a canyon at speeds I didn't think a dog capable of. A coyote was running before them, and he was just managing to keep a lead on them.

A rider came loping behind them in the distance, and I soon could tell it was Billy.

He rode up to us just about the time those dogs latched on to that coyote right in front of our wagons.

"Ain't those dogs something?" Billy was all smiles, and I noticed he was already toting a damned big coyote pelt across his saddle swells.

"Those ain't your dogs, are they?" I asked.

"No, they belong to Archie."

I noticed for the first time that Billy was riding a horse with a Rocking Chair brand.

"When did you go to work for them?"

"Not long ago. It ain't a bad outfit."

"Did Andy hire on too?"

Billy looked back the way he'd come. "He's back behind me somewhere. Archie's horse tripped in a prairie dog hole, and Andy stopped to help him."

"I heard some Englishmen had bought that outfit."

"Yeah."

Word had already spread all over the country about the change in operation at the Rocking Chair Ranch. The new owner, or representative of the owners, was a fellow named Archibald. He didn't know a thing about cows and grass, but he ran a loose ship, and didn't get in his hands' way when they went about their work. What's more, he loved to gamble and drink, and thought nothing of his hands doing the same. He was confident that his foreman would see that the books showed a profit, and spent most of his time chasing coyotes with his dogs, or sitting at a poker table in Mobeetie.

"Isn't Archie some kind of royalty?"

Billy just shrugged. "He's all right. He says he's Duke Archibald or something, but the boys all call him Archie."

A duke must have his vassals, retainers, and men-at-arms, so without regard to efficient payroll, Archie traveled with a cavvy of cowboys everywhere he went. It wasn't long before just about every cowboy in the country wanted to work for the Rocking Chair. The pay was no better, but the allotment of fun sure seemed abundant.

A lot of the boys working for Archie were a little on the wild side, and rumors soon sprang up that many, if not all of them, were taking advantage of the loose management of the ranch and rustling cattle. Not just Rocking Chair cattle, but everything they came across. The Mobeetie crowd loved Archie, but a lot of folks were beginning to think that it wouldn't be long before the Association was sending word back to England notifying them to check their books, talk to their man here, and look over their operation in Texas.

I watched the growling pack of dogs wool that coyote around from several directions. It was a vicious game of tug-of-war. An especially big, yellow dog latched on to the varmint's chest and crouched over his victim while looking up at us with proud eyes and a bloody muzzle. His tail was wagging, and I heard bones crunching in his massive jaws. The last breath went out of that coyote in a ragged wheeze. Despite the fact that he was dead, the excited wolfhounds continued pulling at him.

"That yellow dog's a tough one," Billy said.

"I've never seen dogs like those."

"Archie gave a lot of money for that set. That lean, silky-haired red one is a Saluki cross. They're fast as greased lightning, and supposed to be all the way from Egypt."

"It sounds like he's a man that likes his dogs."

Billy lifted the fresh pelt from his saddle. "Look at this. We caught a damned wolf about an hour ago. This big old lobo was too much for the dogs to finish off, and I had to shoot him."

"I ain't seen a wolf in a while."

"That's because somebody is beating you to them. That five-dollar wolf bounty has half the cowboys in the Panhandle ruining good horses chasing wolves."

"I thought all you had to show to claim a bounty was their topknot with the ears on."

"I would have scalped him, but Archie wants to have his hide tanned to hang on his wall."

"I heard you sold your racehorses to some rich sugarcane man from Louisiana." Long was keeping an untrusting eye on the dogs, as if they might jump on him when they were finished with the coyote.

"That fool loved a fast horse even more than I do. He gave me three thousand for War Bonnet alone, and another two for the rest of my racing string."

I knew from Billy's own mouth that the sale of the trail herd he had driven the summer before had netted him a tidy sum, despite the troubles and delays he'd experienced.

"That's a lot of money," Long sighed.

Billy was once again a mere cowboy, albeit one with a gambler's roll of bills big enough to choke a horse stuffed inside his boot top. His name was going to be the toast of many a cowboy bellied up to a bar by that fall.

"What about you, Long? Are you still making whiskey?" Billy rode his horse among the wolfhounds, hoping he could scatter them and retrieve the coyote.

"No, Fawn made me promise to quit selling the stuff over in the Indian Nations."

"That must be hard on your pocket."

Long still ran just the wagons he could operate himself, but he contracted his own loads. He might have been a one-man gang, but he continued to make money hand over fist.

"I've got me a new line of business," Long said.

"Is that so?"

"Long's going to be the biggest farmer in the Creek Nation before too many more years," I said.

"I thought you had to be a tribal member to own land over there."

Long grinned like a wolf himself. "I've got a cousin who married into the tribe and that got him a big chunk of fine farmland. I put up the money for him to plow it in and seed it."

"Sounds like you've been busy," Billy said.

"I also hired me a white lawyer out of Kansas City to act as my front man. He formed me a little company and got me a contract supplying Fort Reno and Fort Sill with corn."

"You old black devil." Billy sounded truly impressed.

"If the white folks knew half of what I'm

doing they'd come string me up."

Billy looked back again for Andy and their employer. There was still no sign of them. The dogs were finally done with the coyote, and he stepped down and grabbed it up by the hind legs. He tied them with a thong and hung the animal on his saddle horn.

"I'd best go find the rest of my bunch."

We all shook hands and watched him ride away with the worn-out dogs following on his heels. The dead coyote bounced against his leg with its tongue hanging out and flopping in time with the horse's stride.

It seemed that while I followed rutted trails to an uncertain fortune, Billy and Long were rapidly outpacing me up the financial ladder. While Billy was chasing coyotes, playing poker, and no doubt adding to his wallet, I just kept chugging along, determined that hard work would see me through. A month before the interest on my note was due I paid a visit home to spend a few days with my family. I tried to let on like all was well, but Barby pried my worries out of me. No black-hooded torturer of the Inquisition ever made easier sport of a man's mind than that woman did with me.

She suggested I borrow the money from Long, as he was our friend, and we could have him paid back by mid-winter if I kept the road hot. Long would have loaned us the money, but he was gone to the Creek Nation delivering his first government contracts, and besides, he was bound to be strapped from the investment in his farming operation, or so I told her. It wasn't right of us to lay our troubles off on him every time he turned around. Ashamed as I am to say it, it bugged me some that a black man was doing far better than I.

My pride was getting in the way of common sense, and I hated for Barby to believe I couldn't provide for us like I should. I quickly regretted having been unskilled enough to let her discover my worries. We had quite a fight about the matter, and I ended up sleeping in the tepee that night.

It took two days for me to settle the matter with her, or at least I thought I did. She had wanted to visit her father in Clarendon for a good while, and I had a load going that way. I would take her with me and leave her to visit there while I worked to make the loan payment. It was going to take a Herculean effort to make enough money by the payment deadline, but I assured her I would get it done. I felt not one bit of the confidence in myself that I showed to her.

Fawn assured us that she would be all

right alone until Long returned, and we packed Barby and Owen for the trip. The two women hugged like departing sisters, and I came to realize just how close they had grown. I knew Barby was worrying about Fawn having to be by herself as we were traveling south.

My troubles left me for the trip to Clarendon, and I enjoyed the camping along the trail with my wife and boy. My son was growing like a weed, and already tottering about on his hind legs and getting into everything he wasn't supposed to. He had his mother's green eyes, and he reminded me of her when he smiled. That child was the light of my life, even if I sometimes looked at him and thought he was going to look just like Billy.

I left Barby and Owen with Mr. Allen, grateful that I had good excuse not to tarry too long. Father and daughter seemed to have patched up any rift our marriage had caused, but he and I still didn't see eye to eye on anything. He promised to send my family by stage to meet me in Mobeetie one month from the day I left them. I headed for that same town to pick up a load of telegraph poles I was to drop off at intervals along a stretch of the government trail north of the stage stop on the Canadian.

My plan was to drop off the last of the poles, and hurry down to a place east along the Canadian within the Cheyenne Reservation where I knew of a stand of unusually big cedar. I would cut a wagon load of posts, and deliver them back to sell to the soldiers at Ft. Elliott in time to meet Barby there as she arrived by stage. With pay from my two freight trips, and money from the sale of the cedar posts the government was buying, I should have enough to pay my loan. As I traveled I tried not to remind myself of the good chance that what I was doing probably wouldn't work.

I made short work of dropping off my telegraph poles, and cut a beeline for the stand of cedar I had located. Neither the Cheyenne nor government troops on patrol caught me cutting reservation trees. It took me two weeks with an axe to do what a man who knew how to use one could have done in one. But by the end of that time I was headed back to Mobeetie with a wagon load of posts to sell and hands covered in bloody blisters. If nothing else, the trip had taught me that a cowboy's hands don't fit an axe handle.

Triumphantly, I made town the night before Barby arrived, and was waiting for her when she stepped down off the stage with Owen on her arm. I hugged both of them and quickly told them of my success. Optimism had taken a hold of me and I splurged on a meal for us at O'Laughlin's that set me back most of the jingling money I had. I didn't think a thing of it, as I had money coming to me as soon as I made my way up to the fort.

Owen was tired from his trip on the stage, and I rented a room for them with what I could scrape from my pocket. While she lay Owen down for a nap, I hitched my team and went up to the fort to sell my posts.

It nearly took the entire U.S. Army to get me out of there.

"We aren't buying pickets or posts anymore." The smug lieutenant walked out under the shaded porch of the quartermaster's building and eyed my loaded wagon.

"You told me a month ago you were."

"That was a month ago." He was a fresh-faced kid, but his dimpled smile gave me the impression he was laughing at me.

"I was counting on you buying posts."

The young officer brushed at a spot of imaginary dust on the shoulder of his uniform blouse while he looked me over from head to toe. I reckon I did look a little seedy. Sweating in a cedar brake in August heat with an axe in my hand had left my clothes not much more than rags, and the brim of my hat had long since lost its snap to the point I had pinned it up out of my eyes with a small stick punched through the felt.

"You've obviously miscalculated. You had no contract with us that I'm aware of, and I would suggest you try to find another buyer." He was plainly unbothered by my predicament.

"You can shove these posts up your ass." I took a step closer to him, the mad coming up in me.

"Mister," he said it like the word wouldn't fit his mouth, "I am sorry for your tough luck. You do look like you could use some help." He held up his hands in gesture that was supposed to make him appear helpless, but the sneer was plain in his voice.

He was standing a little above me, but my arms are long and I reached out and cracked him on the chin. My left followed my right and I caught him again in the temple as he was falling. I hit him hard both times, and my fists struck with the sound of pounded meat. He folded up in a limp pile on the plank porch with his eyes rolled back in his head, and bloody drool running out of the corner of his mouth. I kicked him once in the belly for good measure, and stood over him waiting for him to move again.

The first sergeant came running around the corner of the building. That was back in the day when you had to be able to whip every soldier on the line to make that rank, and from the size of him I knew what I was in for. He was as tall as me, but twice as wide with meat-hook hands and shoulders like a miner. The long points of his waxed, handlebar mustache twitched while he studied his fallen officer.

"Your lieutenant made a little miscalculation and looks like he could use some help." I rolled the unconscious man off the porch with my foot.

The sergeant ducked his bald head like a bull and charged at me with both fists flying. I did manage to land the first lick, but only busted my knuckles on the top of his hard head. His fists struck me in a barrage of blunt pain and splitting skin. I was knocked down three times before I got my back against the wall of the building. One of my eyes was already swelling shut, and I pawed the blood out of the other and watched him come at me. He was moving more slowly, a malicious grin on his face, toying with me before he finished me off. Two other soldiers formed up at his sides, and from the violent pleasure plain on their faces I knew I hadn't even started taking a beating yet. The sergeant loaded up his right hand, and swung a wide one from way back behind him. I should have been able to dodge that one, but it seemed I wasn't up to snuff.

As it was, I have taken far worse poundings. The good thing about there being three of them trying to kick my ribs in was the fact that they got in each other's way. Soon, they were winded and beating on me had lost its sport. The sergeant had them drag me over to my wagon, and they left me there until I could climb up a wheel and pull myself into the seat.

It took me a few minutes to gather my wits, and to regain some sort of dignity — if there is any such thing to be had for bloody losers. Somebody pitched me my hat, and I set it gingerly on my head. I looked back at the porch, where the two privates were propping the lieutenant up on his feet. He was still drooling and slurring nonsense, and a pump knot the size of a hickory nut was already forming above his right eye. He looked my way blankly as they walked him backwards into the doorway.

"Ain't you had enough?" The first sergeant walked halfway back to my wagon and stopped with his fists resting on his hips.

"I reckon we're about even." I chucked to my mules and drove away with a mock salute thrown at the lieutenant.

Thoroughly routed by the Army, I made my way down the road. I stopped at the creek separating the fort from town and bathed the blood from my face and hands. My head was pounding, and I felt like a team of mules had trampled me. Nothing seemed to be broken, but my fingers told me my face wasn't going to be the same for a long while. That was the least of my concerns right then, and I sat by the water's edge trying to find what, if any, options I had to weigh.

I didn't want to face Barby with the news just yet, and I was too stubborn to just give up and quit. I loitered around town for a while trying to figure out what to do, my swollen, battered features drawing curious stares from everyone I passed. Late in the afternoon, I managed to trade the load of posts to the firm of Wright and Rath for the mule I owed them for. They wanted me to deliver them to the fort after I'd signed off on the paperwork. I just smiled like it was the best news I'd ever heard, and then went outside and proceeded to pitch every last one of those posts out on the ground in their wagon yard.

The company man cussing at me as I drove off lifted my spirits a little bit, so I was over my mad some when I found Barby talking to Billy on the porch of O'Laughlin's. I never got over the uneasy feeling that came over me every time Billy was around Barby and Owen, but I was actually glad to see him that day. Maybe I could enlist his help to go lay siege to the fort.

"You look like you woke up in an alley," Billy observed good-naturedly.

I laughed, but it came to me that I did indeed look like hell. Billy was dressed to the nines in the best of cowboy elegance and style, and I began to feel uncomfortable, realizing just how dirty and beaten I was.

"What happened?" Barby rushed to me and probed tenderly at my face.

"Just a little business disagreement." I brushed off her medical attentions, and put one arm around her waist.

"I hope the other fellow looks worse." Billy winced as he made a careful study of my face.

"For the life of me, I can't understand you men." Despite the frown, she sounded more sympathetic than disapproving.

"A bath, a barber, and a trip to the mercantile will have him good as new," Billy said.

Clothes cost money, and I guess Barby read the look on my face, because she immediately knew that something was wrong. "They didn't buy your posts?"

All I could do was nod, because nothing I could say would make the way things were sound any better. I had two little bank drafts for freight deliveries in my pocket, but they didn't amount to anywhere near what we needed. Barby took hold of my hand at her side, and I hated myself for the comfort that it gave me. I hated whatever weakness in me had brought me to this point where I needed consoling. Billy looked the two of us over while we passed silent sorrow between us. Our worries would have been apparent to a blind man.

"I can loan you the money, and you can pay me back when you've got it," he said.

Part of me almost wilted with relief or hugged his neck, but the other part stiffened when I realized that Barby had told him of our tight finances.

"Thanks, but I don't need charity," I said sternly, and sounded to my own ears like an ass.

"It ain't charity. That's what friends are for," Billy said angrily.

"Thanks, but . . ."

"But nothing. You've loaned me money before."

"That didn't ever amount to a dollar or two, or a drink at night's end. If you really want to lend a hand you can ride with me back up to the post and help me whip those soldier boys."

My arm was starting to hurt where Barby's fingers were digging into my flesh. I looked at her, and I knew that I had to ignore my stubborn pride, because I couldn't face the worry in her eyes one more time.

"Take the money," Billy said.

"All right, but I'll pay you back by Christmas for sure." The relief in Barby's face when I said it was plain as day.

"You'll be a cattle baron by then."

"Thanks, I owe you." I shook his hand.

I soon had a hot bath, a spotty shave, and a haircut. I sported a brand-new outfit from my boots to the new beaver hat sitting on my head, and was carrying enough money in my pocket to cover the bank payment plus a little extra, all at Billy's expense. I wasn't fool enough not to know how lucky I was to have a friend like him.

Barby wanted to retire to our room early for the trip home the next day, and she didn't put up any fuss when Billy drug me off for a drink or two before I called it an evening. We had just barely ordered a drink when Billy waved to a gent in the back of the room with muttonchop whiskers and a big pipe dangling from the corner of his mouth. He was playing poker with a full table, and a couple of girls flirted about his head.

I assumed he must be no other than Archie, and Billy led me over and introduced me. Billy was telling him my name when a low growl stopped me in my tracks and I looked down to see I'd almost stepped on the enormous pair of dogs lying at the Englishman's feet. They were rawboned, grizzled animals with long legs and thick, matted coats of shaggy hair. They looked at me with wild, yellow, ancient eyes, and I knew they were killers just the same as I had seen men who struck me as such.

"I see you admire my wolfhounds," Archie said in his most proper English accent. I thought he intentionally sounded a bit stuffy.

"I'm glad I ain't a coyote."

Archie merely grunted and puffed his pipe while he studied his cards. He placed a bet big enough to run everyone out of the hand, and raked his winnings to him.

"Are you a pugilist, Mr. Reynolds? I do so like to exercise with a bit of boxing from time to time."

"Not so you'd notice."

"Are you a sporting man?"

I had already decided I didn't like him, but I shook my head no. He was the kind who asks questions just to hear himself talk.

"Too bad, I find the Texas game a tad boring at times, and I would like to find someone other than Billy who could test my skill."

Apparently Billy was the only one of his employees with enough cash, or enough balls, to not let the pompous SOB buy every pot. Big-stacking working cowboys who made thirty a month didn't make Archie a Doc Holliday or something. I wondered if he had played with any of the pros in town. I decided from his attitude that he had not, or he had and was sore about it.

"Come on, Nate, there are two open seats," Billy suggested.

"I'll just have a drink and watch."

The whiskey burned the cuts in my mouth and on my swollen lips, but hit bottom with a pleasing warmth that I found myself in the mood for. I watched the game long enough to see that despite my observations, the English duke could play a little. Nobody

462

at the table was in either his or Billy's league.

As the night progressed the cowboys slowly left the game to be replaced by a few of Mobeetie's gamblers looking for all the action they could find. I found myself at the bar with a couple of the boys I knew, and passed the time visiting with them and slowly, steadily getting drunker than I had planned.

Several times Billy looked up and asked me to play, but I refused. I wasn't about to play poker on borrowed money, especially with the crowd then sitting at the table. Nobody there was content with small stakes or played for fun. I'd seen my poker skills humbled on more than one occasion long before and knew I didn't measure up.

Billy was on a hot streak, and he was stacking money before him like bricks. I continued to drink, and the more I watched him win, the more I got to thinking about money. The more I thought about money, the more I thought about having to take money from him in front of my wife. By the time Billy was five hundred ahead I was drunk enough to feel sorry for myself, and mean enough to blame him for his good fortune.

They say there aren't any answers to be

found in a bottle, but an idea so easy it made awful sense came clearly to my slurred brain. Vengeance and redemption lay within my reach, and I felt no shame or remorse for what I decided to do. Without a word to Billy I left the saloon, and headed to the livery. I saddled up my good horse Dunny, and rode out of town headed north at a high lope for the Horseshoe Ranch. I had a bottle in my hand and another in my saddlebags to see to it that I didn't falter or fail in what I set out to do.

I woke Bee Hopkins in the middle of the night, and drug him from his bed. He told me I was drunk, and a damned fool to run such a good horse to a lather in the dark. I laughed in his face, and knew he wouldn't refuse the deal I offered.

By late morning I was back in Mobeetie on another lathered horse, except it wasn't Dunny I rode. I staggered up the stairs to my room, and slammed open the door, blind drunk and crazy. Barby leaped from the bed as I stormed into the room, and turned involuntarily half away from me with Owen shielded protectively in her arms.

"It's me, Barby." I waved the wad of bills in my hand before her eyes like a madman.

"Where did you get that?" Her eyes darted to her valise where I'd put Billy's money the evening before.

Before she could search the bag I was across the room and jerked it from her hands and sailed it against the wall.

"We don't need his money," I cried. "I've got a thousand dollars in my hand right here."

"You're drunk." The disgust in her voice was plain, but I was in no shape to feel guilt, only mad satisfaction.

"Maybe, but I've got money."

"Where did you get it?" She already knew with a terrible premonition that I had done something bad.

I sprawled into the chair by the door, and offered her the money once more. Couldn't she see that I had done it for her?

"What have you done, Nathan?"

As drunk as I was, I couldn't bring myself to say it, for to put voice to it was to admit the wrong and to realize how far I'd fallen from the man I thought I was.

"Tell me what you've done." Her voice was like God's wrath torturing me to admit my sin.

"I sold Dunny," I said. "I sold him, and I'm glad I did it."

I held out the money and begged her with the sight of it to ignore how I had spited my friend and tried to buy her love. I woke up that evening alone with the money still clutched in my wretched, jealous hand.

CHAPTER TWENTY-EIGHT

Even the long cold winter that followed wasn't enough punishment to absolve me of my guilt and torment. As one blizzard after another swept down upon the high plains the bitterness inside me refused to leave, and instead seemed frozen inside of me, branded there by the searing bite of the Arctic wind cutting everyday with its ice-bladed knife at my imperfect heart. Each day that I walked down to the corrals and saw my good horse gone I promised myself to be a better man, but the simple sanity of such good intentions eluded me, and I felt not one bit different.

I told myself a thousand times I must be crazy, and cursed myself for the weakness that would eventually drive my family from me. My jealousy had caused a festering sore between Barby and I, and my petty, spiteful actions would pick at it until she could bear me no more. You would think that a man so blessed with a beautiful wife and child as I was would be at ease with the turning of earth, but I seemed determined to destroy what I held so dear. If life has taught me anything, it's that the entire human race is as crazy as a shithouse rat, and only through denial and false pretense does it appear otherwise. A little bit of Nero prances madly in the heart of us all, ready to burn down Rome at the drop of a hat.

Hidden from the cold behind the icy collar of my buffalo coat, I rode the frozen prairie daily, wondering if it was Billy that my wife loved and ashamed of such thinking. I followed the long drift of the cattle southward, in a vain attempt to see that my meager herd survived the brutal cold. While my family hugged close to the warm hearth of the home fire, I ventured out to ride alone upon the windswept expanses, with emergency as my excuse.

My travels became aimless, and I stayed out days between the end of one storm and the threat of another. The cold, hard lump of my saddle served as a stone pillow for my head, but my sleep in the cold wilderness failed to bring about anything but tortured feet and fingers. On the brink of the coming snow, I rode up to the Association drift fence on the Canadian, half snow blind, and with a wolf hunger gnawing at my guts.

The last snow was drifted high in places along the fence, and cattle lowed sadly along its expanse for as far as the eye could see. The norther starting to blow had more of their kind marching southward, instinct and their dumb, bovine brains driving them with the wind to die a frozen death against Association wire. I could already picture them piled high, bloated and frozen inside snowdrifts they could not escape.

Visibility was slowly getting worse as the wind whipped up snow on the ground to mix with the fresh snowflakes starting to fall from the sky, and I could just make out the forms of a group of riders headed my way. I could tell by the way they sat their saddles that they had been out in the elements as long as I. They came on with chins tucked down inside their coats, and their horses carrying their heads slanted away from the bite of the crosswind, backs humped against the cold and the prod of their riders' insistent spurs.

It was a hard group of men who faced me with weary, sunken eyes measuring the world with no nonsense at all. The clench of their haggard, unshaven jaws was made harder by the cold. There were five of them, and three of them rode Rocking Chair horses. Billy and Andy were among them, and I thought it strange that they should be north of the fence when their range lay south of the river.

It was the first time I'd faced Billy since I'd sold Dunny, and I uneasily sought to decipher if he knew what I had done. If he knew, he didn't show it, or bring the matter up.

"Are you ready to cut wire?" Billy asked, his voice brittle and smoky as a gust chilled his teeth to the quick.

"I am."

I had no tools upon my person, except a rope and my two strong hands, but they came ready with gear more suited to the work. As we rode to a place in the fence they'd chosen, my study of their obvious preparation was enough for Billy to understand the question I was fixing to ask.

"The Association has ordered riders out to keep anybody from cutting their fence and letting the drift through, but only a few old diehards are going to weather this storm when they could be sitting in a bunkhouse tending the fire." His voice carried to me on the downwind side.

"Rocking Chair cattle don't travel against the wind, but a few good men in the north

470

have offered a bounty should any man be brave enough to cut this fence," he added. Money was just added incentive to do what Billy probably would have done anyway, had he come upon the fence that day.

"Why don't they do it themselves?"

"One of them and two of his hands tried a week ago west of here, and got turned back at the point of a fence patrol's guns."

"They'll have to shoot me if they catch me, because I ain't watching my cattle die against that fence," I promised.

"Let's set things right." Billy pitched a loop upon a fencepost.

The fence creaked sharply as chilled metal and wood succumbed to the pull, and a long section of barbwire fell to the ground. While others cut wire with axes and pliers, I slapped my stiff rope against my leg to beat some life into it. With my saddle horn and my horse's strong back, I merrily joined the destruction. By the time the sure-enough blizzard was upon us we had a mile of fence torn down, and were scattered out to the north funneling the drifting cattle into the hole we'd made.

Maddened by our success, we split up in two groups, to open up other sections of fence before the blizzard drove us to shelter. I rode east with Billy and Andy, thinking that most of my cattle would hit the fence in that direction. We worked with the industry of Satan's minions, slaving gleefully in forges of hellfire, impervious to the growing onslaught of bad weather enfolding us in blowing white. By the time we finished our third hole, I could barely see Andy standing twenty feet from me.

"Let them eat the breaks of the river clean, the Association be damned," Andy cheered in the storm. We watched the cattle already pouring through, and knew that if the weather continued the drift might come from as far as Nebraska by winter's end.

I tried to tell him we had better find shelter, but my voice wouldn't carry to him. Billy rode to us, and motioned for us to mount up and go. We followed him nose to tail, sure that he had an idea where to go to keep us from freezing to death. The rush of adrenaline I'd felt earlier had left, and I feared we'd be lost in the snow, blind as if we walked on the pitch-black side of the moon.

We'd drug some sections of fence entirely away, while others we had just pulled down to let the cattle walk over. Billy led us through one of those openings we'd just managed to lay over, and the metallic screech of wire rent the air. Billy's horse viciously kicked out a hind foot snagged in the wire, and lunged his entire weight wildly against the end of it. I was sure I saw the horse go down to the ground, but my own horse was shying under me at the excitement. Billy and his horse were just madly pirouetting shapes seen dimly through the storm.

The wire was jumping and jerking with a life of its own, and I knew Billy was down and his horse still entangled in the wire. I fought my frightened mount through the threatening maze of barbs to find Billy pinned down under his thrashing, crazed horse. The animal jerked madly, each jerk burying the wire deeper into his flesh, and the pain and fear making him fight the pull that much harder.

Before I could take any action wire snapped and gave, and Billy's horse lunged to its feet in a run with Billy dragging the ground wildly, one boot hung in the stirrup. I put the spurs to my horse, and he flew along on the wind in the wake of Billy's bouncing form that threatened to disappear before me.

I managed to get beside Billy's runaway horse, but I couldn't get to my pistol fast enough for I'd belted my heavy buffalo coat tight to keep out the wind. Seconds mattered dearly as my friend was drug over the rough terrain. Before a rock smashed his head, or a wild hoof stomped the life from him I leaped from my saddle upon his horse's neck.

My hands latched on to the bridle, and I fought to keep my legs from under the churn of the running bronc's legs. It was all I could do to hang on, and my efforts to stop the horse only seemed to make him run faster. With one hand over the far side of the horse's neck and holding the bridle cheek piece, I risked falling away by reaching to grab the shank of his bit on the near side with my other hand. A strong pull wasn't enough and I tugged with all my might, succeeding in jerking the crazed animal's head around, and sending us crashing end over end to the ground.

The rolling horse was just a blur to me, and the crushing weight that loomed over me for an instant somehow avoided my body. I scrambled on hands and knees to press myself across the horse's head and neck in a frantic attempt to pin him down. The fall must have broken his neck, because he died under me with a deep groan from his massive lungs and one last violent shudder. I looked around furiously for Billy, but found only his empty boot lodged against the top of his stirrup.

Billy's body was a lump in the snow that I crashed over as I ran blindly back along the way we came. I don't think I could have found him in a million years if I hadn't stepped right on him. I feared the worst, but he stirred under me as I righted myself.

"Are you hurt bad?" I asked.

He groaned and muttered something I couldn't make out, and I knew there was no way that he had avoided at least some broken bones. I didn't know the country well enough to get him to help, and my horse was surely still traveling fast in the direction he was going when I left him.

There are such things as miracles, and Billy shoved off my hands and sat up by his own power.

"I'm just skinned up some," he growled.

Andy couldn't find his butt with both hands in the dark, but he rode a hundred yards in a blinding blizzard right to where we were.

"Can you ride?" I asked Billy.

"I'm all right. My leg's a little stiff, but I think nothing's broke."

Andy dismounted, and despite Billy's protests we shoved him in the saddle. I motioned for Andy to climb up behind him.

"Is your mind steady enough to remember

where you were taking us?" I pressed my head close to Billy's thigh in order that he could hear me.

He merely nodded and kicked the horse forward while I grabbed hold of the passing tail and drug along wearily behind. I don't know how long we traveled, because I was so cold and tired that minutes may have seemed like hours. I badly wanted to live, and I was filled with the simple inspiration to keep my hand wrapped in that horse's tail, even if it meant getting drug when I stumbled.

We started over the lip of a steep grade, and I braced myself against the horse's hindquarters. Blind to my surroundings I thought I felt the ground leveling out, and in that moment I fell and I lost my grip on the only thing keeping me from certain death. My hands grasped wildly ahead of me for the feel of horsehair, but found only the cold, hard ground and snow between my fingers. I braced one knee under me and surged up with the last energy remaining in my cold-weary body. My shoulder smashed against something hard, and a hand slapped my face. Dumb and cold I stared at the face before me, and after a long study recognized that it was Billy shouting at me.

I couldn't understand what he was saying,

but I took hold of him and followed where he led. It seemed we only took a dozen steps and I was lying on the floor of a dugout and Billy was fighting the wind to get the door closed.

Long after Andy had a fire going I lay on the floor, wanting nothing more than the comfort of a long, deep sleep. The hard toe of Andy's boot in my ribs moved me to the fire, and the three of us warmed our shivering bodies before the flames. We were all too cold to speak, and we suffered silently as warmth and life flooded back into our flesh.

Unsure how long we would be trapped, we fed the fire stingily and huddled close to its feeble warmth. The storm lasted the night and into the next morning, and our fire started with a pack rat's nest soon ate up the wood of what little broken-down furnishings the dugout possessed. When the wind no longer howled and hissed over the dugout, Andy rose and looked out the door at the frigid aftermath that was the new morning. From where I sat at the fire I could see between Andy's knees the frozen corpse of his horse lying just outside the door.

The thought of how close a blizzard had come to finishing me off yet again left me without words, and I brooded while Billy and Andy stood at the door and discussed our options for removal. I was thinking of my family miles to the north, and wondering if they too stared into a fire, when Billy sat back down beside me.

"There's no snow falling, and the wind has just about quit," he said.

I felt no relief at the news, and in fact I felt nothing at all, being numb of both body and spirit.

"You saved my life back there," he said plainly. "I thought I was a goner for sure."

"You'd have done the same for me."

"Uh-huh, but I thank you just the same."

"That's what friends are for." And as soon as I said it I knew it was true.

I looked at Billy and knew he was about the best friend I'd ever have, and at the same time I came to the realization that I had to take Barby away from the country where he lived if I were to ever know any peace.

"I won't forget," Billy swore.

And neither could I, no matter how hard I tried.

CHAPTER TWENTY-NINE

My second son was born that winter, and we named him Samuel Houston Reynolds, a fine Texas name if ever there was one. To all appearances he seemed a healthy baby boy, but by the time he was two weeks old a fever and a cough racked his little body. With his condition rapidly worsening, we raced him to Mobeetie in the middle of the night. The doctor there helped us save him, but he was as weak and fragile as fall leaves before the wind.

We were too afraid to get far from the doctor, and I rented us a little house above the Sweetwater for the time being. The child's convalescence drug out longer than I had planned, and spring came with little improvement in his lungs. The winter had cost me too many cattle, and the hot, dry summer that followed just about finished off my hopes of building a herd. I had never liked bouncing along on the seat of a freight wagon cussing at a team of mules for my living. The fear of returning home from one of my long trips to find Samuel dead kept me home so long that we were soon scraping the bottom of the money barrel.

I was loafing in the Pink Pussycat Saloon when a chance at a new occupation called on me. Cap Arrington walked up to me and plainly and simply asked me to go to work as his deputy, for no other reason than he thought I'd performed well in our apprehension of those two bandits a couple of years before. I had always scoffed at the law, but the thought at least merited consideration.

I guess I drove a hard bargain, because he offered me sixty dollars a month, half to be paid by the Association, and 5 percent of his cut of fees, fines, etc. I'd never wanted to be a lawman, but to me, anything beat hauling freight. Cap had to say no more to get his man, and I was ready to start my new profession.

Like me, Cap may have been receiving bonus pay from the Association, but I found him a fair man, even if a little bullheaded in his sense of justice. I didn't consider myself a tough man, and was content to follow his lead and learn the trade. Despite Barby's worries, I didn't get shot those first couple of months, and in fact, did nothing much that could be considered dangerous.

Most of the time Cap seemed content to keep me as his presence around Mobeetie while he rode the countryside sniffing out cattle rustlers, and horse thieves. Other than lending the city marshal a hand in quieting some drunk, I stood little chance of being shot except on those occasions when Cap got a lead on the whereabouts of some wanted man, and called me out to help in the chase. Most of those leads didn't pan out, and my education into handling desperados was slow to say the least.

Along about August, Cap got me out of bed in the middle of the night. I followed him out a ways into the sand hills in my bare feet and drawers, and found a posse holding horses in the dark.

"How long since you've seen Billy?" Cap asked me, and I could tell he wasn't sure if I'd tell him or not.

"I haven't seen him in more than a month. Archie's crew has been around, but Billy hasn't made the rounds here for a while."

I knew Cap would eventually get around to telling me whatever was on his mind; it was just a matter of patient waiting.

"Do you know he killed Colonel Andrews a week ago over in Tascosa?"

I merely nodded that I knew, and let it go at that. The cowboy rumor express was faster than the telegraph at times, and I'd gotten the details secondhand not three days after it had happened.

"You don't want him for that, do you?" I asked.

"No. The officials over that way ruled it self-defense, and I daresay I envy Billy some. I would have liked to have caught that man myself."

I saw more justice in Billy putting a bullet in the gambler than I did in Cap catching him for the courts. The regular law had come to the Panhandle, and Cap couldn't get away with hanging bandits on a whim anymore.

"The grand jury down at Clarendon has indicted Billy and your other friend Andy on charges of cattle theft," Cap said.

"Billy's no rustler."

"We've got word from a stock detective that he is," Cap tossed back at me.

"What detective?"

"Dale Martin."

"Hell, that schoolteacher is the worst stock thief in the entire country, and everybody knows it."

"I guess he reformed. The Association puts a lot of faith in his work." Cap sounded like he knew how little confidence I had in the Association.

"I'll agree that he's caught a few rustlers, but that was probably just to cover up his own thieving."

"You don't have to come with us. In fact it would probably be best if you didn't," Cap offered.

I weighed my options cautiously, and found no easy answers. On one hand I knew Billy wouldn't take this lightly, and wanted to be around to see that he didn't get himself shot by the posse. On the other hand I didn't know if I could bring myself to ride with a party willing to arrest Billy on false charges.

"Best thing you can do is just send word for Billy to come turn himself in. Give him time to get over the urge to fight, and he'll show up soon enough to call us all liars."

Cap shook his head in disagreement. "No, I've got an idea where he and Andy are, and I'm going to have them in Clarendon for the coming session of court in Donley County."

"I don't blame you if you fire me, but I won't have any part of this."

Cap seemed to have the answer he expected, and mounted his horse to go.

"I figured you wouldn't go, and I can't

say as I don't respect you for it. I just hope he's worth your trouble."

"I know him better than most."

He started to ride off with his men, but stopped his horse broadside to me, and paused to ponder what he was about to say. "I know more than enough to judge that I might have to shoot him to bring him in."

"He won't fight you if you give him time to think it over."

"Like I said, I know him better than you think."

Something about his tone of voice made me believe him, and a cold shiver of premonition ran down my spine.

"I trust I know you well enough that you won't try and warn him," he said as he rode off into the night.

I walked back to the house with a bad feeling in my bones. Billy was hell on wheels with a pistol in his hand and his color up, but Cap didn't take any chances. If he wanted you he would wait in ambush with leveled rifles, and if you decided to make a fight of it you would end up riding home tied belly down on your saddle.

The word was Billy was drinking more than usual, and folks said once he got word of Colonel Andrew's presence in Tascosa, he hunted him down like a mangy coyote. I knew that the whiskey had nothing to do with it. When Billy found the colonel in the street, he put a bullet in him because he aimed to set things right. I saw nothing but justice in his action, and liked to think I would do the same to a man who'd stolen from me if I had the chance. No matter how hard I tried to convince myself of the fact that Billy was no different from me, I knew better.

Billy was a bad man to tangle with, but not a bad man in the usual sense of the word. Maybe we of that time just gave that distinction to some men in the way of taking up for our friends. I thought Billy was a good man for the most part, but I knew that he had a streak of something that separated him from most of his fellow men. Those like me might talk tough, but it was easy for us to hesitate when it came time to pull the trigger. Billy's kind never hesitated, and were marked as deep as branded Cain with a willingness to do violence. They have a well-defined limit to the amount of insult they will bear, and are weighed down by no more conscience for their antagonists than a rattler when it strikes.

Cap Arrington and his posse beat the sagebrush for a week in search of Billy and

Andy, but didn't get so much as a whiff of their scent. One fine, bright Sunday morning at the end of that same week I was walking with Barby and the children upon the sandy path to church. I should have been shocked when I spotted no other than Billy himself enter the Lady Gay saloon, but on the other hand, I should have expected no less audacity from the man. Barby had seen him too, and I felt her hold on my arm tighten. I knew she wanted me to pretend I had seen no such thing as passed before our eyes.

Before I'd taken two more steps, I saw another thing that concerned me even more. Cap Arrington's gray horse was tethered in front of the courthouse, standing alongside several others that I was sure belonged to the rest of the posse. In my mind there was but one thing to do before Cap got wind that Billy was in town. I made Barby promise me she would take the kids on to church while I went to talk to Billy.

"Be careful, Nathan. He's a proud man." She clung to me, not wanting to let go.

"I know something about foolish pride." I kissed her and gently sent her on her way.

I just made it to the front door of the saloon when Cap and three men toting rifles started down the steps of the courthouse. I stopped just long enough to make sure they were headed my way, and then ducked inside. Billy was standing at the far end of the bar, and he smiled thinly at the badge pinned to my shirt.

The length of the room was between us, and out of the corner of my eye I saw Andy sitting at a corner table with a Winchester hidden in his lap. Nothing much usually bothered Andy, but it was obvious he was fretting. I would have been nervous too had I been in his shoes with Billy calling the play.

"Never thought I'd see you wearing a badge," Billy bantered as easily as if he were swapping lies on a spit-and-whittle bench.

"Cap's coming, and he's got three guns to back him." I had no time for small talk, and felt fate gave me little time to maneuver.

"I see him coming." He gazed out over my shoulder and through the saloon's front window.

"Turn yourself in, and we'll prove it all a lie." I tried to sound as level and calm as I wanted to appear.

"I'm more of a mind to show them that I'm tired of being picked at."

"Arrington's got you outnumbered."

"How do you figure in the count?" Billy stepped by me to the door.

"I won't let them shoot you down, if I can help it." I followed him across the room.

Andy rose and slipped along the wall to take a stand at the window just out of sight from the street. He was wiping sweaty hands on his shirt front, and his bottom lip was clenched in his teeth. I knew Andy, and no matter how scared he was, he would follow Billy straight to hell, and do his part in the clutch. He was nothing if not reckless, and that is always a thing to be reckoned with.

Billy was standing just to the side of the open door watching Arrington make his way down the street. Billy noticed just like I did that two of the posse had disappeared, and he cast a quick look over his shoulder at the back entrance to the room.

"Where do you stand, Nate? It's time to pay the fiddler." Billy's eyes gave me no room to waiver. "Throw down that badge, and we'll give old Cap a dose of humility."

He knew without me answering that I wasn't going to stand with him, and he turned his back on me to watch the street once more.

"You'd better get home to your wife. It's fixing to get touchy here," Billy said as he slipped his pistol from his holster.

In Billy's mind he'd dismissed my presence, and his thoughts turned solely to the task at hand. I could see Cap and the deputy only twenty yards away and coming nearer. Watching Billy with his pistol hanging at the end of his arm, I knew that it was only seconds before he stepped into the doorway and opened up on the lawmen who thought they had him treed.

My gun came to my hand and I took two quick steps toward the door just as Billy turned halfway around to face me. The impact of my pistol barrel against his head shocked me to my elbow, and Billy folded up on the floor, slobbering and squirming in semi-conscious pain. I whirled to face Andy, who stood with rifle leveled on my guts and a wild, shocked look on his face.

"They would have killed him," I said loudly to him.

For a moment I wasn't sure if Andy was going to shoot me or not, and tried everything I could to talk him down.

"Drop your rifle, and we can beat this thing in court."

"He was your friend, Tennessee." There was as much confusion as there was anger in his voice.

"That's why I did it."

My pistol felt slick in my sweaty palm, and I wondered if Andy was the joker in the deck I hadn't taken account of. I sighed with a gush of relief when he laid his Winchester upon a table and slumped limply into a nearby chair.

"You better not have killed him," he threatened.

Looking down at Billy groaning on the floor, I had no doubts his wound was too far from his heart to kill him. I kicked his pistol across the room and stepped to meet Cap just outside the door.

"They've both surrendered, Cap." I stood over Billy with my gun.

Cap's pale blue eyes studied Billy lying in the doorway. "He ain't going to forgive you for that."

He didn't have to tell me the ramifications of what I'd done. I knew that from watching Billy's face as he managed, despite his throbbing head, to stand and prop himself against the doorjamb. The look he gave me was as simple as it was murderous, and had he a gun then he would have tried to kill me. His eyes left me and locked on to something across the street. There stood Barby holding Samuel in her arms, with Owen staring big-eyed from behind her skirt. Billy cussed under his breath, and I knew that even if I'd had a chance of his accepting the buffaloing I'd given him, he'd never forgive me for Barby and the kids seeing him that way.

I studied Barby where she stood and tried to interpret the look she was giving me for what it actually was. Maybe her perspective of the matter was closer to the truth, because I had no faith in my ability to find my way through the tangled mess that fate had woven for all of us.

"That's all right, Cap. I don't sleep easy anyway." And that was the bitter truth.

CHAPTER THIRTY

Neither Billy nor Andy ever threatened me while in jail or on the long ride to Clarendon, but neither acknowledged my presence with so much as a single word. I rode silent sentinel on the edges of their escort, shunned by the men who had once been my good friends. Once or twice I caught Billy looking at me, and his stare was a cold, hard thing. I cursed him for a pigheaded fool who couldn't tell friend from foe.

We arrived in Clarendon to find that a mob of the rough element from Tascosa and Mobeetie had beaten us to town. They were burning effigies of the county officials, and threatening to tear the town down around our ears. There was a bit of high tension until Goodnight showed up with a crew of his cowboys just in the nick of time. They parked a wagon full of rifles along the main street, and stood around the entire day within handy reach of them while the rustlers, pimps, and murderers decided how far they were willing to take things toward a fight.

That bunch wasn't there so much to rescue fellow criminals as they were to have one last go at stopping the law from coming into the Panhandle. If law and order were allowed to take a hold, their merry refuge far from legal constraints would be no more. I was proud that Billy showed no pleasure in the presence of that crowd, although he knew many of them just as well as I did.

We had just enough firepower that the toughs kept their peace, and a jury was convened to hear what was scheduled on the docket. My belief that Billy's case would be quickly dismissed was ill-founded, and the jury ruled him and Andy guilty of a list of charges a country mile long. The evidence against them was strong on hearsay and weak on evidence, but the jury and prosecutor didn't seem to care. In fact, that was why they stamped them guilty for so many things. The common belief of those gathered to watch the trial was that any decent lawyer could beat the charges, but Billy and Andy would be in and out of court for five years in the process.

I thought Billy would tell the entire court what he thought about them, but he never even said anything other than to quietly answer the questions asked of him as he took his turn on the stand. He denied everything they accused him of, but he might as well have been yelling into a well for all the good it did him. It looked as if Billy and Andy were bound for a long stay in jail, or high bond, and years of lawyer fees. There was no denying that I had brought them to that point.

Through legal shenanigans that only lawyers can understand, a deal was negotiated whereby Billy and Andy agreed to leave Texas if the state would drop all charges. It was a bitter pill to swallow, but they had no other options with so much set against them. Sometime during the night they rode off bound for parts elsewhere, and the court said hallelujahs that justice held sway in the Panhandle.

The next morning I handed Cap my badge, and told him I was done with enforcing the law. He knew that I wasn't cut out for it anyhow, and he gave me no argument as I went upon my way. I stopped in Mobeetie long enough to hitch my team of mules to the wagon, and load up the wife and kids. We made our way to the home place and settled back into life away from town, and badges, and crooked courts.

Despite drought, blizzard, and uncertain market, I talked Long into partnering with me. We bought out a rancher I knew who wanted to recoup a little of the fortune he had lost. We made the deal at a bargain price with a market panic going on, and though the few brands on his books didn't amount to much in numbers, I felt once again on my way to building the ranch I'd hoped for.

We had another addition to the family when Fawn gave Long a pretty baby daughter, and at about the same time Barby informed me that she was pregnant again. With the population of our little settlement booming I couldn't help but wonder what the country would be like by the time all of our children were grown.

I helped Long put in a quarter section of wheat along the creek, although I couldn't see myself farming no matter how Long preached about the future in it. I was content to work our cattle, or build improvements on the ranch. Between the toil and labor I found time to spend with my family in those little moments that don't seem to matter much while they're happening. On hot summer days at dinnertime we would often take a picnic on the banks of the creek, where I swam under the hot sun with

Owen riding on my back while Barby watched with happy eyes.

Sometimes in the evenings, after Barby had read or sung the kids to sleep, we would walk out across the prairie under the night sky, hand in hand like two young sweethearts. I came to know beyond all doubts that she loved me, and if possible I loved her more.

Those were good times, and to all intent and purpose, I looked as if I'd found peace away from the worries of the world. But in the back of my mind was the constant certainty that Billy would come calling one day when I least expected it. More than one person had heard him threaten to kill me in the year since the trial. When a strange sound startled me in the dark, I couldn't help it that my heart jumped beat and my hand reached for the pistol that I made sure never to be without.

I never told my concerns to Barby, and if she came to the same conclusion on her own, she never let it show. If maybe she hugged me a little tighter, or kissed me a little longer when I left for a trip, I accepted it as a sign of how much she loved me, and let it go at that.

And when on that day I saw Cap Arrington loping his horse to me across the plains, I knew just about what he had come to tell me when he was still a mile away. He took his sweet time crossing the creek, cutting for sign along the sandy banks and scanning the area carefully. He made his way up to the corner of the corral, where I was forking hay to my horses. From the sweat and dust caked on his tired mount, I took it that he had come a long ways to see me, and fast.

"Are you craving some of Barby's biscuits, or did you just miss me?" I jabbed my pitchfork into the hay pile and leaned against the top rail of the fence.

"No, I've come on another matter altogether." It was plain to see he was in no mood for small talk. In fact, he looked plumb wary.

"Get down and visit awhile."

"No thanks." He continued surveying my homestead, starting close to the house and working his gaze all the way to the horizon.

"Did you come all the way from Mobeetie just to sit your horse in my yard?"

"I don't suppose you've seen Billy, have you?"

"No." I suspected he already knew the answer to that before he asked.

"Well, he ain't in New Mexico like everybody says."

"You can't believe half of what you hear."

"I rode into Mobeetie yesterday evening and he had just left there."

"You think he's headed here?"

"That's the rumor."

"I don't need you playing nursemaid to me."

Cap grunted once in disagreement and chewed at his mustache. "There's some that say it was Billy that shot up that track-laying crew's locomotive east of Oneida last week."

"Where the hell is Oneida?"

"Little spot down on Wild Horse Lake that the land promoters have staked out. The LX cowboys got talked into voting it the Potter County seat, and those promoters say it's going to be a boom town." Cap scowled as if he didn't believe such talk was anything more than snake oil salesmen pitching foolishness. "A man told me that there's already half a hundred people there. He said the tracks are still a week away and they're already thinking about changing the name to Amarillo before it's even a town proper."

"Well, Billy never did like the thought of railroads coming here, nor farmers either, but I doubt he'd shoot up a train, even if he was on a little Saturday night spree," I said.

Cap paused just long enough to give the

country around him another careful look. "There are also those that say it was him that ran off with some of the Bar CC's horses last winter."

"The Stock Association outlawed him, and that gives every gossip that wants to an excuse to lay every head of stolen Association stock off on him."

"You don't believe it?"

"He ain't the rustling kind."

"But he's got it out for the Association, doesn't he?"

"I wouldn't put it past him, pestering them a bit."

"I've got some other bad news." Cap's face didn't change expression, but he was the kind that could tell somebody he was going to hang them in the same voice he asked about the weather.

"Oh?"

"Andy was killed a little over a week ago. Some promoter hauled in an outlaw horse to Dodge, and offered a fifty-dollar bounty to anybody who could ride him." Cap shifted his weight in his saddle and rubbed at his achy hipbones with both palms. "They say the damned thing reared up and fell over on him."

I watched the wind roll the dust across the yard while I thought of Andy trying to ride a bad horse on a whim. He always claimed he could ride anything with hair, and I knew without being told he'd been laughing when he'd climbed into the saddle one last time. The world had become a little tamer when all the mad, vibrant life of him rushed out from his lungs, crushed between horse and ground. I missed him already.

"A man never knows when his time is near."

Cap raised one bushy eyebrow at me. "I've felt Old Death circling around me a time or two."

"You'd best get down. It's just about time for supper."

"No, I'll be riding on. It's a long ride back to Mobeetie."

"Why are you so bound and determined to catch Billy?"

Cap seemed to give that some thought for a spell. "I guess you could say he bothers me."

When Cap rode away that evening, I watched until he was out of sight, and then saddled a horse and took down my Winchester from its pegs above our door. Owen was playing in the middle of the room, with little Samuel studying his every move. I rough-housed around with them for a bit, and told them to mind their mama while I was gone.

And maybe I risked a little lie when I hugged Barby and asked her to keep my supper warm.

No silly premonition or casting of the bones led me down to wait for Billy at the creek crossing below the house. I knew he was coming for me just as plain as I could tell when a rain was brewing by watching black clouds building overhead. I felt no sense of doom, but I dreaded what I was sure would come.

I was sitting on a cottonwood log when he rode into view just at dusk. As he wound his way down the slope to the crossing I saw he wasn't alone. I couldn't make out the other rider in the failing light, and my hand slipped back the hammer of my gun. Two against one didn't seem to me the way Billy would want it, but no matter, I was determined to beat the odds.

My plan was to stop him on the far side of the crossing, and with the creek between us we could say what needed said and settle what was between us. I was no match for him with a pistol, and a rifle fight in the growing dark was as good as I was likely to get. While I waited I tried to determine just how things ended up like they were, and I had come to no satisfactory conclusion when Billy rode down to the edge of the water and stopped.

"Is that you, Nate?" he asked of the night.

Out of the dark shade of the cottonwoods I stepped to the edge of the creek bank, where the moonlight lit the water, and I cast a long shadow on its sheen. I stared across that universe of stars floating there at the vague shadow of Billy that could have been my twin for all appearances of the night. The other rider with him stopped back in the brush, and I studied hard to see him there. The dull stomp of his horse's hooves, and a hint of shadowed movement in the dark told me where he was.

Maybe whoever it was would sit this one out, and leave it as should be, between just us two friends.

"Hello, Billy."

"I've come a long way to see you," he said, and I didn't doubt that he had.

His horse bobbed its head down for a drink and my tight-strung nerves had me too much on edge. My rifle sprang to my shoulder at the quick movement, and I tensed myself for the bullet I was sure he had already sent on its way. I stared down the long glint of my worn rifle barrel willing myself to hold steady, and knowing that I had already hesitated perhaps longer than I should have. Billy seemed as still as death, and I held on to the faint hope he would just ride away and leave things as they were.

"Hold up there," a voice shouted from the night, and I knew it was Cap Arrington calling out from ambush.

Billy's pistol flamed and cracked twice followed by the dull boom of a shotgun from somewhere down the creek. I watched as he reeled in the saddle, and then another round of buckshot knocked him to the ground. His horse charged over the crossing and passed so close by me that his shoulder brushed against me in the dark. I could feel the wild, hot sweat of him on my arm while I stared across the water at Billy lying there.

I waded the shallows to where he lay in the sand, already certain I would find him dead. He was on his back with both eyes open to the sky above and one hand upon his riddled chest. There was no sign of what force had left him lying peaceful there, for blood is not even so much as a shadow in the dark. I studied him there in his silent repose, and I knew he had nothing left to say to me forever and ever anymore.

Cap came walking cautiously out of the dark with his shotgun leveled in his hands. I thought for a moment to shoot him down, but the urge was as short-lived as it was strong. I turned away from him and studied the place where I thought Billy's ally waited, and I was not quite sure that the night had seen all of its malicious intentions born out. What possessed me to do what I did I'll never know, but I walked toward what my eyes told me could be an enemy waiting in the brush with my gun hanging useless at my side.

When I neared to within no more than a few feet from the horse I could now make out standing there, I recognized an old friend. I wrapped my arms around Dunny's head, and pressed his face against my chest.

"I can't figure why he let go that extra horse, unless he was going to swap to a fresh one to run out of the country," Cap said behind me.

I laughed short and bitter, and led Dunny back down to him. If Billy had killed me he wouldn't have gone anywhere once it was done. Cap couldn't know that, but he was wrong just the same. He might be able to track an outlaw across the hardest rock, but he had no feel for the signs left by human nature, and the awful tricks it played upon us all.

"I'll go get my horse across the creek, and we'll take him up to the house," I said.

We placed Billy across my saddle, and I didn't wait for Cap to retrieve his own mount before I headed for the house. I had no sooner started back when Long rose from the trail before me with his old double barrel resting across his shoulder.

"I'm sorry I got here too late to help," he said.

The truth was, I was glad that he was too late. I wondered how to explain to him that the best of intentions and loyalty weren't enough sometimes to overcome our rugged, bloody hearts, and that killing Billy was indeed no way to save a friend.

Barby was standing in the light of the open door waiting for me and she prepared our table for Billy's body while Long and I carried him into the house. She cried and looked to me to cry also, but I couldn't find a single tear to shed for Billy, or for her either. While she wept I passed the night staring into the fireplace with Billy lying on my table, cold despite the flames that flickered over his face.

Come morning, Cap made it known that he wanted an official inquest to record the shooting and to justify his actions, but he wasn't hypocrite enough to argue very long with our intentions of burying Billy that very day. He had laid low too many men without aid of judge or jury, far out on the wastes. He scrawled out his account of Billy's demise on a scrap of butcher paper, and asked for all our signatures to support his claims. History is as simple a thing as that, and I signed the page.

There was no next of kin that we knew of so Cap left all Billy's possessions with me to do with as I pleased. I intended to bury most of Billy's things with him, or at least what I could. I would give his horse and saddle to Owen when he was old enough to ride, and his fancy spurs to Samuel when he too was of age. Billy's good Sharp's rifle I kept for myself, to keep well-oiled and hanging on my wall.

Long and I dug Billy's grave on the side of the hill above the house at a place I thought he would like overlooking the wide sweep of the plains. The women dressed him in a good suit we found among his travel roll, and they trimmed his hair up neat. I found myself staring at his freshly polished boots, his Stetson laid upon his breast, and I was sure he would be pleased with the way they spruced him up just like he had always liked to look. If he were still alive I would have told him there was no such thing as a handsome corpse.

We wrapped his body with a good quilt, and in silent procession carried him up the hill on the tailgate taken from my wagon.

The wind whipped Barby's black dress about her as she stood at the edge of the grave, and I wondered if all pioneer women kept such things packed away in secret trunks, thus prepared and equipped to see good men placed beneath the ground. Our boys clung to her hands with big, solemn eyes, looking so much alike in every detail that they could easily pass for twins. They both seemed the spitting image of Billy; or maybe it was just the way the sunlight was hitting my eyes. I'd sworn off judging anything life offered, but I couldn't help but consider if the child swelling her belly then would look like Billy also.

Long after we laid Billy low, and all his mourners had gone away, I sat in the grass and studied the fresh mound of earth that now separated him from all but memory. All that I held against him was buried beneath that dirt, and I knew he had drawn a tougher lot than I in the end. Maybe given time, after I had come enough to sit and talk with him about the old days, we would be better friends than ever.

Under the dying light of the setting sun I pulled a sheet of paper from my pocket, and studied it like I had many times since the morning. In my hands I held the bill of sale for Dunny, made out in my name and signed just the day before with Bee Hopkins's hand. I had found it in Billy's breast pocket, with two buckshot holes through its middle, and his own blood staining the yellow paper brown. When I got back to the house I would place it in the little fancy box Barby kept on the mantle, so every now and then I might take it down and remember what very little I'd known of Billy Champion up until the bitter end.

EPILOGUE

Somewhere west of Plum Creek, Texas Panhandle — 1890

The old Ranger kept his eyes upon the skyline and stopped to check his back trail more than once. He did it more out of habit than out of any necessity, for the Indians were all but tamed, and most outlaws of any account had all been hanged or elected to office. But there had been a time when a cautious man lived much longer, and he preferred to exist in the bygone, way out beyond sundown, in that faded land where the broncy ones still roamed.

He stopped upon the brow of a hill, and his pale blue eyes, made paler and watery by long exposure to the sun, took in the land before him. Both memory and vision tracked across that vast sweep of country, and the pioneer heart in him searched for what should be contained within that expanse. It wasn't the grass in the wind that waved before his eyes, but instead a parade of long-ago images seared into his memory so deep they branded him.

The good horse beneath him was restless, and he could remember when he too was chomping at the bit to bring law and order to that last bit of wild Texas. He knew that there was bound to be territory still left wild enough to need his kind of lawman, but he was too old to search it out, and he returned his mind to the task at hand.

Buzzards were circling in the air a couple of miles to the west, and he set out with them as a beacon. He wound his way across the rolling prairie, nose to the wind and cautious hand near his gun. The lines in his leathery face showed his age, but the thought of the pursuit ahead lightened him and he felt twenty years fall away.

He had a report of a murdered man found shot upon plains and left there by the discoverer due to a lack of transportation, or a shortage of concern. It might just be your common, run-of-the-mill murder, if there was such a thing. The old Ranger didn't count on it, because life had taught him that murder has a complexity all its own.

The sign left at the scene of the crime would be faded, and faint, but no matter.

He had been on cold trails before, as vague and impossible as the reasons why people committed the crimes they did. And long ago he'd given up all such speculations of personality and motivation where those he hunted were concerned. Experience had taught him that you never know what kind of man or woman you are chasing, because even the tracks left by the guilty are second-hand hearsay to the truth.

He approached the body warily, cutting a wide circle casting for sign before his horse's hooves marred the ground. The buzzards had just recently arrived, and they flushed upward only at the last minute, reluctant to give up what they too had found. He knelt beside the body and studied the twisted lay of it there in the grass, and put a finger to the bloody hole and busted bone centered in the chest.

Cap Arrington needed no witness to tell what his tracker's eyes told him just as plain. The dead man's rifle was just beyond his death-drawn, outstretched hand, and the bullet that killed him had taken him in the front. Cap worked the action of the rifle and found one empty case in the chamber. It was readily apparent that the killer had given his victim at least a fighting chance.

While his mind absorbed the evidence,

Cap rode back and forth studying the ground between the body and where the killer had fired from. It was a long hundred yards or better to where he found the hoofprints and the spent shell that had taken Dale Martin's life. That was a damned good offhand shot for a man sitting horseback to make.

Lots of folks had reason to want the stock detective dead, but the man who had done the deed wanted to make sure that whoever found Dale Martin's body recognized what he died for. Across his chest lay a hammerless Sharps rifle with the initials "B.C." carved into the stock. It was a hell of thing to believe that a man three years dead could shoot so true from the grave.

Cap chuckled grimly and wished all such crimes were so easily solved. He'd never known Nate was such a marksman, but it seemed like half of Texas had been settled by Tennesseans and they were all shooters by the time they were big enough to hold a gun.

He was getting too old to chase outlaws much longer, and he'd been offered a good-paying job as manager of a ranch. The new job required he run off most of a tough, rustler crew, and toss a certain Englishman out on his ass. That seemed to offer enough excitement and light work for an old wolf like him in his declining years.

He could see no sense in cluttering the books for the next man in office by leaving such a difficult case, so he dragged the body and the evidence over to the nearest wash. Then he caved in the bank of earth over it all to keep it from the buzzards. Damned the buzzards, and damned the prying eyes of men with lesser senses of what constitutes fair play.

And he rode away to disappear into the horizon as all such men do. As he passed down his last long years he recalled the men of the country gone before him to vanish along hoof-rutted trails, like Blue Knife, Billy Champion, and others too wild for a more settled land. Nobody would ever know their long years, dry years, cold years, freedom clouded in dust. The time would come when such men were as rare as dinosaur bones — the last of the old breed, come long before to orphan themselves upon the plains.